THE MAGPIE

Fireflies Publishing, LLC
THE MAGPIE
Copyright © 2017 Oliver Rock
LCCN Number: 2017945631

ISBN-10: 0-9984358-6-4
ISBN-13: 978-0-9984358-6-2

This is a work of fiction. Names, characters, places, and incidents either are the product of the author's imagination or are used fictiously, and any resemblance to actual persons, living or dead, businesses, companies, events, or locales is entirely coincidental.

THE MAGPIE

BY
OLIVER ROCK

TABLE OF CONTENTS

PREFACE

Whilst the room was damp and dark, beautiful clean white light from two neon bulbs achieved their objective of shining clearly onto the thick ten-foot wooden table positioned in the middle of this basement. On top of the old pine table was a crisp thin white linen sheet, speckled with a few blood spots. Lying on top of the cloth was the naked body of a male in his mid-twenties, motionless. The torso was thin but muscular, tanned but lifeless. He had not been dead for too long as there was color still in the flesh.

Despite the room being cold and wet, as you would expect from a cellar, this hadn't impacted the features or good looks of the dead male. He was both masculine and beautiful. He had no stubble, very short brown hair and his eye lids were shut. The man's face fell at a strange angle on the table, as his chin lay on top of his right shoulder. He had clearly experienced a snapped vertebra in his neck.

Apart from background noise coming from cars and cyclists passing by on the streets nearby, you could hear a snipping sound, as fingernails were being trimmed. As each nail end fell off on the table top, it was carefully picked up and placed into a small pot, what used to be an old jam jar.

The person dressed in white overalls and rubber marigold gloves moved quickly round the body, cutting all the nails on fingers and toes and then proceeded to scrub the hands and feet clean with a fine rough edged cloth soaked in alcoholic disinfectant. There were two other containers in the room located on the floor next to the table. One was filled with the victim's clothes, which had been surgically removed with scissors. The other was a much smaller and contained the possessions of the dead male. With the lack of light on the floor, one could only make out a wallet, a gold necklace and a bunch of keys.

The individual silently cleaning the body sniffled to themselves but didn't raise a hand to their face. It wasn't a runny nose that they had but rather several tears coming down their face. The way they worked on the still torso was so routine and clearly not the first time that they had carried out this procedure. As the job was completed, they gathered all the victim's belongings and tipped them without remorse into a black bin liner.

Then there was darkness, as they turned off the two lights and exited the cellar silently.

CHAPTER 1

September 25

7:15 a.m.

It was a typical September morning in Amsterdam as the first light broke through a blanket of dull grey sky. The onslaught of heavy rain pelted down on the old cobbled stones of the 'nine streets' in the center of town, washing away old cigarette butts and fast food wrappers that were scattered on the narrow roads, remnants of last night's festivities. A lone cyclist zigzagged between the litter on Wolvenstraat, almost driving into the five lost English guys who were huddled together in the middle of the street - drunk, disorientated, and white-faced. The cyclist, a young Dutch student, was heading home from a night at her boyfriends' and was in a rush to get back and change for Sunday field hockey. She rang the bell on her bike but to no avail, as the hungover English guys were too busy arguing amongst themselves about the way back to their hotel, and clearly, they had no clue.

You knew they were English as they all dressed the same - shirts or polo shirts hanging outside their perfectly ironed jeans, tattoos, short cropped hair, loud, and annoyingly drunk. The cyclist swerved around them and rang her bell again. Making sure that she was a good ten meters past them, she shouted out, "eikels", as she sped off down the street. The stag party was oblivious to her frustration as they had other pressing issues on their mind - a warm hotel room. Now, they were lost in this maze of narrow crossroads that split the four main canals in the heart of Amsterdam and were getting wetter and colder by the second.

The ringing of the cyclist's bell and the raised voices woke Roos up. She had had a terrible night's sleep. First, the heavy rain hitting the window ledge and beating down on the skylight above her bedroom had woken her at two in the morning. Then, there was the pigeon on her windowsill that was trying to shelter itself from the downpour and didn't stop cooing. Now, at 7:15 a.m., there were the cyclist and the muffled drunks shouting outside.

Lying in bed, she brushed her dark brown hair off her face and lifted her head up so that she could look at the digital clock that sat on the small bedside table. She checked the time and reached across to turn off the alarm. It was set to go off at eight but there was no way that she was going to fall back to sleep now. Roos was still tired but she had too much going on in her head.

Her hair fell perfectly into an immaculate bob cut, thanks to her monthly visit to the hairdresser, on the Spui. This was the sole treat she gave herself other than her weekly manicure, which she really still couldn't justify as a nurse in her third year out of training college. Even without a good night's sleep, Roos still looked pretty, with fresh pale skin, no blemishes, wrinkles or spots. At twenty-five, she took care of her features, using both day and night creams, facial scrubs, and numerous glosses. If only she could lose the last annoying three and a half kilos, she would be very happy. Working long shifts as a nurse, she only had time to exercise a couple of times during the week and on weekends, so she relied on cycling to and from the hospital to burn the extra calories. The extra weight on her thighs and waist troubled her and was at the top of her list of issues to deal with.

Roos looked around the room as she lay in bed. It was a small cozy bedroom with clean white walls, recently painted by her younger brother, who had been trying to earn a few extra euros during his school break. The walls were quite bare, apart from the giant-sized poster of a beautiful lonely lady, looking out of a house as if waiting for somebody. Roos often felt like this woman.

Light began to creep in through the gap between the blinds and the skylight. Soon, the bedroom would be lit by the natural rays from the sun and Jade would wake up as well.

At the end of the bed was a large dark brown chest of drawers. It dated back to pre-First World War. It had been well-cared for over the years and this hadn't changed since it had been passed down to Roos from her parents. When her brother had painted the bedroom, she had given him clear instructions on how to varnish the chest of drawers without damaging the old oak wood, ensuring that it didn't lose any of its character. It was no surprise as Roos was a bit of a control freak and over the top about cleaning. The chest was passed on from her father and grandfather. She liked to think of this beautiful piece of Dutch furniture as her third favorite belonging in the apartment.

On top of the chest sat her second favorite possession - the silver picture frame. The frame had been a gift for her twenty-first birthday from her parents, Bram and Theresa Van Vels. They lived in Amstelveen in the same middle-class house where Roos had grown up. Originally christened Roos-Marijn, which she hated, her parents were the only ones who still called her by her full name.

The frame was A4 in size and was immaculately polished especially over the silver crest. There was no smudging on the glass or marks on the blue velvet on the back. In fact, it looked nicer now than when it was first removed from its wrapping several years ago. The picture frame was positioned on top, close to the edge of the chest, so that it received maximum light when Roos opened the window curtains in the morning.

Next to the picture frame was a medium-sized but perfectly manicured white orchid. Placed in a small pot, the orchid had a clean stem and three white flowers. She looked after the orchid as if it were a terminally ill patient at the hospital. She would wipe the leaves, stem, and petals every day with a wet cotton ball. Roos would water the plant religiously and followed all the instructions about caring for orchids on the internet. This was actually her fourth orchid and despite the tender loving care she had given, she had lost the first three. Roos was determined to keep this one.

Apart from these items, the bedroom was quite bare, which was Roos' intention. As she lay there looking at the frame, she thought to herself that the only thing that had changed was the picture that sat inside the frame. When she had opened the gift four years ago, there was a colorful picture of her brother and parents, dressed in their smartest outfits posing with extremely cheesy grins. The whole family wore glasses and Roos always felt good having made the decision to go to Belgium to have eye surgery. She always wanted to please her parents but there were some instances where she would stick her neck out and go her own way. Having surgery so that she wouldn't have to wear glasses or contact lenses ever again, was one of them.

Roos enjoyed nursing. Working long hours and helping sick people made her feel good. It had also pleased her parents, especially her father, a consultant and renowned heart surgeon at the Vu Hospital. She couldn't have handled the extra years of studying required to become a doctor, and in fact, she wasn't that ambitious. Becoming a nurse was a satisfactory compromise and it made her father happy. He also got to have coffee once a week with his daughter at the hospital when their shifts crossed and if Roos bothered to check the text messages that he would send. They would discuss work, her mother, her brother, and her father's golf game but never anything too serious or personal, like relationships.

Whenever relationships were discussed in the past it would always end in a heated argument with her father raising his voice, her mother getting frustrated and crying, and Roos storming off in a mood. She had gotten so used to these conversations now that when she sensed the topic beginning to arise, she would either sigh and walk off or make a fake smile and suggest that they change the subject. Roos had learnt to hold back her tears, even if it still made her upset inside. Her parents had also learnt not to bring up the subject anymore, especially if they wanted to continue seeing their daughter. They had adored both her previous boyfriends: Thijl and Arthur. Both were nice, clean cut boys, and the same age as Roos. She had dated one when she was eighteen and the other when she was twenty. Thijl had become a journalist and Arthur a teacher, and both had grown up to be great guys but neither was in contact with Roos anymore.

Roos slid out of bed sideways without lifting the duvet in the process. She was wearing a thin, almost transparent, white cotton nightie, through which you could see a tiny string. Her pale skin was smooth, her legs recently waxed and well-creamed, and her toe-nails were perfectly cut and beautifully painted. As she crept towards the bathroom, she sidestepped on the floorboards that didn't creak. She was desperate not to wake her flat-mates. As she slipped into the bathroom, she closed the door behind her without making a noise. Flicking on the light, Roos stared straight into the bathroom mirror, observing her face for any blemishes. Her skin was perfect and her lips rounded and full, never requiring bright lipstick, unless she wanted to draw attention to herself. She thought her lips were a big plus point and perfect for being kissed.

Her eyebrows were well-shaped and didn't need plucking this morning. Happy with her facial features, Roos lifted her arms towards the ceiling and stretched and yawned silently at the same time. She checked her armpits that she had shaved last night and they were still looking clean. As Roos stretched, her nightie also moved higher, revealing the top part of her thighs which disappointed her greatly. The cellulite was unsightly in her opinion. She would need to cycle harder to work and spend an additional ten minutes on the 'step machine' at the gym to try and deal with this. Roos sat down on the toilet to take a morning pee and looked at the small tattoo on the inside of her right wrist, Greek markings that spelt out love. She smiled to herself thinking about her parents, who didn't know that she had a tattoo, and how crazy they would be if they saw it. She liked being a bit rebellious.

Roos got up from the toilet, washed her hands, and took one last glance in the mirror before turning off the bathroom light and creeping back into the bedroom. Gently lifting the white cotton duvet and quietly lying back on the mattress, she couldn't help herself from rolling over to stare at her favorite possession that lay beside her in the bed. She stared across at this amazing slender body that lay intertwined in the duvet, noting the real contrast between the dark brown skin and the pure Egyptian white cotton sheets. Roos liked to think of Jade as a possession but actually she was an obsession.

Jade had everything that she didn't. She was tall, very slim, with beautiful long legs, and a swan-like neck. Her hair was long, thick, and fair in color, with sun-bleached streaks. Her skin was constantly tanned, partly from her origins but also from the continuous long distance trips she took as a KLM air stewardess to South America and the Caribbean. Roos always worried when she was away travelling for work, as she feared that Jade would fall for someone at a party with the flight crew. Whilst she knew that Jade wasn't interested in men, she had the ability to attract anyone and would sleep with them just to play with their mind. In fact, she had confessed to sleeping with a captain in the past that was arrogant and very sure of himself. She wanted to teach him a lesson and after a drunken night of passionate sex, she spent the next three months ignoring him, which brought him back down to earth.

Jade had, of course, experienced relationships in her twenty-seven years of life with both men and women. At the age of eighteen, she came to realize that she preferred women more. She had had five proper relationships with girls, Roos being the fifth. Jade never really showed much emotion except in bed. It was frustrating for Roos as she didn't feel close enough to her.

Before Jade, Roos had never been jealous but this had all changed as soon as they started dating. She dreaded Jade going on these long-haul trips. She knew that most of the air hostesses were not gay. However, there was a small group that was, and they were also pretty and quite forward. Jade was leaving today for a five-day trip to Argentina. Roos wanted to wake her up, but at the same time, she was scared that Jade would be annoyed if she was disturbed. They had had a big night yesterday and both would be suffering from hangovers this morning, especially Jade, who had drunk far too many tequilas. A flirty barman at the Escape Club had spent the evening chatting Jade up, and she had played along, receiving complimentary shots in the process.

Everything about Jade was cool, thought Roos, even her name. Moving the long blonde locks away from one side of her face, Roos could see her perfect cheekbone and pouting lips. Leaning across, she noticed the smudging of ruby red lipstick on her pillow, mixed with fresh saliva. Even this looked sexy. As Jade lay fast asleep on her side, Roos moved her hair behind her ear, so that it fell over her back. This revealed the fine pencil thin Balinese writing that was tattooed at the top of Jade's neck and continued for about ten centimeters down her spine. She had got this tattoo done in Asia four years ago with her ex-girlfriend Brie. Roos had told her that she hated the tattoo but really, she just hated Brie and saw this cool marking as a memory of her ex. Roos quickly placed Jade's hair back over her neck to cover up this annoying ink.

Jade was much more confident of herself than Roos and refused to wear anything in bed. While this made her feel like a prude, Roos did like to feel her naked body next to hers when they slept.

Roos moved her right hand towards Jade's as she wanted to look at their identical tattoos inked on the insides of their wrists, together. This made Roos happy as she knew that they would always have this attachment whatever happened between them in the future. Roos turned Jade's hand over, and noticed frustratingly, that the markings were hidden by the old brown leather wristband Jade wore. In contrast, Roos had her tattoo very visible, purposely not wearing a watch or jewelry, unless she was seeing her parents. .

While the girls made similar salaries, Jade had a more exotic, carefree job - meeting new people, travelling all over the world, seeing more places, and partying in the sun. For the five days that Jade was going to be away, Roos would be bored and needed to find things to do in her spare time. Apart from working extra shifts at the hospital, she would add more gym classes and running to her schedule. She didn't enjoy the fitness training but it kept her mind off Jade and she needed to stay in shape.

Roos knew that she would get very jealous wondering what Jade would be doing and who would be 'hitting on her'. The more she thought about it, the more it made her blood boil. This time, however, it would be worse, as they had just had a heated argument the night before. Jade had got drunk and flirted with not only the barman but also with a tall attractive barmaid. Roos had stayed late just to keep an eye on her prized possession.

Roos kissed Jade's neck but Jade didn't show any sign of enjoying it. Her eyes remained closed and even her body rolled a little further away as if to say 'leave me alone'. Roos lay still for a few seconds pondering over her next move. She decided that she didn't want to wake Jade and was glad that she had kissed her neck and smelt the faint fragrance of perfume, surviving odors from last night's partying. The soft oily skin against her lips and the familiar smell of the perfume turned Roos on.

She got up once again and tip-toed slowly back into the bathroom, shutting the door behind her and then stepped into the shower.

Having dried herself off, Roos went to the top drawer of the old chest in the bedroom to pick some fresh underwear for the day. She stopped for a second to stare at the black and white picture of Jade and Fleur hugging each other in the silver picture frame. The picture was taken on a holiday in France last summer and Roos absolutely adored it.

With the towel wrapped around her body, Roos walked out of the bedroom and down the winding stairwell into the living room. She decided to get dressed there so that she would not disturb Jade. Hanging over the kitchen doorway was a clean nurses' outfit, ready to slip on. Normally, Roos would be more discreet but she could see that Fleur wasn't home yet. Her bedroom door was wide open. Roos didn't know if Fleur had been working last night or was out partying but it must have been a good night either way, as it was now eight in the morning and there was still no sign of her.

Looking through the open doorway to Fleur's bedroom, Roos began to shake her head in disbelief at how messy her second flat-mate was. Scattered all over the floor and bed were stilettos, miniskirts, piles of underwear, and glittering blouses. At least the mess didn't spill out of her bedroom, thought Roos. Fleur's only excuse for being like this was that she was still a full-time student holding a part-time job.

Roos still had time for breakfast but she was so angry with herself for causing the argument last night that she felt like she had to be punished. She decided to skip food and head straight to work. Roos had too many emotions going through her head right now of anger, jealousy, and anticipation. At least her work would take her mind off things for a while. What was Jade going to do when she was away? Maybe she would get involved in one of these KLM drunken orgies? Would she flirt with another barmaid again? Was she fed up with Roos' jealous nature? Maybe, when Fleur got home later this morning, they will meet in the kitchen and Jade will tell her how jealous Roos has become. Maybe, Jade actually likes Fleur and will make a move on her. She felt dizzy and grimaced with all these silly scenarios racing through her mind. Fleur likes guys and in the six months that they had been living together, they had become good friends. Fleur was far too sweet to do that to Roos.

Roos needed to get outside. She put on her shoes and raincoat and left through the front door picking her hospital ID pass and bike keys in one motion. The fresh air would clear her head pretty quickly, she hoped and the ride to work would act as a distraction. As the rain began to fall harder, she thought she was probably going to get very wet and be late for work. That was not a good mix coupled with a head filled with jealous thoughts.

* * *

8:30 a.m.

Arnaud Van Loo sat in a crumpled heap on the stained brown leather seat in his cold dark living room. His small apartment, located on the Tuinstraat in Jordaan, consisted of a double bedroom with a tiny bathroom, kitchen, and living room. The big plus point about the apartment was that it was on the first floor and he only had one small flight of stairs to clamber up and down each day.

Arnaud looked older than his fifty-one years of age, mainly due to his lifestyle of excessive beer, spirits, and cigarettes. His nicotine-stained skin blended in with the caramel color of the worn leather seat on which he had passed out last night. Curled up in a ball on the chair, with his knitted jumper pulled up over his knees to keep him warm, Arnaud snored away.

Whilst the apartment was poorly lit, you could see that it hadn't been decorated for many months. A lot of his belongings still sat in boxes scattered around the living room. These were the same boxes that had been packed eighteen months ago, when he had left his wife and daughter. A high-pitched vibrating noise of glass rattling pierced through his cloudy head. On the seventh set of vibrations, Arnaud opened his wrinkled eyelids to the familiar sound. He knew it wouldn't stop until he did something about it. Arnaud took a deep breath of dusty, smoke-filled air, and squinted knowing that any bright sunlight would make this morning's hangover even worse and turn it into a migraine.

Without looking, he reached over to the small coffee table on the right to find his pager, which had been the cause of the vibrating noise. His main concern was to simply stop the annoying little contraption from rattling violently against the empty glass that it was propped against. Next to the tumbler was an open bottle of gin and five empty bottles of beer. Carefully positioned on the side of the bottles was a large glass ashtray stacked with a pyramid of cigarette butts. The smell of old cigarettes filled the room and made Arnaud's clothes and hair stink. He had a thick curly mop of black and grey hair that was cut four times a year. He didn't have to worry about ever going bald.

This was quite a rough hangover, Arnaud thought to himself, as he slowly came to his senses. His tongue and throat were dry and sore. He would need to get up and take a drink of water from the kitchen tap. Arnaud's eyes were now fully open and he spotted the remote control on the floor by his feet. He had obviously passed out last night and not managed to turn the television off. He reached for the controller and started flicking through the channels trying to find some news, with no luck.

Moving slowly, he leant over to the coffee table and picked up the pager to see who had been trying to get hold of him. It was his office, which was no surprise, but he was beginning to get worked up inside realizing that it was only eight thirty on a Sunday morning. He began gritting his teeth as the feeling of anxiety spread through his body. Reaching in his right pocket for his mobile, he lifted it up to his face so that he could read the font on the small screen. He had one missed call from the station and three missed calls from his colleague, Friso Bos. Arnaud's heart started to beat a lot faster as he noticed that there was a flashing envelope at the top of the screen, indicating that he had a text message. It was from Friso, "Arnaud, please call me asap – urgent."

Arnaud's mind was wide awake now even though his body wasn't. He put both hands on the sides of the chair and pushed himself upright. He needed to go immediately. Seven pager messages, three missed calls and a text on a Sunday morning, his day off, could only mean one thing. He staggered towards the kitchen sink. Arnaud turned on the tap, splashed water on his face and took a few swigs to clear his throat. There was no time for a shower or to change. He would go to the office like this.

Next to the sink was a half-empty tube of toothpaste. He squeezed a small amount into his mouth, mixing it with another gulp of water. Arnaud spat out the water and then put on his coat. Checking that he had his moped keys in his pocket, he headed as fast as he could down the steep flight of stairs to the door. Outside, he swept the rain off the moped seat, his hands shaking, filled with adrenaline. Eventually, managing to get the key into the ignition of the moped, he pressed the start button and sped off down the Tuinstraat in the direction of the Oud Zuid.

CHAPTER 2

September 25

9:30 a.m.

Arnaud arrived at the RAI exhibition center thirty minutes later. He had followed the instructions in Friso's text message and headed to their office on the second floor of the Koninginneweg police station. Once he reached there, Arnaud was told that Friso and the team had not waited for him, but gone straight to the RAI, where Arnaud was supposed to meet them. Whether it was an emergency or not, Arnaud always took his moped everywhere, as it was the quickest way to get around Amsterdam. He was far too lazy and unfit to cycle. And this was an emergency.

The RAI was the largest exhibition and conference facility in Amsterdam. Modern, consisting of five large halls and surrounded by huge car parks, it took up a very large expanse of open space in such a small congested city.

Arnaud slowed down his moped as he approached the first car park on the North side of the complex. Looking ahead, he could see a crowd of policemen, cameramen, and reporters standing by the entrance. They were all pushing against the bright yellow plastic tape that had been used by the police to fence off the large car park area. Checking the faces in the crowd, Arnaud recognized most of them. He was thankful that there weren't many members of the public present. This was probably due to the fact that it was still only nine thirty-five on Sunday morning. Still, Arnaud was surprised to see such a large huddle of people and wondered how information had gotten out so quickly. It was clear that everyone had been expecting this.

Positioned about twenty meters away, Arnaud parked his moped and sat on it with the engine turned off. He waited a couple of minutes to compose himself and take a drink from the bottle of water that he had bought from the news-stand along the way. He had a headache and was feeling very tired. He checked his mobile phone to see if he had missed any more calls or received any further text messages. His hands were trembling, making it hard to read the writing on the small lit-up screen. No one had tried to contact him in the last thirty minutes, which was a good thing. He got off the moped and walked at a brisk pace towards the wall of people.

The rain had started to fall even harder now and Arnaud needed to wipe the constant dripping of water from his face. His thick mop of hair was acting like a sponge and soaking up all the rain. It was falling into his eyes and impairing his vision. He reached into the inside pocket of his tweed jacket and pulled out his police ID and also found a lone piece of gum, which he began chewing immediately. He was wary of how badly his breath smelled of alcohol and cigarettes and didn't want his colleagues to think that he was late because of a hangover. Although, it wouldn't be the first time that that had happened.

Apart from cleaning his nicotine stained teeth, chewing on gum also helped calm his nerves. Arnaud was a big NAC football fan from his home town of Breda, and he had observed that their manager had always chewed gum as a stress release. He tried it himself and it really worked. At times like this, it was essential for Arnaud and he chomped down on it ferociously.

Arnaud approached the first wave of reporters and camera crews from behind. They had their backs towards him as they stared across the car park hungry for information. Most of them had come prepared for the rain with umbrellas. The rest either had hats on or the hoods from their jackets up. Even with shelter from the bad weather, they were all soaked and cold. Arnaud saw this as an opportunity to sneak through the crowd without getting recognized. They would only notice him once he had got past them and through the police barrier. He raised the collar on his jacket and began barging his way through the scrimmage of people. As he got out to the other side, a 'smart arse' reporter from the NRC newspaper spotted him and shouted over to Arnaud, "Detective Van Loo, have you got any information for us at this stage?"

There was silence for a second as other members of the press began to realize that Arnaud had arrived and tried to single him out. Another journalist continued the questioning, "Detective Van Loo, is it number nine?" Arnaud didn't acknowledge the press but kept his head down and continued walking the few extra yards towards the police line. He raised his ID out of courtesy, although it wasn't necessary. They all knew who he was. The wall of police opened up to make way for Arnaud to pass through.

Another shout came from behind him. "Hey, Van Loo, your colleague Bos arrived here an hour ago! What's going on? Is he in charge now? Or was this not serious enough for you to get here earlier?" This wasn't really a question but more of an insult. That annoying high-pitched voice could only come from one guy and that was Toon De Bruin from the Telegraaf newspaper. He was arrogant and a 'nasty piece of work', whose grating voice got on everyone's nerves. Arnaud detested the reporter and the feeling was definitely mutual.

De Bruin had it in for both him and his colleague, Friso, but especially for Arnaud. In a sadistic sort of way, De Bruin wanted them to fail, which would imply that they hadn't caught their guy and therefore, more crimes were likely to take place. It also gave him something more to write about. Arnaud couldn't stop himself from shooting a stare at De Bruin with his eyes half-closed and a full sneer that showed off his yellow teeth gritting together with hatred for the reporter.

Turning away, Arnaud carried on walking past the police who said "Good morning" to him. He looked up and gave them a respectful nod and continued on a few steps, moving further away from the crowd of journalists. He could hear De Bruin's muffled voice continuing to chatter to the reporters around him in that female-like tone. Arnaud couldn't believe that any of the other reporters actually liked that annoying skinny worm, as he was so unpleasant and a real pain.

He stopped for a second to scan the open space ahead of him. The large car park was empty except for a few stray vehicles. Right on the other side, about a hundred and fifty meters away, was a blue Saab car and next to it was a white police tent structure that must have just been erected. That was the scene of the crime, thought Arnaud, and that is where he needed to be.

As he began the long walk across the car park, the wind began to pick up and the rain was now blowing straight into his face. This forced him to squint in order to see where he was going. Arnaud raised a hand in front of his eye line hoping it would help. He could just make out four more policemen standing outside the white tent. Looking from left to right, he could also see that the whole car park had been cordoned off with yellow tape and police were scattered around the perimeter, ensuring that nobody came inside.

Arnaud heard footsteps close behind him and looked out of the corner of his eye to see a police sergeant walking briskly in his direction, and within seconds, was right next to him. He was short, round, and dressed very smartly, which was unusual for an Amsterdam policeman. As they made their way across the car park, the sergeant began briefing Arnaud on the information that he currently knew. He was clearly in charge of this crime scene.

"Detective Van Loo, we received a call at approximately 6:35 a.m. from one of the security guards here, who was going home after his night shift. As the guard headed for his car, he saw the feet of a body sticking out from behind an old Volvo that was parked about fifteen meters away from him."

"Hmm, okay," replied Arnaud. His mind was elsewhere right now, even though he was taking in all the information. For him, the top priority was to see the victim's body and establish if there were any familiar signs: cause of death, state of the body, what the victim was wearing, and any other clues from around the crime scene. Arnaud would be able to tell right away if there were any similar patterns between how the victim had died and whether it was part of a legacy - the work of the serial killer.

"Did the security guard notice anything unusual or see anyone in the car park late into the night shift?" asked Arnaud.

"Errrm. What do you mean, Detective?" replied the sergeant blank-faced. Arnaud was used to these types of silly answers and he regretted asking the question. Arnaud stopped in his tracks and turned to the sergeant, staring at him with an agitated expression. He had already prepared a list of much simpler and more direct questions to ask the policeman.

The rain continued to pour down and Arnaud wiped the dripping water off his face with his jacket sleeve. He began to speak again.

"Was the guard awake all night?"

The policeman replied quickly, "He said so." Arnaud's next question was going to be whether he had seen anything unusual, but before he could ask, the sergeant began speaking again. "Yesterday was the last night of the 'Ideal Home Exhibition' and there were a lot of people and cars coming and going, and a large number of trucks being loaded up with stands and furniture. This went on until the early hours of Sunday morning." Arnaud looked down at his brown drenched brogues, as he was standing in a large puddle, and sighed as he thought to himself about the work ahead of himself and his team.

"Well, we will need to get all the CCTV video footage from the RAI for the last forty-eight hours. Please give it to my colleague, Detective Bos," replied Arnaud.

"Understood, Detective." came the reply, as the sergeant scribbled some notes on a small pad.

Arnaud continued, "And arrange for Bos to interview the guard as well."

"He already has, Sir." replied the sergeant.

This didn't surprise him as Friso was always very efficient and he had come to expect such excellent follow-up work and data-crunching from his partner.

Arnaud then fired off a string of questions to the sergeant. "Where did the visitors come in and out of the exhibition and the car park? Was there anything strange found around the scene of the crime? Were there any other guards on duty or witnesses? Has the forensic team arrived yet?" He didn't expect the sergeant to have all the answers but these were questions that Arnaud wanted him to go and find out. The poor red-faced policeman was busy trying to scribble everything down on his pad, blue ink smearing everywhere on the paper as rain soaked the page.

He closed his eyes for a second to think as he did have one final question for the sergeant.

"Is Dijkstra here yet?" asked Arnaud. Marcel Dijkstra was his boss, who he had worked with for many years, solving numerous crimes together in their district. Arnaud liked Dijkstra, as he normally left him alone to get on with his detective work. They understood each other very well and had a good working relationship. The strength of their friendship, however, was now being tested. Things between them were slowly changing as his boss was getting a lot of heat and criticism from the highest ranked police chiefs in North Holland.

"I believe he is, Detective." Came the reply from the sergeant, happy that he could answer another one of his questions. This wasn't good, thought Arnaud to himself. Whilst he knew that he was well-respected for his methodical approach to detective work, he had a reputation for not being on time. Today he was late again, and the press had seen it, the other policemen had seen it, and Dijkstra would know about it. Arnaud could put up with the criticism that was written about him in the newspapers, but ultimately, it reflected badly on his boss, who wouldn't be happy.

Arnaud began walking again in the direction of the tent, picking up his pace in order to get away from the sergeant, who got the message pretty quickly and let him get on with his work. Arnaud needed to move onto the next stage of the morning's investigation, which was all housed inside the white structure ahead of him. He guessed that the CCTV tapes would be impossible to work through and wouldn't contain any clues. Arnaud knew that whoever had committed the murder, and he was fairly sure he knew who it was, had planned this extremely well. Last night, there would have been so many vehicles moving in and out of the car parks and thousands of people walking around, which would have made it made it extremely difficult to spot any unusual behavior, and he was also sure that none of the cameras were actually directed at the spot where the body had been found. The killer was too thorough in his planning and every move was calculated, leaving absolutely nothing to chance. Arnaud had learnt quickly that this master craftsman left no traces of his actions. He needed to see the body to confirm what he was thinking.

Arnaud approached the entrance to the tent, where the four policemen stood, soaked to the bone. He acknowledged them with his usual nod and then slipped between the thick white plastic drapes that acted as the doorway. These make-shift tents were always used when a dead body was found and where the police needed to shield a crime scene area so that they could search for clues. These structures also made it impossible for others to see what had happened. In this instance, the tent was essential as it prevented any evidence being washed away by the rain.

Arnaud was glad to be inside, sheltered from the heavy storm. The four make-shift walls surrounded a twenty-five square-meter crime scene. The light inside the tent was extremely bright as lamps on telescopic stands beamed down on the two cars that stood in the middle of the room. One was an old Volvo and the other was a relatively new VW Golf. There was an eerie silence in the room as the forensics in their white outfits scurried around, picking up anything that might be a clue and putting them into numbered plastic bags. Flashes from two police cameramen kept flicking as they took numerous pictures around the tent. You could hear the rain tapping away on the plastic roof. Arnaud took off his jacket because it was humid inside the tent and his clothes were already drenched. Being hot and completely wet at the same time was an uncomfortable combination.

Arnaud could see his colleagues standing in a huddle between the two cars, looking down at the ground, and chatting quietly amongst themselves. There was Friso, Dijkstra and two young police men, Jim and Robin, who had been selected to work with them on this case. This was his team, and while Dijkstra oversaw them, he really let Arnaud manage things on his own. Arnaud was a little old-fashioned in his ways and not the best communicator, but he was a very good detective with a strong thought process about solving crimes, leaving no possible scenarios uncovered. He was well-respected amongst the detective community and had an excellent track record for achieving results, until this year.

Arnaud walked round the front of the Volvo towards his colleagues. Between the two cars lay a white sheet on the tarmac covering what was clearly a body from the shape of it. You could also see naked toes poking out from under the end of the rectangular piece of plastic. No socks or shoes. His colleagues seemed pleased to see him, apart from Dijkstra, who glanced at his wristwatch.

Friso stood across Arnaud in his familiar long blue rain jacket. Underneath, he wore faded jeans and a white polo shirt. His younger colleague looked tired, thought Arnaud to himself. He probably had woken up early to play with his two sons so that his lovely young wife, Viola, could have a lie in. Arnaud was very close with Friso. He trusted him completely and while he wasn't as experienced as himself, he was very thorough with his case work and never left a stone unturned. Arnaud had mentored him over the last four years, since he was promoted to detective, and was extremely confident that Friso did things exactly the way he wanted him to. Arnaud noticed that Friso was staring at him, and once their eyes fixed on each other, Friso looked down at the white sheet and nodded.

The nod confirmed to Arnaud that Friso had checked for the cause of death and the state of the corpse. The nod signaled to Arnaud what he had been expecting. It was the work of 'The Magpie', the serial killer that he had tried to understand and track down over the last nine months. The police had nick-named the killer, 'Magpie', because he always took the victim's clothing and jewelry, before dumping the body, naked. It was thought, at first that the killer was attracted, like the bird, to 'shiny' bits. Arnaud's heartbeat was racing and he started to sweat profusely. This was the news that he did not want to hear but had expected of course. The Magpie had struck again and they were no closer to catching him. They were only left to pick up the pieces once more.

Arnaud ushered Friso towards him and he obliged. He leaned across the Volvo trying not to touch it as a forensic was busy scanning the car for fingerprints.

"Grill the security guard again and meet me at the autopsy room in the hospital in one hour." Friso nodded his head in agreement.

Arnaud took one more glance around the make-shift room and then slipped back outside the plastic sheet door. He had seen and heard enough to come to the simple conclusion that if this was the work of the Magpie then there would be no clues left where the body was dumped. He was thorough. Arnaud needed to see the body in the autopsy room and then he would know for sure that it was this serial killer who had struck again. The one who took so much pride in his work and followed the same style of killing every time.

As he walked back in the direction of his moped, he put on his soaking wet jacket and started thinking what they needed to do next. They had no clues and nothing to report apart from there being another victim and that the killer was still on the loose in the Amsterdam area. Arnaud tried to understand what was he doing wrong. His trail of thought was interrupted by a voice behind him calling out, "Arnaud." He stopped and turned around to see Dijkstra, standing there with an annoyed look on his face.

"What do you think? Is it what we expected?" asked Dijkstra. Arnaud said nothing. He didn't need to respond to these questions now.

His boss was getting frustrated, "You didn't even look at the body! And you only stayed for five minutes!"

"Friso did." Arnaud snapped back him. "And he knows."

"Yes, but you are running this investigation Arnaud, and you were late." Then there was silence.

Arnaud turned and walked away. He wasn't going to bite. Dijkstra was right about the last part – he had been late. But whether he had arrived earlier or not didn't make any difference. The outcome would have been the same. Amsterdam was in a panic mode right now, living through something it had never experienced before. The killer was getting confident of himself as the murders continued to stack up. He wasn't scared of the pursuing police or administration and they were no closer to catching him. The Magpie continued to strike every month. Now, there were nine. He planned everything so well and was proud of his untouchable work. He would continue for sure. He was already an infamous serial killer.

Arnaud continued across the car park in the direction of the reporters. He had no choice but to go this way as his moped was parked just behind them. He thought to himself that the car park would have been so busy yesterday with cars and trucks going in and out that it would be very difficult to find the car that had brought in the body and dumped it.

Arnaud needed to think about the drop-off point and why this spot had been chosen by the killer. But he couldn't concentrate right now because of the crowd in front of him, who were getting louder as he approached.

He hated the 'wise guy' reporters who were just looking for a story. They weren't the ones who had to go and see the family of the victims, he thought to himself. They didn't have to attend the post-mortems or witness the identification of the bodies by their loved ones. They were only after the story and the picture, and this was on the front page of every newspaper in Holland. The news was also spreading to other countries in Western Europe.

What he hated most was the pressure by the journalists. They really had it in for Arnaud. 'This detective can't solve a crime!', 'Van Loo spends more time in the bar than in the police station!', 'How many more murders before Van Loo is replaced?' 'Amsterdam needs a new team to catch the Magpie!' 'Van Loo should retire! He has failed us!' Arnaud was sick of it. He had enough stress and he couldn't bear the thought of the killer reading the papers or watching the news and seeing Arnaud being portrayed as useless and a failure. The journalists were giving 'the Magpie' more confidence and at the same time making a mockery of Arnaud.

He was tensing up as he walked past the line of police who blocked the exit of the car park. Arnaud could feel all their eyes on him as he passed by and moved towards the noisy crowd held back by the plastic tape. He was determined not to say anything, at least not at this point.

Suddenly, cameras started clicking and journalists began firing questions at him. This was the last thing he wanted to deal with right now.

"So, is it the Magpie?"

"It is number nine?"

"Come on Detective, give us something."

"What was the cause of death?"

"Are there any clues?"

Arnaud listened as he walked around the crowd, speeding up to get away from them as quickly as possible.

"You know what, he's still hung over from last night, so of course he has no answers!" That was it. Arnaud had heard enough. His blood was boiling. That streaking voice could only be one person. He turned and scanned the heads in the crowd for Toon De Bruin. He spotted him in the second row, tall and thin, with a gaunt white face and thick black-rimmed glasses. What he wouldn't give to punch De Bruin straight in the face. Arnaud was now shaking with rage but he had to stay in control, as the press would have a field day if he tried to attack the reporter. He clenched his fists and kept moving, away from De Bruin and away from the insults and questions. He would get his chance, he thought to himself.

For now, he needed to focus on this case and the first thing to do was to get on his moped and get away from here. The next step would be to find a quiet café where he could drink coffee and collect his thoughts. This was often how he came up with new ideas and directions to try and solve a crime. After this, he needed to go and watch the post mortem and confirm that the Magpie was in fact responsible for the killing. Finally, he could sit down with Friso and discuss their next move.

But for now, he just needed to get away.

CHAPTER 3

1:30 p.m.

Her smart ground-floor apartment had a large bedroom overlooking the Singel. A king-sized bed was positioned in the center of the room sitting on top of a very large Persian rug. It was purple in color and had faded through age and wear but definitely was authentic. The floorboards were the original unvarnished wooden planks and all the walls had been painted a light blue. They were covered in a collage of ornaments and pictures from her travels all over the world. Even though Mariana was only twenty-four, she had been fortunate enough to visit every continent with her parents, at least twice.

Amongst other things on display, was a headdress from Mozambique, a clay pipe from Peru, and an old car number plate, pulled out of a swamp in Florida. One could spend a lot of time in the bedroom studying the vast amount of memorabilia.

The overriding theme on the walls, however, were numerous pictures of a beautiful lady, tanned, exotic- looking, and always wearing a big smile. This was her mother. A giant sized Brazilian flag was pinned to the ceiling directly above the bed. This was important to Mariana and it was the first thing that she saw when she opened her eyes in the morning. It reminded her of her love for Brazil and also of her mother, Bruna, who was originally from Sao Paulo. She had passed away five years ago.

Mariana had just woken up and she rolled on top of Jan and sat up. Her slender but muscular legs were positioned on either side of his torso. She looked down at Jan knowing exactly what she wanted. He stared up at her 32C pert breasts and not at Mariana's face, which annoyed her, although she didn't show it. Her breasts were just as brown as the rest of her body, the result of three weeks of religious sunbathing at her father's holiday home in St. Maxime. Her skin color was naturally dark because of her mother's heritage and hours of baking in the sun simply turned it a muddy brown.

Mariana loved to have sex when she first woke up in the morning, and today was no exception, although it was already early afternoon. She had been dating Jan for just over one year and as she looked down at him she thought to herself that she was attracted more to his body than his facial features. Jan was a pale-faced working class lad from Badhoevedorp, a small town about eight kilometers from Amsterdam. Their backgrounds couldn't be more different.

She was the daughter of Dr. Akkermans, a very well-known judge in Holland, who was from 'old money'. Her late mother was this beautiful vivacious woman who her father had met on his travels the year after graduating from University.

When she was growing up, her father was always working and was never around. It had been her mother who had spent all her time with Mariana. Mariana had been given everything including a lot of love. Since her mother passed away, she still got everything she wanted, apart from love.

Jan, on the other hand, had been brought up in a small town outside Amsterdam with his parents, who ran a bakery that had been passed down to them by his great grandparents. They had a simple but hard working life and he was much-loved by his family. His most exotic vacation had been a camping trip to the Black Forest in Germany with his parents ten years ago. This proved to be a very difficult holiday as they couldn't speak a word of German. Mariana, in contrast, had been everywhere and spoke six languages fluently.

Jan had no intention of taking over the family business although they didn't know this. He helped his parents out now for 'pocket money'. That and the house cleaning jobs made it possible for him to survive financially while studying History of Art at Amsterdam University. Mariana and Jan met at the University's Tai Kwon Do Club. She had been impressed by his black belt and quiet confidence and for being the toughest student in the club. They had sparred together and Jan had taught her a throw, which resulted in him pinning her to the ground and sitting on top of her. His power and strength had attracted her even if she saw him as being inferior to herself. After the class, she had invited him for a drink and he had ended up at her apartment having passionate sex.

Now she was straddling him, naked. Mariana didn't have the strength to pin his arms down but she was able to grip his body very hard, pinching him as she began to grind her buttocks over his belly button and hard penis. His eyes were now wide open as he stared up at his girlfriend's beautiful face. Jan was in awe of her and couldn't believe that he had been able to get such a stunning girlfriend. In fact, he always asked himself the same question, 'what does she see in me?' This was his first true love, and he wanted this relationship to last forever.

Mariana had her eyes closed. She was lost in her own thoughts but at the same time was in complete control of this situation. She always was.

Jan was beginning to breathe heavier and started to make dull groans of desire wanting to be inside Mariana. She would, however, decide about that and for now she was riding on top of him harder and harder but with no penetration. She liked this foreplay but also wanted to show him who had the power. You could hear the scraping of his pubic hair against her naked flesh. The friction hurt her soft skin, but she also liked it, as she knew she was close to being in ecstasy. This scratching noise became lighter as Mariana became wetter and wetter, her juices acting as a natural lubricant as she continued to rub herself on top of him.

She bit her bottom lip to avoid moaning out loud with pleasure. With her left hand, Mariana reached behind her and grabbed Jan's throbbing penis and slipped it quickly inside her. She was so wet that with one push Jan was all the way in. Mariana groaned louder not being able to conceal her excitement. She speeded this riding motion, moving harder and faster. Taking hold of Jan's left hand, she placed it on her breasts, closing his fingers so that he could squeeze one of her hardened red nipples. Taking his right hand, she lifted it up and put it round the front of her neck encouraging him to squeeze her throat tighter. She loved the feeling of being in submission, or being tied up, especially when she was about to come. The crazy thing was that she was in complete control, making him almost strangle her. It was becoming difficult for her to breathe with her windpipe half closed.

Jan knew the routine, but didn't complain, as she would have an orgasm every time. The goal for him was to make sure that he came before she was finished. With a final flurry of bouncing motions up and down, she speeded up her grinding and then screamed loudly with pleasure. Mariana rolled off Jan immediately. She had come and frustratingly, he had not. This did happen sometimes as she was actually a very selfish lover.

She sat up on the side of the bed, with her back to Jan, staring at a picture on the wall of herself with her parents skiing in Villars, fifteen years ago. What wouldn't she do to bring back her mother and replace her father? Her thoughts were disrupted by a glance at her wristwatch that lay on the bedside table. The vintage Cartier watch showed that it was 1:50 p.m., which made her twenty minutes late for lunch with her father.

"Shit!" shrieked Mariana, as she reached across to pick up the beautiful gold watch that used belong to her mother and tied it round her wrist. She didn't really care what her father thought about how she led her life but punctuality was important to her, a point that her mother had stressed a lot. It was also very important to her father and she couldn't face a lecture for being late today.

Jan leant across the bed and gently stroked Mariana's slender but muscular back. As expected, he didn't get a response. He reached down to the floor by the bed and retrieved the remote control. Pointing it at the fancy plasma on the wall at the end of the bed he turned on the television and flicked through the channels and stopped at the news. The channel was broadcasting from the RAI exhibition center, where a female reporter was speaking into a microphone in the rain.

"We have had no confirmation from the police yet but it looks like the Magpie has struck again. We know for sure that there is a dead body, as an ambulance reversed into the police tent to pick up something, presumably the victim. The ambulance left twenty-five minutes later and drove to the Vu hospital where the autopsy will be carried out. Detective Van Loo and his team were at the RAI earlier interviewing potential witnesses and spending most of their time inside the police tent. The body was found by a security guard in the early hours this morning."

Jan sat up in bed and lodged a pillow behind his neck for support so that he could listen comfortably to the news. Mariana still had her back to him and the television as she looked down admiringly at her mother's watch. Then, she stood upright and headed hastily towards the bathroom. Jan's eyes switched away from the news and focused in on her naked figure as she moved across the bedroom. He couldn't help staring at her tall slim frame. Mariana was extremely fit as a result of the weekly yoga and Tai Kwon Do classes that she took. There wasn't an ounce of fat on her body and at five foot ten inches she could easily be a model, especially with her naturally tanned skin, beautiful face, and bone structure. Her bottom cheeks were small and rounded like a peach and as she walked you could see the light between her legs all the way up to the top of her thighs. She didn't have a hair on her body. 'God, she's gorgeous,' thought Jan as he watched her disappear into the bathroom, shutting the door behind her and turning on the shower. He still couldn't believe that she was his girlfriend.

Jan had become hard again but turned back to the television to watch the news and to take his mind off it. His ears pricked up as he listened to the television reporter. Jan began to shake his head as it was clear that they didn't really know too much regarding what had taken place. They even started repeating themselves explaining that it had to be another one of the serial killings. Their reasoning behind this was that there hadn't been a body dumped in September yet and as we were nearing the end of the month this had to be the one. The reporter then went on to tell the Magpie's story and that there had been a murder every month since the beginning of the year. In Holland, this was common information, so the reporter apparently had no new news to report.

There was no mention of whether the body was male or female or whether a missing person's report had been filed recently that matched this victim. Jan shuffled like a crab down the bed to get closer to the plasma screen, as the news showed shots of Detective Van Loo passing the wall of reporters and ignoring their onslaught of questions. Everyone knew who Van Loo was, including Jan. As he sat upright on the bed with his legs crossed you could see Jan's stomach muscles piercing through his skinny torso. He was wiry in physique but very strong.

Jan lost his concentration for a second and looked up. Mariana was standing at the corner of the bed, staring at him, with a stern expression on her face. She had a white cotton towel wrapped around her body and was holding a smaller towel, which she used to dry her dark brown wet hair. The color and thickness of her hair matched her Amazonian roots.

She had long and thick perfectly groomed locks, which looked far too immaculate for a student.

In her posh Dutch accent, with a hint of foreign twang, Mariana spoke to Jan in her usual disinterested tone. "I'm late. Let yourself out. I need to rush to my father's." She turned and dropped both towels and then walked towards her double wardrobe. Selecting a pair of jeans, a black lace string, and a cream-colored blouse, she had her outfit picked out for today. Mariana wasn't shy as she bent over to put on her underwear and jeans. Jan stared at her as everything was on show. Mariana didn't even think twice about bending over naked in front of him. She knew that she was gorgeous, and anyhow, she simply didn't care what Jan thought of her at all. She was very confident of herself.

Mariana went across to her dresser and selected a pair of diamond stud earrings from a glass bowl that sat on the top. Putting them in her ears, you could see that while they were small they were also very real. She also wore a small silk scarf that she tied in a knot around her neck. It was red, orange, and white in color and looked extremely expensive. She always wore this type of scarf and Jan didn't really like it. This was not a normal item of clothing for an Amsterdam student and made her stand out from the crowd. It was a sign of wealth and showed that she liked to be different. Jan would not dare question her about it, as he was scared of how she would react. His believed she wore these scarves because every picture of her mother also had one tied around her neck in exactly the same way. In fact, most of the scarves she used belonged to her mother. Jan wanted to surprise Mariana with one last Christmas but had walked out empty-handed, horrified by the price.

Jan turned back to Mariana who was pouting and staring at herself in the mirror. She put her hair up very quickly using an elastic cotton band and then applied one stroke of lip gloss as she pulled a moody face, still transfixed by her own reflection. With one squirt of perfume to her neck, she turned and headed out of the bedroom towards the living room, without looking at Jan or saying goodbye. He could hear her taking a drink of water in the kitchen and then putting on her shoes.

"See you at class on Thursday," she called out, before slamming the front door behind her. She was gone. Jan waited for a few seconds and then got out of the bed and pulled the window curtains slightly to one side so that he could peek outside. He could see her unlocking her bike and then cycling off down the canal road in the direction of her father's place. He would see her at Tai Kwon Do on Thursday. Jan lay back on the bed for a second, frustrated. They had been together for over a year and he didn't feel any closer to her today than when they first met. He loved Mariana dearly, but she wouldn't let him in. She was a closed book with a lot of issues, probably stemming from her mother's death. She certainly didn't show any feeling of love towards Jan but he sort-of accepted this. He convinced himself that they had been together for quite some time so she must at least like him a little bit. For now, that was good enough for Jan.

Jan broke out of his deep thoughts and sprung up from the bed. He, too, needed to go home. He was also in a rush. He slipped on his clothes that lay in a pile by the bed. There was no time for a shower because he needed to get back to help his parents with the dough preparation for the following week. Today was the most important part of the week's work for the family business and Jan was an integral part of that, together with his sisters, Doreen and Imke. He wore an old blue t-shirt and a pair of faded jeans. Walking into the living room, Jan put on his hooded sweatshirt and white Converse trainers. He was ready to head home. He never liked to leave, as when he was alone, he didn't feel like he really had a girlfriend. Mariana gave him no reason to think anything different. Until he saw her next Thursday, she would not text or call him. Sometimes he felt that she just used him for sex.

The living room was simple and spacious but filled with expensive furniture. Apart from one door leading to a second small bathroom, there was another one that went from the living room down to a storage room. Jan thought that Mariana was lucky having a father who basically bought her anything she wanted and especially fortunate to have her own apartment. She was spoiled by Dr. Akkermans and didn't appreciate him.

Leaving the apartment, Jan shut the front door and walked across the cobbled road to his small white van that was parked right outside by the canal. He took one last glance back at the apartment and then unlocked the van's door and got in. The van actually belonged to his parents and was used to deliver the fresh bread to the local supermarkets and village shops around Badhoeve-dorp.

As Jan did most of the deliveries, he had full access to the van, which was probably the only perk of the job. He could drive into Amsterdam for lectures or to see Mariana whenever she would let him. The van made his life a lot easier. Unfortunately, Mariana refused to get into it, as she felt embarrassed being seen in a baker's van. This annoyed Jan, but he had learnt to put up with her pompous nature. In some ways, she had made him extremely ambitious and now he wanted more for himself than just working in the family business.

He sped off down a narrow canal road in the middle of the city. He would take a small detour and go past Mariana's father's house on the Keizersgracht, before heading for the motorway and then home to Badhoevedorp. It was unlikely that he would catch a glimpse of Mariana in Dr. Akkermans' large town house but the thought of being near her again made him content. Jan's parents would be disappointed with him for being home late but they had gotten used to it over the last year. Mariana had changed him. He had become more insular, sadder, and less loving towards his parents and sisters. These were not the normal emotions that you would expect from someone who had found love.

* * *

6:00 p.m.

Arnaud knocked on the door of the autopsy room. It had a 'busy' card on the wall next to it, so he didn't want to enter until he was sure that he was about to attend the right autopsy. Friso opened the door slightly and popped his head out. Seeing Arnaud, he opened it fully to let him in, then turned and walked back to the middle of the room. The steel handle was very cold as Arnaud held it and shut the door softly behind him.

Arnaud had been in this particular room on numerous occasions over the years and eight times just this year. It didn't ever get any easier attending autopsies, and the ninth one of the year was just as traumatic as the first. There was silence in the bare room. He could see the long steel table on which the body lay, still covered. As Arnaud walked across the room, he was hit by a strong smell of disinfectant. Next to the lifeless body was a smaller table which held an array of knives and surgical tools. .

Dr. Kuipers greeted Arnaud, who he had grown to like very much. The doctor was a small middle-aged surgeon who gave a very 'matter of fact' account of everybody he had to look at. It was his job and he didn't seem to get emotional about touching the dead victims or cutting through their flesh and organs. Arnaud didn't know how he did it but was pleased to have him on the case, as he got straight to the point and always gave a very clear explanation of his findings.

Also in the room, standing next to Friso was Dijkstra, who was looking extremely tired and somber. Arnaud was surprised to see him but it proved that he was under a lot of pressure, just like the rest of them.

The doctor flicked a light switch on the wall that shone onto the operating table. The sheet covering the body was a violet color and you could make out the shape of the man beneath it.

Arnaud shuddered as he looked down at the tray of stainless steel knives, saws, and pliers that lay on the small table next to the doctor. They all served a purpose and sadly, Arnaud had seen them in action numerous times before.

The doctor looked across at the three detectives and then with one sweeping motion pulled the sheet all the way off the body. Using a small steel instrument as a pointer, the doctor began to go through his initial findings. As the doctor started speaking, Arnaud stared at the body for the first time, trying to see any familiar signs that would make it clearer to him who had done this.

"The body arrived here as it was found." began the doctor, "Naked."

This was the first box ticked thought Arnaud to himself. The Magpie had dumped all the bodies with no clothes on them. This victim was a slim muscular male, medium build, of average height, and in his mid-twenties. His skin was very pale, verging on grey. There were no markings on the body, as it lay there, almost in a frozen state.

"Time of death," continued the doctor in his monotone, "approximately forty-eight hours ago."

"Like the rest." Dijkstra spoke out, stating the obvious. All the Magpie's victims were dumped about two days after the person had gone missing.

"Cause of death," said the doctor, pointing with a scalpel to some bruising around the side of the victim's neck. "A broken vertebrae, again."

It was now confirmed, in Arnaud's mind, that it was the Magpie who had struck again. Everything was the same. He didn't deviate even a bit from his killing pattern. Why would he? The killer was effective in his work. As Arnaud walked around the body, the doctor continued talking, giving a robotic commentary of his findings. Arnaud saw a lot of similarities between himself and the doctor: no bullshit, very detailed, and straight to the point.

"It still seems strange to me," continued the doctor, stopping to sigh and think for a second. "That again, there does not appear to have been any struggle or resistance from the victim." The doctor had a baffled look on his face as he had clearly pondered over this before.

"The only bruising is around the second vertebrae in the neck, which was snapped."

The doctor stopped speaking and looked up at the three detectives. They were all thinking the same thing. They had all seen this before. There had not been any markings on any of the other eight men found dead this year. All the victims seemed to just let it happen without putting up a fight.

Arnaud scanned the hands of the dead person. They were perfectly clean with no scratches on them. A finger on the left hand had indented flesh around the area where presumably a ring was worn. Noticing what Arnaud was looking at, the doctor began speaking again.

"It does appear that the victim had been wearing a ring." He then pointed to the earlobes of the victim. "He also has his ears pierced and the markings on the skin would indicate that perhaps he was wearing earrings as well."

Arnaud interrupted directly facing Friso, "When we have an ID on this guy, please check with his friends if he wore a ring and earrings. It may help with potential witnesses, once we find out where he went missing."

Friso made a note in a small black book, which he then slipped back in the inside pocket of his raincoat. Every killing this year had been a male and their bodies had been dumped naked with any jewelry removed.

"It looks like both the fingernails and toe-nails have been cut and cleaned thoroughly. Also, his hair appears to have been washed after the killing, from the strong smell of a fragranced soap ." said the doctor.

Arnaud looked at the victim's hands and feet again and noticed that the flesh was very red compared to the rest of the body, indicating that they, also, had been scrubbed hard with strong disinfectant.

The killer had been very thorough, as usual, cleaning the body after death to ensure that there were no DNA or other traces left.

Arnaud felt pity for the victim, staring at the still corpse with its eyes and mouth closed. He wished he could give more information to the public about the cause of the death. He wanted everyone to know that young men were at risk and that the killer seemed to get his prey without any struggle involved. This would surely scare the public, and possibly deter men from going out alone. Apart from victim number four in April, who was fifty-three, all the others were at the prime of their lives; between the ages of eighteen and forty-one.

He couldn't reveal too much, at least, not yet. Arnaud and his team had decided not to give away too much information around how the Magpie was killing his victims. This was partly because they didn't know the specifics themselves but also because they didn't want to give the killer a feeling of satisfaction or accomplishment. He was clearly getting more confident as he continued to take a new victim every month and followed the same method each time. The Magpie was successful and whatever his motivations were, he was getting a taste for this now, and also knew that he was no closer to getting caught.

Arnaud had tried putting more undercover policemen on the streets at night, wired up, and matching the basic profiles of the victims but so far it hadn't worked. At the start of every month, they would have fifteen undercover policemen in the bars around Amsterdam during the evenings. There was no pattern around where the victims were last seen by friends or witnesses or to where the bodies were subsequently dumped. As the days of each month went by, without a murder, they would increase the number of undercover policemen and normal policemen on the streets, knowing that their chances of catching the Magpie statistically went up. He struck every month and Arnaud believed that he wasn't going to change this, as it was a statement of his success. He was in control and nobody was ever going to catch him.

Again, this hadn't worked so far, but Arnaud had the backing of Dijkstra and the most senior management within the police force, so they would continue this tactic. They had no choice. They needed to do something.

Arnaud looked over at Friso.

"How close are we to getting an ID on this guy?"

"I should have the missing persons' report soon and we will be releasing a picture of the victim's face to the press shortly," replied Friso.

Arnaud knew that as soon as the victim's picture was passed on to the newspapers, they would get an ID from friends and family. This was a difficult time to deal with but at least they could move onto the next part of the investigation process. Once identified, they could find out where he was last seen and hopefully start interviewing potential witnesses.

Arnaud turned to Dr. Kuipers and thanked him. The doctor nodded and then Arnaud left with Friso and Dijkstra. As they walked out of the hospital Arnaud told his colleagues that he was going to the office. Friso said that he would come as well. It was now 8:15 p.m. Surprising both Arnaud and Friso, their boss said that he would join them. Dijkstra was looking quite upset at the moment and clearly, he had found the autopsy very disturbing. This was the first one that he had attended regarding this case. It had obviously brought home the nature of this trail of murders to him.

As Arnaud walked towards the moped, Dijkstra called out to him.

"I am going to make sure that we can increase the number of undercover police on the streets. I just need to get approval."

He was clearly emotional after today's events and obviously was frustrated like Arnaud and Friso. Dijkstra was normally weak when it came to dealing with the politics in the police force, but for once, he was backing his men and willing to push for what they needed. This news pleased Arnaud as he got on his moped. He watched his two colleagues split up and head for their own cars. He would see them soon enough back at the office.

* * *

8:35 p.m.

Arnaud arrived at the police station at almost the same time as Friso and Dijkstra. As they each walked into their own offices, they saw the two young policemen, who were helping them with the case sitting behind Friso's desk.
"Hi Jim. Hi Robin," said Friso.

They were reporting into him, as they were responsible for interviewing minor witnesses and data crunching. Arnaud didn't have either the time or the patience for that.

They looked eager to speak and Arnaud beckoned them to do so.

"Okay, any luck with the identification?" asked Arnaud.

"Yes," replied Jim. "The victim is Thomas Deckers, twenty-eight years old, from Weesp." He looked down at his notes to make sure that he got all the facts right. "He went missing on Thursday night."

Friso interrupted Jim. "Why have we only just found out about a missing person's report when he has been missing for almost three days?"

"Well, his friends thought that he must have gotten lucky with a girl or gone home early." Robin chimed in now. "They didn't think that he was in any danger."

Robin spoke up again. "It wasn't until a couple of his friends saw the news today and tried reaching Deckers that they started getting worried. As none of his friends or family had spoken to him since Thursday, they decided to contact the police and then they were passed onto us."

"So, we have witnesses?" said Arnaud.

"Yes," replied Jim and Robin at the same time.

"He was out with friends for a night in Leidseplein," said Jim. "And was last seen at approximately eleven-thirty in a club by one of his friends."

This was now getting interesting, thought Arnaud, as there were friends who were with him that night and could have seen him with someone. There were also many witnesses in the club who might have seen something or someone that could turn out to be a vital clue.

"Ok," said Arnaud. "I want you two to interview the victim's family and also the friends who were out with him last Thursday night." Arnaud didn't need to say it but Friso would oversee this. "I will see you guys in the morning."

He turned and headed for the door. Arnaud wanted to go home and think. It had been a long day and there was a lot to take in. His stress levels had also gone up a few notches and he needed to calm himself down. He would have a couple drinks before going to bed otherwise he'd never be able to sleep. Before he managed to reach the office door, Dijkstra spoke up.

"Arnaud, we will need to make a statement to the press tomorrow morning and identify the victim. You and I should do that."

Arnaud hated doing this. It wasn't the sharing of the information, but the probing questions that followed from the pushy reporters, that he detested. He would have to try and be as pleasant to the rude journalists as he could and respond to their questioning, without giving too much away.

"Ok," said Arnaud as he left the office, without turning back around.

Arnaud needed time alone, time to plan for tomorrow. What was he going to say on camera to the press? What would the public think? Had he failed again? Would the killer be watching him being interviewed? What would his ex-wife and daughter think? These questions ate away at Arnaud as he walked down the stairway to the garage. He also wanted to think about what the Magpie's next move could be. There were just over four days left in September and then the killer, if he stuck to his pattern, would potentially strike again. Arnaud started up his moped and headed home to contemplate.

* * *

9:40 p.m.

Sitting in his living room, Arnaud didn't turn on the television or radio. He didn't want to hear anyone else's views on this latest murder, which would of course, be on every channel. Pressure continued to mount, and add to his frustrations. He wasn't any closer to ending the killer's run of success. It was right now, the bane of his life.

The apartment was cold and dark, as usual. He was pleased that he couldn't make out the picture on the mantelpiece of his daughter and his estranged wife. His daughter Anna, who was now fourteen, was the only thing in his life that he really cared about. Arnaud went to visit her once every three weeks in Arnhem, where she now lived with her mother. Anna was proud of her dad and loved him dearly.

Arnaud took off his jacket and dropped it onto the small sofa in his living room. He then slumped back down into the old leather seat. This was always his seat of choice. He had fallen asleep so many times in it that it was comfortable and had shaped to fit his body over the years. Arnaud threw his keys onto the small round wooden coffee table that stood to the right side of the leather seat. He then leant across for the light switch to turn on the lamp that sat on top of the small table.

Without looking, he reached for the bottle of gin that was positioned on the floor next to him. Arnaud proceeded to pour himself four large glasses of gin and then gulped them one by one. Within thirty minutes, he was fast asleep, and snoring softly. He would now have six hours of freedom away from this job that lately had a stranglehold on him. The case was suffocating Arnaud slowly, and he saw no way out. Nine months into the year, and they still had no idea who they were chasing and therefore were no closer to catching the killer.

The rain started again, falling down heavily against the windows of his Jordaan apartment. The wind began to whistle through the narrow streets of this older part of Amsterdam and up into the cracks of the sash window frames in his living room. The noise was melodic, almost singing Arnaud a lullaby and helping him to stay asleep.

CHAPTER 4

September 26

8:55 a.m.

The Morning After

Mariana rolled over, yawned, and opened one eye to look at the time. She pulled her left arm from under the blanket so that she could see her watch. She lay back and smiled to herself as the watch always brought back great memories of her late mother. It had been a fortieth birthday present from her father. On the back was inscribed, "To my darling Bruna. Love always, Ate." She had thought about changing the back of the case many times but it probably would have upset her mother, so she never did it.

She had stayed the night at her father's house in her old bedroom. She sometimes did this to appease her father when he was disappointed with her or when she needed something, which was usually money. On this occasion, she had slept over because he had been upset with her for being late again for lunch yesterday.

Mariana always kept the windows open in her old bedroom. It was on the top floor of their five-story canal house, located on the Golden Bend of the Keizersgracht. The bedroom gathered a lot of dust as it wasn't used often and fresh air was essential. She also slept better in a cold bedroom. Her father, Dr. Akkermans, was very old-fashioned and insisted on all the beds in the house being covered with traditional blankets. Mariana didn't actually mind this as she had grown up with blankets rather than a duvet, however, she wouldn't admit this to her father. She always mocked him for being dated in his views and very 'old school'.

Probably the nicest thing about staying at her father's house was that she would get to see Rina, the live-in maid. Rina had worked for the Akkermans' family for nineteen years and was always very nice to Mariana. She would wash and iron her laundry and cook wonderful food. Rina had been Mariana's nanny since she was six years old and still treated her like a princess, although not so openly in front of Dr. Akkermans. Mariana liked being spoilt.

Rina had been very close to Mariana's mother, as well. Bruna had confided in her when she was having marital problems with Mariana's father. Bruna was distraught for seven whole years when Dr. Akkermans had an affair, and Rina was always there to listen and help where she could. She was very caring towards Mariana and had promised her mother, when she was in the late stages of her breast cancer, to always look after her daughter. After Bruna had passed away, Rina continued speaking Portuguese to Mariana. This had been another promise that she had made to her mother. Rina was from a different part of Brazil, a small town south of Rio. As she was Brazilian, she had shared a close bond with her mother and now with Mariana.

Nowadays, Mariana and Rina continued to speak together in Portuguese most of the time. However, Mariana made a real effort to speak it whenever her father was in the same room with them. She did this to annoy him, as his Portuguese was poor at the best of times, and he certainly would not understand everything that they would be talking about. This would frustrate Dr. Akkermans, with him being such an educated, clever man, and it was something that Mariana had over him. Mariana liked this and always talked with Rina about him in Portuguese when he was close by, making jokes and often being very rude. Rina always tried to be respectful to Dr. Akkermans and would only give a small grin of acknowledgement to Mariana at one of her most rude remarks. If Mariana went too far, Rina would give her a quick stern look.

Mariana knew that Rina would now be in the kitchen, preparing breakfast for them. She needed to get dressed and go downstairs quickly as breakfast always began promptly at nine and her father was very strict about that. Mariana had been late for lunch yesterday and hadn't seen her father that annoyed for a long time. He was an extremely punctual man and expected everyone else around him to be, as well. Dr. Akkermans hadn't spoken to her during the whole meal and instead just read his paper. After the late lunch, he had stormed off into his study to look over cases. He had even slammed a few doors in the house, which was very unusual, as he normally never showed any emotion. Dr. Akkermans was a quiet, methodical man most of the time, and yesterday he made it clear how annoyed and disappointed he was with his daughter.

Mariana liked to annoy her father but he was her 'lifeline' right now and she needed to remember to be extra nice. He bought her the apartment on the Singel, financed her studies, holidays, and everything else. Soon after her mother died, she had left high school and she started smoking marijuana and hanging out with some strange people. Dr. Akkermans had tried to be strict with her but it didn't work as she would disappear for days on end. He decided to send Mariana to a finishing school in Switzerland to try and change her ways. Although she actually enjoyed the experience, living in a school with other wealthy children from all over Europe, she told her father that it was unbearable just to make him feel guilty. After a year in Switzerland, she became bored and begged her father to let her study in Amsterdam. Mariana claimed that she had changed and convinced Dr. Akkermans to buy her an apartment. Although he didn't believe her for one second, he did feel sorry for her and of course, had succumbed to her wishes.

Mariana always blamed everything on her mother's death as she knew that this was the best way to get to her father. As Mariana grew older, she looked more like her mother. She was fully aware of this and the melancholy it brought her father. Dr. Akkermans knew that his daughter was complicated and didn't really like him, because she felt that her mother had gotten cancer through her stress and worry over her husband's affair. Because of his guilt, he had spoilt Mariana hoping that he could make her happy and that maybe one day she might forgive him.

Dr. Akkermans was sure that Mariana wore her mother's silk scarves and jewelry to remind him of her. This coupled with the fact that she even put her hair up in the same way as her mother, made it very difficult for him not to dote on Mariana. She always got what she wanted. Mariana knew that she was beautiful, a younger version of Bruna, but with a lot more attitude. The neck scarves were always rolled up and tied in a knot at the side, exactly the same way her mother had worn them. Mariana had ten of these colorful silk scarves, all of which had belonged to Bruna, and had been presents from her father.

Mariana got out of bed and stood upright and stretched. Raising her arms above her head and standing on tip-toes, she could touch the bedroom ceiling with her skinny tanned fingers. Her muscles were a little stiff from the Tai Kwon Do lessons this week and the passionate bout of sex yesterday. She didn't need to have sex again for a few days and saw Thursday, after their martial arts class, as good timing. Wearing nothing more than a white vest and her underwear, Mariana skipped out of her bedroom and across the hallway of this decadent old canal house into the bathroom. Like her apartment, this house had pictures and unusual objects hung over all the walls on every floor. Dr. Akkermans rarely had time to travel these days because of his high-profile role as one of the top judges in Holland. Therefore, most of the pieces on the walls were old.

This wonderful town house was positioned on one of the most prestigious part of the Keizersgracht. It was now too big for her father to live there on his own even though Rina kept it immaculate. Dr. Akkermans stayed there because of all the good memories he had from the past with his family, as well as the image that came with living in such a location. He also thought that his daughter liked coming back home from time to time and this made him happy, even if he wouldn't admit this to her. Also, having such a large house kept Rina very busy and fully employed. He wanted to give their dear family friend security. Apart from her delicious cooking, it was also a status symbol for him to have a full- time maid.

The house had six bathrooms in total, and the one on the top floor had some special memories for her. When she was sixteen, she used to smoke marijuana out of the bathroom window and then creep back into her bedroom, stoned. Her parents never knew that she used to smoke upstairs, although Rina had found the old joint ends on the window ledge. She didn't tell her parents but tried to convince Mariana to give up smoking. When she was seventeen, she had sneaked a boyfriend upstairs to her bedroom and when her father had heard them having sex, she had hidden the boy in this bathroom in a cupboard under the marble sink. He was never found and she had denied the whole thing to her parents.

Mariana looked in the old bathroom mirror above the sink and was happy with what stared back at her. She saw a slim, tall, tanned beauty. She took off her watch and rings and placed them on the white marble surface next to the sink. The two rings that she wore on her index finger had belonged to her mother. One was a platinum band encrusted with diamonds. It was subtle yet exquisite. The other was a worn silver band that had been her mother's wedding ring. The third was a gold signet ring, which was given to Mariana on her eighteenth birthday and she wore it on her little finger. It had a blue face with the family crest cut in to it, picturing an eagle with two crossed keys.

Mariana filled the sink with warm water and with cupped hands she washed her face. Pulling a cheesy smile in the mirror, she checked out her perfect, white teeth. Then, she took a toothpick and prodded into the gaps between them. She noticed blood on her gums and sucked it away immediately. Mariana then pulled out some cotton wool pads and dipped them into a small pot of facial cream. Unsparingly, as her father paid for all of her beauty products, she pampered her face for a further ten minutes. Mariana took one last look in the mirror, and after a deep breath, she decided that she was ready to go downstairs to face her father.

Putting her jewelry and watch back on and slipping into a tight pair of black jogging pants and a white slim fitting t-shirt, she walked back across the hallway and headed for the stairs. She was sure that the high-pitched creaking of floorboards would be heard downstairs by her father, and he would know that she was awake and would be coming down shortly for breakfast.

The coiling stairwell took her down the whole five flights of stairs. A lush crimson carpet covered the wooden stairs and even though her father knew that she was awake, he didn't hear her approach the ground floor. As Mariana walked on the black and white marble-tiled hallway towards the kitchen, she felt the cold stone under her feet give her chills, especially since she wasn't wearing any socks. At the end of the hallway, she looked into the large kitchen and saw Rina standing over the AGA, preparing scrambled eggs. This was her favorite. Mariana smiled and skipped into the kitchen. She stopped behind Rina and gave her a kiss on the cheek.

Speaking in Portuguese, Mariana said 'Good morning' to Rina. The maid didn't turnaround but smiled and greeted her back in her mother tongue.

In the middle of this huge kitchen stood a long oak dining table and at one end of it, in his familiar position, sat Dr. Akkermans. He was a very imposing man, extremely tall and thick-set from lack of training and too much good food and wine. He had rowed most of his life and represented Holland on a number of occasions and also in the Olympics. However, since getting arthritis in his right knee about three years ago his exercise regime had stopped, and he had put on quite a bit of weight.

Immaculately dressed in a crisp white shirt, washed and ironed by Rina, Dr. Akkermans wore his familiar gold cufflinks, engraved with his initials, AAA, Ate Arie Akkermans. He also wore a dark blue silk woven tie with a thick Windsor knot. He was a good-looking man with a tanned handsome face that was always clean-shaven. Dr. Akkermans had a prominent pointed nose that was not so big but red at the end. Too much Scotch and fine red wine were the cause of this. He had thick silver-colored hair, oiled and slicked back over his head and cut just above his shirt collar. His appearance made him look both wise and important, and he worked hard to maintain this image.

Mariana looked at her father and thought that he had gotten even more tanned since returning from his late summer vacation in the South of France. She assumed it must be from all the golf he played at the Kennemer in Zaandvoort. This was the other passion in his life, apart from being the top judge in the country. Mariana walked behind her father and around the table towards the other end where Rina had set up a place for Mariana to eat breakfast. Mariana touched her father's shoulder as she walked past him. She felt his big athletic muscular frame, even if it was a little softer these days. This was as much affection as she was going to give him right now.

Mariana took her seat and stared down the other end of the table at her father and managed to pull a fake smile. He was, however, not looking at her but still hunched over reading all the newspapers that he had laid out in front of him in a mosaic. Various papers were tactically positioned and opened to specific pages and articles, so that Dr. Akkermans could skip between the various pieces quickly and take in as much information as possible in a short time. He looked like a military general overseeing maps and battle plans.

Between large bites from his heavily-buttered toast and loud slurps from his mug of tea, Dr. Akkermans muttered to himself as his head flicked from one newspaper to the next. His legs were so long that they stuck out from either side of the table revealing dark blue pinstriped trousers. They were well-pressed like everything else he wore.

Dr. Akkermans breathed in loudly as he finished reading another article and looked up over the top of his small gold-rimmed circular glasses perched on the bridge of his nose. As he focused in on Mariana he also managed to pull a semi-smile.

"How are you today, Papa?" Mariana spoke softly across the table, deciding to start the conversation. If she needed something, she would call him Papa, and if she didn't, then it would be Ate. He also knew the pattern to her affections and was fully aware of how she played with his emotions. Right now, however, she didn't need anything but she did feel like she was in his 'bad book' as she was late for lunch yesterday. At some point in the not so distant future she would need an injection of cash from her father and it made sense to try and win him over now.

Dr. Akkermans sighed again and looked away from his daughter back down at the papers that lay out in front of him.

"I am fine, my dear, but Amsterdam is not." he replied in his deep voice, and very posh tone. His use of words was very clear and straight to the point, just as if he was sitting in a courtroom delivering a verdict.

"It would appear that this serial killer has struck again. It's all over the papers."

"Oh no," Mariana replied, only semi-interested in what her father was saying. She had seen the story on the news yesterday. She looked over at Rina and smiled, which was her way of telling her that she was ready for breakfast.

Rina walked over with a plate of scrambled eggs on toast. She always tried to give Mariana big portions as she thought that Mariana was too skinny and needed plumping up. Mariana loved her cooking but never ate it all. She had gone from being slim to very slender and muscular. Mariana was very hungry and started cutting the scrambled eggs and toast up into small manageable pieces. As she took the first mouthful, she glanced over at her father, who was still looking down at the papers and shaking his head in response to what he was reading.

Mariana spoke up, trying to make conversation again. "I can't believe that they haven't caught him yet." Her father looked up from his papers and replied, "Well, they don't even know if it's a 'he' my dear." He cleared his throat and continued, "Although, it probably is. I would say, however, that it's alarming that the team investigating the case do not seem to be making any progress."

Dr. Akkermans picked up a newspaper with his right hand and then continued in an aggravated voice.

"These newspapers actually have no new information. They don't confirm if the victim is a male or female or if it's actually the work of the Raven."

"Magpie, Papa." Mariana interrupted him. "Magpie." She said again. Correcting him gave her great pleasure although she didn't want to show it at the moment. He didn't acknowledge his mistake but continued on with his rant.

"Or whether they have any clues about the cause of death." He shook his head again in despair. Bothered by the lack of information in the papers, Dr. Akkermans grabbed the remote and pointed it at the old square television that sat on a shelf in the kitchen on an adjacent wall. On the first channel that came up, there was a reporter talking about the RAI murder. First, you saw clips of the exhibition center and the crowd of reporters that were huddled there all day on Sunday. Then, the pictures changed to a 'live' image of the same group of camera crews and journalists standing outside the police station on Koninginneweg in the Old South part of Amsterdam.

Three detectives walked outside the front entrance of the police station to address the crowd. It was clearly the start of a press conference and Dr. Akkermans recognized Arnaud Van Loo.

"Perfect timing," said Mariana's father, as he moved his seat forward in the direction of the television and turned up the volume.

Dijkstra spoke first, "Yesterday morning at 5:17 a.m., a body was found in the main car park by Hall Two at the RAI Exhibition Centre. The victim is a white male from Weesp named Thomas Deckers. He was twenty-eight years old. The family of the deceased has been notified." The senior detective looked under stress and he took a moment to collect his thoughts. The reporters were silent as they waited for him to continue. "It would appear that the cause of death was a broken neck. We are still looking into when and where the victim was last seen and need to interview more witnesses before we can reveal any further information. All that I can say, further, is that the investigation is ongoing."

Because Dijkstra had finished his well-planned speech, the journalists started screaming a barrage of questions at him. Every reporter was trying to get their question heard and they were clearly disappointed with the small amount of new information on the case. It was actually very difficult to hear any question clearly. The one word that kept being repeated in all the shouting was 'Magpie'.

Dr. Akkermans continued watching the television intensely as Dijkstra raised his hand to quieten the crowd. He then pointed to a female journalist in the front row and waited for her to speak.

"Is it the work of the Magpie, Detective?" the lady from the NRC newspaper spoke up. There was silence as everyone waited for the senior detective to reply.

"It would appear that it is part of the ongoing investigation of the trail of murders that have taken place in and around Amsterdam this year. Yes."

The reporters were clearly annoyed by Dijkstra's politically correct response and a string of further questions were fired at the three detectives standing in a line. So far, Arnaud and Friso had not said anything. The crowd of journalists was getting louder and louder.

In the kitchen, Mariana's father started shouting at the television, also annoyed with the detective.

"Of course, it is linked to all of the other murders this year." Mariana's father continued his rage. "There has been one killing a month and this poor bugger is the Magpie's victim for September!" his voice was now very loud as he got more annoyed. Mariana could see that Rina felt uncomfortable with her father shouting. She also didn't want to hear him ranting away.

"Papa, can you turn it off, please," asked Mariana politely. "I am trying to have breakfast with you and don't really want to listen to this."

Her father seemed to ignore her as he remained fixed on the screen. The noise from the television went quiet as Dijkstra began to speak again to the attentive angry audience, who looked like they were getting ready to pounce on him.

"The victim appears to have been killed a number of days ago so there are definitely some similarities to the previous killings."

Once the crowd realized that was all he was going to say, the questioning started again. The detective then raised both his hands and shouted above the reporters' voices, taking them by surprise, but getting them to simmer down pretty quickly.

Dijkstra continued, "That's all we have to say right now. We need to get back to work and continue this investigation. Anyone who saw anything unusual around the RAI in the last forty-eight hours, please contact the police. Thank you."

With that, the three detectives turned and walked back into the police station. Camera lights were flashing and reporters were shouting as they huddled in closer to the entrance of the building. The noise of the crowd got even louder as they shouted both questions and insults at the three men who had made their exit. There was a lot of anger and frustration in the air. There was no real story to report. Dr. Akkermans picked up the remote and pressed the off button as he shook his head once again.

"That Detective Van Loo didn't even speak! I thought he was supposed to be running this investigation!" Dr. Akkermans made a loud tut and then turned back to face his daughter. She was gone.

Rina walked over to the table to clear Mariana's plate and cutlery. She had eaten very little. They could both hear Mariana's footsteps running up the stairs in the direction of her bedroom. Dr. Akkermans looked at Rina to get her reaction. Rina clearly looked annoyed but said nothing as usual. Dr. Akkermans was her employer and she respected him very much. She also knew that even though he was quite 'pig-headed' in character, his daughter was not the easiest person to deal with. He put his big hands on the tabletop and pushed himself up. Dr. Akkermans brushed the crumbs off his clothes and took one last swig from his tea. He then walked to the doorway leading out of the kitchen to call after his daughter up the stairwell.

"Mariana!" there was silence. "Mariana, darling." There was still no reply. She was upset with him. It wasn't the first time and it certainly wouldn't be the last. Putting one hand on his hip and running the other hand through his slicked back hair, he sighed with despair. He didn't know how to handle his complicated daughter. Dr. Akkermans walked back to the kitchen table and picked up the papers and carefully folded them one by one. With a nice neat pile under his arm he headed to the other doorway leading out of the kitchen into his study. This is where he spent his time when he wasn't in his office or in the courts. Here, he would study cases, think and read newspapers and journals.

His mind was on his daughter right now. When would he see her again? Was she really upset with him, or just playing a mind game? When would she come and stay again? He decided that he would call her later today, once she had cooled down. That often worked best.

Mariana regularly came over on Friday's for dinner or a drink after her boyfriend left for his cleaning jobs. He thought it was a shame that he very rarely got to meet Jan. Was it because he once made a comment about Jan's parents running a bakery? He couldn't think of any other reason why Mariana didn't want them to meet. Dr. Akkermans thought that he seemed like a nice guy, if only a little quiet. It had been almost six months since they had met. He wished that he could rewind the clock and not ask Mariana about her boyfriend. But this was the case with a lot of things. It seemed like Mariana disapproved of everything that he said. "Damn it!" said Dr. Akkermans to himself.

His trail of thought was broken by Rina's knocking on the study door. She walked in with his morning cup of coffee.

"Thank you," said Dr. Akkermans as he watched Rina place the large mug on his desk in front of him. She turned around and headed back out of the study shutting the door behind her leaving the sad judge to read, think, and be alone.

CHAPTER 5

11:15 a.m.

Roos sat on a bright red sofa in her pretty little living room staring at the small television. She was wrapped up under her duvet cover. Her mouth was wide open and her eyes transfixed on the screen. She could not believe the story being told on every channel. She had been watching the news covering the latest murder for about one and a half hours. The curtains to her 'nine streets' apartment were closed and apart from the small coffee table lamp and the light coming from the television, the living room was very dark. She didn't want to miss any of the updates and it was good to watch the news in such a setting.

Fleur walked into the living room wearing a tiny pair of pink shorts and a skin-tight t-shirt. Roos averted her eyes from the television for a second to look at her, and as usual, she couldn't believe that her flat-mate would wear clothes that were far too small for her. Fleur had very nice legs but they were slightly too orange, she must have just applied some tanning cream to them. Her nails were painted silver with sparkling bits in them. Fleur's t-shirt only went down to the bottom of her rib cage and you could see her tight mid-drift and a gold belly button ring. Through the t-shirt Roos couldn't help but stare at Fleur's erect nipples, which stood out because of the cold living room.

Fleur had 34DD breasts, which she had paid for herself last year. Even though she was a full-time student she had managed to get a job at the prestigious Amsterdam brothel, Yab Yum. This enabled her to live in the center of town, finance her degree, and pay for her partying and luxurious treats, like these silicone implants. She was a free spirit who had fun with whatever she was doing, whether she was partying, having dinner with friends, or even when she was working at Yab Yum.

Jade and Roos were always surprised that Fleur never had a boyfriend as she wasn't a lesbian like themselves. She would explain that she got enough sex at work and if she wanted more she had her toys. And if that wasn't enough, it was very easy for her to chat up a guy at a student bar and go home with him, which she often did. Anyway, she didn't need or want a boyfriend right now because she had too much going on in her life at the moment.

Fleur grew up in Zwolle, in the East of Holland, on her parents' farm. When she was nineteen, she moved to Amsterdam but ended up studying in Utrecht. She wanted to study journalism and Utrecht was the only place to do this. It became quite an expensive arrangement so she had to get a part-time job. She was out clubbing one night with friends when she met another girl who was a student at the University of Amsterdam. When they started talking she told Fleur that she had this part time job in Yab Yum. She explained that it was well-managed, luxurious, extremely well paid, and fun. You could drink champagne all night, do drugs for free if you liked, and get paid a lot of money to sleep with one or two guys a night. The clients tended to be Russians, Arabs, and wealthy businessmen who were stopping over in Amsterdam for a night. That was it. Fleur was sold on the idea.

She started working there a week later, and 'Pearl', as she came to be known at work, earned four hundred euros an hour. She loved dancing, partying, and sex. Now she was being paid for all three. She could also afford to commute to Utrecht for classes and have a great lifestyle living in the center of Amsterdam.

Roos didn't know how she could do this job. Fleur always told her that she didn't hate men but needed them for one thing. Money.

Fleur brought two cups of tea into the living room and placed them on the coffee table between the sofa and the television. The low table began to wobble as the cups were put on it. As Fleur bent over her tiny shorts showed off her red lace underwear between her legs. Normally, Roos wouldn't be able to resist looking at such a sight as she secretly fancied Fleur, even though she was straight. Not at the moment. Roos was too focused on the news, which had shocked her.

"It's so scary!" Fleur said suddenly, also staring at the television. "I am glad that I'm a girl as he clearly only cares about killing guys!"

"You should still be careful when you go out nowadays," replied Roos, "You never know, he may turn to women eventually!"

Fleur stared at Roos and took in what she said. She always listened to Roos even though they weren't very close. She valued her opinions on things as she was a lot more responsible than herself.

Roos carried on, "Anyway, there are plenty of other weirdos in this city to watch out for!"

"That's true," Fleur replied, "I am nervous about walking outside on my own at night."

Fleur had asked for a pick up and drop off from Yab Yum recently. They had offered her the company limousine, which she had turned down at the last minute. She didn't want to draw too much attention to herself while leaving the house. Most people knew she was a student as Fleur was very social and talked to everyone, especially her neighbors. Disappearing at night in a blacked out, stretched Mercedes would definitely turn a few heads and people would start asking questions.

Fleur's thoughts went quickly from discussing the killer to how tanned her arms were, which she liked to look at. Unlike her legs, they looked naturally brown but the manager at Yab Yum had commented over the weekend that she needed to tone them up a little. She had a membership at the local Splash Gym and was planning on going there after tea to work on her triceps and biceps. She didn't have University classes today so she thought that she would go for a light spray tan as well this afternoon.

"Fancy coming for a tanning session later?" Fleur asked Roos.

Roos continued watching the news. She felt sick from the story. Not scared, just sick. This, coupled with the fact that Jade was away in Argentina for five days on a long haul with pilots and pretty airhostesses, made her jealous as well. Feeling sick and jealous was not a good combination. They hadn't parted on good terms yesterday either.

"Hey Roos," Fleur spoke louder seeing that Roos was still not paying attention to her. Fleur walked in front of the television blocking Roos' view. Roos was now staring straight at her sexy flat-mate wearing next to nothing. Normally, she would feel embarrassed at being caught looking at Fleur but she had a knot in her stomach right now. Roos looked down at the floor putting her head into her hands. Her mind was elsewhere.

"Yeah, sure." she replied, without really thinking about what she was saying. She was now looking across at Fleur. Fleur's long blonde hair with red streak extensions fell down over her shoulders and covered part of her face. You could still make out Fleur's big smile indicating that she was amused by her distracted flat-mate.

"Errm," continued Roos, "I mean no. I can't. I have to work later." This was pretty obvious as she was already wearing her nurse's outfit, which was partially hidden underneath the duvet. Roos was just confused right now and her mind was elsewhere.

"I'm sorry, I can't. I have to work." Roos repeated herself. She then put her hand on her stomach and frowned. "But I don't feel well so maybe I should stay home today."

"Oh, poor you," replied Fleur, "Is it that time of the month?"

"No, I just don't feel good. I mean, I feel sick."

Fleur walked over and sat down next to Roos and gave her a hug. "Can I get you anything? Do you want an aspirin?"

Fleur's left boob squeezed against Roos's arm shaping itself around her bicep perfectly. Roos was distracted momentarily surprised how hard the silicon was. The brick in her stomach brought her back to reality quickly.

"I will be fine, thanks. Maybe I just need to rest and have a day in bed." Roos then pictured the scenario where she would get bored lying in her bedroom all day. She would probably start thinking about the news and then move on to thinking about Jade. She would become jealous again and then would feel even worse. She had made a decision. Roos stood up suddenly catching Fleur by surprise and making her fall backwards on the sofa a little.

"I should really go to work. I'm not really sick, just a bit run down." said Roos who was now looking at her watch. She had thirty minutes to get to the hospital for her shift.

"I gotta go now, otherwise I will be late." With that Roos picked up her keys from the coffee table and headed for the front door. Fleur watched her putting her coat on in a rush and said, "Roos." Her flat-mate turned around to face her. "Are you sure that you are okay?" Fleur felt sorry for Roos. She looked unhappy, unwell, and in such a panic.

"Yes, thanks. I'm just not feeling a hundred percent."

Fleur continued to speak, while she had Roos' attention. "Dinner tonight? I'm working till nine myself but could squeeze in a quick bite at seven thirty if you like?" There were a few seconds of silence as Fleur waited for Roos to answer.

Roos opened the front door and then turned back again and spoke. "Errmm, yes, maybe. I will text you later." With that she shut the door behind her and was gone.

Roos walked over to her bicycle to unlock it. She heard the front door opening and turned to see Fleur standing there like a Barbie Doll. Her long hair was shining and her boobs were sticking out. She had everything that a guy dreamed of, thought Roos.

It looked like Fleur was waving goodbye with one hand raised upwards and moving from side to side. As Roos looked closely she could see that there was something in her hand - an object.

"You will probably need this," shouted Fleur, "especially if you want to text me later."

Roos couldn't make out the object in Fleur's hand but from what she had just said she presumed it was her mobile phone. She reached in her pockets to check but it wasn't there.

Fleur was expecting a smile and at least a thank you. Instead, Roos looked furious as she stormed across the street like a raging bull just avoiding a moped and a cyclist, which managed to swerve around her. Reaching out, she snatched it off Fleur.

"That's mine." screamed Roos. "You shouldn't be looking at it!"

"I wasn't," replied Fleur, shocked by her flat-mate's aggressive tone. "It just helps to have it if you need to text me later."

"What text?" snapped Roos without thinking. She clearly wasn't listening to what Fleur was saying.

"Huh?" replied Fleur, with a confused face.

"It is my phone and you shouldn't touch it and definitely not read my texts!" Roos carried on shouting in her high-pitched tone. She seemed uncontrollable.

"But I haven't read your texts!" Fleur raised her voice to get Roos' attention and held her hand at the same time. Roos stared into Fleur's eyes to see if she was lying. Fleur looked back at her, blank-faced and surprised by her out-of-character behavior.

Fleur broke the silence, "Are you sure you are okay to go to work? Maybe it is a good idea to take the day off?" She said with a sincere face. Fleur was telling the truth. Roos believed her. She hadn't read any of her messages.

Roos pondered for a second as she continued looking at Fleur. Of course, she hadn't read any of her text messages, she thought to herself. The mobile had been left on the coffee table, out of sight, for no more than ninety seconds. She managed to pull a fake smile trying to signify an expression of 'I'm sorry'.

Roos spoke up, "I'm fine and sorry for the way that I have been. I'm just not myself right now."

"No problem." replied Fleur. She was so easy going. "Go to work but if you start to feel any worse come home." Roos nodded in agreement. "Let's text later." continued Fleur.

She kissed Roos goodbye on the cheek. Then quickly went back inside shutting the door behind her. She was cold from standing on the doorstep with hardly any clothes on.

Roos went back to her bicycle, which was lying on the ground with her keys in the wheel lock. She put her phone into the pocket of her jacket noticing that she had only fifteen minutes to get to work now, the exact time it took to get there with her bike. As she started cycling frantically up the street she couldn't help thinking about her phone. It had lots of saved messages on it, including love and hate texts from Jade. They were private and for her eyes only and she didn't want to share them with anyone.

CHAPTER 6

September 26

8:15 p.m.

The Command Center

The five men sat in a circle behind their desks in deep thought. There was complete silence in the office assisted by the double-glazed windows. They needed this peaceful environment to think and brainstorm. They had to find out if they were missing any clues or other important signs. It was like a game of chess that they were playing for almost ten months now, but with severe consequences every time they made a wrong move. The second hand on the ugly wall clock clicked away in the quiet office. They had been sitting there all day.

Positioned on the far wall of their office was a giant size map of Amsterdam and Amstelveen. It was surrounded by a patchwork quilt of pictures and notes that had been stuck on any blank space that was left on the wall. The mix of black and white, and colored pictures were of the murdered men – all the victims of the Magpie. Next to each large head shot of each victim was a smaller picture of the crime scene and their naked bodies, just as they were found. Next to these were notes regarding important observations of each body: cause of death, had the finger nails been cut, had the body been cleaned, were there any scratches or marks on the skin?

There was also a resume style piece typed up about every victim detailing who they were, where they lived, what they did for work, friends and family, places they visited often, etc. They felt that this write-up was very important even though it hadn't really helped so far, Arnaud hoped that it would assist them in eventually building a profile of the killer. Why did the Magpie pick these men and what was his motive? Arnaud wanted to get in front of the Magpie and he thought that this was the only way he would have a chance of catching him. They had done a lot of background work in an attempt to track down this beast.

From each victim's picture, that surrounded the main part of the map, were two pieces of string. One string was red, which was stuck on the wall connecting the picture to the location on the map where a victim had gone missing. The second piece of string was blue and this ran from each picture to the place where the individual's body was found.

The map had become a spider's web over time but an organized one. The team understood every picture and piece of string that was on the wall. They spent hours every day staring at it trying to establish why things were happening in this pattern and attempt to work out what the killer's next step was going to be.

So far, their successes had been very limited, and they had often wanted to tear down the paper mosaic on the wall. This was understandable. What were they missing? Why were they not making any progress? Their only explanation was that they were dealing with a very well organized psychopath, who had planned everything right down to the final detail. They had a moral obligation to the city of Amsterdam, and now their country, to keep on going and to continue looking for the one clue that could potentially be a major breakthrough.

It was a well-drawn map highlighting all the events of this year. Their whole investigation was based around this wall and their office was the control center for the case. If the press and public could see this, they would surely be impressed and realize how much work was being done by Arnaud and his team. It was, however, top secret and for nobody else to view.

The team had listed a number of other similarities between the killings. All of the men were between eighteen and forty-one years. The victims had all been in bars on the night they went missing. Maybe, they were picked up by the killer in the evening because it was dark and there was a low chance of being seen by somebody else or being seen on CCTV. Obviously in a bar, the killer would have more time to choose and could hand-pick his victim.

As the year had gone on, Arnaud and his team had gotten approval to place more undercover policemen in bars and clubs around Amsterdam. The Mayor had also put more CCTV cameras on the main streets in Amsterdam and Amstelveen in order to spot the victims leaving bars and hopefully see them being followed by the Magpie. So far this hadn't worked. The killer clearly studied his victims and the surroundings where the snatch would take place.

Arnaud and the team had a list of unanswered questions, which they had written on a flip board at the front of the office in thick red felt tip pen. How did the Magpie get the victims away from where they were last seen? Why was there never any sign of resistance from the victim? What did he do with the victims for the two to three days between catching them and dumping the bodies? Why did he keep them for a few days? Why take all their belongings? Why did he always go for men? Did he hate men? This was a strange question as none of the victims were gay.

They went through the list every day to raise any new ideas. These questions kept them awake at night, as the pressure mounted. This case had received international interest now, and the European press was following Arnaud's team. The question being asked more frequently was whether Arnaud needed to be replaced. The argument that saved Arnaud and kept him in the role of leading the hunt, was that he and his team had collated a lot of information so far and it didn't make any sense to make changes at this point.

It also helped that Dijkstra had a close relationship with some of the top management in the Dutch police force. He had made it clear that despite their lack of progress a change of team would not be able to do things any differently or better and would get them no closer to a breakthrough. He met with the senior members of the police force regularly and they were well- briefed on what Arnaud and his team had been focusing on. It was indeed clear to everybody that they were covering all the bases and were just dealing with a very calculated and cunning killer. It would also look terrible from a public perception standpoint if they changed the whole investigation team at this point as it would signify that they were making no progress.

Dijkstra was highly regarded in the police force and was also a friend of the Amsterdam Mayor, Cohen. The team had been granted another six months to make a breakthrough. Dijkstra had relayed this to Arnaud but they had agreed to keep this to themselves for now and not share it with the rest of the team. There was already enough pressure on them and they didn't need any more.

He also knew that Arnaud was both a good guy and an excellent detective. He had sacrificed his marriage and time with his only daughter so that he could focus on the case. He had aged tremendously in the last nine months. The least Dijkstra could do was to stand by Arnaud and support him and the rest of the team as much as possible even if they weren't getting any closer to catching the killer.

The office was heavily lit up and all the blinds in the large square room were closed. All the furniture in the room was dated and very much standard police order. The room was off-white in color and some parts of the ceiling had damp patches visible where the paint was peeling off. The office was furnished with Arnaud and Friso's desks as well as a large double desk for the two younger policemen. Dijkstra, who actually had his own office, had even set up camp in the main room. Most of his time was now spent supporting and monitoring the team and also speaking to the press and senior management about any progress. He wanted to make sure that he had complete color on what was going on at all times.

Apart from the main wall, covered with the map, all the others were bare. A few police graduation certificates for the team members were scattered around. Next to Friso's desk was a silver trophy, which he had won three years ago, for captaining the station's five a side football team in the annual North Holland competition. Friso was a good-looking guy and very fit. He was also smart and was often asked why he continued to work for the 'grumpy Arnaud'. He never saw a reason to answer this as he knew that he had learnt a lot from him. He was loyal and a friend, and despite their lack of progress this year Arnaud had an excellent hit rate when it came to solving crimes. Their bond was strong.

Arnaud paced the room along the ten-meter gap between where his team was sitting and the map on the wall. He was frustrated with their lack of progress. What were they missing? When he was in deep thought, he always rubbed his chin and scratched his thick curly hair. All of Arnaud's colleagues could see that he was desperately going through ideas in his mind trying to unravel a missing link.

What did they know for sure? Once a month, since January, a murder had been committed. There was no pattern on when it would happen. There was also no consistency about where the victims went missing or where bodies were dumped. Corpses had been found in the center of the city, in parks, and also near housing estates. One thing was consistent; the Magpie didn't leave any traces. He was very thorough. The time was always the same between when the victims disappeared and when the body was dumped - two to three days.

None of the victims were severely assaulted or had their bodies cut up, apart from two who had had their teeth pulled out. It became apparent later that the teeth extracted had gold crown fillings. None of the murdered men were sexually assaulted.

The Magpie got his nickname because he removed anything that had any value from the victims. Arnaud and Friso had visited all the second-hand jewelry stores in and around Amsterdam hoping to find some of the victims' pieces, but to no avail.

What did the killer do with the valuables, and why did he take everything? They had discussed this point in detail with a team of psychoanalysts who had been trying to build a profile of the Magpie. There was no real explanation for this. It definitely wasn't done because of the monetary value of the missing items. The March murder was a thirty-year old man. He had worn a lot of cheap gold jewelry that clearly had no value. It was all stripped from his body.

Where did the Magpie go with the body for two to three days and what did the Magpie do with it? It was clear that he took all their clothes and jewelry from them and cleaned the corpse. This was obviously done to avoid any clues and DNA being found on the victims. The one thing Arnaud and his team were sure of was that the Magpie must have his own house or storage space. A space where he could take the victims, kill them, and then strip and clean their bodies. Storing a dead corpse for a few days was no easy task, especially without anyone else noticing something suspicious.

Arnaud often thought to himself that the Magpie couldn't possibly live in Amsterdam, as a neighbor would surely see something strange going on and inform the police. After all, it seemed like the whole city was on a knife's edge. Surely, somebody would see something if he lived on a crowded Amsterdam street. This was, however, just a hunch and he had no sound evidence.

The cause of death was always suffocation or a broken neck. None of the corpses had scratches on them or any sign that they had been in a fight or resisting an attack. Again, the group's conclusion was that the killer was a very strong guy.

The two young policemen, Robin and Jim, stared at the infamous wall. Friso and Dijkstra were looking up at the ceiling, in deep thought, and Arnaud just scratched his head running through ideas in his mind.

"So, anything new?" Arnaud broke the silence. Even though there were five of them in the room, the question was really directed at his trusted right hand man, Friso. Friso responded immediately as he started walking towards the map on the wall. He pointed at the most recent picture of this month's victim.

"Thomas Deckers was out having drinks on Thursday night with some friends."

"How many friends?" asked Arnaud.

"Five, they were all from Weesp, except one, who lived in Amsterdam. They were celebrating a birthday."

Friso took a moment to think and then turned to face his colleagues and continued speaking, "They started drinking a few beers in the bars around Rembrandtplein at six in the evening and then walked up to Leidseplein at 8:30 p.m. They spent the rest of the evening together in the Palladium Bar on the square. Around 11 p.m., they all left to get something to eat from a local Febo Snack Bar. Around 11:40 p.m., they moved on to go to the Surprise Bar, which is just around the corner."

"Did his friends see him talking with anyone unusual during the evening before they went into the Surprise Bar?"

"Not that they can remember. Every bar they went to was packed and they were all talking to other people. When they got to the Surprise Bar, they split up as they started dancing and chatting up girls. They are mainly a bunch of single guys. All of them were quite drunk and have no recollection of him disappearing."

"I can't believe no one saw him leave!" Dijkstra spoke up, a little frustrated. They all turned to stare at Dijkstra. The two young policemen stood up as if they were getting ready to speak. One had his notebook out and the other walked over to get his laptop. He turned it round so that everyone could see the screen.

Robin, who stood by his laptop, spoke first, "We got the CCTV tapes from the Surprise Bar. One camera is positioned behind the bar and points to the dance floor, and the other camera is outside by the entrance door of the club."

Jim flicked through the notes he had made during the day, while Robin turned on the tape recording of the camera inside the club. The picture was in black and white but very clear. They all looked at the computer screen as Robin fast-forwarded the tape to an appropriate clip of the victim dancing close to the bar, appearing very drunk. The footage went on to show Thomas Deckers speaking with three different girls separately in the club, two of whom, he kissed later. The young policeman had done a good job of editing the tape and highlighting the most important parts, thought Arnaud.

Jim began speaking, "The club was full and it was impossible to track the victim all the time, especially when he left the bar area. We made a plea on the news today for anyone who was in the Surprise Bar on Thursday evening to come forward. Anyone who may have spoken to Thomas Deckers. We are hoping that these girls will call. One girl has already made contact with us and we interviewed her earlier. She is a twenty-one year old student from the Hogsechool Holland in Amsterdam."

Jim paused to look at his notes and then continued, "Apart from being in shock today, she said that she was so drunk on Thursday night that she can only vaguely remember kissing him. She couldn't recall any conversations or seeing him leave. She said that she also spoke to a few other guys that night so didn't really spend much time with Thomas. Anyway, she wasn't particularly helpful."

"That's because she was out of her mind." said Arnaud sarcastically. "What did the other two girls look like?"

"Unfortunately, the camera did not get a clear picture of their faces." replied Robin. "But they are both young and wore sexy clothes. Have nice figures."

"That's useful!" Arnaud was in one of those moods, getting more agitated with the lack of clues.

"No face shots then?" interrupted Dijkstra. "No face shots," confirmed the young policeman.

Robin spoke up. "It didn't help that one was wearing a long wig that completely concealed her face." He pulled up freeze frames on the same screen of both girls with as much detail and picture clarity as possible. They all moved in closer around the laptop screen to focus on the two girls as Robin zoomed in on their bodies and heads. Both girls seemed medium height, slim, with amazing figures.

One had long light-colored hair, which was as much as you could make out from the black and white tape and wore an extremely short, tight dress. She had also worn open high heeled shoes. The other girl wore an 'over the top' party-wig that was long and thick and completely covered her shoulders and the sides of her face. She also wore skinny jeans and a strapless tight vest that looked like it had been painted on.

"Was he seen speaking with anyone else?" asked Arnaud.

"No, we have been through the tape and he only speaks with his friends and these three girls." They all stared at the freeze-frames knowing that they didn't really have much to go on.

"Why don't we put these pictures in the newspapers tomorrow and request these girls to contact us?" Arnaud saw this as more of an order rather than a question and decided to reply. "What's the point of that? We don't have a clear picture of either of them. We will be mimicked by the press if that's the best we have to go on."

Friso and the two young policemen looked down worried about a confrontation between Arnaud and Dijkstra.

"Okay." said Dijkstra, giving a nod to Arnaud, accepting his opinion. "Can we print the pictures of the two girls that we haven't been able to contact yet and add them to the map wall?"

"For sure," said Arnaud. Jim had already started walking towards the printer to pick up the shots of the girls. Arnaud continued, "What time did Deckers leave the club?" He looked over at Jim and Robin expecting them to switch to the next clip of the footage. The two young policemen looked over at Friso hoping he would speak on their behalf.

"This is the strange thing," said Friso, "He didn't leave the club." Before he could finish the sentence, Arnaud interrupted him with a raised voice and a bewildered face.

"What do you mean that he...," began Arnaud. Surprisingly, Friso spoke over him, "Well, not through the front entrance at least."

Arnaud looked even more confused than before and waited for Friso to continue.

"We have gone through the tapes a number of times and checked all the people leaving the club. There is no sign of Thomas Deckers."

They all paused in thought, looking blankly at Arnaud.

Arnaud spoke up again, "Any other exits?"

"There are two fire exits, although neither alarm was triggered. It's possible that they would have left the club through the toilet window, as it is about fifty by fifty in size." said Jim nervously.

"But why would he do that?" asked Dijkstra, stating the obvious but desperately wanting to be involved in the discussion. Arnaud closed his eyes, as if to ignore his boss' question and spoke up again.

"Okay, go back and check for fingerprints on the toilet windows and interview the security and doormen to see if anyone was seen hanging around the fire exits."

Arnaud stopped for a second to think, scratching his curly hair again. "Was somebody in the toilet collecting tips?"

Jim replied, "Yes, we spoke with him and he said that he saw nothing unusual. He also admitted to leaving the toilets quite regularly to go and chat up girls in the club."

Arnaud didn't look impressed. It couldn't be possible that in such a small club with so many witnesses no one would have seen anything.

The Magpie couldn't be that good. "Okay, we need to find out how he got out of the club and why he didn't use the front entrance." The others knew that this was a key point but they didn't have an answer right now. They all looked around at each other and then back at Arnaud.

He continued, "We need to interview everyone that worked in the club that night. Even the cleaners, who come in the morning to tidy up."

"We have already spoken to everyone." said Friso. "Apart from the cleaning staff, which we will get to immediately. So far, none of the people working that night saw anything unusual and nobody can remember seeing Thomas Deckers." Friso paused to take a deep breath, knowing that his comments were making Arnaud more frustrated. "Neither of the fire exits were tampered with, let alone opened." He looked up at Arnaud to see his reaction.

"Well, I want you to check the fire exits for fingerprints as soon as possible. Maybe one of them was touched. This poor guy was not invisible and had to get out of there somehow!"

Arnaud sounded annoyed and desperate. How was it possible that they couldn't find which exit Thomas Deckers had left through? If they could only spot him on camera or get a witness then they might be able to see if he left with somebody. Had the Magpie been in the club or did he find the victim roaming the streets of Amsterdam drunk after leaving the club? Arnaud was convinced that the killer would have been in the club. He didn't leave anything to chance and would have identified his prey and made contact with him prior to an attack. One thing was for sure, they couldn't allow their lack of progress to get out to the media.

Friso spoke, trying to cheer up the team's mood of despair and demotivation. "It's clear that we are tightening the noose around the killer's neck."

Dijkstra looked across at Friso as if to say 'How so?' The two junior policemen listened attentively to Friso. Arnaud sat with his head cupped in his hands but he was listening.

Friso could see that he had everyone's attention and so he continued, "If you look at the nine victims, two were last seen in Amstelveen, one in Abcoude, one in Ouderkerk aan de Amstel, and five in Amsterdam." He paused, staring into the eyes of his colleagues before continuing. "The last five were in Amsterdam. I know that I am stating the obvious, but it's becoming harder for the killer to strike. There are too many wary eyes looking out for him now and the villages and smaller towns are virtually impossible for him to operate in, without being seen."

Friso continued, "He is also going to crowded places to pick up his victims. You can see this from the last three that have happened in Amsterdam. We have to keep focusing on the center of the City, and if possible, increase the surveillance in this particular area."

"We don't even know if the killer was in the Surprise Bar and have no witnesses who saw him or the victim!" said Arnaud.

Dijkstra spoke up, "True, but there is something very funny about the victim not being seen leaving the club through the front entrance, especially if the other exits were locked and alarmed." Arnaud nodded his head acknowledging his boss' comments as he was also baffled by these points.

Friso continued, "Also, the murders are happening later and later each month, which shows you that it is becoming harder for the Magpie to pick his next victim and make contact. I would also propose increasing the surveillance and number of undercover police on the streets in the last ten days of the month." He looked at Arnaud and Dijkstra for comment.

Friso was right, thought Arnaud. That was a good evaluation of what they knew. Jim spoke up, "What do we do for the rest of the month? We now have three weeks to wait."

Friso didn't reply, caught off guard by this comment. Of course, they would continue investigating and carry on the surveillance work.

Arnaud stood up and spoke at the same time. "Send me those CCTV tapes." This was directed at the two junior policemen. "Also, get the tapes from every other bar that Thomas Deckers was in that evening. See if you can spot him making contact with anyone else before he went to the Surprise Bar." This was a good point that none of the others had thought of and Jim and Robin acknowledged Arnaud's orders.

Arnaud then walked up next to Friso and spoke softly. "Friso, apart from overseeing the interviews of all the staff at the club, I need you to find these other two girls. They must have seen something. If nothing else, they must have seen him talk to someone else, some other guy. They must have seen him leave the club." Arnaud looked and sounded as if he was under so much pressure, and extremely desperate. Friso nodded. Friso also knew that these girls were important witnesses and hopefully held the key to some important clues. He also knew, however, that they had such poor pictures of the two girls that unless they came forward in response to the news requests for them there would be no way possible to identify them or find them. They were so close to some valuable points that would help the investigation progress, yet still so far from actually catching the killer.

Why didn't they have any undercover police in the Surprise Bar that night?, Arnaud thought to himself. It was just bad luck, of course. He just needed a small break. Anything. Arnaud was feeling a lot of tension in his shoulders. He could feel another headache coming on. He knew that this was caused purely from stress. He also knew that after the headache would wear off, depression would set in. This was a familiar pattern for him, all resulting from his work, and the lack of success with this case. The Magpie was his life right now and was slowly wearing him down.

They had had similar team discussions this time last month, which had all come to nothing. This month, they could potentially have lots of key evidence all situated in an enclosed small space. This club had many witnesses in it and perhaps also the Magpie. Something didn't add up, however, and that was how Thomas Deckers had got out of the club without being caught on camera or without being seen by anyone. Arnaud needed to be alone to think. He must be missing something.

Arnaud turned and headed for the exit door followed in hot pursuit by his boss.
"Where are you going Arnaud?" asked Dijkstra.

"Out." came Arnaud's short reply.

"Why? Where?" continued Dijkstra.

"I need to think."

Arnaud was telling the truth. He thought and went over cases and clues best when he was alone, drinking a beer and smoking a cigarette. This was best done at home in the Jordaan, where he felt comfortable and more relaxed. He couldn't be seen out in a bar, just after another murder, with the Magpie still on the loose. In his living room, no one could see him and he could drink a few beers, which would calm his nerves. In doing this, he would be able to think more clearly.

Arnaud could feel his boss walking closely behind him. He turned to face Dijkstra, putting on his jacket at the same time.

"I will call you later." Arnaud spoke up. This was a polite way of saying 'back off'.

With that, Dijkstra turned and headed back to the office to be with the rest of the team. He knew it was best to leave Arnaud alone. He could oversee the other guys who had plenty to do. Dijkstra also wanted to take a look at the CCTV film again.

CHAPTER 7

October 5

8:00 a.m.

Tuinstraat, The Jordaan

A few days into the month, Arnaud had mixed feelings about waking up in his Jordaan flat. He was pleased that there had been no missing persons' calls or any signs of another murder. He wanted to believe that the extra undercover police on the streets were really making a difference, but he was also realistic and knew that the Magpie would be striking again later in the month. He was also extremely disappointed and couldn't accept the fact that nothing had come from all the video footage in the Surprise Bar or from any witnesses that were present that night.

One other girl had responded to the press adverts. She was the one with the long blond hair with the short tight dress and high heels. The twenty-six year old's input was not helpful at all. She could remember speaking with Thomas Deckers and thought that he was even more drunk than she was. He had been slurring his words heavily and was having problems standing up straight.

She also mentioned that she fancied him but some other girl had been whispering in his ear constantly. When the other girl finally took him to a dark seating area in the club, she gave up on him and went back to dancing with her friends. When Friso had shown her the picture of the girl in the wig, she confirmed that this was the one that Thomas sat with in a corner of the Surprise Bar. She couldn't, however, give any more information on what the girl looked like as her long wig had mostly covered her face. All she said was that the girl seemed very persuasive and had an amazing body. She wore very sexy clothes and danced well. She didn't appear to be with any friends. When she saw the victim kissing this girl, she completely gave up on him and lost interest. That was it. Apart from this, they had no more information to go on. Arnaud got very frustrated every time he thought about it.

It was now October and they were no closer to catching the serial killer. The Magpie was in complete control. Arnaud and his team knew it, the police knew it, and so did the public. Annoyingly, he was reminded every day by the press. Arnaud got out of his bed wearing his old white boxer shorts and t-shirt and went to peek through his window to look out at the weather, and to see if there were any reporters standing downstairs on the Tuinstraat.

There were four members of the press waiting outside his front door - two newspaper reporters, one radio guy from BNA, and an annoying photographer from a Dutch gossip magazine. Arnaud had become familiar with all of their faces. This highlighted the fact that Arnaud was under the spotlight at the moment and this ongoing murder hunt continued to be the story of the year.

Bright rays of light coming through the window pierced his hungover eyes, and Arnaud sighed and sat back on the bed. His back cricked as he hit the mattress and the bed springs pinged at the same time. The bed frame and mattress were forty years old, a 'hand me down' set from his late mother. Arnaud never saw a need to replace this as he rarely slept for very long and didn't have a girlfriend either.

As always, Arnaud checked his pager and mobile phone for messages. There weren't any. This was the time of the morning that he would get a 'barometer' reading on how the rest of the day was going to pan out. Arnaud felt relieved and semi happy as this meant that nothing had happened last night.

Arnaud shaved, and took a shower. Having managed to run a comb through his thick curly hair, he got dressed. Fastening the old leather belt on his trousers, he realized that he had lost a lot of weight this year. This was clearly from stress, replacing food with a liquid diet of beer and gin, and a lot of cigarettes. He always put off going to see the doctor to get his weight loss checked for fear of being told that he had a terminal illness. Bowel cancer had taken his father's life sixteen years earlier.

Actually, the worst that Arnaud ever felt was a sore throat or a bad headache, both brought on by his own doing. For once, he was feeling hungry and had an urge for breakfast so he went downstairs to cook something. Opening the fridge, he wasn't surprised to see that it was pretty much empty. Apart from half a carton of orange juice and six eggs, well past their 'sell by' date, there was only a good stock of beer in the small ten-year old fridge. He took a swig from the orange juice carton and quickly made the decision to go to the local café for some food.

Café De Prins was a seven-minute walk from his apartment. This was one of the two places, apart from his home, that actually he felt safe going to and relaxing in. He always went to Café De Prins for food, whether it was breakfast or lunch, and Café De Twee Zwanntjes for drinks in the evening and sometimes in the day. They were very much local cafés for Jordaan people who kept to themselves, which Arnaud liked and needed.

Café De Twee Zwaantjes was located next door on the Prinsengracht to Café De Prins, which was convenient. After having something to eat, Arnaud always liked a few drinks and he didn't need to walk too far. More importantly, when he left 'the two swans' he was normally pretty drunk and it helped that his walk home was a short one, which he could do with his eyes closed and he often had. Apart from both establishments being full of locals who never bothered him, they also had his favorite barmaids. Noor Lumas worked at De Twee Zwaantjes and Tessa worked at Café De Prins, whom he would see shortly.

Looking out of the kitchen window, he could see that even though it was sunny and the sky was blue it was obviously very cold. People walking past his apartment and the annoying reporters all had hats and thick coats on. Clambering back upstairs, Arnaud could feel his knee joints ache with every step that he took. Grabbing an unfolded brown v-neck jumper from the closet in his bedroom, a present from his daughter last Christmas, he put it on and headed back downstairs. Admiring the jumper, as he pulled it down to his waist, he realized that it was the only one he had that really fit him and which looked half decent, without any holes in it.

Arnaud reached for his long jacket that was hanging over a chair in the kitchen and walked towards the front door that opened up onto the Tuinstraat. He stunned the four reporters outside by saying, 'Good morning. How are you all today?" He carried on walking past them in the direction of the café. The reporters were in shock because Arnaud had actually said something to them and also because he seemed 'upbeat'. Strangely, they remained standing still and did not pursue him or reply with any questions.

Arnaud turned left out of his front door and left, again at the first crossroads down the thin street called the Tweede Boomdwarsstraat. At the end of this street he would arrive at the Prinsengracht on his left. Turning right onto the canal, Arnaud had a one-minute stroll to Café De Prins. As he walked in, he spotted a vacant small table with two stools which he grabbed immediately, as the café was pretty full already. After taking off his jacket and placing it over the free stool next to him, he picked up one of the café's papers to read the news.

The great thing about Café De Prins was that nobody even blinked an eyelid at Arnaud. They were local people from the Jordaan who got on with their own lives and didn't judge or comment on others. They protected their own, and Arnaud was one of them. This was probably a trait that was ingrained into them from the war, when the Germans occupied Amsterdam, and the Dutch resistance movement looked after one another and ran their operations against the Nazi's out of the Jordaan.

Arnaud breathed a sigh of relief as for once he wasn't on the front page of the newspaper. He flicked through the Telegraaf and thought to himself that it was really turning out to be a good day after all. Looking up from his paper, Arnaud scanned the bar to find his favorite waitress, Tessa. Although he had known her for many years now he had no idea what her surname was. It didn't really matter. What he did know was that Tessa was a big fifty year old Jordanese woman, born and bred in Amsterdam. She was both tall and on the heavy side and had been married and divorced three times. From each marriage, she had had two children, which explained the size of her frame.

Arnaud could relate to Tessa as she didn't judge, and was level-headed about marriage and life. She was a real person and saw eye-to-eye with Arnaud. She had also been serving him snacks for the last thirteen years. Looking up, trying to get Tessa's attention, he made eye contact with Mr. Blokker, a seventy-two year old man, who basically lived in the café. He was a lonely old man with sagging skin on his face, like a tired hound with blood-shot eyes. Mr. Blokker's jaw and lips moved around with a sour-tasting expression on his face, as if he was chewing on a wasp. Arnaud smiled at him with respect and the old man nodded back in acknowledgement. This was quite surprising as normally he would look down and ignore everyone around him. He knew who Arnaud was and Arnaud saw him as how he would be in thirty years' time. Although, he hoped he wouldn't be as sad as Mr. Blokker.

Tessa saw that Arnaud was trying to order and she shouted to him across the café in her flat Amsterdam accent.

"Your usual, Arnaud?" which meant, at this time of day, a black coffee and a white bread roll spread with butter and aged cheese.

Arnaud smiled and nodded in response. As Tess turned and headed over to the kitchen Arnaud checked out her figure. He thought to himself that if she lost ten pounds she would look quite nice. After all, she had long well-groomed hair and a pretty round face. He was disturbed from his trail of thought by some abrupt noise from outside the café. He peered out through the steamed-up windows to see that the reporters had finally made their way over to the café, to see what he was doing. Annoyingly, the four reporters were now seven. Arnaud got up from his stool and moved to the other side of the small round table so that he could have his back to the window. He didn't want to be disturbed or photographed whilst having his breakfast.

Arnaud ate the bread roll very quickly and slurped down his coffee. After wiping his mouth with a paper napkin, he stood up and put on his raincoat. Reaching into his pocket, Arnaud pulled out seven euros: five euros fifty for the food and drink and a one-and-a-half euro tip for Tessa.

As he made his way towards the exit door, he passed Mr. Blokker who was looking down into his coffee mug. Stepping out of De Prins, Arnaud turned left and started walking briskly in the direction of home. Actually, he wasn't intending on going back in to his apartment, he just had to pick his moped keys. Passing the reporters, Arnaud pulled a nervous smile in acknowledgement but didn't say anything this time. He was caught off guard by one of the journalists calling out to him.

"So, Arnaud, you have a fan!"

This statement caught him off guard and his eyes glazed over not knowing what the guy from BNA Radio was talking about. He could see that clearly all the reporters were in on it and were staring at him waiting for a response.

The radio reporter continued, "The blogger!!" He looked very surprised that Arnaud didn't appear to know what he was talking about.

"I'm sorry...," replied Arnaud, not having a clue on what they were talking about.

The journalist continued, "The blogger on the website 'Amsterdam Living' who keeps posting comments that you are a great cop and about how you are slowly moving in on the killer behind the scenes." The journalist could not believe that Arnaud was unaware that he had a secret admirer.

Arnaud realized that even though he genuinely didn't know about this blogger or website, he needed to pretend that he did.

"Oh, that one." he replied, showing little interest but inside his heart was racing. Arnaud decided to keep on walking, shrugging off the recent conversation because he was worried that the reporters would catch up and realize that he was completely confused. He was also desperate to get home and check out this site. Who was writing these blogs? Was it the Magpie playing games? Arnaud speeded up, fueled by this interesting twist and potential lead. He needed to know more and didn't like surprises. Why had Friso not mentioned this website or blog?

Turning onto his street, Arnaud could hear the speedy footsteps and chatter of the journalists behind him. The BNA reporter continued calling out to the detective, that he was pursuing.

"Detective, let me read you a quote: This detective is Amsterdam's own super hero!" Arnaud opened his front door and snuck inside. He didn't bother taking off his jacket, but instead, headed straight for the computer in his living room, which was already turned on. Sitting on the old wooden stool he googled the website 'Amsterdam Living'.

Arnaud scanned the home page for information. It was a genuine website for people who lived in and around Amsterdam. He could see that the goal of the site was to highlight things to do in Amsterdam: upcoming events, concerts, and museums. It also had various chat rooms discussing new bars, restaurants, and clubs that had recently opened in the city. Arnaud was impressed with the site and could see how it would attract people who wanted to stay in touch with what was going on.

Then he saw it. Under the tab for blogs, there was a title that stood out. 'Is Amsterdam a safe place?' This particular chat room had been active for a couple of months now and had picked up a lot of readers and bloggers. There were in fact one hundred and eight different people who had written comments on the subject, which amazed Arnaud. Reading through the comments, he could quickly see that while the subject was not directly about the Magpie, all the comments had been about the killings this year.

As he continued to scan through the comments, Arnaud pulled his mobile phone out of his pocket and pressed speed dial one, which was for Friso. Before he could get the phone to his ear Friso had already spoken.

"Hi Arnaud."

"Have you seen this site?" Arnaud replied immediately. "We should be monitoring it regularly, checking out every comment for possible clues."

"You mean the 'Amsterdam Living' website. We have an admin person in the police checking it daily and reporting any suspicious comments to Robin and Jim."

Friso had answered Arnaud's questions, although he wasn't finished on this matter and felt that he should have been told about this earlier. He didn't like surprises and he also thought that there really could be some valuable information to be found on such a blog. Perhaps the killer even read it...

"You have an admirer." said Friso.

"So I was told this morning by some journalist who was stalking me." replied Arnaud. He continued to search through the comments on the site for the secret admirer.

"Friso, how can I see this person's comments?" asked Arnaud. Friso knew that his boss wasn't great with computers and could picture him straining his bad eyes over the small font on the site.

"Check out the blogger called 'Happy Single'. She is the biggest user of the blog and writes admiring comments about you but also, sometimes, gives views on the Magpie and what she thinks his plans are."

"How do you know it's a she?" asked Arnaud, not liking the fact that Friso was making assumptions.

"She actually says she is one on a number of occasions." replied Friso confidently. "She mentions that she feels safe in the city as the killer is only after men and he won't change his killing pattern as that would give the impression that he has failed."

Arnaud immediately thought that this blogger's comments weren't stupid at all and made good sense. He actually agreed with her opinion on the Magpie and suddenly felt annoyed again that he had only just been made aware of this site. It could be very useful to their investigation. However, he didn't want to moan now. He wanted to study the site, and in particular, the comments and opinions of 'Happy Single'.

The first few lines from this blogger were very flattering.

"Leave him alone. He's a great detective."

"Detective Van Loo is getting closer to catching the killer."

"The killer is finding it harder to strike and that's because Detective Van Loo is tightening the noose."

These defensive comments from the blogger were already beginning to worry Arnaud. He thought that if the killer actually read them it may anger him and spur him on to kill again more quickly. He also didn't want to give the press any ammunition. They were putting him under enough pressure as it was.

"Do we know who it is?" asked Arnaud with his mobile phone to his ear. "This, Happy Single?"

"No," replied Friso. "She signs into the blog as anonymous and has not left her email address. Anyway, it's just a blog."
"So, there is no way we can identify her?" Arnaud asked naively, his lack of IT knowledge very apparent.

"Nope," replied Friso, who was a little fed up with Arnaud's questions and sudden interest in this site. Friso had been on it for two months already, along with the rest of the team. He could sense that Arnaud was excited.

"You know, this site could lead us to the killer." continued Arnaud. "Why has..." He was cut short by Friso.

"Come in to the office Arnaud and we can talk about it. As I said before, we have been monitoring the website for two months and there has been nothing worth mentioning to you so far." Friso had lost his patience with Arnaud, and spoke respectfully back to him, but in a way that he would understand that they had better and more important things to discuss right now. Arnaud needed to trust him that they shouldn't spend too much time discussing this blog but focus on bigger issues.

There was silence and then Arnaud replied, "Okay, see you in half an hour."

Arnaud put his mobile phone back into his pocket and continued looking at the website. He genuinely thought that there could be some very useful information on the blog but for now he just wanted to read and not really hunt for clues. He wanted to try and build characters in his mind of the different bloggers that had been chatting about this topic. Normally, he would listen to Friso when he was so sure about something, but in this instance, Arnaud had a hunch and would need to make his own conclusions regarding the site.

Looking at his watch, he realized that forty minutes had flown by and he was already late for his meeting with Friso. Arnaud quickly went outside, got onto his moped and sped off down the Tuinstraat. On his way to work he thought more about this blogger, 'Happy Single', and some of her comments. He couldn't believe that she could be just a bored housewife who felt sorry for him. He was surprised that she had written such doting statements, as she didn't know him. "Leave him alone. He's a sweet man who is doing his best for his community. Give him time. Arnaud cares. Nobody else could do better than Detective Van Loo." Indeed, when he thought about these statements, Arnaud could see why Friso didn't take the blog too seriously. But he had to go with his own instinct and read the whole blog in detail.

One thing that struck him, as he was pulling up to the police station was the fact that 'Happy Single' never referred to the killer as the Magpie, unlike everybody else on the blog. She just referred to the killer as somebody. It seemed clear that the blogger didn't want to give the killer any recognition of iconic status or achievement with a title, just in case he read the site. This made him believe that she was actually a very smart individual. Anyway, he would spend more time studying the site once he got upstairs in the office with Friso and the team.

He chuckled to himself, which rarely happened, out of disbelief. There was something available to the whole world, this website, which could have critical information and clues for this case that they had taken for granted. Up until an hour ago, Arnaud knew nothing about it. How could they be so stupid! Here was a forum, where people could be anonymous and come forward with their opinions. Here was a window to the world that they could look into and one that the killer had access to as well. Arnaud needed to sit with his team and get them to understand that this was potentially a gold mine that they had been sitting on.

CHAPTER 8

October 5

3:00 p.m.

The Bakery, Badhoevedorp

Jan finished the next three trays of dough balls and slid them into the stainless-steel giant industrial oven. That made it twenty-five trays for the afternoon so far. He raised his white apron to wipe the sweat from his unwrinkled forehead. He couldn't use his hands, as apart from it being unhygienic, his fingers were covered in flour and sticky dough. His head looked a little ghost-like. Jan had quite a gaunt face anyway but he was looking particularly pale because of the flour that was in the air.

The bakery business had been in the Meijer family for three generations and had been successful, growing steadily over the years. Meijer Brood was well known in and around Amsterdam as a quality supplier of bread to cafés and small supermarkets. Their produce had a reputation for being tasty, well-priced and reliable. Their bakery was located on a small industrial estate about half a mile from his parent's house in Badhoevedorp. His two sisters and his brother-in-law, who was married to his older sister, Doreen, also worked in the business but more on the administration and sales side. Jan and his parents ran the dough preparation and baking. Jan also had the job of delivering the bread. This, he didn't mind, as he was 'an early bed' anyway and he also got the luxury of using one of the Meijer Brood vans whenever he wanted.

Jan had spent his whole life growing up in Badhoeve-dorp and working in the family business. He could prepare any type of bread, loaf or cake. Working long hours at the bakery always provided him with sufficient spending money to be able to have hobbies and to be able to go on holidays with friends over the last five years. His parents were simple people; nice, honest and hard working. They worked every day of the week, apart from Sundays because of their religious beliefs. Jan was the only member of the family who wasn't overweight. His father was tall and very fat. His mother was small and round and his two sisters were of average height but both on the heavier side. They could blame their size on the amount of bread that they consumed. Jan had seen his whole family grow over time and he was desperate not to follow in their footsteps. For now, Jan was tall, slim, and very muscular. All the training that he had done over recent years, weight lifting in the garden shed, cycling around Badhoevedorp, and the Tai Kwon Do classes had kept him very strong and slender at the same time.

The other promise that he had made to himself was to never work in the family business once he graduated from University. His sisters sort of knew Jan's intentions but his parents didn't. His father was very traditional and would want a male to run the business once he retired. Jan didn't want to tell his parents quite yet as he knew they would be very upset. He didn't think there was any point breaking the disappointing news now as he had two more years at the University. He would still work at the bakery for a while. He needed to.

Jan had aspirations to have his own art gallery one day. His plan was to try and get a job with a curator in one of the great museums in Amsterdam once he graduated. He loved the old artists like Vermeer and Van Gogh but preferred the Cobra movement and in particular Corneille, Constant, and Appel. A job in any of the museums in Amsterdam was his dream. His bedroom was littered with History of Art books, which were not tidied up or put in any order. His parents never commented on his messy bedroom or his University studies, as they didn't really understand the art world.

The family house was a simple three up and three down semi-detached terrace property in the middle of Badhoevedorp with perfectly manicured lawns in front and the back. Jan's parents took pride in keeping their house clean and tidy. They had even put a nice extension at the back of the house to create a conservatory, where they spent most of their time when they weren't at the bakery. Jan had always had his own bedroom, whereas his sisters had shared a room, until recently. Doreen had moved out when she got married. Now Imke had the room to herself next to Jan's bedroom.

Jan loved his parents and sisters but couldn't bear the idea of copying their lifestyles. They seemed so content with their simple boring way of living and he had to get out. Jan spent three quarters of his time sleeping at home and the rest staying at his darling girlfriend's apartment. If it was up to him, he would spend a lot more time with Mariana, but that wasn't his decision to make and there was no way that he was going to ask her.

Mariana controlled the relationship. She decided when they would see each other and even when they would speak. He had learnt not to call her as she would rarely pick up the phone. Instead, Jan would text and he knew that she would eventually reply. He sometimes felt that she used him just for sex and a shoulder to cry on because she rarely showed any emotion.

Jan was a self-conscious young man but he knew that whilst he was only okay looking, he did have a good physique. He was also very good at Tai Kwon Do and he knew that his strength impressed Mariana, although she would never admit it. He also thought to himself that Mariana must like him for more than the sex and his strength but he could never work it out. Was it because he came from a completely different background than hers? It had to be something as she could get anyone she desired. She was beautiful, exotic-looking, dressed elegantly, was extremely intelligent, and had an amazing figure. Mariana also had a way about her that would attract men instantly. Jan was, in fact, sure that she had cheated on him once or twice but she would never admit it. She liked to see him get jealous so Jan refused to bring the subject up.

Mariana realized that she had Jan exactly where she wanted him so he did his best not to show any feelings or emotions when they would chat at bars and restaurants every time they went out. She wasn't particularly nice to him, and Jan pondered over the reasons why he liked her so much. Apart from the obvious attraction he thought she maybe his way out. He felt that Mariana would push him to get out of this boring suburban life style that had been mapped out for him since birth.

Jan had slept with six girls in his life and Mariana was so different from all of them. Apart from the color of her passport and the fact that she spoke Dutch, she was extremely foreign in all her ways and he liked that. Jan liked that she didn't conform. It was also a challenge for him to keep her and to make sure that she carried on wanting him even though it was a strange relationship. The longer they stayed together, the closer he thought he was to getting away from working in the bakery for the rest of his life.

In his heart, Jan knew that he wouldn't be able to keep her forever. She would marry the son of a wealthy Dutch family or a foreign man with an exciting lifestyle who would fly her around the world, just as her father had done to her mother many years ago. With either one, they wouldn't be able to win her over if they showed her too much love. Not showing any affection was the way to keep Mariana interested. He knew this very well now. One thing was for sure, Mariana would always call the shots and be in control. She would choose whether to break a guy's heart and not the other way around. Jan was also fully aware that he was obsessed with her and that he would be there whenever she wanted him. He knew that it wasn't good for the relationship but she was like a drug and he couldn't help but idolize her. He just tried not to show too much emotion.

Mariana had been to his parents' place twice in their fourteen-month relationship and she made it clear to him that she detested Badhoevedorp. Jan had wanted her to meet his parent's none-the-less. By inviting her over, he hoped that she would also ask him to visit her father's house for dinner or drinks. Jan was impressed by Dr. Akkermans. He had been invited over to the town house on the Keizersgracht four times and all were brief visits apart from one dinner. Jan thought that Mariana might be embarrassed of him and also didn't want him to see where she had spent a number of years growing up. She didn't talk about her past and never wanted to open up to him. She was indeed a 'closed book', and a psychiatrist could probably spend a lot of time pulling back the layers of her complicated life and background. It would probably be very good for her to see one but there was absolutely no way that Jan was going to suggest it. Their relationship was run by Mariana and when they spent time together it was just the two of them and no one else. Jan knew there was no long-term future in this.

Jan's parents found her very strange and laughed and joked about her that she acted like royalty and a morning of preparing dough for the ovens would sort her out. They couldn't believe how immaculate she was in appearance. No student wore diamond earrings, silk scarves, and a vintage gold watch. They were right but Jan didn't expect them to understand. They had never seen anyone like this before and had nothing at all in common with her. His parents had constantly laughed with his sisters, in front of him, "what does she see in Jan?" This had stopped pretty quickly as they could see Jan becoming sad because he knew that it was true. A question he couldn't even answer himself.

Jan didn't care what his parents thought. He had different dreams compared to them. They had never studied or traveled. His sisters were worried for Jan as they could feel his sadness and see his obsession with Mariana. They knew she treated him badly and it would end in Jan having his heart broken eventually. They cared and loved their brother even though they knew he had different aspirations than them. Jan was the opposite of his sisters, he was clever and ambitious.

Jan had completed all the bread preparations for the day and now had to tidy up. He wiped the flour off all the stainless-steel surfaces and then swept the floor with a broom. Making two neat piles on the floor, he used a dust-pan and brush to sweep the flour and then collected the small bits with sticky dough throwing it all in the bin.

The ovens were burning bright, baking the trays of bread rolls. He mopped the rest of the kitchen floor keeping an eye on the bread. He was wearing flour-covered blue and white checkered trousers and a white t-shirt that was two sizes too small for him. You could see his rippling torso beneath it. You could also see large sweat stains under each armpit and on his back resulting from a hard day's work in the extremely hot kitchen.

He needed to tell his mother, who was sitting in the office next to the kitchen, that he was done and that all the bread that was baking were set on timers. He had to drive back to the house and take a shower before he did anything else. He also needed something to eat as he was starving and it was already three in the afternoon. After this, he would finish his art history essay that was due tomorrow. Then, he could drive in to Amsterdam. Mariana had invited him over tonight but hadn't mentioned whether it was for dinner or just for sex. He didn't know whether to feel excited or sad.

He had only seen her once this week at Tai Kwon Do class and later at her apartment. She hated cooking anyway, especially for him. He didn't want to think about this too much and was just happy that she had invited him at all. Before he could see Mariana, he needed to clean one of the three apartments that he did on a weekly basis in Amsterdam. He didn't have time for these cleaning jobs but made time, as it got him more money that he could use for dinners and drinks with Mariana. Hopefully, a winter holiday too. He was late for his weekly cleaning job in the city and couldn't put it off another day.

Realizing that he still had a lot to accomplish before he could meet his beautiful girlfriend Jan raced to speak to his Mom. He was in a rush.

CHAPTER 9

October 5

9:00 p.m.

Yab Yum, Amsterdam

As you walked up the steps to the front entrance and onto the pristine velvet carpet in the hallway, there was a strong aroma of perfumes blending together, signifying a number of women inside. The three Japanese businessmen who had just been dropped off at the high-class brothel in the blacked-out limousine walked nervously into the establishment. They were in their late forties and early fifties and were small and thin in physique, like most Asian men. They had been out for a long dinner and were clearly drunk after a few glasses of wine and some beers. They had remained, however, smartly dressed as if arriving at the house of their first prom date.

They nervously followed the manager of Yab Yum, Ralph Van Beek, along the marbled walled corridor to a set of double doors that opened up into a bar and lounge area decorated with purple satin sofas and mirrored walls. Welcoming the businessmen into this bar, Van Beek smiled at them with white bleached teeth. He had worked at Yab Yum for more than twenty years. He had initially started as a bedroom cleaner, moving onto bar work, and finally, for the last eight years he had the ultimate job of brothel manager. For a fifty-year old man, Van Beek took a lot of pride in his appearance with an over-the-top sun bed tan and a slightly shiny double-breasted grey suit. He was balding but tried to hide this by carefully placing strands of wispy silver hair greased back.

Van Beek was very proud of what he did and the attention he paid to his appearance. He expected the brothel girls to do the same. He also felt that appearances were everything and in being as hospitable as possible would result in lots of tips for him. He was right. He got paid very well to run this establishment.

It was the ultimate location in Amsterdam where men were pampered and fulfilled their fantasies. Most of the clientele were overseas businessmen that were visiting Amsterdam or very wealthy Dutch guys. All the concierges at the top Amsterdam hotels knew where Yab Yum was located and would make a discreet call to the club's manager on behalf of inquiring guests. A Yab Yum limousine would then pick up clients from anywhere in the city and bring them to the beautiful white townhouse positioned in the middle of the Singel canal.

The only clue that this building housed an exotic paradise with beautiful women of the night was the lantern outside that lit up the entrance and the two cuddling doves painted on it. This was the emblem of Yab Yum. The second giveaway for anyone passing the building was the two-meter, broad-shouldered doorman with no neck. He would come outside to open the doors of the parking limousines that were dropping off clients. This scary-looking character was dressed in a tailored dark suit and long wool coat. He always had well-groomed hair and was cleanly shaven, revealing a chiseled square jaw. He never spoke but just nodded at guests and was probably Eastern European, very tough and not to be messed with. The brickwork and paintwork outside the building was immaculate and the purple velvet carpet started from the matting outside the main entrance.

Ralph Van Beek ushered the three men into the busy lounge area to a corner table. The small sofa and seats surrounding their table were also purple velvet, just like the carpet. There were about fifteen businessmen in the lounge and three waitresses serving drinks. The waitresses were dressed smartly in mid-length black skirts and stockings, with low-cut white blouses. They would take drink orders from a selection of vintage champagnes from the tables and go over to the bar area, where a tall old bar man would then retrieve the appropriate bottle. It was a very good and lucrative bar business.

Once the Japanese trio had ordered a bottle of Krug, the waitress poured them each a glass. Van Beek walked over to show the men a different menu and talk them through it. As he pointed to various offerings on the card, you couldn't help but stare at the manger's dark brown fingers and the numerous rings he wore. He even had a gold ring on his little finger with a large diamond in it. It was expensive but extremely tacky. Van Beek leant over the table and spoke slowly to the Japanese businessmen explaining how Yab Yum worked and the varying costs for different services.

"We have a range of rooms at different price ranges available that you can rent for the evening. Now, all the rooms are suites but some are bigger than others and some have a number of beds. Some even have extra luxurious items in them like a sauna and a jacuzzi." Van Beek paused to let the men take in what he was saying and to see if they had any questions.

"Okay, okay." said the oldest of the three men loosening his tie and sounding extremely excited. The other two Japanese men just stared at Van Beek with their eyes popping out of their heads.

"Now, for the girls," continued Van Beek, "They range from twenty-one to twenty-five in age. All speak English and all are white, apart from Zoe who is from Suriname, and Ruby and Maxi who are both Indonesian."

The oldest Japanese man, who was clearly the boss, interrupted Van Beek by pointing at the white girls' names on the menu. They had already made up their minds on what they wanted for dessert.

Van Beek started speaking again, "You can see that there are no prices on the card as the girls will decide how much they are going to charge you depending on the services you take. For example, if you would like a massage there will be an additional cost for that."

Obviously, this was how the club made its money by racking up the charges. Van Beek could see from their facial expressions that these additional services were not part of the Japanese men's agenda. The men gulped down their champagne and beckoned the waitress to refill them. They were clearly in search of some Dutch courage.

"And how many girls would you like?" Van Beek asked calmly.

"Errggh." replied the older man looking over at his colleagues for their opinions. "Free, one each." he answered nervously.

Van Beek understood 'free' to mean 'three' as this was hard for a Japanese person to say.

"Okay." replied Van Beek with a cheesy smile. "You can always have more later." But he knew that these men were not regulars and didn't appear experienced in this type of entertainment either, so they would be done shortly. This was the perfect client for Yab Yum as they paid for a full night's service but would use it only for an hour. They would then leave and new clients could use the services of the establishment.

With everything agreed upon, Van Beek stood up from the table and bowed to the three men.

"I wish you an enjoyable evening."

He then turned and walked away in the direction of the exit door of the lounge area. Like a general in the army, Van Beek made two clear signals to the staff who were watching him like hawks. The waitress was the first to react. She brought a second bottle of Krug to their table and quickly took the cork out. Even though the businessmen hadn't finished the first bottle, they were not going to complain, as their minds were elsewhere right now. They were also too busy looking at the waitress that was serving them as she had a large cleavage that got bigger every time she bent over to top their glasses.

Van Beek's second signal had been a tap of his fingers on the bar as he left the room, which was a signal to Brum, the barman. He responded by picking up the telephone and speaking into it for about thirty seconds. This was a call to the lady who prepared the suites upstairs for clients who were about to use them. Van Beek would personally take care of selecting the girls that would be entertaining the three Japanese men. This was part of his job that he liked doing the most as it showed his power over the girls.

After about twenty minutes, the waitress escorted the three men out of the lounge area. She told them that it was time to go upstairs and she would bring their champagne to the suite shortly. They followed her past the bar and out to the hallway by an old wooden stairwell. She took them up to the second floor in the direction of their suite. They chuckled nervously amongst themselves excited but at the same time pretty drunk. As they followed the waitress up the final steps, they all stared at the slit in the back of her black skirt. They could see her lace stockings and tanned thighs as she walked sexily in front of them.

The slit in the skirt and the stockings were planned of course; all part of the service and finishing touches to the Yab Yum experience. Unfortunately, for the men, the waitress was not for sale but was there to get the night started by serving drinks elegantly to them.

As they reached the door to their suite she explained that they could order more drinks or snacks via the phone in the room.

The waitress opened the large oak-paneled door to the suite and beckoned them to enter. As the men walked in, they were surprised to see a beautiful large room of approximately one hundred square meters. There were two cream-colored sofas in the front part of the suite where the waitress told them to sit and wait. Like naughty school kids they did exactly what she asked them to do.

"Enjoy your evening gentlemen. I will be back later." With a lovely smile the waitress bid them farewell and closed the door behind her. She was gone.

The men sat silently for the next ten minutes as they looked around the large room trying to imagine what would be happening shortly. Next to them was a plasma screen on the wall and a small shelf with a selection of porn DVDs, just in case clients got 'stage fright' or needed some assistance to get in the mood. The walls were painted in a brilliant white color and the carpets were purple, just like the rest of the building. There were three beds in the large room. One was an old wooden four-poster bed with cream cotton sheets with fake rose petals sprinkled on it. The other two beds, down the far end of the suite, were round and free standing: one was covered in a purple silk sheet and the other had a white silk cover.

Even though the room was very luxurious, it didn't have a jacuzzi in it. They could only be found in the three presidential suites on the top floors of the building, which were normally hired out by middle-eastern clients or Amsterdam gangsters.

There was a knock on the door and this stopped the three Japanese men from muttering. They bolted upright and froze still in sitting positions staring at the door to the room wondering who was on the other side of it. They were all nervous and scared. In a high-pitched tone and with a slightly shaking voice the older Japanese man spoke out.

"Kwom in."

There was an eerie silence for a few seconds, when everything was still, and the men just waited staring at the door. Then, the brass round door handle started to turn and the door opened slowly with a creaking sound. Still, nobody entered the room. You could hear one of the younger Japanese men swallow loudly, worried about what was about to happen. After another ten seconds of silence, three women entered the room, strutting across the floor in stilettos and walking in different directions as if they were about to start a well-choreographed dance performance.

Following them into the room was the waitress, carrying a silver tray with six champagne glasses. She placed it on a side table next to one of the sofas and then headed for the door. She left the room and closed the door behind her without the men even noticing. The three women were in their early twenties, all Dutch, and each of them had slender sexy figures.

One of the girls walked straight over to the four-poster bed next to the sofa. She was about five foot eleven in height and had long brown hair that had beautiful waves in it. She wore a black silk see through nightie that barely covered her buttocks. When she leant forward slightly, everything was on show. Her bottom was small but muscular and pale in complexion. Through the nightie you could see that she was wearing a tiny black string and she had a pair of 32C breasts that stood very pert. When she lay down on the bed, you could definitely tell that these were fake as they simply didn't move. She slid up the mattress towards the pillows and then turned around to face the three men.

She had small features but big lips accentuated by a lot of lipstick. She smiled innocently at the men sitting opposite her on the sofas as if she was shy. She focused in on one of the younger men with her dark brown eyes and then lifted up her right hand and beckoned him to come over to the bed with a curling finger. The message was very clear, and the youngest of the three Japanese men stood up and ran his hand through his short black hair before shuffling nervously across the room, past the sofas and over to the side of the four-poster bed. He was transfixed by this long red painted fingernail that was drawing him towards her. As he approached the bed the woman sat upright on her knees like a rodeo rider and leant across to the small man and kissed him softly on the cheek purposely breathing deeply into his ear. With two hands, she sleekly took off his tie and dropped it on the ground. She then proceeded to undo the buttons on his white shirt as he stood rigidly still mesmerized by the handy-work of this fast-moving goddess.

The second girl who had entered the room walked around to the back of the sofa and then sat her long slim body down on the arm rest next to the other young business man. Instead of looking at her he stared nervously straight ahead unsure if she had come to sit next to him and what she was going to do next. She deliberately slipped backwards over the armrest of the sofa and fell on to his lap with her head facing up towards his. The man almost jumped out of his skin and then looked down at the beautiful young woman whose head was lying on top of his groin. She smiled at him and then in a silly voice said, "Ooops, sorry." She then spoke Japanese and said "Youkoso." Looking petrified, he plucked up the courage to mutter back to her in a high voice "Konnichiha."

His eyes and mouth were both wide open. She didn't know if he was going to laugh or cry, a sign of a 'first timer'. As she looked into his eyes and continued to smile she knew that this client wouldn't be here for too long, which she preferred, of course. The man relaxed a little bit and started to check out her slender body as she lay there in front of him. She was wearing a skin tight white vest through which you could see her small breasts and very erect nipples. He started thinking that maybe he had excited her and this turned him on. Below her short vest, you could see her muscular abs and her naval. She had the mid-drift of a gymnast. Looking further down her body he checked out her white hot pants and the v shape that was very visible between the tops of her thighs. He was becoming very excited and the girl sensed it as she could feel something growing harder at the back of her head. She lifted her arm up and started stroking him through his trousers. Looking up at his face, to check if he was enjoying this stimulation, she noticed that he was completely distracted and looking the other way at something else behind the sofa.

She too looked across at the older Japanese man, who was sitting on the other sofa, and noticed that he had also moved his focus away from her and was staring in the same direction as his colleague. The young prostitute sat upright to see what was going on and to find out what was more interesting to look at than her, although she already had an idea.

There was a click sound as the third girl who had entered the room turned on the stereo system. They all stared at her bending over adjusting the volume dial. Her tanned firm legs were propped up in a pair of shiny black stilettos with red soles. She wore an extremely short silk white nightie and matching string. As she leant over the men could see everything and they all stared with their mouths wide open. They admired her beautiful body that was completely bald.

As the music started the two other girls began moving their heads to the beat of the Latin dance music. The third girl stood upright and turned around to face the crowd. She walked behind the back of the other sofa and ran her hand through the greying hair of the elder man who was sitting on his own. His eyes followed her every move. He looked on nervously but excited as he knew that he had got the 'prize catch'. She then walked to the front of the sofa and stood directly in front of him staring down with her hands on her hips. She wasn't as tall as the other two girls but her body was amazing. Her hips started moving back and forward to the music as she continued to watch his face, which looked hypnotized. She was wearing a short black-bobbed wig, which made her look quite Japanese. Unlike the other two girls she didn't wear any make up. She didn't need to. She was very beautiful.

She lifted her hands and slipped off her nightie to reveal large pert fake breasts and a body to die for. Her belly button was pierced and covered with a pink shiny stone that moved around as she danced. She could see that the man's eyes were going from side to side as she gyrated to the music. She bent across and grabbed the man's tie and pulled him towards her. He was still sitting but their heads were now touching. Softly, she whispered sexily into his ear, "Hi, I'm Pearl."

She then turned around still holding onto his tie and started walking away forcing the man to stand up from the sofa and follow her. She led him by his tie to the other end of the room, like a puppy dog, towards the round beds. The man shuffled along behind Pearl staring at her naked buttocks and legs that strutted down the room in time with the beat of the music. Her bottom cheeks were so pert and tight that there was no wobble to them. She ushered him onto the round bed with the white silk sheets and sat next to him. She whispered into his ear again. "Let's party." Pearl started to caress his neck and shoulders. His small frame was motionless and his muscles seemed very tight, which probably came from him being nervous.

"How about a massage?" said Pearl as she started to run her left hand up his thighs towards his crotch. She could tell immediately that he wasn't hard yet and hoped that it wouldn't take too long to finish him off. First, she needed to get him naked as the man had not responded to her offer for a massage. She took it upon herself to undress him and go ahead anyway.

Pushing him back onto the bed she sat on top of the fully-dressed man and started to undo the buttons on his shirt. He liked the way she looked. Whilst the complexion of her skin was smooth and soft it wasn't pale enough for a Tokyo lady. Pearl could see that he was still very nervous so she grabbed his hands and placed them on her firm silicon breasts. He gripped them hard, scared to let go. He clearly hadn't experienced anything like this before.

He continued to stare at her beautifully toned body as she slipped off his shirt and started undoing his belt buckle. She could see through his dark grey suit trousers that he was getting erect, even if it was just a small lump.

Pearl had only been working at Yab Yum for a few months but had quickly learnt how to undress a man in seconds. The Japanese guy's body was shaking with excitement as she undid the zip on his trousers. He was clearly out of his comfort zone so he tried to make conversation with her.

"What is your real name?" came the high-pitched question, in badly-pronounced English. She was often asked this and didn't really understand why as it didn't really matter if Pearl was her real name or her work name. Her only explanation for this question was that nervous clients were trying to make conversation and feel that they had some form of relationship or bond before the deed was done.

She didn't know if they felt sorry for her but they definitely didn't need to as she was the richest student in Amsterdam and Utrecht. She was also having a lot of fun. She could drink as much champagne as she wanted, do cocaine and ecstasy if the clients requested it, and had so much cash that she could buy whatever clothes and accessories she desired. What more could she want. She had also learnt to orgasm very quickly so that all her clients would think that they must be doing something right if they could make the lady of the night climax!

She looked down at him one more time and with a cute innocent smile spoke softly to him.

"I already told you, it's Pearl."

She managed to fake a giggling laugh and then flipped him gracefully, but with force, over onto his front with his face down on the silk sheets of the round bed. The man was surprised at her strength but remained very excited as he was expecting a good massage and hopefully her hands would wander. She sat on top of his back and started giving him a hard massage working down from his neck through his shoulder blades and along his spine. She could hear him moan and shriek as she pushed down forcefully on his upper body muscles. He had a thin neck like a skinny woman and Pearl thought to herself that she could snap it as easily as breaking a chicken's neck, just like she used to do when she was younger, helping her mother prepare Sunday roasts, at her parent's farm. She could tell that the man liked the pressure of the massage even if it was causing him pain. He started biting the silk bed sheets as she continued to push down hard on his thin muscles.

She shuffled backwards onto his legs and reached across to the side of the bed for a small bottle of baby oil. As she sat there naked, on top of the man's calves, she took a moment to scan the room to see what the other two girls were doing. Her friend, who was with one of the younger business men on the four-poster bed, was giving him a blow job but kept stopping as the condom kept slipping off his small penis. Pearl laughed to herself as that didn't look fun at all and she could see Jasmine getting annoyed. The man was moaning loudly, tied up with silk ropes to each post on the bed, lying in a star position.

On the sofa, Star sat naked on top of the other Japanese man, bouncing up and down and groaning with fake pleasure. This was also funny to see as she was so much bigger than the guy with her long legs wrapped round his skinny torso. Star's long hair covered the man's face so Pearl couldn't see if he was enjoying it or not. She got the impression that they were both almost finished with the men and so she also needed to get a move on. Greasing up her own hands with baby oil, Pearl started applying the lubricant all over the man's lower back and buttocks. Very quickly his bottom started moving up and down in a sexual motion.

She ran her hands down to his inner thighs where she started stroking him with her oiled fingers. Massaging all the way up between his cheeks and touching his ball sack. The man was shaking with excitement and making heavy panting noises. She noticed that he had very little hair on his body for a man. Every time he raised his buttocks and body upwards she moved her right hand underneath him and around the shaft of his penis greasing it up. She could feel that even though he was fully erect his penis couldn't have been more than four and a half inches in length. She was glad that they hadn't gone down the route of intercourse as it would have been pretty boring.

Pearl could sense that he was close to coming with the groaning noises he was making. She quickly turned him over and with ten seconds of quickly jerking his penis he gave a shriek and then squirted three times. Pearl very sportingly caught the sperm with her cupped left hand and then reached across to the side of the bed for the wet wipes that were next to the bottle of baby oil. She cleaned her hands and the tip of his penis. The tired Japanese man looked up at her and spoke softly, "Thank you Pearl."

"You are welcome." she replied as she stood up off the bed and put her nightie back on. She thought to herself that this had been a success as she hadn't even taken off her string and would still get paid very well. She picked up a glass full of champagne that sat on the carpet and drank it down in one gulp. It was a sort of celebration to a job well done.

This was a really quick night's work, thought Pearl to herself, as she wiped a few beads of sweat off her forehead. As she did this, she felt a few strands of her fair colored hair fall down from under the short-bobbed wig. She couldn't be bothered to put them back up and hide them as the night was done. The role play was over and her client was fully satisfied.

Looking around the room Pearl could see that her colleagues were also finished and had put their underwear back on. She walked back down the room towards them passing a large mirror on the wall. She stopped for a moment to check how she was looking. As she stared into the mirror she thought to herself that she was young and pretty without a wrinkle on her face. Her eyes were big and blue and her light brown eyebrows were thin and well-manicured and their color matched her hair. She had beautiful big lips and she blew a kiss to herself before walking on towards a silver button that was positioned on the wall by the door to the room. This button was used to let the waitresses and cleaners know that the girls had finished with the clients. They could come up and clean the room of any leftover snacks and drinks, and bring the bill for payment.

Pearl pressed the silent bell on the wall and then quickly walked back to her man who was now sitting on the side of the round bed fully clothed trying to put his tie back on.

She approached him and spoke politely.

"Don't rush, take your time."

She had her stilettos on which made her seem even taller as she towered over the small man. She bent over and gave him a kiss on the cheek and whispered to him, "Thank you for your custom."

She always was very polite to the clients even after sex as she thought that it might result in bigger tips. With that she turned again and headed for the exit. She opened the door and let her two girlfriends leave the room first. Before she shut the door behind her, she turned back to face the older Japanese man who was now standing up at the other end of the room, and she called across to him.

"Oh, and my real name is Fleur!" She winked as she said this and then left immediately. Shutting the door behind her, Fleur was gone.

CHAPTER 10

October 8

2:30 p.m.

Arnaud walked out of the doctor's office on Beethovenstraat and looked at his watch. It was time that he head back to the office on Koninginneweg. He had just been for his bi-annual doctor's appointment, which he hated turning up for. Nothing had changed with his conditions, which was good in one way but it also meant that he still had high blood pressure and continued to suffer from mild anxiety attacks.

Every now and again he would take a Xanax with a beer in the evening to calm his nerves. However, in general, Arnaud preferred to use a sleeping pill with a couple of shots of gin in the early evening to get his mind off things. It would also knock him out. He had expected his conditions to worsen this year as a result of the events that had taken place in and around Amsterdam over the last ten months but they hadn't. Dr. Berkhoudt had been in the same fraternity as Arnaud and had prescribed him even stronger sleeping pills anyway.

Arnaud headed over to his moped and sped off down the Beethovenstraat in the direction of his office, which was approximately eight minutes away. There was a lot of grey cloud cover and Arnaud didn't have his raincoat with him. He wanted to get to the police station as quickly as possible to avoid the rain. Parking just outside his office building, he got in through the front entrance just before the rain started to fall. Pleased with his timing, he walked briskly up the stairs to the floor of his office.

Arnaud had arranged a meeting with the two young policemen assisting them with the case, to go over data collection, research, and most important to Arnaud, 'the blog'. As Arnaud entered their office, Jim and Robin looked up attentively at him, keen, ready to listen, take orders, and work. It was clear that they both respected Arnaud highly and felt very lucky to be part of the investigation team that was working on the biggest murder hunt in the history of The Netherlands.

Friso was also in the office, which didn't surprise Arnaud, as he was always working. Sitting behind his computer, Friso glanced up at Arnaud and looked back down again immediately. Clearly he was busy, thought Arnaud, which was a good thing and was best left alone. Friso's work ethic was the most detailed and diligent of the whole team.

Arnaud made himself a coffee from the vending machine and sat next to Jim and Robin to start working. Arnaud placed his coffee cup down on their shared desk and emptied two sachets of sugar into it. Stirring his coffee, Arnaud began to speak.

"Okay guys, as we discussed already, I think it's important that we not only monitor this website but actually take it a step further."

As he spoke, Arnaud noticed Jim and Robin's faces focus even more, as well as Friso's ears prick up.

He continued, "I believe that there is more on this blog and probably other websites than we really think. The likelihood is that the killer is a bit of a loner and will spend quite some time on the computer researching future kills. Remember, he is very calculating. He is also a very famous serial killer now and will likely take an interest in reading about his work and success on the internet and in the press."

Arnaud took a swig from his coffee and paused to think before speaking again. Friso was now sitting back in his chair and had stopped what he had been working on to pay attention to Arnaud's every word.

Arnaud breathed in deeply and started speaking again, "We are dealing with a serial killer who is both, cunning and extremely disturbed. He plans his strikes very carefully, then disappears with the body for about three days, does whatever he does with the victim, kills them, and then dumps the corpse without a trace."

Robin interrupted Arnaud, "What should we be looking for on the internet then? What do we know?" Arnaud stood up and faced his team like a professor about to give a lecture. "He targets only men and probably hates the male sex. The Magpie is strong enough to take down young men. He keeps the body for up to three days and works on it uninterrupted. Therefore, he probably has his own place where he can hide the victim. The Magpie also has a thing about hygiene and cleaning the body and stripping the victim of their jewelry. He isn't going to stop as he knows that he is good at what he does now and has a taste for it. Also, he doesn't have a problem working on a dead body as he does this for a number of days before dumping it. Finally, the Magpie is very smart and thorough, and plans everything exceptionally well and still hasn't been seen."

It was clear that nobody had any questions so Arnaud continued, "What has this one particular blog told us? Are there any different opinions to our trail of thought? Any other views or clues?" Arnaud looked at his colleagues for answers.

"Well," said Jim, "Happy Single has been saying that she believes that the killer is a girl."

There was silence as everyone stared at Jim. Friso was a bit surprised by Jim's comments. They had discussed this view and had dismissed it. In fact, as not everything on the blog could be taken seriously, Friso was a bit annoyed that Jim had spoken up on this without consulting him first. He felt that it made him look stupid by saying something like that.

Jim continued, "The way the killer cleans the bodies and cuts their hair elegantly and clips their nails so neatly has all the traits of a female's work."

Arnaud finally responded, "Good. Very fucking good!"

He was impressed and excited by Jim's comments. Not that he necessarily agreed with Happy Single but they needed to think outside the box and look for at other possibilities. After all, they weren't really getting anyway at the moment so they needed to try other things.

"There you go guys. It is possible that the killer is a female but I wouldn't agree with the view that only a woman would clean and cut the nails and hair of the victim meticulously. We know that the killer is calculated and a perfectionist and even a man could clean the corpse well in order to get rid of any DNA. What else?" continued Arnaud. "Friso, please write these ideas down on the flip board."

He handed him a marker pen. Turning back to the two young detectives Arnaud spoke again, "Come on guys, what else? Come on!" Raising his voice despairingly, Arnaud focused in on Jim for more points.

"A lot of bloggers are agreeing with Happy Single that the Magpie has an accomplice. The general opinion on the blog is that it's too much work, even for a strong guy, to take the body away, hold it for a few days, and then dump it with no sign of resistance on the corpse or without any witnesses."

"Good." replied Arnaud.

He didn't agree with the comments but he wanted his team to brainstorm at the moment. Arnaud looked across at Friso, who was standing by the flip board and nodded at him.

Arnaud turned back to the two young men and said, "Anything else?"

Robin spoke up this time, "Happy Single thinks that the killer takes all the jewelry off of the victims to strip them of any happy memories or gifts from their lives. Therefore, she thinks that the Magpie is an unhappy person, scarred from their past."

"Well that's a tough one to take a view on as we would be making a lot of assumptions in agreeing with this opinion," said Arnaud, although he did think to himself that this made complete sense.

The blogger, 'Happy Single', was a clever person and it was becoming clear to him that most of what she said was quite probable.

Arnaud continued speaking. "Write it down please, Friso, but just to be clear, this blogger 'Happy Single', never refers to the killer as 'The Magpie'."

They all nodded at Arnaud in agreement.

"It's getting tougher for the killer to strike." said Jim.

"We know that!" snapped Arnaud, in response to the first obvious comment.

There was silence again and Arnaud thought that the guys were running out of ideas.

"Okay, was there anything new on the blog yesterday or today that was of interest?"

Robin spoke up, "Just comments about you and the team on whether we are doing a good job or not."

"Well," said Jim, "It's clear that Happy Single is a secret admirer of yours. Some would say that she's even in love with you, Arnaud!"

Arnaud's eyes opened wide with Jim's silly comments.

Jim continued, "She won't let anyone say anything bad about you and defends you all the time. Do you know her? She must know you as she seems so attached to you!"

Arnaud took these comments as a joke and stood up to go over to chat to Friso. Jim carried on speaking, stopping Arnaud in his tracks.

"She even knows that it is your birthday in three days!"

Arnaud was in shock. Why were people discussing his birthday on the blog? How did they find out his birth date? Who was this 'Happy Single' blogger? Did she really know Arnaud and did she really like him?

"How can we find out who these bloggers are?" asked Arnaud. "Who is this Happy Single?"

"You can't." Friso spoke for the first time. "That's the beauty of a blog. You can hide your identity and remain anonymous."

"Well, let's keep monitoring the conversations and any other blogs discussing this topic." Even Arnaud, who didn't want to commit any specific viewpoint regarding this serial killer, was beginning to think that maybe the Magpie was really a woman. If this was the case, it changed everything and they would have to retrace their steps and previous evidence and clues. He had Happy Single to thank for influencing and changing his opinion, whoever she was.

* * *

7:10 p.m.

You could cut the atmosphere with a knife in Roos' apartment. She hadn't spoken to Jade for three days now and Roos was getting angrier by the minute. Since Jade had come back from her last long haul flight, there had been a problem between them. Jade was sitting silently on the sofa in the living room putting on nail varnish and watching a bad US chat show on the television. She was wearing a pair of pencil jeans and a tight white t-shirt. The expression on her beautiful face was stern with a slight frown, giving off the persona that she was not to be messed with right then. It was clear that she was pissed off and everyone in her vicinity could feel that.

Roos was busy slamming doors in the apartment and scurrying around from room to room trying to keep herself busy. She was so upset with Jade at the moment, but didn't want to talk through things about why they were arguing so much. Basically, Roos had such a jealous nature that it was driving a barrier between them. Where was Jade going in the evenings? Who was she going out with? This was driving Roos crazy and making her very angry with her girlfriend.

The doorbell rang, and Roos knew that it must be the cleaner. She rushed down the stairs and through the living room to open the door. Right now, she would do anything to keep herself busy and distracted. She was right. The tall wiry figure of Jan Meijer stood in front of Roos with a smile on his face. It was the easiest clean-up job he had, as Roos was a tidy freak. But she was also mad and he knew that she and Jade were having problems.

Roos had one of her moody expressions on her face but also one that made her look a bit sad today. They must have been arguing again, was the conclusion that Jan drew as he said, "good afternoon", and walked past Roos into the living room. Roos slammed the door behind Jan and ran upstairs back to her bedroom, crashing that door shut as well. He could tell that they must have had a falling out and were not speaking. He headed to the kitchen to start cleaning there. This was probably the best place to begin, away from both of them.

He had been cleaning their house for over a year now and couldn't remember a time when there weren't any issues between them. If it wasn't for the fact that Roos paid so well, he wouldn't do this apartment. He was scared of both Roos and Jade, and thought they were both crazy.

Fleur, in fact, was the only normal one of the three girls living there and she was always really nice.

Jan normally spent most of his time chatting with Fleur, when she was around, as the house was so tidy that he ran out of things to clean after being there for more than thirty minutes. Today was no different than any other time that he was at this apartment. When Roos and Jade were there, he knew that fireworks would start.

Roos sat on her bed, biting her nails, and in deep thought. She couldn't blame the fact that they had a flat-mate, Fleur, as the reason for their problems because she was hardly ever there. Maybe, Jade was just getting bored with her. Maybe she had found someone else. After all she was taller, slimmer, more beautiful, more fun, sexier, not jealous, and carefree! All of these thoughts were eating away at Roos and making her more and more irrational and angry. In the past, they would solve their lover's tiffs by going out, getting drunk, and having passionate sex. They would normally talk it over the next day and then make-up with terrible hangovers. This time, however, it was different.

Roos' hand was bleeding from where she had been scrubbing the tiles on the bathroom floor. She had grazed her knuckles, which had also begun to swell. She stood up from her bed and decided, suddenly, that the best thing to do was to go for a walk and clear her head. She put on her long raincoat and before leaving her bedroom she combed her immaculately bobbed hair and took one last glance in the bedroom mirror.

She wasn't entirely happy with what she saw but rarely ever was. Roos sucked in her cheeks and held in her tummy for a pose and acknowledged the fact that she had nice boobs that were easy to notice through her thin raincoat.

Surely, Jade hadn't found someone else, she thought to herself again. Roos thought of herself as a pretty 'seven and a half out of ten' girl who was good in bed. This was difficult for Jade to beat but other girls weren't as crazy or as jealous, which counted for something as well. At least, there was nothing to stop Jade from looking.

"Okay, enough Roos!" she said to herself as she headed for the stairs down to the living room. Picking up her mobile from the coffee table in the middle of the room, she deliberately bent down for a second to obscure Jade's view of the television. Annoyingly, Jade didn't flinch.

"I'm going out, Jan." said Roos, still standing in front of the television. "I've left some cash for you upstairs on the dresser in my bedroom. Thanks for today and see you next week."

Jan stopped cleaning the kitchen surfaces to turn and face Roos and smiled as if to say thank you for leaving the cash. If he could get away with just faking a smile, clean the house, get paid, and exit without being in the middle of one of her fits he would be happy. Anyway, Roos didn't even give Jan a chance to reply. She left the house and slammed the front door behind her, almost smashing the glass window at the top of it. Jan glanced over at Jade, who still hadn't shown any reaction to her crazy girlfriend leaving the apartment, but was concentrating on putting a second layer of red varnish on her fingernails. It was clear that she had no interest in speaking to Jan and he didn't know what to say to her anyway.

Of the three girls, she was the least talkative but the most attractive, thought Jan to himself. Jade was tall for a girl and much taller than anyone that Jan had dated in the past. She was a couple of inches bigger than Mariana, which he liked. She had also dabbled with guys in the past, which intrigued him. Her face was stone cold as she stared at her finger nails, showing no emotion or feeling after Roos' rant and exit.

Jan still had to clean the living room and Fleur's room and then he would be done. He knew that there would be nothing to clean in Roos' bedroom or bathroom. He decided to start with Fleur's room next. He was scared of getting in Jade's way while she watched the television in the living room. She might not react as passively as she did towards Roos.

Fleur's room was always a mess. Jan would normally pick up all the clothes and make a pile, and then give the floor a quick vacuum. Fleur didn't really care and she was happy with whatever Jan did. He bent over and started picking up underwear and sexy outfits off the floor and throwing them into her laundry basket. Once he had completed this, he got her duvet off the ground and gave it a shake before laying it back on the bed. As he did this, a vibrator flew out from under the duvet and fell to the ground. Jan picked it up with a smile on his face and placed it under Fleur's pillow. She was definitely a fun-loving girl who was clearly mad about sex. Jan really liked Fleur but for whatever reason he wasn't really attracted to her. He didn't really know why this was the case as she was very pretty and had an amazing figure. He also got on really well with her. Maybe, it was because she wasn't complicated.

Fleur had invited him out with her friends a couple of times in the past to go for drinks. He had always found an excuse not to go. He thought that they would think that he wasn't trendy enough to go clubbing with them. Fleur was bubbly and fun and Jan was bland and stiff after all. What was the point anyway, he was madly in love with Mariana and didn't want to risk her getting annoyed or jealous with him.

Jan put Fleur's study books in a neat pile on her desk and rearranged her dance CDs in an orderly fashion next to the big stereo system. Unlike the rest of the apartment furniture, everything in Fleur's room was expensive. She could afford it, after all. Jan knew that she did some exotic dancing in a strip club but that was as much detail as he had got. He didn't pry as it was none of his business. Also, he was too shy and polite to ask her anything else.

Finishing her room, Jan moved back into the living room to start there. He began by picking up some DVDs off the coffee table when Jade spoke up.

"You can leave this room."

Jan froze and looked up at Jade. She never called him by his first name, unlike Roos and Fleur.

"Are you sure?" he replied with quiet voice. He swallowed with a dry throat and waited for her response, a little scared of her reaction.

"Yep." said Jade.

That was it. She didn't look up or show any change in expression and continued looking at her nails.

Jan didn't want any confrontation with Jade as he always felt awkward around her. He circled the living room in order to avoid any more conversation and headed upstairs to Jade and Roos' bedroom. As was always the case, their bedroom was spotless. He never understood why he bothered going in this room as there was never any cleaning for him to do. The bedsheets were pressed and neatly folded and it was ready to be photographed for a magazine on 'ideal homes'. Even Roos' jewelry was immaculately laid out on top of the dresser in a clear line. She was such a control freak.

It was very easy to see which side of the bed Roos slept in. Apart from it being scarily organized, there were always two or three ironed nurse's outfits hanging on the outside of the wardrobe door. It wasn't that Jade's side of the room was a mess but it just wasn't immaculate. Jade's wardrobe doors, in contrast, were wide open and bulging with lots of very sexy colorful outfits. Jan thought that Roos probably tidied up after Jade, which would certainly annoy her. He shook his head in disbelief still not able to understand why these two girls were living together as, apart from their sexual preferences, they couldn't be more different. He thought about his girlfriend for a moment as their situation was exactly the same. Mariana was also so different compared to him in every way.

Looking around the room for something to clean, Jan noticed a small ball of fluff next to the laundry basket. He flushed it down the toilet and went to pick up the money that was left for him on top of the dresser. There was nothing else for him to do there, so Jan went back downstairs, grabbed his jacket, and headed for the front door. He turned to say goodbye to Jade who was still lounging on the sofa.

"Right, I am off." said Jan.

Jade replied by giving Jan a sad smile as if it was the last time that they would see each other. As he left the apartment he thought to himself that maybe the girls were going to split up. He didn't really care if they weren't together as it was probably for the best. Jan was more concerned of the economic impact it would have on his financial situation. Would they still need him to clean the apartment? The answer was probably yes, as it was Roos' place, and she was the cleaning fanatic who loved Jan. Anyway, maybe it was just another 'lover's tiff' and they would stay together. He got in the baker's van and drove off down the canal at full speed. He was late.

* * *

10:00 p.m.

Mariana paid the taxi driver who had stopped just outside her father's townhouse. The driver was pretty annoyed that he had been called to do such a short fare. Basically, he had taken Mariana from her apartment on the Singel to her father's place on the Keizersgracht. Mariana tipped him two euros but still the total fare was only nine. He got out of the taxi at the same time as Mariana and went around to open the boot. He pulled out two black dustbin bags full of laundry, which he dumped on the path next to the canal street. She would have to take them up the stairs into the house on her own, thought the Turkish man.

As she opened the large front door to the townhouse, she could see her father's head popping out of the entrance to the kitchen, at the other end of the long hallway. He was pleased to see his beautiful daughter home again but also a little surprised as she had been around recently. The visit seemed too close to the last one, not that he was complaining. Dr. Akkermans then noticed the two bin liners that she had dragged in off the front steps and realized that she had a lot of washing to be done, which was clearly the reason for the visit.

"Hi darling!" he shouted down the hallway to his daughter. Then commenting on the bags of laundry he continued, "Your washing machine has broken down again, has it?" His head then disappeared back into the kitchen, but he didn't stop talking, and as usual, he started complaining. "You know, you really need to stop buying these cheap Asian ones and get a good German washing machine!"

"You buy these appliances for me, Papa!" snapped Mariana, realizing that he was about to go into one of his rants. She continued, "And I thought I was saving you money by selecting Korean and Japanese ones."

"Ah, yes. I can see that you are doing me a favor." replied Dr. Akkermans sarcastically. She couldn't see him but knew that he was now distracted, probably sitting at his favorite seat in the kitchen drinking a cup of tea and reading the paper.

Mariana was hot and bothered, and red-faced from carrying the bags full of laundry. She was not used to doing this type of work and detested it. She also wasn't in the mood to deal with her father's lecturing and opinionated views. Looking up at the first flight of stairs, she really didn't want to take the bags up there to the laundry room. She also knew that Rina was out and didn't want to ask her father for help. She would have to get on with it on her own.

Mariana was wearing black legging tights and a long blue t-shirt that covered her behind. She slipped out of a cashmere cardigan in an attempt to cool down. She even took off the white and gold silk scarf that was tied tightly round her neck and placed it on top of the cardigan on a single antique chair that was in the hallway.

Picking up the bags, one in each hand, she dragged them up the stairs to the first floor and into the laundry room. Flicking the light switch on and emptying the contents of the two bin bags on the floor, she realized that she had three wash loads to do. Mariana filled the machine with the first load. Then she closed the door and slumped down onto the floor by the washing machine, knowing that she was going to be there for a while. It would take about two hours to wash all the dirty clothes and she didn't want to leave it. She also didn't want to go downstairs and talk with her father, so she decided that she would stay in the small laundry room itself. As she sat on the floor, she looked at her naked arms and noticed that she had a large red scratch on her left wrist. She didn't know how she got this. Perhaps, it was from the zip of her jeans, which she had taken off earlier and was now in the washing machine. Maybe, the scratch had come from her watch, which she had also taken off before she had come to her father's house. For once, Mariana had no jewelry on at all, which was unusual for her.

She was tired and aching. Maybe she was coming down with something. She caught her reflection in the glass door and, for once, felt ugly. She needed to rest and the best place to do that as well as get pampered was at her father's house. Knowing that Rina would be around first thing in the morning she decided that she would stay the night but finish washing all her laundry first. She wouldn't speak with her pig-headed father. She couldn't handle his self-righteousness now. She would stay slumped here in a heap, alone.

Within twenty minutes, Mariana was fast asleep curled up in a ball on the carpeted floor. The first wash hadn't even finished and she was out for the count.

* * *

11:00 p.m.

Arnaud was sitting at his favorite table in his favorite bar, Café De Twee Zwaantjes. He was also being served by his favorite barmaid, Noor Lumas. She was quite plain looking as she was overweight and wore middle-aged clothes, she wasn't attractive. For a lady in her early thirties, it was surprising that she didn't care about her appearance. She always seemed to have greasy hair and oily skin, and never wore makeup. Arnaud knew that Noor didn't have a boyfriend and put her lack of caring about her appearance down to the fact that she also worked at the local supermarket to earn some extra cash and was also studying for a PhD in Sociology. She clearly didn't have any free time to make herself look attractive, which she could easily do.

This didn't matter to Arnaud as he liked her for lots of other reasons. She was clever, soft spoken, a good listener, and poured a great glass of beer. Arnaud often referred to her as his 'free shrink'. He could go to this little brown café and be left alone to think, and if Noor was working, she would be there for him to answer any questions that he might have. He confided in her, probably more than anyone else.

Noor clearly liked Arnaud more than just a client of the café. She felt sorry for him and always wanted to help him. They were both lonely people and that was their strongest bond. She would always tell him when he was looking tired or stressed and Arnaud would then open up and explain what was bothering him. The problem was normally related to the murder hunt and so Noor was privy to information that even the public didn't know, because Arnaud would often let information slip when he had had a few drinks. He trusted her and needed to share his thoughts and emotions with somebody. The 'Two Swans' was both Arnaud's getaway and hideaway, where he could open his release valve. Coming here, however, wasn't completely free as he had a large bar tab, which he would settle at the end of every month.

Tonight, Arnaud was in a relatively good mood. It was three days before his birthday and work was taking a new turn in the right direction. He felt that they were making some small steps forward with the case. He had told Noor about the website and the interesting information that was unfolding on the blog. New opinions and public views had broadened his horizons and he even explained that he was beginning to think that the Magpie could be a female. Noor knew that he hadn't shared this information with anyone else outside of his tight knit team of detectives and she couldn't help think that Arnaud trusted her more and perhaps, even liked her more than just as a friend. Arnaud asked her for another gin, and as she poured it out into a small glass, she thought to herself that Arnaud was more upbeat and confident about the case, and maybe a little drunk.

Having given the glass of gin to Arnaud, who starting sipping it immediately, she checked out his tab for the night: seven beers and four gins. This was quite a lot but not excessive for Arnaud and certainly not an unusual quantity that would make him act or speak irrationally. Noor knew that the alcohol helped him relax and sleep so she never commented on his drinking habits. She was also too shy to ask Arnaud direct questions as she had feelings for him. She just believed that the more he opened up, the more he must trust her.

It was now 11:50 p.m. and the bar was almost empty apart from Arnaud and two old guys who were sitting in a corner of the café. Arnaud was looking tired and she wanted to get home soon as well. She was thinking of asking for last orders from the three men. As Noor went over to speak with the two pensioners, she heard Arnaud's phone vibrate on the wooden bar. Whilst speaking with the old men, she saw Arnaud heading for the exit in a mad rush. With his keys and phone in one hand and his coat in the other, he almost fell over as he scrambled for the café entrance.

Noor quickly made her way over to Arnaud who was now opening the door to leave. He appeared to be staggering and out of breath, which was worrying as she really didn't think he was that drunk. As he left, she could see from his face that something was wrong and the fact that he would go without saying goodbye, was also disturbing and out of character. Following him out of the bar, Noor watched him clamber on top of his moped and fumble around trying to put the keys in the ignition. Surely, he wasn't going to drive in this state, she thought to herself. But clearly something was up.

"Arnaud!" she shouted, trying to get his attention. He still hadn't managed to start his moped.

"Arnaud, are you okay?" He didn't respond. Noor attempted to jog over to him losing her breath almost immediately.

"Arnaud!" she had made it over to him and placed her hand on his forearm.

He looked up at her, startled and almost in tears.

"It's happened again." he said with a trembling and slightly slurred voice. He continued, "The Magpie. It's happened again. He has struck."

The message was very clear and Arnaud looked terrified. She had never seen him so vulnerable and weak. But Noor knew what this meant. She knew what Arnaud was talking about. She was, however, more concerned about the state that Arnaud was in, than another murder.

"Arnaud, you can't get on your moped now." She was almost ordering him. He managed to start it up and he revved the throttle and the moped jumped forward a couple of feet. Noor gripped tighter on the arm of his jacket. She began shouting at him out of desperation.

"Arnaud, you have had too much to drink. You can't take the moped now. Please get off!" She realized that her pleas were falling on deaf ears. He looked over at her once more. His face was wrinkled and distraught.

"It's him. He has struck again. I have to go."

Those were his last words to her. With that he revved the throttle again and sped off. Noor couldn't keep her grip on Arnaud's jacket and she spun round with the momentum of the moped bolting forward at full speed. As she watched him disappear in the distance, she became very worried about Arnaud crashing into a car or falling off the moped and into the canals. It was night time and nobody would find him if that happened. She then stopped to think for a second and it dawned on her what Arnaud had been speaking about. She froze and a chill ran up her spine. The October murder had happened. Someone must have gone missing or a body had been found. It was clear that it was serious as Arnaud looked shocked and had been summoned to go somewhere immediately.

Noor ran back into the bar in a panic. She needed to serve a last drink to the two old gentlemen and close the café as soon as possible. She wanted to race home and search the television channels for news. She would also scan the internet for any stories. Most important of all for Noor was to get on the 'Amsterdam Living' website and read the blog that she spent so much time looking at. Little did Arnaud know, Noor's username was 'Happy Single'.

Noor was the one who defended him and praised him on the site. She was also the one who gave her views and opinions on the killer's profile. In doing this, she had put the idea into Arnaud's and his team's heads that the Magpie was a female. She was surprised that it hadn't crossed Arnaud's mind, that Noor was his secret admirer. She used all the information that he shared with her in the café, took time to think it through, and then posted her ideas on the website. In a way, she felt that she was really helping him through the blog. But now she needed to get home to see whether the news of a killing or a missing person had been leaked to the press. If it had, then the daggers would be back out for Arnaud and she would need to protect him once again.

Noor also wanted to be alone so that she could analyze the news and see if she could work out any new clues. She knew that they were reading the blog constantly now. She wished that she could tell Arnaud that she was Happy Single, then they could have open conversations about the case and what she thought about the Magpie, but she couldn't. If he knew that she was the blogger, he would also know that she was madly in love with him. She couldn't face this as she wouldn't be able to handle the possibility of rejection, if he didn't like her. At least for now, Happy Single would have to remain anonymous and she would just have to be a shoulder to cry on and a friend that served drinks to Arnaud at the café.

Noor had tears in her eyes as she continued to worry about Arnaud. She hoped that he was okay and had made it to wherever he had been summoned. She decided to send him a text, hoping he would let her know that he was fine. 'I hope you got there safely, wherever that is. Take care, Noor.' She was pleased that she had sent it. Now, she turned back to the men in the café who had finished their last drink. She started turning off lights in the bar to speed them up and to get them to leave. They got the message pretty quickly, stood up from their table, and put on their coats. Noor walked over to the front door of the café, ushered the men out and bid them good night. Shutting and locking the door behind them, she went back behind the bar to cash out the till and put the night's takings into the safe. When she was done, she grabbed her coat from a hook on the wall and left.

Outside De Twee Zwaantjes, Noor walked to her bike and unlocked it. She cycled the short ride home to her rental flat on the Marnixstraat. Walking up the two flights of stairs to her second floor apartment, she realized that she was very tired. She got into the studio flat and rested her coat on the small sofa. She then headed over to the tiny desk to work on her computer. Holding onto the mouse, she noticed that her chubby hand was trembling. This was a combination of fear and exhaustion. She was also perspiring from the short but speedy cycle ride home. Brushing some long black strands of thick hair off her face, she focused in on the screen and flicked through the tabs of favorite pages and sites that she always looked at. These consisted of newspaper sites, the 'Amsterdam Living' page, a couple of other blogs, and a dating website, which she didn't really use or have any success with.

There was nothing. No new missing person report or murder was announced. Either it was too soon or maybe it just hadn't happened yet. The second option was not viable to Noor, as she bit her nails and thought through things. The way Arnaud had reacted to his text messages and phone call, and the way he had sped off could only mean one thing.

She would just have to wait and see. She knew that she wouldn't be able to sleep for a while as she was too worked up about what had potentially happened. She needed to know. There was no way she could sleep now. She was also worried about this man that she cared for.

She leant back on the chair by the desk and switched on the lamp next to her computer, as the only light was coming from the terminal screen. The new light shone across the walls of the tiny living room, and Noor moved her head from side to side, studying things on the walls. She had created her own murder hunt in the small apartment. The walls were covered in cuttings from newspapers of the murdered victims, pictures of Arnaud and Friso, and her own notes scribbled down on little pieces of paper. She even had a map of Amsterdam and Amstelveen on the wall above her sofa with comments written all over it.

The layout of all the documentation was not quite as professional as Arnaud's team had created in the police station but it was detailed and to the point. She knew what she was doing and had different ideas from Arnaud. Some ideas were more correct than the detectives' presumptions. The police had come to realize that. She had created her own think tank and the blog was her communication channel. Her plan had worked. All she needed to do now was continue feeding her ideas to the detectives so that they could eventually catch the killer.

As she looked at the map, she wondered to herself where the next murder would take place and where she would need to mark another cross on the paper. Noor was very upset, not only because the Magpie had struck again but also because Arnaud was struggling. She had not seen him look like that before - old, vulnerable, and helpless. She needed to think and work out how best to support him. Were there going to be any new clues for her to pick up? If so, how would she communicate these through the blog to Arnaud and his team? The less she did, the more she felt that she was failing Arnaud and letting him down.

She also needed to convince Arnaud that he should be looking for a female. Arnaud continued to refer to the killer as a man and Noor was convinced that this was the work of a girl. The murderer was extremely calculative and probably strong but the way she cleaned the bodies, cut their nails and hair made Noor strongly believe firmly that the Magpie was a girl. And if she was right, this female killer needed to have an accomplice. It was the only way that the Magpie could move the body around unnoticed.

She pulled herself together and got up to take a shower. This would help her stay awake. She was also hot and sweaty and if she was going to spend a long night in front of the computer, she wanted to feel comfortable. She paused to take one last glance at a newspaper cutout of Arnaud on the wall above her desk. He was looking stern and powerful, gritting his teeth and frowning, as always. He was standing in the rain wearing his usual long jacket and his thick black curly hair was a mess. This gave her motivation. She headed into her small bathroom and turned on the shower. It was going to be a long night for Happy Single.

CHAPTER 11

October 9

12:25 a.m.

Arnaud arrived at the front entrance of the police station. He stepped off his moped, wobbled slightly before getting his balance back and then raced to the front door, which was locked. Pressing the bell, he was met within a minute by Friso, staring through the glass at him. He had been expecting him and opened the door for his boss. As they headed up the stairs to the first floor, Friso began speaking softly in Arnaud's ear with a calm voice. Arnaud wasn't in the mood for calm however.

"Speak up Friso, damn it!" said Arnaud, attentive and aggravated. "I can't hear a word you are saying!"

Friso had fully expected this type of concerned and irritated reaction from Arnaud and didn't react to it. When they arrived at the double doors to their office, he stopped and pointed inside to a small group of people who were sitting around the desks of the two younger policemen, Robin and Jim. It looked like Robin was asking the questions, while Jim was listening and making notes. A small red light glowed from the tape recorder indicating that it was recording, as the four of them talked back and forth in the open office.

As Arnaud and Friso entered the room, drawing closer to the group, they could see that the two men sitting across from Robin and Jim were distraught. They were both in their mid-twenties, spoke articulately, and sounded university educated. Their voices were trembling and just in their facial expressions one could sense that they were very scared. Wearing chinos and faded polo shirts with the collars up and stained blazers sitting on the backs of their chairs, it was easy to come to the conclusion that they were final year students.

Standing at the back of the room in order not to disturb the interview process that was clearly going on, Arnaud turned to Friso and raised his eyebrows expecting to be filled in as to what had happened.

"So, the young guy on the left over there, with the short blond hair, is Thomas Van Poel. He was at the Spa Suiver today in the Amstel Park." began Friso.

"I thought that was a tennis center?" replied Arnaud quietly, so as to not disturb the interviewing that was going on across the other side of the room.

"It is but they opened a very modern and large spa there as well earlier this year. He had gone there with his best friend, Floris Heidstra, around two in the afternoon today. They spent some time moving between the various jacuzzis, steam rooms, and saunas in the complex."

"Is the other chap being interviewed the 'best friend'?" asked Arnaud, trying to paint a storyline in his head and picture of the day's events.

"No." replied Friso sternly. He swallowed deeply and whispered back at Arnaud. "That is Floris Heidstra's brother. Floris has gone missing!"

The two of them stopped and looked at each other as Arnaud digested what Friso had just told him.

Arnaud wanted to be clear on his facts and spoke up to confirm things with Friso. "So, the young guy over there with the blond hair was at the spa today with his best mate who is now missing." Friso nodded in agreement. Arnaud continued, "And the other lad over there is the brother of the missing chap?" Friso nodded again.

Friso composed himself and then continued speaking, "After approximately one hour, they decided to go to the outside part of the spa that had a heated swimming pool, a lounging area, and a very large mixed sauna."

Friso looked up at Arnaud who was listening to every word that he was saying and flicking his eyes across at the interviewees constantly. He could see that he was getting Arnaud's full attention and continued speaking.

"He then left his friend, Floris, for a couple of minutes to go outside the sauna to take a cold shower. When he went back inside, Floris was talking with a girl who was sitting opposite them at the back of the sauna."

Arnaud butted in, "Any more information on the girl?"

"Not really. She was sitting high up in the corner of the sauna away from them so it was very dark and she was well hidden."

"Damn." said Arnaud quietly.

"But…" replied Friso, wanting to continue.

Arnaud looked into his colleague's eyes in anticipation to what Friso was about to say. "Go on…"

"Well, he couldn't see what she looked like but did note that she came across well-educated and of Dutch ethnic background. She also sounded quite young and had nice legs." Friso stopped speaking and waited for Arnaud to respond.

Arnaud paused in thought for a second and then spoke up. He couldn't stop thinking about what the blogger had been saying regarding the killer being a female. It was eating away at him.

"Nice legs! Is that it? God damn it!" He looked down and scratched the top of his head and then stared up at Friso again. "How young?"

Friso was used to Arnaud's temper but could see that in this instance he was more frustrated than annoyed. He answered in his usual calm voice and manner.

"He thinks between twenty and thirty-five." Realizing that this was quite a large age spread and would aggravate Arnaud even more, Friso continued speaking, wanting to give Arnaud as much information as he had collected.

"Apparently, her legs were very long and toned and her toe-nails were painted."

Arnaud fired another question back at his trusty colleague. "Hair color?"

"He couldn't see, Arnaud. We have already been over to the spa and looked around. Even though its night time now we put lamps outside the sauna to imitate the day-light and it's very difficult to see inside, especially in the far corners. It's a very large mixed sauna and this is quite deliberate. The darkness of the room provides a level of concealment for the guests, which makes it quite private and more relaxing for them."

Arnaud was in deep thought and his mind was working overtime. He was thinking to himself that it was indeed very deliberate. He was also beginning to contemplate the possibility that the person they were looking for was actually in fact a female. Maybe the blogger had been right all along with her assumptions. Maybe the Magpie was a girl. It didn't make sense that a beautiful young girl could take these men down but all the new evidence was pointing towards the Magpie being a female. If this was the case, they had wasted a lot of time searching through previous evidence and CCTV footage for a man. They would all have to be reviewed, thought Arnaud.

The female, if she was in fact the killer, had selected the sauna very carefully as she could operate inside and pick up a potential victim, without being seen.

Arnaud looked straight back at Friso and continued with his questioning.

"What was her figure like? How tall was she?"

Friso responded again, shaking his head slightly. "Like I said before, she was sitting on the top shelf in the far corner of the sauna and the witness couldn't really see her. He could only make out the bottom half of her legs as they draped down over the lower benches in the sauna that had some light."

The two detectives stood there, while Arnaud collected his thoughts.

"Okay. What else?" He asked; keen to hear if Friso was holding back some good information or clues.

"They were busy chatting between themselves."

"Who was speaking?" asked Arnaud with an impatient tone in his voice.

"The guy who is missing, Floris Heidstra. He was in the sauna with his friend, Thomas Van Poel, who is the young man sitting over there with the blonde hair."

Arnaud glanced across again at the two men being interviewed. Friso carried on speaking, anticipating what Arnaud's next question was going to be. "Floris Heidstra is a twenty-five year old graduate student from Delft, now living in Amsterdam with his brother. The brother is sitting in our office right now, next to Thomas Van Poel."

Friso pointed at the other interviewee who had unwashed, short thick brown hair. Arnaud stared at him and checked out his appearance. He was clean-shaven and quite stocky, probably about five foot nine inches tall.

"The brother, Jeroen Heidstra, is the missing person's twin."

Arnaud squinted his eyes and checked out the brother more closely.

"His identical twin." concluded Friso. Arnaud looked back at his colleague, thinking for the first time that they had some interesting information.

"So we know what the missing person looks like." asked Arnaud, although he was saying this as more of a statement rather than asking a question.

Friso realized this but answered him anyway. "Correct. They are spitting images of each other in every way: facial features, physique, and even the way they dress."

Arnaud looked back at Friso and spoke again. "So, where was the brother, Jeroen, when Floris was at the spa with his best friend?" This really was a question for Friso and he had the answer ready, as he had done the necessary homework.

"At home, studying for his Masters in Philosophy. His twin had graduated the previous summer with a degree in law, and their friend,

Thomas, had also been at the University of Amsterdam. Both were now interviewing with Dutch law firms for graduate positions."

"Okay....." replied Arnaud, waiting for Friso to continue. He was pleased to see that Friso had done a lot of the background work already.

Friso carried on speaking. "So, the friend, Thomas, realizing that Floris had sparked up a chatty conversation with the girl who was sitting in the shadows, decided to leave them alone and go back to the inside section of the spa to the swimming pool. Before leaving the twin with the girl, Thomas told him that he planned to head out of the complex in twenty minutes and cycle back into the center of town."

Friso could see from Arnaud's expression that he was listening to his every word.

"Was there anyone else in the sauna? Any other witnesses?"

"Not so far. Thomas said that it was virtually empty, as you would expect during the afternoon on a week day."

Arnaud was beginning to think that this could be the Magpie that they were dealing with here, as it seemed to be well planned. She had found a quiet spot to pounce, away from lots of potential witnesses. If they were indeed facing the serial killer then she was right on point again, calculating her every move. It was becoming increasingly clear that they were looking for a female.

Friso continued, "Then, as Thomas was getting showered and dressed in the changing room, Floris walked in with a big smile. He was extremely excited, as the girl had suggested that they go for a drink together. She was keen to meet up that night which made Floris think that she really liked him. Anyway, he had given her his number and she had promised to call him later that day."

"How did she take his number down in a naked sauna?" asked Arnaud.

"Good question, I had asked the same thing. Don't know, is the answer."

He continued with his story. "Thomas had joked with his friend about how he was going on a date with someone that he hadn't even seen. Floris had laughed and responded that he was waiting for her to get up and leave the sauna so that he could check her out but he was so hot and sweaty that he needed to leave before her. Anyway, he commented that she must have been pretty with such nice legs and he liked the excitement of a blind date. He had also found the forwardness of the girl appealing."

"I guess that was pretty forward." Arnaud chimed in. "What happened next?"

"Well, the two guys left the spa and cycled into town together and that was the last time Thomas saw Floris."

"So, we don't know if the missing twin actually met the girl or not?"

Friso nodded his head to confirm that they indeed did know that the twin had met up with the girl.

Seeing his colleague's response, Arnaud continued. "So, actually, it is probably a little too early to assume that this Floris is indeed a missing person and a potential victim?"

"Agreed." replied Friso with another faint nod.

Arnaud felt slightly relieved and thought that even though it looked like this had been the selection process for a Magpie victim, they were 'jumping the gun' and maybe they were just dealing with a twenty-first century girl meets boy dating scenario.

Friso needed to complete his summary of the events and began talking again.

"The missing person lives with his twin brother and always calls or texts him if he is going to be home late. They are extremely close. In fact, the brother told us that they text each other at least ten times a day."

These comments deflated Arnaud's optimism somewhat so he interrupted Friso by speaking up.

"Maybe he lost his phone or left it at home!"

He didn't want to believe the possibility of it being the Magpie anymore and thought Friso was making too many assumptions.

"Floris had called Thomas from his mobile when he was waiting for the girl to show up. He was sitting in the café called The Gruter on the Prinsengracht, where the mystery girl had arranged to meet him at 8:30 p.m. The Gruter is a student bar."

Friso's detail and information gathering was impressive as always, thought Arnaud. Friso paused to look down at his note pad and then continued speaking again.

"On the call, Floris joked that the girl had called him and requested him to reach The Gruter a little early in order to find a table for them by the window near the exit door. They laughed a little about her strange request but didn't think anymore of it."

"That's strange." interrupted Arnaud. "Why?"

"It gets stranger." responded Friso, as his hand holding the notepad started to shake a bit.

"Floris was chatting with his best friend on the phone when he suddenly stopped speaking as the girl had arrived."

Arnaud started firing questions again, cutting off Friso.

"Did we get a description of the girl? What did she look like? Did the friend hear her talking with Floris?"

"The whole thing becomes more suspicious, Arnaud. The girl was standing outside the bar and got Floris' attention by knocking on the café window. Floris had told his friend over the phone that he needed to go as she had arrived and was beckoning him to come outside."

A shiver went down Arnaud's spine as his view had changed again on what had taken place. This was all too calculated. She had selected her victim in the day without being noticed and then plucked him from a busy student bar at night without being seen. Arnaud thought that this had been a clever move as she had not gone into the café and so wouldn't have been caught on the cameras. He was beginning to think again that it could have only been the Magpie.

"Mmmm," replied Arnaud, "She clearly didn't want to be seen, which means no witnesses. Very clever."

Arnaud thought that there was a strong chance that it was indeed the work of the serial killer. He didn't want to get too worked up as they needed to wait until tomorrow lunchtime to see if the missing twin would return home. He could, after all, have stayed the night with this girl at her house and they would have nothing to worry about. In his gut, however, this scenario was not what Arnaud thought had happened.

"Anyway," continued Friso, breaking Arnaud's deep thoughts with an excited tone. "The last thing that he said to his best friend on the phone was that he would text him and his twin to say how the night was progressing. He had promised to give them an update by eleven to let them know if he would stay at the girl's house or if he was going to bring her back home."

Arnaud looked at his watch and replied, "Yes, but that's still only an hour and a half ago since he should have contacted them. Maybe he was busy and got lucky with the girl and is just late in texting his brother and the friend."

Arnaud didn't actually believe that the brother was okay but wanted to play devil's advocate. Friso shook his head and replied.

"The twin and Thomas both said that he is a fanatical texter and it was very out-of-sorts for him not to have contacted them, even if it was only ninety minutes over the agreed time. Also, they tried to call him and his phone was turned off."

"So…" interrupted Arnaud. "He might actually be busy!"

"No, Arnaud. Apparently, he never turns his phone off even during the night as he is always messaging friends and tweeting. The friend and his twin are worried as this is completely out of character for Floris. That's why they contacted us. They are convinced that something bad has happened. They are sure that Floris is in danger."

Arnaud stood silent for a few minutes, composing his thoughts. He agreed with the conclusions that the two guys were coming to with regards to Floris being in grave danger. This didn't add up and it certainly looked like it was the work of the serial killer. Having said all of this, they still needed to wait and try not to panic.

Arnaud spoke up. "Well, we can't do too much right now Friso. It's too early, although I do think there is good cause to be concerned. Let's give it another twelve hours and then react. In the meantime, do we have any other information that would be useful for filling out the missing person's report?"

Friso spoke up again, just remembering one final piece of information.

"One other thing, Arnaud, apart from having a good description of what he was wearing during the day and also in the evening, his twin brother told us that they both wore exactly the same watches. They never took them off. They were a present from their parents for their twenty-first birthdays. We have taken a polaroid picture of the twin brother's one as a reference. Jeroen said that he was sure that his twin brother would have kept the watch on in the sauna as well."

Arnaud had goose bumps on his arms and a chill ran down his spine. This was the second piece of information that made him think of the Magpie. Of course, it was no hard evidence but still he associated expensive and shiny things with her. He was certain now that the killer was a female. Again, there was silence and Friso could see that Arnaud was turning over all the information in his head. He had kept the best information for the end and spoke up in a proud voice.

"One final thing, Arnaud. The last thing that the missing twin said to Thomas, on the phone when the girl arrived was that she was pretty. Very pretty."

"Well that is subjective. That is a matter of taste."

"Agreed." responded Friso. "But we know she is not ugly."

"True. I don't suppose he mentioned anything else about her age?"

'No."

"Okay, good job Friso."

Arnaud was very pleased with the information that his trusty colleague had collected. His mind was working overtime, and Arnaud was genuinely worried, but he knew that he couldn't draw conclusions or panic too soon. There was another moment of stillness as Arnaud thought to himself and Friso waited to hear what his boss was going to say next.

"Okay." said Arnaud. "We are not going to take any sudden actions on the back of what has happened so far. Let's wait until lunch time, later today, to move. We know that this girl is approximately between twenty-five and thirty-five, potentially good-looking, and has nice legs. We can assume that she probably has a nice figure as well. She is also probably a white Dutch female, as she spoke with no accent."

"What we can do now is go back to the spa and get the CCTV tapes for the entrance and exit. We can see all the girls who went into the spa yesterday and then focus on the ones that left after the missing twin and his friend. We need close-up pictures of all the girls and not just the pretty ones. I would also interview everyone that was working at the spa yesterday."

This was why Friso worked with Arnaud. He was happy to put up with his short temper and old-fashioned ways, as he learnt so much from his detective work and quick thinking under pressure.

Arnaud continued, "Try to find out who came in around the time that the guys arrived and see if they were members. The management of the spa will cooperate with us and let you see the age and addresses of any members that fit the description of the girl. Also, see which females signed into the spa and were not members. We can check out all the names, although, I would expect that if it actually is the Magpie that we are looking for, then she would have signed in under a false ID."

Arnaud thought for a second and then carried on. "Also, ask the staff that was working during the day if they noticed anything unusual. Not just the reception personnel but also those who were cleaning the saunas and steam rooms during the day."

"Yes, understood. I know that the spa is not just for members only. In fact, less than fifteen percent of the people that use the spa are members." Friso knew that this would disappoint his boss.

"Mmm, that's a shame. We could have been really close to catching her. But, that would have been too easy and too careless of the Magpie."

Arnaud was done for now. He didn't want to stay in the office any longer. He turned and began walking towards the stairs.

As Arnaud reached the first stairs, he turned back to Friso. "Focus on the CCTV tapes and let's try not to give anything out to the press yet. We don't want to scare anyone. It's too early and we just don't know enough yet."

Arnaud walked down the stairs slowly and Friso turned to head back to his other colleagues and the two young chaps being interviewed. He stopped as he heard Arnaud shout up the stairs.

"And Friso." There was a pause. Friso didn't need to respond, as Arnaud would know that he would be listening.

Arnaud continued, "We also don't want the brother and his friend panicking. Please stay with them at all times as we don't want them going home or speaking to the press, etc."

"Understood."

Arnaud was gone. Friso could hear him start his moped and speed off down the street.

Arnaud shut the door of his house behind him and headed straight for his bedroom. It was two in the morning and he was exhausted. The booze from the night before was wearing off and Arnaud was feeling dehydrated and a little hungover. He took two aspirins and washed them down with a swig of water from the bedroom sink. Arnaud needed to try and get some sleep as tomorrow was going to be an eventful day.

Was this most recent missing person incident going to be 'a storm in a tea cup' or the real thing? He could not stop asking himself this question.

As Arnaud got undressed and slumped into bed, pulling the covers up to his chin, he pondered over the facts that he had collected this evening. He believed that they were, in fact, dealing with the actions of the Magpie once more. They would know in the next two days if this really was the work of the serial killer. He knew that if Floris had left the bar to meet the Magpie then Arnaud and his team were already too late to save him. He was probably dead already. They would find out soon enough.

Of course, Arnaud didn't want this young innocent student to have been lured into the waiting hands of this seductive beast, as his destiny would have already been decided. However, Arnaud was excited as he knew that if a corpse was dumped in the next forty-eight hours, then they would be making progress in the hunt for the Magpie. Hopefully, with the CCTV footage tomorrow, they would even be able to get a full facial shot of the killer. A shiver went down Arnaud's spine again as he lay curled up in his bed in a white vest and baggy Y fronts.

Arnaud lay there still, in deep thought, realizing that it was morally wrong of him to wish that the young man had been killed, just so that it would help his murder hunting progress. He shook his head trying to get this sick thought out of his mind. What was he thinking? What had all this come to? Arnaud continued to think and reason with himself. He was now sure that he was chasing a female killer.

Arnaud was asleep.

CHAPTER 12

October 9

6:00 a.m.

Arnaud opened his eyes earlier than usual, apprehensive but surprisingly wide awake and without a hangover. He felt nervous and couldn't sleep anymore. Looking at his old wristwatch, he was stunned to see that it was only six in the morning. It was possible that the watch had stopped, which sometimes happened if he forgot to wind it up. He normally didn't wake up so early, however, he had never lived through a year like this before. It had been a period of constant stress. Arnaud would also know very soon, if the tenth murder of the year had taken place in Amsterdam.

Arnaud thought to himself that he was going to call Friso even if it was really too early. He was sure that he would be up-to-date with any current news as Jim and Robin would have stayed with the two young witnesses in the office all night. If it transpired that Friso was still asleep, well, Arnaud didn't feel too bad waking him up. He needed to know if there had been any developments during the night. Whilst the spa wouldn't have opened yet, he could certainly encourage the younger detectives to head down there shortly to collect the video footage.

He reached across for his jacket that lay next to him on the bed and delved inside to a small pocket where his mobile phone sat. The red battery sign was flashing in the top right hand corner of the screen indicating that he had very little power left on the phone. He had forgotten to turn it off last night. Hopefully, he had enough battery left to call Friso.

Focusing back in on the blurred screen of his mobile phone, Arnaud noticed that there was also a flashing envelope in the left-hand corner. He had a text message. Arnaud was getting worked up already as he reached back into his jacket pocket to retrieve his glasses. Having put them on, he opened the message. It was from Noor. 'Hi Arnaud. It's me. I hope you are okay. Have been worried about you. Please let me know if I can help with anything or if you need to talk. Noor x.'

While Arnaud thought of Noor as a friend, a good person to talk to and a 'relief valve' for him, he found the text annoying. Arnaud used Noor as a sounding board to bounce ideas off of regarding the hunt and he trusted her but he didn't need her probing right now. Arnaud sat up on the side of his bed and stretched in an attempt to wake himself up. He didn't have time to think about this. He scrolled through his phone's address book and pressed on Friso's number. After about four rings, Friso answered the phone with a muffled croaking voice, signifying that he had indeed just been woken up.

"Hi Friso. It's me. Is there any news?"

"Nothing as yet."

Arnaud thought for a few moments and then spoke again. "Mmmm, okay. Well, I think I will head over to the office then."

"It's too early, Arnaud." said Friso.

"I know but we have a lot to do," replied Arnaud, anxiously.

There was silence again and Arnaud could make out the annoyed whispering of Viola's voice in the background. Viola, liked Arnaud, but got fed up with the number of hours her husband was away from home, working on this dreadful case.

"It's really early. God damn it, Friso." She whispered angrily. "Let him do some work on his own for once."

"Sshh." came the muffled response from Friso.

Arnaud didn't really care what Viola had to say. It wasn't his fault that there was this vicious murderer on the rampage in Amsterdam. But she was right. He did need Friso to help him with the data crunching and 'leg work'. Friso was great at collating information from witnesses and filtering out the important facts from the ones that were irrelevant. Arnaud didn't have the time or energy to do this and relied heavily on Friso for the role.

Again, Arnaud didn't know what to say. "Well, I guess I will see you later." came his response.

"Yes, Jim and Robin stayed in the office all night with the witnesses and have been writing up the statements as well as making a list of all the people that need to be interviewed from the spa. One of them will be heading over there in an hour to collect the tapes. They were going to call me if there was any news but so far I have heard nothing."

"Okay, Friso. Why don't you have a lie in and I will see you later."

He realized Friso was on top of things and started to feel a little guilty about waking him up. He also knew that today was going to be a big day for him, but for now, there was very little Friso could do until they got the tapes and had all the spa employees into the station for questioning.

Friso felt that this reaction was very unlike Arnaud. Maybe his boss was tired. Maybe he was unhappy with him. The thought of Arnaud being disappointed in him really worried Friso, as he worked hard to gain his respect. Maybe he had just heard Viola in the background of the phone call complaining and felt guilty. This was probably unlikely. Whatever the reason, Arnaud had clicked out of the call and was gone.

Now, Friso was nervous. He was annoyed and turned to his wife who was lying next to him.

"Why did you have to say that Vi?!" Friso sat up in the simple light pine double bed, shaking his head. You know Arnaud is under a lot of pressure!"

"Well so are you!" snapped his wife back at him. "And you also have a young family that has barely seen you this year!" Viola was also angry, and this was the time to let Friso know it.

"And I haven't seen much of you either!" she continued.

Friso stood up from the bed, naked, and headed to the bathroom. He was normally a sweet husband and extremely calm but right now he did not have the patience to deal with his wife's rant. If Arnaud was going to the office right now, then so was he. Friso didn't want to miss out on any new developments with the case and needed to be there as Arnaud's right-hand man.

He couldn't be bothered to take a shower this morning as he wanted to get out of their apartment as quickly as possible. He dressed back into the clothes he wore yesterday. They lay in a neat pile on the bathroom floor. Fully dressed, Friso lowered his head into the sink and splashed some cold water over his face to wake himself up. He cleaned his teeth as he stared into the bathroom mirror. Unshaven and looking tired, he thought that if they did manage to catch this Magpie then it would all be worthwhile. It would be good for his career, for his family, and for his and Arnaud's morale.

Friso headed back into the bedroom and leant over his wife to give her a kiss goodbye. He could never stay annoyed for long. She looked at him and then turned the other way making it clear how she felt right now. Her head sunk into the pillow and she pulled the duvet over her whole body. She was upset and a kiss was not going to solve anything. Friso didn't want to go through the reasons why he was working so hard again. He didn't have time. He sighed and crept out, exiting quietly through the apartment door, making sure that he didn't wake up his children.

Arnaud arrived at the office at 6:50 a.m. The two young detectives were still busy behind their desks surrounded by papers detailing the witness statements and empty coffee cups. The caffeine overdose had kept them awake.

Robin and Jim looked up, "Morning, Arnaud." They said in unison.

"Hi guys." replied Arnaud impressed with their work ethic. Arnaud scanned the room as he walked up to them. He could see that the missing twin's brother and friend were asleep on the floor in one corner of the office, using their jumpers as pillows and their coats as covers. He spotted their mobile phones lying next to them on the ground. Both were turned on, as the screens were lit up.

"So, any news?" continued Arnaud, expecting a 'no'.

Surprisingly, he noticed that both the young detectives were smiling and were excited. Arnaud walked towards them to see what they had up on their computer screens. He was desperate to know what the two men had found and why they were looking so proud of themselves. This didn't happen often.

"Well, no news yet from the missing twin," said Jim.

"That's not good." replied Arnaud beginning to fear the worst even though it was still early in the morning. It was feasible that Floris could still be with this girl on the date.

Robin began to speak, "We got hold of the spa manager late last night and he came with us to the spa security room. He gave us the CCTV tapes. We have spent the last three hours going through them, checking everyone by the entry and exit turnstiles."

Both of the young detectives looked over their shoulders at Arnaud to see his reaction. He was staring at their computer screens with wide open eyes and a small smile on his face. He clearly was very keen to see what the footage might reveal and was pleased with their proactive work.

"Why didn't you tell Friso that you had managed to get the tapes?" asked Arnaud, knowing that his second in command was not going to be happy that they hadn't checked in with him.

"We thought that we should let him get some rest and we would do some early filtering of the footage." replied Jim, realizing that they had probably made a mistake, even though they had acted with the best intentions.

Arnaud agreed with them and he didn't discuss it any more. He wanted to hear what else they had to say and if they had found anything interesting. That was far more important right now.

"Are they the only cameras by the turnstiles?" asked Arnaud, looking back down at the computer screens. The footage was coming from a camera that must have been positioned next to the entrance to the spa.

"Fortunately, yes." replied Jim. "However, we can be sure that anyone who went in and out of the spa yesterday will be on these tapes as these turnstiles by the reception are the only way to enter or exit the building."

Both detectives stared at Arnaud to see his reaction and what he had to say next.

"Ok fine. Good. Carry on."

Robin spoke up, "So we asked the twin's friend, who was with him at the spa, what time they left. He said about forty minutes after Floris had come back to the changing rooms, after leaving the girl in the sauna. So, we started watching the footage closely from sixty minutes before the guys left the spa, just be sure. We've studied it from that point until it closed yesterday. Therefore, we have definitely captured the time period in which the girl must have left."

"Ok, that makes sense." said Arnaud. "Go on."

Jim was pointing at the far left of the three computer screens that were positioned across their desks. He tapped away at his keyboard, and on this screen was a black and white picture of the two young guys exiting the spa through the turnstiles. Arnaud squinted to focus in on the detail of the picture and was pleased to see that even he could clearly see Floris and Thomas. Arnaud was tensing up with excitement. If this was the work of the Magpie then they must surely have a very clear shot of her on the tape as well.

Robin began speaking as all three of them continued staring at the monitors.

"There were twenty-six females in total that left the spa one hour before the two guys left and till the end of the evening when the spa closed."

Much to Arnaud's pleasure, Robin clicked on his keyboard again and twenty-six small freeze frame shots came up on the middle screen of all the females who left during that time frame. The two young detectives looked back at Arnaud, who was raising his eyebrows and moved closer to the screen in order to focus in on some of the small images. Noticing this, Robin tapped away on his keyboard and nine of the pictures suddenly disappeared. Seventeen photos were left on the screen, which Robin then enlarged as much as possible. Arnaud looked at the young detective for an explanation of what he was doing.

"We narrowed the search by eliminating all the women who looked like they were over forty years of age and clearly couldn't be the girl that we are looking for. This was easy to do with some of them as we checked which ones were members and then got access to their birth dates. For those who are not members, which were the vast majority of the ladies, we simply enlarged the shot of their faces and it was easy to see who was older. For any that were borderline, we kept them in."

Robin looked back at Arnaud once again to get his reaction. Arnaud remained focused on the middle screen.

Jim started to speak next, "Of the seventeen females, we decided to exclude the four that were of ethnic descent and the five that were substantially overweight. Simply looking at the camera footage, you can make out the Turkish and Moroccan females as well as those that were too big to fit the description of the one that we are looking for."

Robin held the mouse in his right hand and clicked on it. A further nine pictures disappeared from the computer screen, leaving only eight pictures, which were then enlarged to fit the PC monitor.

"Okay, said Arnaud in approval. He was getting excited realizing that they were homing in on what was quite possibly a picture of the Magpie.

Jim continued, "So of the eight that were left, four are members and we have their details from the spa. I will bring them in for interviews."

"Good." replied Arnaud.

"And of the remaining four, two left the spa around eight p.m., which was long after the time when the guys had exited and too close to the time when the female was supposed to meet with Floris at the bar. It is just not physically possible that it could be either of them. Therefore, we eliminated both of these girls from the investigation."

"Find out who they are and interview them anyway." said Arnaud.

The two younger detectives nodded. Jim looked at Robin, who then pressed a button on his keyboard to eliminate a further two pictures, leaving six black and white shots on the screen. He then enlarged these and pressed down on the return key. A printing sign came up on the screen and noise started up from the office printer that was positioned in the corner of the room. Jim walked over to the printer and retrieved the pictures out of the tray.

As he walked back to his desk, where Robin and Arnaud sat, he noticed that the twin and his friend who had been sleeping on the floor were beginning to stir. Tip-toeing past them he got back to his desk and laid the pictures in front of his colleagues. These were blown up freeze frames of the six females that were still possible suspects.

The three detectives looked over them in silence, trying to pick up anything unusual on the shots of the women. Robin then moved four of the pictures to one side of the desk and explained that these were the members that they were going to pull in for an interview. All three of them were just focusing in on the two remaining pictures laid out on the other side of the desk.

If they were really dealing with the Magpie in this instance then there was no way that she would be careless enough to pick up a victim at a spa where she was a member and have her identity easily traced. That wasn't her style and they all knew it. Indeed, it really had to be one of these two other girls. Arnaud leant over the shoulders of Robin and Jim, who were sitting in front of him, so that he could focus on the two remaining pictures. She had to be one of these and they all knew it. They were close.

There was silence again. All were thinking the same thing. Which one was she? One was a very attractive female that looked like she was in her late twenties. From what you could make out from the black and white photo, she seemed quite tall and thin, and had long fair hair; all the traits of a typical Dutch girl.

In the other picture you saw absolutely nothing, which was very surprising and this made Arnaud suspicious. The photo was of a female with tight jeans on nice slim legs. She wore a loose sweatshirt so it was hard to establish much about the upper part of her body. Her head was down and turned away from the camera, as if she knew exactly where the camera was positioned. She was wearing a woolen hat, and if she had long hair, it must have been tucked up under it. The hat had an A&F logo on it, which Jim explained stood for Abercrombie and Fitch, a trendy fashion brand. It was very difficult to put an age range on her although she was probably not older than thirty. She appeared very fit and had a slim figure.

"Great!" said Arnaud, sarcastically. He picked up the photo from the desk to look at it more closely. There was nothing else to see apart from the fact that she carried a bag over her shoulder with no brand name on it. This must be her, Arnaud thought to himself.

"Can you bring her up on the screen? Also, do we have footage of her entering the premises earlier in the day?" asked Arnaud.

He was surprised to see that Robin had this part of the tape recording ready to show him, which made him realize that they were all focused on the same thing.

Again, they all stared on the middle monitor and watched the recording of this female entering the spa earlier in the day. The whole time she kept the woolen hat on and her face turned away from the cameras. This had to be deliberate, thought Arnaud to himself. As the girl approached the reception and paid her entrance fee, she kept her head down the whole time. They really had nothing to go on.

Robin continued speaking, "All we can be sure of is that she arrived at the spa at 5:02 p.m., which was about an hour before the two guys. You can see from the footage of her when she entered the building that she is definitely quite tall, relatively thin and does appear to have nice slim legs. Apart from this, we have nothing else to go on."

Arnaud sighed with frustration. He knew that they needed to do a lot of work around interviewing the short list of girls, even though he was pretty sure that this was the very one that they were looking for. And he was also pretty confident that there was no way they would get to interview this one, as they just couldn't identify her. If it was really the Magpie then she had done her homework, scoping the premises and being fully aware of where all the cameras were. In doing this thoroughly, she had avoided giving any clues away regarding her identity.

"Well, we need to interview as many of the girls as we can, both, the members and the non-members that we are able to put a name to." said Arnaud.

Robin and Jim could hear in his voice that he was frustrated. It was going to be a lot of work for nothing. They all knew it.

"And you will need to interview all of the staff working at the spa today. Don't just get the reception staff in for questioning but everyone who was working yesterday from the sauna cleaners to the canteen staff."

Arnaud continued, "It's possible that someone saw something. She had to get changed in the ladies changing rooms. She had to walk to the sauna. Someone must have seen something. Take blown-up pictures of the unidentified girls with you to the spa to show the staff."

"Yes, Arnaud," replied Jim. "But it has to be this one, boss!"

He was also a little frustrated realizing how much data crunching and interviewing they were going to have to do in order to officially eliminate all the other girls from the investigation. Once this process had been completed, they would still not be able to identify the last girl.

"I know what you are saying makes complete sense, but we can't leave any stone unturned and we have to make sure that we cover all the bases."

Jim and Robin nodded in agreement, knowing that Arnaud was right.

"Can you print a blown- up picture of just her head, please?"

Arnaud could hear the printer starting up and he walked over to collect the photo. As he was walking over to the machine, he noticed that the twin brother and his friend were both sitting upright. They looked very tired. Clearly, they were both extremely worried and anxious. Arnaud looked at them and nodded. He continued walking over to the printer to pick up the picture and then turned and headed straight back to his colleagues. He wondered how much of their conversation the two civilians had heard.

He lay the paper down on the desk in front of Robin and Jim and spoke at once, "Let's get all the background work done and then we can find this girl." They were all on the same page, which pleased the young detectives.

Arnaud didn't sit down again but walked on past the detectives' desks and over to the water drum. He took a small cup of water and washed down his prescription tablets. He was feeling both excited and worked up right now. He thought that they had the killer on camera even if they didn't have a clear-faced shot of her.

Arnaud went back to the desk area and sat down with the young detectives. His mind had already moved on to some more unanswered questions.

Arnaud was in deep thought. He couldn't understand how this girl, if she was really the Magpie, could take down these young fit men. Some of the victims had been tall strong guys who exercised regularly. It just didn't seem possible that this female could do it alone. He was sure that she had an accomplice. Who was helping her? Was she drugging them? Was she seducing them and waiting for them to fall asleep first before killing them? All of these questions had to be answered if they were going to get closer to catching her, but Arnaud realized that he couldn't rush this process, and a great deal of other investigative work needed to be done first.

The three detectives' concentration was broken by the noise of the office door opening suddenly. They looked up to see Friso entering fresh-faced. As he approached the desks where they were sitting, Arnaud stood up to greet him.

"Hi Friso. How are you? I hope that I didn't wake you this morning."

Arnaud was still concerned that he had caused a family rift at Friso's apartment by calling so early. His voice sort of sounded sincere and guilty.

Friso didn't respond to Arnaud but stopped and turned to face the twin and his friend who were now standing up.

"Morning guys." said Friso to the two students. "Hope you managed to get some sleep."

He turned to where Arnaud and the other detectives were sitting, and focused in on Robin.

"Get them coffee, please, and why don't you do a breakfast run?" said Friso.

Turning back to Jeroen and Thomas, he spoke again. "What would you like to eat?"

Robin came walking over to the young students to take their order. There was a café next door to the police station and it was easy for him to go and get them some breakfast.

Friso turned to Jim and began speaking again. "Okay, grab your coat. We need to get to the spa and retrieve these tapes."

"We already have them." replied Jim. Arnaud could see Friso's face turning confused and then annoyed as his young detectives had not followed orders, and called him when they had some developments in the case. This was Arnaud's cue to step in.

"The spa manager got in contact not long ago and dropped the tapes off. We have been sifting through them. The boys wanted to wake you but I told them to let you get some sleep."

Arnaud thought that the young detectives had done a good job and didn't deserve a roasting now. He also needed full teamwork between the four of them today as they had a lot to get done.

"Errgh, okay." replied Friso, not quite sure how to react.

Anyway, Friso was more interested to hear what they had to say and what was on the footage. He walked behind the desks and stood next to Arnaud, staring at the screens and the one single piece of A4 paper that lay in front of them. There was silence as Friso watched the recorded footage of the girl entering the spa. Every thirteen seconds it ran again.

Looking down at the enlarged black and white photo of a girl wearing a woolen hat, Friso quickly realized that it was the same female on the paper and the tape. This must be her, he thought to himself.

The silence said everything, and like Arnaud, he knew that this girl was probably the Magpie. Arnaud and Friso had worked so closely together especially over the last year. They had fought, argued, and had sleepless nights, all resulting from this case and their lack of progress. Now, they had a breakthrough, even if it was just a small one. Friso was warming up inside. He tapped Arnaud on his right shoulder softly as a sign of acknowledgement as if it to say, 'we are getting there, mate'.

Looking straight at Robin and Jim, he began to speak, "So, one of you needs to get all these girls in here for interviews today. We want to try and see all of them within the next twenty-four hours."

Friso continued, "One of you needs to focus on speaking with the staff at the spa and try to find out if anyone noticed anything unusual yesterday."

Again, Jim and Robin nodded in response.

"It's too early to start showing pictures of the potential female suspect or the missing twin to staff at the spa. We don't want it getting leaked that someone has been abducted. We may have our own views on this and we don't know for sure that this is actually the girl. Also, we can't be certain yet that Floris is officially a missing person."

Again, they nodded and spoke up in unison, "Okay Friso, we are on it."

The two young detectives got up and went straight to work. Friso was confident of their ability to get these important tasks done. He went back around the desks to sit next to Arnaud. Friso stared at Arnaud for a minute while he mulled over an idea and then spoke.

"I have an idea." said Friso quietly. "Why don't we pull up the pictures of the prime suspect at the spa from yesterday and compare her to the girl that we have on film from the footage at the night in the Surprise Bar."

Why hadn't he thought of this, Arnaud was thinking to himself, excited once again.

"Sure." said Arnaud.

Friso pulled the keyboard and mouse towards him and started digging into another file that contained all the films from the Surprise Bar. Within a minute, they had two blown up images of their suspect from the spa positioned on the screen next to the girl from the nightclub. The two men stared silently at the pictures. In one shot you had the female in the dark club with the wig on, which covered most of her face and all her real hair. The other picture showed the girl leaving the spa through the turnstile and wearing the hat.

Both Arnaud and Friso were thinking the same thing. It just wasn't possible to say whether they were looking at the same girl in the two pictures but it was clear that both females were aware of the cameras, and were trying to conceal their identities as much as possible. They had done this successfully through the headgear that they were wearing and also by turning away from the cameras. The fact that they did this in both instances made the detectives think that it was definitely the same person.

If only they could prove it was the same girl. As they stared back at the monitors they could make out that both pictures showed that both girls had a slim figure and were quite tall. If you zoomed in on the photos, you could see that both had slender hands and necks. It was quite easy to estimate that they were in their mid-twenties. In fact, a lot of boxes could be ticked. The detectives just didn't have a good visual on the faces, which was deliberate, of course.

Friso printed two copies of each picture, one for Arnaud and one for himself. Arnaud didn't want the print-outs up on their wall map just yet. He didn't want anyone coming into their office making the assumption that this was their target. Nothing could be leaked. He was also against the idea of letting Dijkstra know that they had made this breakthrough. Arnaud trusted Dijkstra but he couldn't be sure that he would not tell his superiors about this in order to get a 'pat on the back' and win some recognition of the team's progress. Arnaud didn't care about the politics. He just wanted to catch this serial killer. Anyway, they also needed to get a lot of interviews done first in order to eliminate the other girls from the investigation. Then, they could be sure about who they were targeting. Hopefully, by the end of the day, this would be done.

Jim and Robin picked up the important things they would need for the day from their desks: notepads, phones, a small digital camera, voice recorders and put them all in their coat pockets. They were going to be busy all day. The two young detectives nodded at Friso and Arnaud and then headed for the office door. Friso was going to the spa, and Robin would be joining him after picking up some breakfast for the missing twin's brother and his best friend. These two guys were wide awake now and sitting on some chairs by the other side of the office.

Arnaud beckoned them over to the desks where he was sitting with Friso. He asked them to sit opposite him and started to speak softly and sympathetically.

"I am very sorry to say this but it is more likely now that something has happened to Floris. We still shouldn't panic but we need to get ready to make a missing person's statement that we can release to the press at 9:30 a.m."

The two young men nodded at Arnaud with sad faces. He continued to speak, realizing that they were taking in everything that he was saying to them, "Now, have you told anyone yet? We need to control the message that gets out."

Jeroen and Thomas looked at each other and then the twin spoke up. "Not yet, but I do need to tell my parents. I don't want them finding out from a news flash."

"Agreed." replied Arnaud. "Friso will make sure that you get to your parents' house later. Then you can brief them on what has been going on."

"Okay." replied Jeroen, shaking with worry, knowing full well that his parents would fall in to a state of panic, as soon as he broke the news to them.

Arnaud continued, "But you need to tell them that they need to keep quiet for now about this story. We have to control what information is given out to the press. And I don't know if you were listening to our conversations earlier but we may be on to some good leads and this information is extremely confidential for now."

The two boys seemed to get the message and nodded again at Arnaud acknowledging his requests. Arnaud carried on speaking, "Now, we have to prepare the missing person's brief, as well as put together a case file on your brother for our own records. Do you have any current pictures of Floris?"

Again, the two guys looked at each other, and this time, Thomas replied. "He is very active on Facebook and we could take some pictures from there."

"Good thinking." said Friso. "Let me help you select some good pictures."

"Okay." said Arnaud, "After breakfast, Jim and Robin will be bringing in a lot of girls who were at the spa yesterday for interviews. Jeroen, if you can recognize any of them from yesterday please let Friso know. This may be the tone of their voice or perhaps the shape of their legs or ankles. Anything. Anything that draws likeness to the girl from the sauna yesterday."

"Okay." replied the best friend. He looked at the paper on the desk and spoke up. "Can we see the picture of the main suspect?" It was clear that they had been listening to Arnaud and Friso's conversations earlier.

"Sure." said Arnaud. Friso pushed the two freeze frames over to the young guys who studied them and then stared at each other with frowns. They then looked at Arnaud and Friso despondently.

"But you have nothing to go on." said the brother with tears in his eyes. His voice was trembling. "There is no way you can recognize this girl."

Arnaud spoke up sternly seeing that the twin was crying. He leant across the desk and grabbed his arm. "We will catch her. Mark my words, we will catch her."

Arnaud needed to get out of the office so that he could think.

Friso paused for a second and whispered back to his boss, "I am going to oversee the interview process in the office today for all the witnesses and potential suspects."

Arnaud turned to the twin and his friend and spoke once more. "Friso is going to take care of you. I know it's a very difficult time right now, but please try and help us with the investigation as much as possible. I will be back here later to see you."

With that, Arnaud was gone.

* * *

4:00 p.m.

The next five hours were spent interviewing staff from the spa and women who had been visiting the spa yesterday. All, apart from three females, had given a statement. Nobody had seen anything unusual. It was a tiring process, asking the same questions, recording and writing down all the answers but they had gotten through most of it. The more women they spoke with, the more obvious it was that the girl with the hat was indeed the Magpie. None of the interviewed females recognized her picture, exiting the spa through the turnstiles.

Nobody had noticed her yesterday and that wasn't by chance. Friso was sure that she remained unidentified for a reason. Friso was picturing her in his head, gliding around the spa turning her head at anyone who was trying check out her figure or face. She had to have planned this so well. It was the work of a professional.

There were still two other girls, besides the key suspect, that hadn't been identified yet. Neither of them were members of the spa but they did have very clear pictures of their faces as they were entering and exiting the building yesterday. Jim and Robin had asked the spa to keep an eye out for these girls, and if they came back, to make sure that they contacted the police immediately. The back-up plan was to put their photos in the national newspapers and ask them to come forward. They wouldn't do this for a few days, however, as it would create more panic than was necessary right now.

The twin brother and his friend were looking even more miserable, as the day drew on. They had moved themselves into one of the two small glass offices next to the main room. This was actually Arnaud's private office, although he never really used it. They looked out of the goldfish bowl at all the witnesses being interviewed. The blank faces of the spa staff and women that were there yesterday told a very clear story. They had nothing to report. There was a lot of shaking of heads and you could lip-read a lot of 'no' responses from all of them. It was not good news.

It was now 4:10 p.m. and the twin still hadn't heard anything from his missing brother. Both Jeroen and Thomas were crying and blubbering uncontrollably. They sensed the same thing as Friso and the two young detectives had. This was no longer a missing person's case that they were dealing with. Most of the witness interviews and suspects had been completed, and it was almost certain that they were looking for this serial killer again. Everything was the same. In the next forty-eight hours, the truth would come unraveled. If they were thinking correctly, then Floris' body would be dumped somewhere, naked, in or around the Amsterdam area.

Arnaud had spent the whole day in De Twee Zwaantjes, drinking coffee after coffee, smoking almost twenty cigarettes, and eating only a small brown roll with aged cheese. He needed to be alone to think. He also did not want to get in the way of the interview process at the office. It needed to be done quickly and efficiently but at the same time in a very thorough way. It had been a good day of thinking through the case and all of the evidence.

He had also come to his favorite bar to see Noor. She was a bit stand-offish today, probably because she had sensed his annoyance at her recent text messages. Arnaud knew that she was genuinely concerned about him and cared for his wellbeing. Most of the time he liked it and saw her as one of his few friends.

Arnaud didn't find Noor attractive, but he liked her attention. She had kept his coffee cup full all day and got him lunch and bar snacks whenever he was hungry. She knew that he was busy thinking and didn't want to bother him too much.

Arnaud sat on the wooden stool, thoughts and ideas racing through his mind, high on a mixture of caffeine, nicotine, and adrenaline. How could this girl in the pictures possibly pick up or move around a dead body on her own? She was slim and feminine, and certainly not a body builder. Even if she was fit and strong, corpses are dead weight and very difficult to carry or drag along. As the day drew on, he was convinced that she had to have an accomplice. They would need to check all the footage again. He would also need to get Friso and the rest of the team to question all the potential witnesses at the spa and the staff if they saw any other suspicious individuals walking around the saunas and jacuzzis. They could be hunting down two girls or a girl and a guy. The best friend of the missing person would also have to be questioned again to see if he saw anyone else hanging around the sauna where the contact had been made with the Magpie.

Arnaud sat up and smiled to himself. He felt happy and content. He had processed a lot of information in his head and made progress with the case. If the girl in the two pictures was indeed the same person and was also the Magpie, then she must have an accomplice. This was a big development, the more Arnaud thought about it the more convinced he was. He would tell Friso and the rest of the team when he got back to the office later tonight. Arnaud was an experienced detective and while he was quite sure of his assumptions, he would continue eliminating possibilities after looking through Jim and Robin's data crunching.

Arnaud and his team were now using the website as a 'think tank' and a font of information and debate. If one had the time to sift through the emotional messages, you could find some really useful ideas on the blog. Jim and Robin would filter this information and present it at the end of the day to Friso and Arnaud.

Arnaud toyed with this this idea for a while. If they contacted the blogger on the site, maybe they might get scared. Anyway, people reading the blog might see that the police were trying to make contact with Happy Single. This may prove to be very risky for their image. Arnaud could just see the headlines in the papers, 'Police helpless! In need of a blogger's advice to help hunt down the Magpie.' It was clear though that this website and blog were picking up steam as more people had started to read it and participate in the conversations. Arnaud had been informed by Friso that the blog was now getting more than a thousand hits per day. He was also not surprised to be told that Happy Single was becoming quite popular. After all, the hunt for this serial killer was the most talked about news in Amsterdam and The Netherlands.

Arnaud had spent the last ten months trying to work out who the Magpie was, and now he was desperate to find out who Happy Single was. He would address this in the office tonight. He would need the other detectives' help to see whether it would actually be possible to make contact with the blogger under the radar. No one could know about this.

As he put some money on the table to pay, Noor spoke up. "Where are you going, Arnaud?"

"Back to the office," replied Arnaud, looking at the bill and realizing that she had only charged him for about seventy percent of what he had actually eaten and drunk throughout the afternoon. He left her a good tip and stood up from the table.

"Well, keep up the good work, Arnaud. You guys seem to be getting closer to catching her."

"Thank you, dear."

With that, he left. Arnaud got outside the café and was hit by a strong cold wind biting his face. It was dark already and the temperature had dropped considerably. He closed his coat buttons and headed over to his moped. Arnaud was keen to race back to the office to share his thoughts and also to see how the interview process had been going throughout the day. The fact that no one had contacted him meant that they were still busy, and that there had been no news worth bothering him with. This was good in a way thought Arnaud as he started up his moped because that meant that their analysis was right.

* * *

6:10 p.m.

Arnaud arrived back in the office just after six. It was a lot quieter than he was expecting. All the people that the team had been interviewing had left and by the look on Jim and Robin's faces it had been a non-event day. The two young detectives looked up briefly and then returned to recording interview reports. Every time they completed a report, they would print it out and then attach a polaroid photo to it with a paper clip. There was nice pile on each of their desks. As Arnaud walked towards them he noticed Friso in one of the glass offices sitting with Thomas and Jeroen.

"Anything guys?" Arnaud said, his question directed at Jim and Robin. They looked up again briefly and shrugged their shoulders.

"Well, this is good news." responded Arnaud. They looked up again at their boss as he walked round the back of their desks behind them. He picked up the two A4 still shots of the key suspect and started to speak.

"We now know with certainty that this is who we are looking for." He took the two pictures and walked to the wall with the map on it and pinned them up on the side of the collage. He turned to face the two young detectives and spoke.

"This is the Magpie."

After a couple of minutes, Friso came out of the meeting room. He looked exhausted, just like Robin and Jim. It had been a long day and Friso had spent his time comforting the twin and his friend. They had become more distraught, as the day went on. They hadn't heard from Floris and now were sure that he was in grave danger.

Friso pulled up a chair and sat down next to Arnaud, Jim, and Robin.

"So, what now?" said Arnaud, staring into the eyes of each of his three colleagues.

Friso decided to speak up. "Well, we have interviewed everyone now apart from her." He didn't need to point to the wall or even say the Magpie's name. "We have even had contact with the other two girls that couldn't be recognized earlier. All are accounted for and can be wiped off the suspect list."

Arnaud was pleased that they could actually eliminate everyone now from the investigation and nodded slowly in approval.

Friso continued, "Nobody can remember seeing our suspect coming in or going out yesterday. I can't believe she sneaked past everyone. We have two more days to wait. If it is the Magpie, the body will be dumped within three days. That will be the eleventh."

There was silence as all three detectives stared at Arnaud, who had his hand over his mouth and looked as if he had seen a ghost. "That's my birthday. The eleventh is my fucking birthday." A cold shiver went down Arnaud's spine, as he took in this fact.

"She knows that it's my birthday and is showing all of us that she is in charge. She decides, when to take, when to strike, and when to kill."

"So, this is planned." said Friso.

"Yes, she is fucking playing with us." Arnaud was losing his cool, as he realized that this whole case was taking over his and his team's lives and it was just a game to the Magpie.

"Maybe it's a coincidence." said Friso.

All of them stared at Friso as if to say don't be so silly. The Magpie was not about luck, chance, or coincidence. Everything was planned and calculated down to the last detail. All they knew after ten months was that it was a slim, pretty Dutch girl. She was good, very good, and she knew it. What were her motives? What was her background? Why always men? Why did she strip them and take all their belongings? Only she knew.

The latest unanswered question was, why on Arnaud's birthday? She was clearly studying the head detective and obviously wanted Arnaud to know this.

If this twin didn't turn up tomorrow, which was highly unlikely, then they would need to notify the whole police force to be on the lookout for the body to be dumped. This would be the next opportunity to catch her. Then the story would be leaked to the press and Arnaud would have to deal with that aggravation. He thought to himself that even if the press didn't get wind of the story, he would have to do a television and radio interview on the eleventh, anyhow. This was so planned. Arnaud was sure that she would be at home, wherever she lived, watching Arnaud on his birthday, explaining the latest killing and answering pushy questions from the journalists. On the eleventh they would have to release the pictures to the press and television channels of this girl in the club and in the spa. The Netherlands would know then that the Magpie was a female.

Arnaud thought that maybe someone would recognize her figure or the way she dressed. If not a friend, maybe her neighbor would see her. Even though they didn't have a face shot, maybe she would be spotted. The A&F hat was not Dutch after all and it might jog someone's memory. Amsterdam was a small city. The Magpie was a girl of disguise but someone must know who she was. Arnaud came out of his deep thought and looked at his watch. It was already 8:20 p.m. He was tired and wanted to go home to prepare for tomorrow.

He looked up at his colleagues and spoke again.

"Tomorrow we will notify the police force and the press. Let's get in front of this and not waste any time. The Magpie won't be expecting us to notify the newspapers and TV channels until the last minute, so let's get ahead of her next move. And her next move will be to dump the body on the eleventh. We release the two pictures tomorrow and what information we know about her. The more information we can share, the more chance we have of somebody spotting her. Get some sleep tonight guys, and good job today."

Friso could see that Arnaud had gone into overdrive mode. He was figuring out their plan of attack. Arnaud nodded at Friso and then stood up and left the office. He headed down to the garage to get his moped.

Arnaud arrived home to a dark living room, with a flashing red light on his phone answering machine. He walked over hesitantly, cupping his hands and blowing them in an attempt to warm them up. He pressed play and listened to the two messages. The first was from the Volkskraant, who wanted to interview him for their weekend magazine. He didn't bother writing the message or number down to call them back. They never wrote anything nice about him, in fact quite the opposite. After the news that would break tomorrow, he was even more opposed to giving any more interviews than were necessary. He also didn't like the thought of the Magpie reading a story about him or his answers to probing questions from a journalist.

The second message was from Noor. Arnaud thought it was strange that she had called his home number, as she knew that the best way to get hold of him was on his mobile phone. Also, he couldn't remember ever giving her his home telephone. It must have been on one of those drunken nights when he was feeling sorry for himself and pouring out his life story, about his failed marriage, his daughter, and his tough job.

Noor was a friend but why was she trying to contact him so much at the moment, wondered Arnaud. He had spent the afternoon in the café with her so it was odd that she wanted to chat so soon again. He knew that she sort-of liked him, but what else was it? Was she worried that he was getting too depressed or stressed? Maybe she thought that he was going to do something stupid? Maybe she was just interested in hearing the developments in the case. Arnaud sat at his living room table in darkness, doing his usual self-interrogation. Maybe, she was just being caring and sweet. Anyway, for now he had bigger, more important things to think about.

He needed to sleep and decided that he would call her in the morning. Tomorrow, he would have to face the press, something he really hated. He wanted to be on his game, especially if the Magpie was watching. He was becoming more obsessed with this killer, which was not surprising. She was also becoming obsessed with him, playing a game around his birthday. The thought made Arnaud even more stressed. He pulled himself upright and headed for the stairs and up to his bedroom.

CHAPTER 13

October 10

7:00 p.m.

Fleur left the house, upset and fed up. As she walked away briskly, she realized that she hadn't even bothered to change or dress up to go outside. Normally, she would always do that. But not this time. She just needed to get out of there. Roos and Jade had been arguing again. It had become unbearable for Fleur to stay in there with them going at it.

The usual arguments would start with a disagreement and then a few jealous remarks from Roos, followed by Jade ignoring her, and then both of them shouting at each other. This time, however, it had gone to a whole new level with Jade slapping Roos across the face with a loud clapping noise shooting across the living room. Roos had found a large colorful lace bra in the laundry, which was clearly not Jade's size nor a color that she would wear. Roos confronted Jade and accused her of having an affair or a fling on her recent long haul trip. As usual, Jade just ignored Roos and sat on the sofa. Roos completely lost control of herself and pushed Jade and started screaming at her, calling her a selfish bitch.

When the violence began, Fleur just kept sitting on the sofa next to Jade and closed her eyes, putting her hands over her face. She didn't want anything to do with their blow-ups. Jade had proceeded to stand up and slap Roos across the face. Surprisingly, Roos was not stunned by this reaction instead it ignited her anger even more. She licked off the blood that slowly dripped from her bottom lip and then reached behind her for a small piece of Delft pottery. Turning back to face her girlfriend she flung the small piece of pottery at Jade's head. Fortunately, it missed and smashed against the back wall.

As the pot broke into a thousand pieces, it triggered another rage between the two girls as they ran at each other grabbing hair, yanking, and screaming. Punches were flying as they fought and clawed each other. Kicking, scratching, and shouting followed and it didn't look like they were going to stop. Fleur stood up in tears and tried to stop them.

"Stop! Stop! Please stop!" she shouted, trying to squeeze herself between them.

She attempted to pull their hands off of each other's hair. After about a minute, Fleur moved away from the crazed girls who were now wrestling on the ground, each trying to get the better of the other. Fleur realized that they were not going to end this fight quickly. She had had enough and wasn't staying to watch it. They clearly had so much tension built up inside and were now letting it out. Fleur headed towards the front door where her coat was hanging on a rail. She slipped on a pair of boots and grabbed her coat. She needed to get out.

Slamming the front door behind her and wiping the tears from her face, she could feel adrenalin pumping around her body. Fleur could look after herself and had needed to several times in the past. However, she was upset and shocked to see so much hatred between two people. These girls were not meant to be together, she thought as she tried to compose herself. They were so different and the jealousy that brewed up inside Roos was beyond explainable.

As Fleur started walking away from the house, she began thinking about the cause of the fight. Where was that bra from? Had Jade really had a fling? Maybe Roos had planted it on purpose, just to have an excuse to confront her girlfriend? Maybe this was how passionate lesbians behaved when they were angry with each other? Fleur didn't know the right answer and really did not care. She was fed up with their arguing and fighting. She was young, single, and wanted to have fun. She didn't want to come home to this fighting every night. It made her sad.

As she walked along the Singel in the cold night air, she realized that she needed to move out of the house. For tonight, she would stay at her friend's place who lived on the Utrechtsraat. Bridget was also a student and worked at Yab Yum, as well. Fleur started walking faster as she was getting cold. She could share Bridget's bed or sleep on her sofa. She didn't have a boyfriend either so hopefully it would be possible for her to sleep in her bed. Fleur was wearing grey jogging pants and a hoodie beneath her long black puffer jacket. She didn't have any socks on though the boots were keeping her feet warm. She needed to go to University tomorrow, so she would have to return home early in the morning to get a change of clothes and her books. Maybe she could get up early enough and pick her stuff before her flat-mates woke up. Maybe only one of them would be there when she returned. As Fleur walked quickly over Leidsestraat, she inspected her hands. Annoyingly, one of her perfectly manicured fingernails had broken off. It might have happened when she was trying to separate the girls. Bridget would have a spare fake nail and a variety of varnishes that she could use to fix this, she thought to herself.

Fleur couldn't stop thinking about how the fight would end. There had been so much emotion that had boiled up between them that she wouldn't be surprised if one needed to go to hospital. Maybe the fight was still going on now. Fleur began running towards Utrechtstraat. She wanted to get these thoughts and the girls out of her head. She didn't want to think about it or them anymore. This was tomorrow's problem to deal with.

CHAPTER 14

October 11

8:20 a.m.

Arnaud woke up and looked out of his bedroom window. It wasn't raining on his birthday. It was, however, grey outside - overcast and windy; a normal Amsterdam winter morning. There was ice on his window, highlighting how cold a night it had been. He had slept exceptionally well considering what today was going to entail for him. He could see that the usual suspects were already standing outside his front door. It didn't matter what was happening with the weather, they were always there. This, however, wasn't the main point of interest for the journalists today. They were more concerned and eager to hear about the missing guy, Floris Heidstra, and the expectation that the body would be dumped and found today.

From the faces outside, he could see that the reporters from all the main Dutch newspapers were present. In fact, Arnaud recognized all of them and could also see that annoying rat of a journalist, Toon De Bruin. He gritted his teeth and squinted his eyes as he focused in on the skinny reporter making small talk with the people around him. Arnaud looked at the time on his mobile phone, which he was squeezing in his right hand, imagining it was Toon De Bruin's neck. It was 8:25 a.m. He had three text messages on his phone as well, which he then read as he sat back on his bed. They were all birthday texts; one from his daughter, one from Friso, and the last one from Noor.

Arnaud sat down on the edge of his bed in his white t-shirt and boxer shorts. He wanted to spend a few minutes replying to these texts. Yesterday had been a long day and his birthday was going to be the same. This was his only chance to not think about work and the one time when he could be nice. To Friso, he just wrote thanks, as he would see him shortly and didn't need to say any more than that. To Noor, he also just wrote 'thanks.' Over the last few days, he had also spent a lot of time with her, and he didn't need to say anything else. To his daughter, he wrote 'Thank you sweetheart', and then paused to think for a second. Whenever he thought of his daughter, he choked up, as he believed that he hadn't been a very good father and he missed her dearly. He finished the message by writing 'Papa loves you, x'.

With that, Arnaud got up, threw his phone on the bed and headed for the bathroom to take a shower. His neck and back were aching, probably from the stress. The hot powerful jet from the shower on his shoulders proved very relaxing and he spent a little longer in there than usual. As he stood under the shower, he went through yesterday's events in his mind. The day had started with a press announcement at nine in the morning. Arnaud and his boss had spoken to the local journalists and television news channels. They had explained that there was a new missing person and a potential Magpie victim, Floris Heidstra. They continued to explain where the missing twin had disappeared and appealed for any witnesses from the spa or the bar, where he met her later, to come forward.

The bombshell was then dropped on the public. Arnaud held the two black and white photos of the suspect, who they believed to be the Magpie. While the pictures didn't reveal too much, he was making it clear that he was sure that the Magpie was female. It had been extremely difficult for the two detectives to complete their briefing, as the noise inside the police station erupted. Journalists and TV reporters had new information on the case. This information had taken everyone back by complete surprise. The serial killer was a woman!

Surprisingly, this was seen as a success and progress for Arnaud and his team. No one was shouting any questions about the probable victim number ten of the year. They were more concerned about this female responsible for causing havoc on the streets of Amsterdam. The press saw this as a major breakthrough. Arnaud didn't get it, as they weren't really any closer to catching the killer. But it didn't seem to matter, the journalists were happy. They believed Arnaud was making a step forward in the hunt for the serial killer, and he wasn't going to try and change their opinion. He had enough to deal with and a friendly set of reporters was better for him.

The pictures of the Magpie were all over the television news yesterday as well as on the internet. There were also pictures of Floris Heidstra, splashed everywhere. His body was expected to turn up today. Friso had guided the missing twin's brother and his friend through a number of press interviews, which had gone well with only a few tears. Arnaud was interested to see if any new witnesses would come forward today, in response to these interviews and pictures. He wasn't hopeful. Probably the best outcome of yesterday's addresses to the reporters was that Arnaud and his team had been granted an additional two hundred and forty undercover policemen for the case. He would let Friso and his boss decide the logistics around the best way to deploy this additional support in the bars and clubs of Amsterdam.

In November, they would have to plan how to position these policemen in Amsterdam and the surrounding towns, with them playing the roles of innocent men, trying to attract this calculative killer. Arnaud wished he could get the additional staffing today, as they could help with the search for the victim's body. This information, about the extra police on the case, however, would not be made public knowledge. Arnaud didn't want to deter the Magpie from striking. The less the press knew about their operations around catching the Magpie, the better. Arnaud and his team had the undercover police wearing subtle jewelry; a watch, gold necklace or an earring. All were under instructions to keep these items visible at all times while sitting or waiting in bars. These were the things that they hoped would attract the Magpie.

For sure, the Magpie would know that they must have upped their team on the ground and have additional police working on the case, and be plotting ways to draw her in. If it didn't catch her, it would certainly make it harder for her to attract potential victims. Even if she was able to strike, then it would also make it more difficult for her to dump a body. Arnaud was convinced that they had a higher chance of catching her when she was dropping off a corpse than when she was actually making contact with a potential victim. Arnaud couldn't stop thinking that the Magpie must have watched the news yesterday and seen the pictures that they had of her. She would have also heard the description of her that they shared with the press. Would this send the killer into hiding? Arnaud doubted that.

Apart from spending time yesterday with the victim's twin and friend, Friso had been extremely busy briefing the task force on their locations in Amsterdam. All were to be on the lookout for the body drop. Jim and Robin had been busy all day going through the footage again with a fine toothed-comb and reading all the interview reports a second time. They were trying to see if they had missed something. They also continued monitoring the blog on the Amsterdam Living website.

The blogs were giving Arnaud and his team a lot of praise for making progress with the murder hunt. There were a lot of compliments for Happy Single about how right she had been about everything. The press had also published an article about her. Who is Happy Single? There had been several comments in the papers yesterday about whether the Magpie had an accomplice or not. This idea was a thought generated by Happy Single.

As Arnaud washed his hair. He mulled over the one thing that was eating away at him. This was the fact that the body was going to be dumped today, on his birthday. Arnaud was convinced that this wasn't a coincidence.

Arnaud dried himself off and got dressed. Looking in the bathroom mirror, he thought that he looked alright for a forty-nine year old man. If it wasn't for the bags under his eyes, he might even pass for a guy five years younger. He looked tired and stressed, but that was to be expected. Arnaud liked having long hair, but this was too messy for him and he needed to get it cut. It was the last thing on his list to do, with everything else going on right now, but he would make sure he would get it done before the month ended.

Arnaud was keen to get to the station and talk to his team. Today was going to be another busy day. He went downstairs into his living room, put on his coat, and checked that the moped keys were in his pocket. He took a deep breath and ran his hand through his hair, composing himself before going outside to face the press. He had become adept at answering questions, although he was always worried about being confronted with a reporter that would hit a raw nerve and throw him a question that he couldn't answer.

As soon as he clicked open his front door, the cameras started flashing and the questions began being frantically fired at Arnaud thick and fast by the reporters.

* * *

10:00 a.m.

Noor had been awake for about thirty minutes. She had stayed in bed late this morning as she had worked later than usual last night. She sat at her computer in the living room reading the morning news on the internet. She was also listening to Sky Radio playing in the background, while enjoying a mug of red berry tea. Noor had to do a short shift at Albert Heijn Supermarket this afternoon and then De Twee Zwaantjes this evening. She was working as many shifts as possible at the moment because she was saving for a three-week cruise around the Mediterranean, visiting Greece, Turkey, and the Balearic Islands. Noor had a keen interest in Greece, having studied Ancient History at the University of Delft.

Her tiny studio apartment, on the Marnixstraat in the Jordaan, was warm and cozy. On the living room wall, above her PC, were various pictures of Greece's beaches and ancient buildings. This was very different from the other wall in the room where she had stuck the map of Amsterdam with her notes and pictures from the murder hunt. At the other end of the room was a small sofa and television and her bed was by the window. On the wall above her bed were two posters of Greek gods, Apollo and Aphrodite. She saw Aphrodite as the goddess who would hopefully bring her luck and love. She loved Apollo, the God of War. He was her hero and the man of her dreams, just like Arnaud. The fact that she didn't have a relationship with him was beside the point. She could fantasize and dream about her perfect man.

Noor had three keen interests at the moment. The first was keeping up her communication and thoughts on the Amsterdam Living blog. The second was supporting Arnaud and being there for him all the time. Noor also spent a lot of time on dating websites, chatting with men but not often meeting them. For a girl who was not good looking and overweight, as well as being a bit strange, she was extremely fussy. Online dating was the third interest and the one she was the least good at.

The two websites that she was subscribed to as a member were eHarmony and Match. She used Happy Single as her code name on these sites as well. Noor knew that she was very picky, and really didn't mind just chatting with guys and not actually meeting them. She was also very insecure and always worried that if and when they actually got to see her, they wouldn't find her attractive, and the relationship would be over before it even started. Noor was fully aware that she was no oil painting but she was happy to wait for Mr. Perfect who was out there somewhere. Anyway, in the meantime, she had Apollo to stare at and Arnaud to look after and support.

She had been on a few dates in the past after extensive email courting. Once she had exchanged emails with a guy a few times, who she felt was credible, nice, and intelligent enough for her. She would arrange to meet them at a museum or at the cinema. This was of course very tactical from Noor's side. Something and somewhere where the man wouldn't have to focus on her all the time, but she could discreetly analyze him as he watched the film or a stared at a piece of art work. This would give her time to work out if the guy was real and kind.

Of the seven dates that she had been on over the last four years, five had been one offs, and it was the guy in all instances who had not wanted to go out with her again. She had liked most of these men but she was sure that they were simply not attracted to her. This was disappointing, as they had all stated on the website that appearance came a distant second to personality when looking for a match. Noor felt cheated and angered by this, as she had so much to offer to the right man in terms of love and intellectual compatibility. If only someone would give her the chance.

The other two dates had been with weirdos. One didn't stop talking about his mum the whole time and still lived with her. The fact that he was a Professor of Latin at the University of Amsterdam was beside the point. Noor had been scared off after being invited back to his small house to find his mother sitting in the living room drinking a cup of coffee.

The other date was with a middle-aged man who was actually very nice. However, he mentioned during the date and subsequent emails that he had a fetish for fat women. She quickly became fed up with him, because he couldn't stop going on about how much he liked her big arms and double chin. He also made her upset and annoyed so she reported him to the website and cut off contact. Clever and normal - was that too much to ask for? She hadn't had sex for seven years. This wasn't the main reason to find a partner but she did want children at some point.

As time passed, Noor was worried that she would never find Mr. Right. Therefore, until one of these websites would come up with the perfect guy for her, she would occupy herself by defending the next best thing to Mr. Right. Noor hoped that one day, when this whole case was over, she could tell Arnaud that she was the blogger who had been trying to help him all this time. Maybe he would be annoyed that she had not told him this in the first place and take offence that he had been tricked. Maybe Arnaud would grab Noor in his arms and ask her to marry him. She pondered over these possibilities. Whatever the outcome, this was a long time away from happening as the Magpie was still on the loose.

She sat in her very baggy white and red pajamas, a present from her parents last Christmas. Noor wondered whether she was going to reply to all the "Congratulations" messages to Happy Single on the blog. She even had a couple of messages that were quite flirty, hinting that they wished their girlfriends were as clever as Happy Single. Noor thought these were nice compliments but messages that she was not going to respond to.

Noor was quite distracted sitting in front of her computer. She had one eye on the blog and the other on dating sites. She was very excited as she had two new potential matches on eHarmony. This was unusual for her as she had put such detailed requirements on what she was looking for. She had started to believe that it was impossible for her to find a suitable match anymore and was considering making her filters more flexible. All the same, she had two matches. Now she was glad that she hadn't changed anything. As she sat there with a big shy grin on her face, Noor didn't know what to do first. Read though the match responses and send them replies or start responding to some of the emails she had received on the blog. Decisions, decisions…

After a few minutes of silent thought, Noor decided that she was going to reply to all the emails on the blog tomorrow. She needed time to sift through all the responses and answer them properly. Noor took the blog and her role very seriously. She was pleased to get so many compliments, but at the same time, she wanted to make sure that she didn't get carried away with them and forget the real reason why she was involved in this blog. She was there to support Arnaud, and help him catch the killer. Anyway, she liked replying to questions and comments and now she had something to look forward to tomorrow. She was never 'in demand' and it was time to make the most of it.

Noor decided that she was going to wait until tomorrow as well to check out the two messages on eHarmony. She was very excited to look at them but knew that she wouldn't be able to stop herself from replying to both immediately. This was never a good move, as she didn't want to come across too keen. She would also need some time to read descriptions of the men in detail, to see if they were for real or time wasters. This process couldn't be rushed. For once, people would have to wait for her. She giggled to herself and smiled. Excitement filled her completely. Noor liked the novel feeling of being wanted.

Noor stared at her blank computer screen, in deep thought. She could see her fat face as a dark reflection on the monitor. Her hair was uncombed and greasy and definitely needed a wash. She would hopefully see Arnaud at the Twee Zwaantjes tonight and wanted to look her best. She had a lot to get done before she left for her shift in the supermarket. Noor needed to take a shower, get dressed, have some breakfast, and make her way to work; all in under an hour. She stood up with a smile on her face and headed for the bathroom.

* * *

11:00 a.m.

Arnaud arrived at the police station and was met by a flood of press and news cameras blocking the front entrance. It was public knowledge that this was the building that housed the command center for Arnaud and his team in the hunt for the Magpie. It wasn't public knowledge, however, that there was a side entrance into the building, which opened via an automatic sliding door. Police cars could go in and park this way. It was also Arnaud's method of sneaking into the building undetected. Arnaud didn't fancy answering questions right now, especially as he had to do a full report and interview later today. He put his head down and pulled back on the moped's throttle, taking a wide berth around the crowd and speeding up into the Emmastraat. He had a small gadget attached to his keys. When he pressed the button the sliding doors on the side of the police station opened. Arnaud drove in quickly and parked his moped next to some police cars.

Skipping off his moped and briskly walking up the spiral staircase, Arnaud made his way to the second floor and then strode down the long hallway to his office. As he got close to the door, he could see the back of his boss, Dijkstra, through the glass window who was standing talking to Friso and the rest of the team. Had they found the body? What was Dijkstra doing in there? Was he planning to get rid of Arnaud? He didn't really think that but Arnaud was suddenly feeling a bit paranoid and insecure. It wasn't often that Dijkstra would talk with the rest of the team without him there. He took a deep breath and opened the door, banging Dijkstra's back in the process, and making him jump.

"Morning guys!" said Arnaud, as he walked passed Dijkstra towards his own desk. He took his coat off before sitting down on top of his desk and facing the rest of the team.

Friso and the two young detectives looked over at Arnaud and spoke in unison, "Happy Birthday, Arnaud!"

Arnaud managed to pull out a smile.

"Oh, it's your birthday." said Dijkstra, a little surprised. "Well, congratulations, Arnaud! Friso and the guys have been explaining to me the positions of the search teams for today, as well where we plan to deploy the extra undercover police in and around Amsterdam over the coming month. A very thorough job, I must say." It was clear that Dijkstra was running out of things to say.

"So, what is the plan for the rest of the day?" continued Dijkstra.

He wanted it to seem like he had some authority over the team even if he and the rest of them knew that this wasn't the case.

"We wait." replied Arnaud. "We just wait."

"Well, okay guys." He turned and walked towards the exit door from the large office. Before he left the room, he spoke once more. "Keep up the good work and please keep me informed."

Arnaud broke the silence. "So, as it is my birthday, I'm going to make tea and coffee."

The team looked even more surprised as Arnaud brought a small box from under his desk and continued to speak. "And I have the cake as well."

This even took Friso back as he knew Arnaud was a fair guy but this joyful generosity that was going on right now was definitely out of character.

As he distributed the cake to his team, Arnaud spoke up once more. "So, no news?" Arnaud knew that he was really answering his own question, but said it anyway as he wanted to hear what the guys had to say.

Friso was the first to reply. "No news, just a lot of calls from the press asking for updates."

Robin switched on his computer and then began to speak. "There has been quite a lot of chatter on the blog, Arnaud."

Arnuad looked over at Robin's screen as the young detective continued speaking.

"There has been a lot of praise for Happy Single for getting the story right so far. The website is getting more and more hits and even the press is writing about Happy Single. They are starting to discuss the blogger's views around the Magpie having an accomplice."

There were a few moments of silence and then Friso spoke next, as if on behalf of Arnaud.

"But we can't make that assumption, guys. We must not assume that there are two killers. We just don't know that and we don't have any proof. Anyway, we have seen the killer on CCTV. We know who she is and she seems to work alone. There is no sign of an accomplice."

Everyone was staring at Friso. Arnaud thought about what Friso had said and acknowledged his opinion. Robin nodded his head in acknowledgement to Friso's comments and then continued speaking.

"Well, the blog and the press have put us in their 'good books' for now as they feel that we are making headway with the case."

"Guys, be clear about one thing. We aren't really making much headway. We just have some breathing space and we should make the most of this time while the press is off our backs!"

Everyone nodded, all in deep thought but realizing that their bosses' planned course of action was the right one. Arnaud continued talking.

"Has anyone spoken to the twin or the friend today?"

"No boss." came the reply from all three of them.

"Poor guys. They must be feeling like shit. All the same, we can't allow the press to get to them." continued Arnaud.

"Agreed." replied Friso, who then drank the whole cup of tea in two gulps. He stood up and grabbed his jacket off the back of his chair.

"I'm going to pick them up. Thanks for the cake, Arnaud. See you guys in a little while."

With that, Friso left.

* * *

4:00 p.m.

Fleur sat on the sofa pretending to read an article in her Hello magazine. The magazine was shaking, caused by Fleur's unsettled, nervous hands. She was trying anything to avoid having eye contact with Roos. She was scaring Fleur by darting around the house like a neurotic housewife, searching for something to clean. Roos was on a mission, scurrying from room to room with a large black plastic bin liner in one of her hands. She was throwing anything that could be associated with Jade into the bag, whether it was a picture, an item of clothing, or even something that they had bought together for the house. You could see by the mad focus in her eyes and the muscles in her jaw line, highlighting her clenched teeth, that she had one thing that she wanted do today. She was desperate to get rid of anything to do with Jade, and wipe her ex completely out of her life.

It was officially over between them and the fight that took place two days earlier had been the final straw. It had gone on for over an hour and what had begun with shouting and name calling, had ended with hair pulling, punching, scratching, and biting. They had always had a futile and passionate relationship but knowing that it was really over gave them the opportunity to show their growing frustration and even hatred for one another. Fleur was so happy that she had left the house that night as she wouldn't have been able to witness such a cat fight. Looking at the scratches and bruises on Roos' arms and face was bad enough, and made her cringe.

Fleur needed to work out what she was going to do now. If she stayed in the house with Roos, then she would have to put up with her being a nightmare for the next six months. As Roos frantically cleaned the living room, Fleur studied her injuries. She had a large scratch on her left cheek that was so bad that it might even scar. Her bottom lip was cut and swollen, probably from a straight punch thrown by Jade. Her bob, which was normally immaculate, had an uneven side to it. Her left forearm was bruised and very blue, and her right hand was covered in fresh scratches, caused by Jade's long fingernails. Fleur swallowed deeply, as she tried to picture the fight and the damage that they had inflicted on each other. Both girls were fit and this coupled with their angry tempers was a bad mix. She could only imagine what Jade must be looking like right now. She was probably as beaten up as Roos. Fleur would let the dust settle for a day or two and then call Jade to check on her.

Fleur held her breath for a second as Roos stopped in her tracks, closed her eyes, and reached for her cell phone that was in her jean pocket. Dropping the bin bag on the floor, Roos searched for a telephone number, bringing the small screen of the phone closer to her face. Having dialed it, Roos closed her eyes once more and put the phone to her ear. As she waited for someone to answer, Roos bit on her fingernails. Surely, she wasn't calling Jade, Fleur thought to herself nervously and then she breathed a sigh of relief, as Roos spoke out.

"Oh, hi, it's Roos." There was silence.

"Hi, it's Roos." she said excitedly again, speaking a hundred miles an hour. There was another moment of silence and then Roos continued talking.

"Yes, hi Jan. I was wondering of you could come around later and clean the house."

Fleur thought that Roos had really gone crazy. The house was already immaculate. She had been cleaning all day and Jan had been to their apartment just two days ago! There was absolutely nothing for Jan to do. Psychologically, Roos must have needed someone else to clean up any last signs of Jade. Fleur was getting scared of her mad flat-mate, as she spoke into the phone once more.

"Yes, today please. It has to be today, Jan. Errm, that is if you have time."

She was almost begging him to come over, as a tone of desperation came through in her voice. Jan being there was clearly important for Roos. Roos opened her eyes for a second as she listened to Jan's response. She then focused in on Fleur sitting on the sofa, who very quickly switched her focus back to the magazine that she was pretending to read. Fleur carefully took a sneak glance over at her flat-mate, who was now looking at her watch. She then started speaking to Jan again.

"Okay Jan. That works. Tomorrow morning at ten. See you then."

Roos pressed a button on her phone to end the call and then pushed it down into the front pocket of her jeans. She closed her eyes once more and swept her tidy hair back off of her face. She had sweat on her forehead, probably from all the cleaning that she had been doing today. She then opened her eyes, turned around and left the living room, heading upstairs to her bedroom. Fleur was relieved to have a moment alone.

Roos stood at the entrance to her bedroom and quickly scanned the inside of the room. It was, as always, spotless, but just a little emptier than normal. She had already taken down pictures of Jade, and thrown them, along with all her clothes into the bin liner and two sports bags that belonged to her ex. These bags lay by the bedroom door. She had even cleared out the big tray of jewelry that sat on the desk next to the double bed. All that remained was her earrings, bangles, and necklaces, neatly laid out on display, on one side of the tray. Her side. Roos wanted it all gone as soon as possible and she was planning to ask either Fleur or Jan to drop it off at wherever Jade was staying. The instructions were to be very clear; never come back to the house again.

Roos closed her bedroom door and lay down on the bed for a second next to a neatly folded pile of laundry. She thought to herself that she needed to put the fresh-smelling clothes away in her drawers but that could wait for a few moments to be done. She wanted to think for a second, while she was alone. Roos could feel her heartbeat slowing down as she began to relax a little. Tiredness swept over her. What had gone wrong between her and Jade? Why did she wind her up so much and make her so jealous? Did she do it on purpose? She knew in heart that it was over between them but did Jade really not have any feelings for her anymore? Roos' eyes began to well up as the reality dawned on her that she may not see her ever again. Was this all her own doing?

She immediately wiped away a couple of tears that ran down her cheek, smudging the faint blusher that she had put on this morning. Roos was pleased that she hadn't cried in front of Fleur. She didn't want her to see her emotional. She knew that Fleur was still friendly with Jade and she dreaded the thought of her ex finding out that she was sad. As she lay there on her bed, she felt angry and resentment towards Jade again. Roos began to think that the best thing for her to do was to meet another girl, even if it was just for a one-night stand. She would love to bring a girl back home and have Fleur witness this. The thought of Jade knowing that she had met someone would surely anger her. If nothing else, it would give the impression that Roos was definitely over her relationship. Maybe she should try and meet a guy? That would probably be easier and would definitely mess with Jade's head if she ever knew about this. Roos would make sure that she found out through Fleur.

Roos bit her nails aggressively as she devised a plan. It was clear that she was not over Jade at all. How could she be if all she could do was think about her, and think of ways to upset her and make her jealous? Maybe it was actually Jade who was already over her! After all, she was a lot more outgoing. She was fully aware of the fact that Jade could pick up men or women very easily. Maybe she was doing that right now? Roos was getting angry again as she dwelled on her jealous thoughts. She continued biting the nail on her index finger, which was almost gone, and was now bleeding. Perhaps Jade was in bed with another girl at this very moment. Someone who was prettier than her and that Jade had really fancied. They would probably be kissing and cuddling, laughing and having fun. Her blood began to boil again. She bolted upright and jumped off the bed making her way over to the bathroom.

Roos' heart pounded as she walked towards the mirror. She could see her tired angry face as a reflection. Her eyes were bloodshot and looked like they were about to explode. Roos didn't really like her own looks at the best of times and right now she couldn't stand her reflection. As she stared back at herself, she thought that her unattractive features would make it difficult for her to meet another girl. This was all Jade's fault, she cursed. Jade had upset her. Jade had made her tired and exhausted. Jade had bruised, cut, and scratched her face. How she wished that she could inflict more pain on Jade. She wanted to hurt her and damage her ex's looks. Scarring her would prevent her from meeting other women. She dreaded the thought of Jade getting another girlfriend, another sexual partner.

Roos licked her swollen bottom lip and wished that she could hurt Jade. Even though she knew that she still had feelings for her, Roos realized that their relationship was over for good. She needed to move on and hatred was a good emotion for her to have in her head right now. Even though she was so angry, she began to come to her senses and realize that actually she couldn't do anything to harm Jade even if she wanted to. She had a job as a nurse and she needed to keep her life in order. Without her job, she couldn't live her life or pay for the mortgage on her house. If anything happened to Jade, everyone would blame her for it. She would be the obvious suspect; the jealous ex-girlfriend.

Damn it, she was so helpless and alone. Jade had ruined her life. Roos let out a large scream of frustration and anger, and punched the bathroom mirror with her right fist clenched. Putting a crack down the middle of the mirror, she let out a muffled yelp as pain spread all over her right hand that was now swelling up and throbbing. Two of her boney knuckles began bleeding. With her left hand, Roos turned on the cold water and placed her right-hand underneath it. She began sobbing as the pain got worse. A small stream of blood disappeared with a whirlpool of water into the plug hole. Roos shook her head and splashed some cold water from the tap over her face. What was she thinking? She couldn't do anything to Jade, even if she wanted to. She realized that she was thinking crazy thoughts. She needed to get outside and take her jealous mind off of her ex.

She assessed the damage to her shaking hand. She was sure that she hadn't broken any bones but it would be badly bruised for a few weeks. Bringing her fist to her lips she licked the seeping blood off the cut knuckles and closed her eyes in an attempt to contain the pain. She thought about Jade once more. She had made her do this. It was Jade's fault that she had a damaged hand and that she was so unhappy. She would get her back for all the pain that she had caused her both mentally and physically. But Roos would have to plan this carefully. She didn't know yet how she would do it but she knew she would get revenge. As Roos stared back at herself in the cracked mirror, she spoke softly under her breath.

"That stupid bitch is not going to do this to me and get away with it. Nobody is going to do this to me!"

Her voice sounded both crazy, as well as, calculated. The thought of coming out of this mess on top and making Jade pay for it, calmed Roos down. She began to feel a bit better as she rearranged her hair with her undamaged left hand. Second by second, she became more composed. She thought about what she was going to do this evening while putting a plaster over her cut knuckles. Feeling relaxed, Roos took a deep breath and then decided to go back downstairs. As she walked into the living room, she could see that Fleur had gone out. Roos thought that she must have been scared and fled after hearing the glass breaking upstairs and her scream. She hoped that Fleur hadn't left for good. Perhaps she was frightened and fed up of her ranting and hysterical behavior?

Even though she felt that Fleur would have to just accept that she was highly-strung and a bit mad, she was worried that she had gone too far this time. Roos went into Fleur's bedroom to make sure that she wasn't there. As usual, the room was a complete mess with clothes, underwear, and make up all over the place. It annoyed Roos that Fleur was always so messy though she was pleased to see that she hadn't taken her stuff and moved out. She must have gone for a walk, thought Roos, which was okay and to be expected.

* * *

9:45 p.m.

Sitting on his own, Arnaud drank his sixth beer in De Twee Zwaantjes. Looking at his watch, he was surprised that Friso hadn't called him yet. They had clearly not found the body. It was very dark outside and unless a corpse was dumped in a public place, it was unlikely that they would find it tonight. There was, of course, the possibility that the body wouldn't be dumped today. Maybe the Magpie was playing with Arnaud on his birthday. Arnaud thought about this and concluded that it was plausible. If this was the case, then she would be sending him a message. The Magpie was in complete control. She decided when to strike and when to release the next victim. The work of a seemingly evil magician.

Arnaud was a little drunk now and his mind was becoming fuzzy. When he drank too much he would start to think deep and dark thoughts; views that didn't necessarily make sense. However, once every now and again, it was in these periods of alcoholic dozing and despair that he would come up with a good idea; something that hadn't crossed his mind before. Arnaud was pulled out of his trance by a soft pat on the shoulder from Noor. He looked back at her with his eyes half shut. She asked him if he wanted another drink and he nodded with a small smile. He knew that he wouldn't be paying for these beers on his birthday. Whilst he was tired and preoccupied, waiting on the expectant phone call from Friso, he wanted to make the most of another free drink.

As Noor looked down at Arnaud, he thought that she hadn't been her usual self this evening. Normally she doted on him and he would have expected her to be over the top sweet today. This was, however, not the case. Noor appeared distracted, as if she had something else on her mind. Arnaud couldn't think what this could possibly be. He knew that she liked reading, listening, comforting him, and working between the café and the supermarket. She didn't have anything else to do with her time, thought Arnaud.

Unbeknown to him, however, she had a lot going on in her life right now and she was very distracted. Noor was filled with excitement, as she contemplated what she was going to do first when she had finished her shift. Was she going to go on the blog and reply to the numerous emails that she had received? She would have to respond to all the compliments, as well as, offer new commentary surrounding the murder hunt and the impending body drop. She, of course, enjoyed the role she had made for herself on the blog and felt a lot of responsibility for it. She took time preparing the responses in detail. Her other option was to go home and log onto the dating websites. She had butterflies in her stomach, thinking about who had tried to connect with her as a match and potential date. This was such a rarity and she couldn't wait to find out more.

Hopefully, if she liked what she saw on eHarmony she could arrange a skype session. She didn't want to get ahead of herself but she was really looking forward to checking her matches. She still adored Arnaud but she knew she had to keep looking elsewhere for a guy. This middle-aged stressed detective was so sweet, however, she couldn't wait forever and realized that he probably didn't even know how much she actually liked him.

Arnaud looked up at Noor with a tired smile and shook his head and whispered, "Thank you." Noor could see that Arnaud was pretty drunk now. She smiled back and then picked up some empty glasses and headed back towards the bar. As she walked away, he realized that she had made an effort to dress up tonight, probably for his birthday. Whilst he felt a little guilty for not noticing earlier and commenting on her appearance his mind was already elsewhere. This would be his last drink. He was fully aware that the phone could ring any minute and he would be urgently requested to come to some spot in and around Amsterdam as soon as possible. He would need to have his wits about him if he had to race off on his moped.

Arnaud's mood during the day had fallen into one of depression as this waiting game had come to the inevitable outcome. Even though there was still the smallest possibility that the missing twin had gone on an unannounced holiday with this girl he had just met, the likelihood was that the body would be dumped this evening. The best Arnaud could really hope for was that the Magpie would be caught while dumping the body. This was now unlikely to happen as it was now pitch dark outside. There were more undercover cops on the streets, however, the Magpie was almost certainly not going to mess up. She was too professional.

Arnaud changed his mind and decided to skip the final beer. He stood up from the table and waved goodbye to Noor. As he made his way to the exit door, he thought to himself that he would go home, sleep, and get the rest that he needed. He would leave both his phone and his pager on maximum volume so that he didn't miss the expected call from Friso.

The weather outside couldn't be any worse. It was extremely cold, windy, and raining. He could see the white funnel of warm air coming out of his mouth and nose as he breathed. Arnaud pulled the collar of his coat upwards as he walked quickly down the canal in the direction of his apartment. He wanted to get home as soon as possible.

He staggered into the living room and slumped down onto his favorite chair, drunk and out of breath. Arnaud flicked the switch of the old lamp that stood on the coffee table next to him. Also, sitting on the small table was half a bottle of gin. He started scratching his cheek as he toyed with the idea of having just one quick drink from the bottle. It was a battle for him to refrain from taking a swig, which made him realize what an alcohol problem he really had.

He would almost always have a few drinks when he got home at night. Tonight he couldn't, he was beginning to get very irritated and his hands were shaking. This internal fight was making him more depressed. How could he get rid of the heavy feeling of anxiety without having a couple of sips from the bottle? He had too much on his mind and wouldn't be able to get any sleep at all. He thought about what his life had ended up being. At forty-nine years old, he was divorced, unhealthy, and a stressed cigarette-smoking alcoholic. Whilst he had become a successful senior detective in the police force and often felt that he was doing something worthwhile for the Amsterdam community, it was at a huge cost. Arnaud was under a lot of pressure and scrutiny to catch this murderer, something he had failed to do so far. He had nothing in his life to be happy about, apart from his daughter, whom he didn't really know or see anymore.

Arnaud had tears in his eyes. He had been living this life alone for three years now. Why suddenly the tears, he thought to himself. Was it because of the fight he was having with himself not to reach for the bottle, or maybe it was the suspense of waiting for the phone to ring. He was also exhausted, and at 10:35 p.m., he dosed off into a deep sleep.

* * *

October 12

1:10 a.m.

Arnaud woke up with a jerk. He was curled up in a ball on the seat in his living room, still wearing the clothes from the night before and with his coat wrapped around his torso. He was surprised to see that he hadn't received any messages on either his phone or his pager. Both lay neatly next to him on the coffee table. He then began to think what had woken him up so suddenly. Unable to come up with an answer, he started to ponder over why they had not been able to find the dumped body yet. Was it a good thing or a bad thing? He tried to think straight but then got distracted by a small open window in the other room that kept banging in the wind. It was blowing a gale outside and he could hear the heavy rain beating against all the windows in his apartment.

Maybe the twin was still alive. What were Friso and the rest of the team doing now? Was the Magpie playing a game? What was her next move? No body had been found on his birthday. He drew comfort in this and drifted back to sleep quickly, without the need for a cigarette or a drink.

CHAPTER 15

October 13

Every newspaper in the Netherlands and every television channel was reporting the same thing. Yesterday, on October 12 at 10:20 a.m., the body of a young man was found dead at the bottom of a canal in the center of Amsterdam. Twenty-three year old, Floris Heidstra, was reported missing on October 8 by his identical twin brother, after apparently going out for drinks in Café Gruter that evening.

Floris' naked body was found at the bottom of the Browersgracht by the corner of the Willemstraat. He had a belt tied around his waist with weights attached to it. This allowed the corpse to sink and stay on the bottom of the canal. The cause of death was unknown at this stage.

There were no witnesses to the body being dumped and no confirmation regarding what time the victim was dropped into the canal, although it appears that it was only a few hours before the body was found. There were no markings on the corpse. The cause of death was yet to be determined. This murder was being linked to the serial killings of the Magpie and while the police had not yet confirmed this, it had all the signs of murder number ten of the year.

Police were asking for witnesses to come forward who were in or around the Café Gruter on the evening the victim disappeared and also if anyone saw anything unusual yesterday around the Browersgracht in the early hours of the morning.

The detectives running the murder hunt had also come with a new twist to the case by releasing some still shots of the suspect who they were now saying was a female. The Magpie was a girl!! Again, the police were asking witnesses to come forward who might recognize this female who they are saying was the same girl that was in the nightclub in September where the previous victim had disappeared.

CHAPTER 16

October 28

It was another day in the office for Arnaud. Another day with his team going through the year's events around the ten deaths that had taken place in Amsterdam. Another day trying to find any piece of evidence they may have overlooked in this case that was still haunting them. They would brainstorm on a daily basis but no new ideas were coming up. They had hit a wall. The more they looked at the old interviews with potential witnesses, the more Arnaud realized that they were getting nowhere. The Magpie had left no clues and couldn't be traced. Arnaud was feeling completely helpless in trying to solve this murder hunt and the stress and fatigue was showing. His team could see it and so could the press and the public.

Everyone realized that Arnaud and his team were no closer to catching her. Dijkstra, was still very supportive, keeping any heat from the management within the police force away from them. They were all in this together, along with the head of the Dutch police, the Mayor of Amsterdam, and the Prime Minister. They all needed the Magpie to be caught and the killings to stop, as much of the rest of the European news channels were now watching Holland and this case.

With lack of progress in the murder hunt, the team was getting frustrated and depressed. Arnaud in particular was feeling very low as he took complete responsibility for not catching the Magpie. He looked like he had aged dramatically in the last few weeks, resulting from lack of sleep, too much alcohol, and a cocktail of stress and depression. He constantly had bloodshot eyes and heavy bags under them. He had started taking more Xanax and sleeping pills, which was also not good for him. Friso and the rest of the team wished that they could make a breakthrough with the case, not just to get closer to catching the killer but also to help cheer up Arnaud. He desperately needed some good news to get him out of this rut.

There were three days until the new month, which meant three days to go before the Magpie would start selecting her next victim. It had been such a clear pattern throughout the whole year, and everyone knew this but it only added to the pressure on Arnaud.

Arnaud looked up from his desk at Friso and the rest of the team. He could see that Friso was busy typing up a new report from the two witnesses who had been in the Surprise Bar on the night that the September victim went missing. These two girls had recently come forward, claiming that they had seen a pretty girl in the toilet wearing a wig, who was putting on some bright red lipstick. The girl was apparently tall and slim, but the wig didn't give much away about her face. Even though these witnesses didn't really add any new evidence, the statements had to be written up.

Jim and Robin were sitting across from each other and playing cards to kill some time. Arnaud didn't mind them relaxing, as they worked so hard without much gratification.

"Guys, I'm going to take an early day, and go home to try and get some sleep." Arnaud told the rest of the team.

"Okay." replied Friso. "We will go through the old tapes from the Surprise Bar again and try and spot these two new witnesses in the club to see if we can get some fresh footage of her coming out of the toilets." They all knew whom Friso was referring to.

Friso got up from his desk and went over to the printer to pick up the witness statements, which he then gave to the young detectives. He spoke softly to them, explaining that he wanted them to read through the reports and then try and identify the two girls on the tapes. Jim and Robin both had glum expressions on their faces, as they knew that the rest of the day was going to be very mundane. They would have to watch this videotape again in slow motion, which they had viewed hundreds of times already. What new information could they possibly find that they hadn't spotted before? They were simply going through the motions and 'ticking boxes' yet again. Jim and Robin were completely done with watching the footage of both the spa and the Surprise Bar.

Arnaud had gone. He had been leaving the office early recently to get some rest. There had been nothing new. He used his usual exit from the police station around the side of the building to avoid any lurking reporters.

Arnaud got home and crashed on his sofa. He was mulling over the last comments that he had read on the blog today from Happy Single. The blogger was being quoted by the newspapers even more recently and was portrayed as the 'Online Detective'. Happy Single's most recent comments expressed that while the killer was a young lady, she was also a loner with an accomplice. The blogger was convinced that she must have a car with which she could easily transport the dead victims and dump their bodies. Happy Single also thought that the Magpie must have her own home or a private space where she could hide the body for three days, undress it and clean it.

The latest opinion of the blogger was that the killer must be using a drug to sedate or kill the victims. Otherwise, she surmised, there would be more scratches or markings on the bodies from fighting. Arnaud thought of that the most, and what the blogger had said made sense. Unfortunately, there was insufficient evidence to prove these points or even make these assumptions. As a detective, he had to go on facts and clear evidence, something which he had very little of at the moment.

Arnaud's personal view, which he shared with the rest of his team, was that the Magpie targeted and picked her male victims in dark discreet venues where she could seduce them without being noticed. She would then get them back to her house in the night and drug them or tie them up and then kill them. He agreed that in order to do this she must live alone or with an accomplice. However, when she was committing the murders, there was no sign of drugs in the systems of the dead victims. Arnaud was fully aware that the autopsies were carried out at least seventy-two hours after the victim had gone missing so it was possible that any sedative or drug that killed the men had washed out of their blood stream. There weren't any markings on the bodies from a blow or being tied up. This was the part of the investigation that Arnaud couldn't get comfortable around. He wasn't really sure about what had gone on.

Within twenty minutes, Arnaud was fast asleep on the sofa, fully dressed and snoring loudly. It was 3:45 p.m. on a grey afternoon in Amsterdam.

* * *

4:00 p.m.

Noor sat at home in her small living room, behind her desk with a shy smile spreading across her pudgy face. She was feeling very romantic and nervous at the same time, as she emailed back and forth with the guy who she had selected from the two matches that had come up on eHarmony. She hadn't met him yet but they had exchanged personal emails and were communicating via text messages too. They had also had spoken on the phone a few times, which had gone well in Noor's opinion. Anyway, she had plucked up the courage to ask him to meet with her, and he had agreed to do this, which was a real confidence booster for Noor. Obviously, he had a good feeling about the relationship as well. Unfortunately, he couldn't meet till November as he was travelling for work this month. She actually didn't mind this, as she wanted to lose a little weight before their date and also have enough time to get a makeover. She was a bit worried that he might not be attracted to her, even though they had exchanged photos.

Noor felt strongly that he must really like her for who she was. He wasn't in a rush to meet her, as often was the case with online dating, where the guys just wanted a sexual encounter. He seemed very happy to email, text, and chat for now, so they could get to know each other better. Jonathan Spyker was tall and slim, and quite plain looking with brown fair hair. He lived in Arnhem and worked as a sales representative for the Benelux region. That was why he had to travel a lot. Noor was happy with a plain-looking guy, and he seemed very kind and considerate. Most importantly for Noor was that he was caring and thoughtful, and interested in her life. This was everything that she had ever wanted from a guy.

It was a shame that they couldn't skype as Jonathan's laptop didn't have a webcam. It was also difficult for them to talk a lot on the phone because of his work and travel. Noor was happy for now with emails and texting. Jonathan had sent her a number of photos of himself, which she had enlarged and printed in color on A4 paper. As she looked up from her computer, she would stare directly at a mosaic of pictures of her man. She even had a couple of pictures stuck up on the wall next to her bed. They made her feel content.

Noor felt sorry for Jonathan, having such a hectic job in sales. She hoped that she could be a calming influence on him in the future, just like she had been for Arnaud. Jonathan was an only child and definitely seemed a bit lonely and quite shy like her. She didn't really understand how he could be in sales. Whilst he had sent her numerous pictures, she wanted more. Unfortunately, he wasn't on Facebook or MySpace like her. This made her realize how lucky she had been to find him on a dating website. Like Noor, it had transpired through their conversations that he had had only two sexual encounters. Unlike hers, however, they weren't one-night stands.

Jonathan had had two very serious relationships in his life. One had been with a girl at high school. They were together for two years. The second relationship was with a girl called Evelyn who he had met at his first job after University, seven years ago. They had worked together and had a relationship on and off for three and a half years. Noor was jealous of the fact that Jonathan had had two serious relationships. She was, however, pleased that he had been honest and told her all about his past. Noor was concerned that this most recent girlfriend was still trying to contact Jonathan. Whilst he had told his ex that he wasn't interested in her anymore, she was apparently keen to go out with him and rekindle their relationship. This made Noor anxious and she was keen to meet with Jonathan as soon as possible. She dreaded the thought of him getting back with this Evelyn.

Noor had made it clear that she wanted to see him soon and they had agreed to meet in November when he was done with his traveling and work commitments. At least if he was working hard, then his ex couldn't really bother him too much, thought Noor. In the meantime, she was committed to going on a strict detox and diet. She had never done this before and she was determined to stick to it. After all she had an end goal. She wanted Jonathan badly and would do whatever she could to get him.

* * *

8:00 p.m.

Jan had just received a text message from Mariana. She had requested Jan to pick her up immediately from her father's house, as she couldn't bare spending any more time with him. Jan thought to himself about how strained the conversation must have been between the father and daughter. He knew that Dr. Akkermans had planned this dinner with Mariana more than two weeks ago and he had asked their housekeeper, Rina, to prepare her favorite meal. From the ranting in Mariana's texts, Jan realized that she had had enough of his head-strong views and forth right opinions on everything, especially regarding her. She thought that her father was so pig-headed.

Jan got in the bakery van and headed for the center of Amsterdam. As he drove in the direction of the canals, he imagined the questioning and lecturing that Mariana must be getting from her father right now. Dr. Akkermans commented on everything that she did, from her future plans to her studies and weekly movements. He couldn't understand how, as a student, she could spend so much money, living in Amsterdam. What did she do with it all? He also always lectured her about not coming to see her wonderful old father more often, especially as they lived less than fifteen minutes apart.

As Mariana sat at the other end of the kitchen table from her doting father, she knew that until Jan arrived, she had nowhere to turn. Her father's tall imposing upper body leant over the oak table in her direction, supported by his long muscular arms that had acted as scaffolding under his huge chest. He was, as always, dressed immaculately in a perfectly pressed light blue business shirt and silver cufflinks, encrusted with orange gem stones. Mariana hadn't seen these before and couldn't stop staring at them. In fact, this proved to be a good way to take her mind off what her father was saying. Of course, she would never compliment her father but she couldn't help but admire his immaculate and classy dress sense. He always dressed elegantly, whether she was coming around or not, and he took such pride in his appearance. It was part of his intimidating persona, which Mariana hated so much.

The kitchen light was off, and various candles were lit and positioned on the table and surrounding shelves. Light flickered off the gold-rimmed spectacles that were balanced on the bridge of her father's large protruding nose. His face was sad right now, which she believed he could pull at the click of a finger; part of his mind games and also a useful expression that he had in his armory for court. He stared at Mariana with one silver bushy eyebrow raised, waiting for a response from his beautiful daughter.

Mariana couldn't turn or hide from him. She didn't have answers for her father either, and even if she did want to respond, she refused to show any reactions or emotions to him. Mariana really didn't think that she needed to justify her actions or lifestyle. He was her father and he should help her and provide support, especially financially, even if she had a lavish lifestyle for a student. After all, she was scarred by her mother's death. Indeed, this was the main reason why he always let it go in the end and gave her whatever she wanted.

Mariana could also put on an act, and while she had had enough of her father for today, she looked down at the table with a solemn face, her arms crossed in a defensive way. She had managed to secretly send Jan a few text messages under the table.

Jan hadn't bothered to change from his outfit that he wore in the bakery. He knew that when he got one of these messages of desperation from Mariana, he needed to go immediately. She detested these evenings at her father's house and he knew she appreciated him coming to her rescue, even if she never said so. He also knew that these random opportunities to see her and spend the night at her apartment were not that frequent so he wasn't going to miss out on this chance. As he drove on this familiar route from Badhoevedorp to Amsterdam, he tried to brush the flour off of his t-shirt and blue checkered trousers. He always wanted to look his best for her even if he was still wearing his baker's uniform.

Going as fast as possible along the dark roads, he had his windscreen wipers on full speed in an attempt to clear off the heavy rainfall. Jan desperately hoped that Mariana wasn't going to be too upset or angry. There was always the possibility that she would tell him that she didn't want him to stay the night, if she was in a really bad mood. Normally, however, after a bust up with her father they would have passionate sex and Mariana would do something that she very rarely did: ask Jan to cuddle with her. This almost never happened so he cherished these occasions. As he pulled up outside Dr. Akkermans' townhouse, he parked, but kept the engine running. Jan immediately sent Mariana a text to say that he was outside. Within seconds, the front door opened and out came Mariana, coat in hand, running down the stairs and into the passenger seat of the van.

"Just drive." was the first thing she said, without even looking at Jan.

He could hear immediately from her voice that she was distraught and angry. Mariana stared straight out of the front windscreen of the vehicle, knowing that her father would be peering at her from his house. Jan looked across at the tall, handsome figure that stood by the open door, hoping that he would get a wave of acknowledgement.

"Just fucking drive!" screamed Mariana. She was now staring straight at Jan, with fire in her eyes. Jan was used to her crazy outbursts, and so did the only thing that he could do in these situations, which was to follow orders. He sped off down the canal in the direction of Mariana's apartment.

Parking outside her building, they both ran towards the front door to avoid getting soaked by the winter rain. Mariana reached inside her bag to get the keys to open the front door. They quickly moved inside the apartment and Mariana headed briskly towards the bathroom, undressing as she walked. It was no surprise to Jan that she immediately turned on the shower and stepped into the cubicle. He had once dared to ask her why she always took a shower after visiting her father's house. Her reply was that his place was so dirty and dusty, but this was clearly not the real reason. It was probably because she detested her father so much that she felt that she needed to shower and wash away anything to do with him after arguing. Whatever the psychological explanation for this, her cleaning process did seem to work and begin to calm her down.

Walking out of the bathroom with a towel wrapped around her slim body and another towel curled up into a turban shape on her head, Mariana headed for the living room. Falling gracefully onto the sofa, she picked up the remote and turned on to the RTL5 channel.

"So, how was your day?" she asked Jan, continuing to focus on the television screen.

He was surprised that she spoke in a very relaxed tone. It didn't sound like she really cared but was just trying to make polite conversation.

Jan replied, "Fine, I've just been working at the bakery all day so I'm pretty tired."

Mariana cut him off short from finishing what he wanted to say. "I can see that."
She looked over at Jan who was still standing next to the sofa. She checked out all the flour that covered his clothes.

"You can take a shower if you want."

"Do you mind if I stay?" he asked timidly, not knowing how she was going to respond. "I have to clean Roos' apartment tomorrow morning, so it would make it easier for me if I could stay over."

"If you like." replied Mariana, not really interested in what he was saying or whether he would end up sleeping there or not. She remained focused on the television screen, so he decided to take a shower after all.

As Jan walked towards the bathroom, he heard Mariana speak up behind him.

"How are those crazy girls?"

He knew exactly who she was referring to as he always kept Mariana updated on the highlights of his week; visiting Roos' apartment to clean and seeing what were the latest goings on in this real-life soap opera. Mariana was also interested in their lives, probably because they were just as unusual as she was. Jan turned around to face Mariana but she was still staring at the television.

"Well, Jade has finally moved out and Roos is becoming crazier and more neurotic by the day. Their apartment is spotless but she doesn't stop cleaning it and wants me to do the same!"

Mariana interrupted him, and he could see that she had a smirk on her face. "So why is she asking you to go and clean the apartment then?"

"I don't know." replied Jan. "She is just obsessed about the apartment being clean all the time but there is really not much for me to do when I go there."

"Maybe she likes you." said Mariana

"She's a lesbian." replied Jan, stating the obvious but not sure why Mariana was saying this as she knew Roos' sexuality.

"I know, but maybe she wants to try a man now that she is single." It seemed to Jan like Mariana was just testing him and trying to push his buttons.

"I don't think so." he replied with a half-annoyed expression on his face. Mariana was staring straight at him to see how he was reacting to her questioning.

"Mmmm." said Mariana as she thought to herself. Jan was surprised how interested she was in these girls and their lives all of a sudden.

Mariana continued, "How is that other girl?"

"Fleur?"

"Yes, Fleur."

"Well, from what I can tell, I think she is getting really fed up in the apartment living alone with Roos."

Mariana interrupted him, "She is not a lesbian, is she?"

She was continuing along this route of either testing Jan or trying to wind him up. He wasn't sure which.

"Maybe she likes you?" said Mariana.

"I don't think so. Anyway, she is never really there so I don't see her that often." He looked up at Mariana, who had appeared to lose interest in this conversation and was watching television again.

"Why not? Where is she the rest of the time then?"

"She is a full-time student and has a night job working at Yab Yum." He cleared his throat and then continued, "It's a brothel."

Mariana was now staring back at him with an annoyed expression on her face.

"I know what Yab Yum is." Mariana continued with an angry tone, "How do you know that she works there?"

"I've just heard her talking on the phone and with her friends when they come around." Jan didn't know how she was going to react next.

"Well, I hope you don't listen to all my conversations." Mariana paused for a second and then continued, "I expect that she is very good in bed then. What do you think?"

Jan didn't respond and instead walked into the bathroom to take a shower. He didn't understand why she was trying to play games with him. As he washed himself down, he wondered what the rest of the night would entail. Would she be too pissed off about her dinner with her father that she wouldn't want to have sex? Was she going to continue questioning him about Roos and Fleur? He knew that she wasn't really jealous about Fleur and was just trying to wind him up and get a response out of him.

Sometimes he wished that she was genuinely jealous, because that would mean that she actually liked him. His love for Mariana was so deep and he fought with himself everyday not to show it. She knew that she had him just where she wanted him. His biggest fear was that she would let him go one day. However, being told that he could stay over was always a good sign that it wasn't going to happen anytime soon.

It seemed that in times of trouble she could rely on Jan and call him for help. There were not many people in that position, as she didn't allow people too close to her. Maybe she did really love him. He would never know. For now, he was content with the fact that he could sleep next to her for the night.

CHAPTER 17

October 28

11:00 p.m., Yab Yum

Fleur had just changed into a long, revealing see-through red dress at work. She wasn't supposed to be at Yab Yum this evening but had been called in at the last minute because three new clients had just booked a suite. They were investment bankers on business from New York and had requested five girls for the night. Kim, who was one of the other girls working tonight, came into the dressing room and said hello to Fleur. She was a twenty-four year old single mum and was so skinny that you would have never thought that she had had a baby. Kim explained to Fleur that she had been in the bar downstairs with these guys and they were big spenders as they had already drunk four bottles of vintage champagne. Fleur was pleased that the maître dee had called her up tonight to work as it was an opportunity to earn big bucks.

As she applied bright red gloss to her full lips, Fleur realized that if there were only three guys and five girls she wouldn't be expected to have as much sex as usual for a night working at the upmarket brothel. She was happy about this as she was tired and hoped that she could get away with doing some dirty dancing, a lot of flirting, and maybe just one blow job. Whatever the outcome, they had signed up for a whole night with all the 'bells and whistles' and had committed to spending a minimum of fifteen thousand euros. This allowed them, once they got the suite, to have as much to drink and eat as they wanted, as well as free cocaine, although this wasn't advertised, but rather known by word of mouth.

From her previous experiences with American men, Fleur saw them as quite conservative although very loud. They would talk a lot, do a few high-fives with their buddies, and then 'wham, bam, thank you, mam.' It would be over. As she stood up and checked herself out in the long mirror in the dressing room, Fleur sprayed a little perfume to both sides of her neck and on her dress. She had decided not to wear a wig tonight but instead put her hair up into a tight ponytail, which showed off her pretty face.

The other girls were now already on the fourth floor with the bankers so Fleur quickly put on her three-inch heels and headed for the elevator to take her upstairs. Her dress looked amazing. The bottom part flowed beautifully around her legs, while the top half was very tight, revealing all her sexy curves. The back of the dress was cut low so that you could see the muscles and spine press against the flesh as she walked. As you can imagine, it drew a lot of attention when she entered the suite on the fourth floor.

House music was blaring out loudly in the room and the four girls and the three clients were dancing with glasses in hand, spilling champagne all over the beige carpet as they jumped around. The men had their shirts open and it was very apparent that they were drunk. Loud, slurring words, groping, and kissing the girls every time they moved close to them. As they danced terribly around the room, Fleur observed that, unlike most American clients that she had met previously, these guys were in good shape. This was probably a function of their age, all of them being no older than thirty-five. They also fitted the stereotype: young investment bankers from New York, working hard, playing hard, and spending the rest of their time in the gym.

As was always the case when Fleur walked in the room, especially when she was late to the party, the clients stopped what they were doing and froze. Mouths wide open, all three of them stared at Fleur as she strode past them and made her way to the drinks cabinet to get a glass of champagne. The other girls didn't mind Fleur getting all this attention.

They were used to it, and in this instance, it gave them some breathing space as the men focused in on her.

Fleur leaned over the drinks table and the three young men glared at the back of her low-cut dress. They seemed hypnotized as they all homed in on the same thing. You could not only see the beautiful pink flesh of her back but also the start of a colorful tattoo at the bottom of her spine, and the mere glimpse of a tiny black thong, as well. Even the other girls thought Fleur was extremely sexy.

Amid the wolf whistles and 'wows', Fleur poured herself a glass of champagne. She noticed next to the flute glasses a small mound of cocaine and remnants of some lines that must have just been snorted up. These guys were not holding back, she thought to herself, and had clearly come for a party.

One of the men took his hands off of the young redheaded Polish girl that he had been dancing with and made an A-line for Fleur. The girl readjusted her dress and hair as the client walked away. This guy was of Italian decent as he had short dark hair and tanned skin. He was wearing fitted navy blue suit trousers and a brilliant white shirt that was wide open, revealing a muscular torso covered with a hairy chest. He still had a striped tie on, loosely hanging around his neck.

Fleur hadn't turned around yet but could sense him walking towards her and getting very close as she could now feel his breath on her back and neck. After a few seconds, he grabbed one of her bottom cheeks quite hard and Fleur immediately turned around to face him. In a sexy way, she took his hand off of her and then waived a finger in front of his face as if to say 'you naughty boy.' In reality she didn't appreciate his aggressive groping and needed to set the record straight.

"Now, now mister." said Fleur in a soft voice. "Not so fast. We have all night."

Fleur took a moment to check out the guy's appearance. Whilst he was good looking, his pupils were dilated, and his mouth was making a chewing motion, a clear sign of cocaine use. His breath stunk of alcohol and she could see that he wasn't smiling. Sensing that he was disappointed by her reaction, she took his hand and led him towards a circular water bed in the middle of the suite. As they walked, he kept trying to kiss her on the neck and grope her breasts. Even though he was very drunk, it hadn't taken him long to realize that she had a rather full pair. Fleur was able to resist his wandering hands by just walking a little faster.

They approached the round scarlet-covered bed and Fleur turned to face the drunk man, whose eyes were half closed and he had a big grin on his face.

"Ok big boy, what do you want?" said Fleur in a deep voice and pulling a sexy stare.

There was an awkward silence, as Fleur looked at the handsome young American who was not responding but just smiled even more, revealing a perfectly white set of bleached teeth. Perhaps he was going to fall asleep as soon as they lay on the bed, thought Fleur to herself. That would be a relief. He was, however, so wired from the cocaine, that this was probably unlikely. She turned her face to the side slightly as she waited for him to reply. She couldn't bear the stench of alcohol and cigar smoke on his breath.

The client raised one of his hands to Fleur's face and stroked her right cheek softly. He then began to speak in a controlled quiet voice.

"Whatever I fucking want, bitch."

Taking Fleur by surprise, he pushed her head with such force backwards as if he was doing a bench press in the gym. The strength of the man's shove made Fleur fall backwards onto the bed. All the breath flew from her lungs as she hadn't expected this reaction from the guy. Fleur's heart was beating extremely fast as she realized that she wasn't in control of the situation any longer. She wanted to try and roll off the bed but before she could sit up fully he had sprung on top of her forcing her to lie flat back down again.

The guy held her head down with both his hands by her ears and passionately kissed and bit at her neck. She realized very quickly that he was a strong, fit guy as she couldn't get out of his grip. They rolled from side to side as Fleur tried to wriggle out from underneath him but to no avail. She was getting quite frightened by his forceful behavior. The drunk man then moved himself into an upright position so that he was sitting on top of her belly. Fleur couldn't really feel his weight as they were lying on a waterbed that just buckled inwards with the extra weight.

"Playing hard to get, are we?" whispered the man with a crazed smile on his face.

He leant towards Fleur and tried to kiss her on the lips. She managed to move her head to the side, despite being wedged into a vice by his hands and arms. He then dug his tongue into her ear, which felt disgusting as he was slobbering. Fleur could feel real panic come over her and with this also came rage. She had never had to endure this type of aggressive behavior from a client at work before. She needed to react quickly before it got out of hand. She started kneeing him as hard as she could in the back. Her knees were boney, and whilst every impact hurt her, she also knew that it would be inflicting pain on the guy's spine and back muscles. After the third blow, she could see his face turn from one of sexual excitement to a grimace.

The man responded to the continual kneeing in his back by sitting upright on top of Fleur and then swinging his right hand downwards, slapping her hard and loud on the left side of her face. Fleur was stunned and in shock by this powerful blow and she lay there dizzy and paralyzed momentarily. She could taste blood flowing inside her mouth. He had clearly cut her lip. The client realized that Fleur was not fighting back and saw this as his chance to lean forward to try and kiss her. He grabbed both sides of Fleur's head again with his hands so that she couldn't resist and then stuck his extended dripping tongue into her mouth. She still couldn't move and as a consequence had to taste the mixture of cocaine, cigars, and alcohol on his saliva.

Fleur didn't know what to do, as she lay there underneath him helpless and in pain. She hoped that the other girls would see what was going on and sound the alarm for the doormen downstairs. Unfortunately, the music was turned up loud and everyone was too busy enjoying themselves to notice anything strange happening at the other end of the room.

As he continued snogging Fleur forcefully, he released his right hand from her hair and moved it down towards her navel, which he started stroking. His hand then moved lower and slipped inside her underwear. Fleur needed to react fast before he found her vagina and while he only had one hand holding her down. She had spent the last thirty seconds composing herself and working out her next move. She needed to take action now.

Fleur started groaning as if she was enjoying his touching and stroking. She moved her hands up to his head and started grabbing his hair and then his ears. He didn't stop her from doing this as he thought that she was responding to his caressing. When she had a firm grip on his hair with both hands, she started to kiss him back passionately. He let his guard go slightly and she saw her chance. She got hold of his bottom lip between her teeth and bit down hard until she could feel that she had gone all the way through it. The man couldn't move as she held tight onto his head with both hands. He screamed loudly and blood gushed from his mouth all over Fleur's face. She then let go of his head and he bolted upright, crying out in pain and shock. She had a few moments to calculate her next move as he moved his hands up to his mouth to assess the damage. His bottom lip was hanging off his face like a loose piece of cooked chicken skin.

His eyes were closed as he held onto his mouth with both hands shaking. Fleur leant forward and reached up to grab hold of his ears. She then pulled his head back down towards hers as hard and fast as she possibly could. As she yanked his head downwards, she made sure that his nose crunched directly onto her forehead. At impact, you could hear the bone crack in the man's nose and his skin split at the same time. She had achieved her goal of smashing the cartilage in his nose. More blood gushed down over her face. Fleur let go of his ears and he sat backwards, screaming in agony and covering his face with his blood-covered hands.

Fleur was completely calm and collected as she used a corner of a bedsheet to wipe the blood from her eyes so that she could see more clearly. She then kneed him in the back again and as he shunted forward she grabbed his balls through his trousers with her right hand, and yanked on them as hard as she could. The client was now in absolute agony as he shrieked like a young helpless child. When she let go, the man rolled off of Fleur and curled up on his side next to her on the bed, feeling his private parts. He was now crying loudly in pain.

Instead of getting up off the bed and running away for help, Fleur jumped on top of the guy and reached for his tie. He was so preoccupied covering his balls that she could easily tighten up the silk knot to the point that she could strangle him. As she pulled harder on the tie, she could see his face turning purple, and she could hear the man was now fighting for his breath. She knew that within ninety seconds he would be dead. However, she didn't want that for him and also not for her. After about ten seconds, she let go of her grip on the silk tie and got up off the man. He loosened the knot and breathed in deeply. As he gulped for air, he began crying again, pathetically, and more blood dripped out of his mouth. His face was a real mess, bloody and broken, with some flapping skin hanging off his mouth that used to be a bottom lip. He wouldn't forget this night in a hurry, thought Fleur to herself, with a small smile on her face.

Getting her breath back, Fleur stood up over the man and leant forward to whisper into his ear. The man was still curled up in a bloody ball.

"So, did you get what you fucking wanted?"

She didn't wait for an answer, as she knew that there wasn't going to be one. Instead, Fleur turned and walked away from the bed and towards the drinks cabinet where there was a service bell and a panic button for times like this, although it was a bit late on this occasion. She could see that her four colleagues and the other two clients were now standing up in the corner of the room staring at her with grief-stricken faces. All of them seemed to be in shock at what they had just witnessed. As the injured client screamed loudly, they all turned their focus over to him. Their faces looked stunned and their eyes and mouths were wide open.

The other girls didn't know whether to feel sorry for Fleur or the guy, as both were covered in blood and it wasn't clear who was injured. The client's two colleagues also began sobbing as they were in shock and clearly hadn't witnessed anything like this before. In the back of their minds they were worried about what the repercussions of this nightmare would be. If this got back to their bosses it would definitely be career-ending for them. They also didn't know what was going to happen next, as Fleur pressed a small button on the wall, which didn't make a ringing noise and was definitely not the service bell. They began to panic as they imagined some enormous doormen busting into the room momentarily to clear this mess up and kick their arses. Everyone's focus was back on Fleur as she ran her blood-soaked hands through her hair and then straightened her dress. She checked out her body and arms as she leant against the drinks cabinet. Fortunately, she didn't have any big scratches although her wrists were sore from being held tightly and would probably be bruised tomorrow. The onlooking crowd was amazed at how composed Fleur appeared.

As she stood there waiting, Fleur thought to herself about what the outcome of these events would be. She knew that she couldn't get in trouble from what had just happened. The client started it and he was messed up from the alcohol and class A drugs. In court, he wouldn't stand a chance but it wouldn't even get that far. Even though Fleur had caused grievous bodily harm on the man, he would never press charges. He would definitely not want any public disclosure. His career would be ruined, as well as, any relationship he might have back home in America.

Fleur would just have to explain to her bosses at the club what had happened. Even though she was completely right, they wouldn't be too happy about the damage inflicted on the client, even if he deserved it. Their view would be that this was one customer who wouldn't be coming back. Nonetheless, Fleur was very popular at Yab Yum with the guests and they would want her to continue working.

She was sure that they would be surprised that she had actually inflicted a lot of damage to the guy's face, so she would just have to act extremely upset and distraught. Fleur would explain that she had luckily made a direct blow to the client's nose with her knee. His features were such a mess that they wouldn't be able to work out exactly how his face had been smashed to pieces.

Within sixty seconds, two giant doormen rushed into the room, with stern faces ready for action. Fleur wiped the blood off her face with some tissues and pretended to sob; trying to give the impression that she was very upset. The henchmen spent a few moments assessing the situation and then jumped on the three American guys, grabbing them by the hair and putting their hands behind their backs. It was clear they were not resisting being held by these two giants, who led them quickly out of the room via the fire exit. Fleur knew that this went down a stairwell out into a back street where these guys would be roughed up and be told not to come back to the establishment.

Fleur headed for the changing rooms where she jumped into the shower to wash all the dry blood off her body and out of her hair. She got dressed in her casual clothes and downed another glass of champagne, which she had taken from the suite. Fleur now needed to go to the manager's office to let him know what had happened. Van Beek liked her very much and would only feel sorry for her, and Fleur knew this. She put some cold water on her hands from the tap and wiped it on her eyes, to make it appear that she had just been crying.

The manager of Yab Yum believed everything that Fleur explained to him and gave her double pay for tonight. Her goal of making Van Beek feel sorry for her had worked perfectly. He also interviewed the other girls working that night and they all explained that the clients were very drunk and they hadn't really seen what had happened as they were at the other end of the room. Van Beek was comfortable with their account of the night's events and drew a line in the sand concerning this matter. He was always going to stand behind his girls whatever had happened.

Fleur left the building and kissed the doormen on her way out, thanking them for their help. She was looking very pretty and relaxed. She got in the limousine that was waiting outside on the canal for her and was driven home. As she lay back in the stretched vehicle, she checked her skin again for scratches and bruises. She had come out of the ordeal unscathed. Her forehead, however, was a little sore from the impact of the head butt. Fleur wondered to herself how this drunk client would have to explain his broken nose and severely damaged lip to his colleagues back in New York. This brought a smile on her pretty face as she headed home, seven hundred euros better off after a night's work.

She looked at her watch to see that it was 1:20 a.m. Fleur needed to go straight to bed as she had to attend the University in Utrecht first thing in the morning.

CHAPTER 18

October 29

9:05 a.m.

As always, Arnaud followed his usual pattern for waking up in the morning. He rolled over and reached for the half-filled plastic bottle of water that sat on the floor by his bed. He would then take a couple of swigs. This cleared his dry mouth and throat, polluted always by excessive drinking and smoking. He would then attempt to focus in on his wristwatch to see what the time was, and normally, see how late he was going to be for work. It was 9:05 a.m., so it wasn't so late, but he wouldn't get to office before ten today. As was always the case, he would be the last one on his team to make it in.

Arnaud felt relaxed this morning, probably because he didn't have a bad hangover. He had slept surprisingly well and woke up thinking that today was going to be quiet and non-eventful, especially since it was not November yet. It was unlikely that there would be a smash and grab or any sign of the Magpie. She had done her strike for October and was surely planning the next one.

Through his dusty old blinds, Arnaud could see frost on the window sill and a bright blue sky outside. He reached for his pager and mobile phone from the small coffee table next to his bed. He turned them both on and lay back against his pillow, waiting for them to come to life. What happened next sent his heart rate and mind into overdrive, as he had one almighty adrenaline rush. Both his pager and phone started a frantic chorus of vibrations and beeps, coming from missed calls and new text messages.

Before he picked them up, he tried to compose himself and stop his hands from shaking. He was worked up to a point where he felt that he could have a heart attack. He was short of breath as he attempted to stop himself hyperventilating, which had just started.

Arnaud took a deep breath and grabbed his phone and looked at the display. He had five missed calls and two text messages. He quickly clicked on the on the first message.

"Hi Arnaud. Please call asap." It was from Friso at 6:10 a.m.

He then managed to click on the second text that came in at 6:30 a.m. With his shaking index finger, he saw that Friso had messaged again

"Arnaud, please come to the office as soon as you get this message."

Arnaud felt nervous, excited, and panic-stricken all at the same time. He didn't need to listen to any of the voice messages, as he knew as much as he needed to at this point. The most important thing now was to get to the office as quickly as possible. First, however, he needed to try and calm himself and stop the heavy breathing and shaking. It wouldn't help him in any way and would make it dangerous for him to drive his moped. He also couldn't think straight in this current frame of mind.

He stood upright and put on the same clothes that he wore yesterday, which were lying in a pile at the end of his bed. He was now functioning on auto-pilot, getting ready to leave his apartment. He walked into the bathroom, went to the toilet, cleaned his teeth, and splashed cold water over his face. After taking a few sips of water from the bathroom tap, he headed downstairs.

Arnaud tried not to think too much about what Friso had to tell him. After all, he had no idea what information and clues the team had found. He was sure of one thing, however, that they couldn't have possibly caught the Magpie. He also didn't want to get too excited as he had been disappointed so many times in the past. The most important thing was that he should get to the office quickly and safely and then be ready to listen to a full debriefing from Friso. Arnaud put on his jacket and wrapped a scarf around his neck. He went outside to his moped with his keys jingling in his hand.

He arrived at the police station at 9:50 a.m. and skipped past the usual crowd of press by the front entrance and headed through the automatic doors on the side of the building. The reporters were there not to interview Arnaud anymore, as this angle was exhausted. It was more on the off chance that there might be some new news to report for the ten-strong crowd that camped outside the Konningineweg station. Arnaud left his keys in the moped and ran upstairs to second floor and along the narrow corridor to his office. As he approached the glass door, he could see that the two young detectives were standing behind Friso, who was sitting at his own desk, staring at his computer. Arnaud squinted through the glass window to get a clearer picture. They were all in fact focusing in on the same computer monitor.

Arnaud couldn't see Dijkstra and was pleased that Friso hadn't notified him or got him involved as of yet, whatever the news was. Even if they had caught the killer, Arnaud would be the first person that Friso told. He was loyal to Arnaud and valued his friendship, leadership, and commitment to this case, which the four of them had been living and breathing for the past ten months.

As Arnaud opened the door to their office, and headed towards them, his three colleagues looked up and spoke together with excited faces.

"Arnaud! Hi, Arnaud!"

He could sense that it really must be good news, whatever they were looking at on the computer screen. He could definitely sense a feeling of success and achievement in the room. The office was very light as bright rays seeped through the blinds on both sides. Arnaud could see dust particles glowing in the air, giving the office a magical feel to it.

He stood in front of Friso's desk for a second, admiring the three faces of his team members. They had worked so hard together this year, as well as fought, cried, dreamed, and argued; all with the same goal. Now they had faces baring big smiles, expressions of pride and finally some achievement. Arnaud was reading so much into their faces and current personas that he suddenly got worried that he was in a crazy dream. He came to his senses and quickly made his way round to the other side of Friso's desk where the three guys were positioned. He needed to stop the speculating. He needed facts.

Having gotten around to the same side of the desk as the rest of the team, Arnaud put one hand on each shoulder of Jim and Robin and spoke in a controlled manner.
"So, guys. Tell me."

The guys didn't speak at first but continued to focus on Friso's computer screen. This forced Arnaud to look closely at the black and white still frame on the monitor. This was clearly what the breakthrough was all about. Arnaud quickly realized that they were looking at a shot from inside the Surprise Bar and he concluded that it must be a freeze frame of the footage from the night that the Magpie struck in there. He immediately felt deflated, as they had been through this film so many times in the past and he assumed that there couldn't possibly be any new clues that they hadn't picked up on before.

Friso spoke up while still looking at the screen and controlling a mouse in his right hand that was playing around with the tool bar at the top of the monitor. Friso rewound the footage.

"So, we decided to go through the film one more time to check every individual who went in and out of the club." He took a deep breath and then continued.

"The goal was to see if the Magpie had changed her appearance before leaving the club. We know, after all, that she likes wigs and hats, as we have her on camera wearing both at different times."

"Okay." replied Arnaud, with a slightly impatient tone to his voice.

"We were brainstorming last night between the three of us and we thought that we do know that she likes to conceal herself, and she does this through head gear of some type. So, we decided to check out all the people once more as they left the Surprise Bar and focus in on those wearing hats and caps."

Arnaud didn't know where this was going but he was starting to feel depressed, as he couldn't see how any of this would result in any new leads. Friso could sense his boss' impatience so he continued, "Now, because of the poor quality of the CCTV picture, it's very difficult, and almost impossible to tick off every individual that was in the club that night, especially since quite a few of them left in a crowd at the end when the club closed."

The two young detectives were nodding in agreement with everything that Friso was saying. He clicked on the mouse again and fast-forwarded the footage and then paused it on a still black and white shot of a tall skinny guy coming out of the club.

Friso spoke up once more. "However, we managed to find this unusual male leaving the club at 12:41 a.m."

Arnaud studied the shot of the slim built guy leaving the club wearing jeans, trainers, a thin jacket, and a baseball cap low over his face, concealing his features. As he stared at the screen, Friso was busy pulling up another shot of the same guy entering the club at 9:32 p.m. He put the freeze frame up next to the existing shot so that it was easier to look at them both at the same time and compare. It was definitely the same guy but when he entered he wasn't wearing a baseball cap. Because of this, you had a clear view of his face and it was Thomas Deckers. Arnaud swallowed deeply as he drew his own conclusions from what he was looking at. The Magpie must have given him a cap in the club to conceal his identity when he was leaving and in doing so she was also hiding herself!

All three of the detectives turned around staring at Arnaud.

"Interesting." said Arnaud.

They had made a breakthrough. His hands were shaking once more as adrenalin pumped through his veins. Arnaud's heart and mind were racing as he had a lot of questions for Friso.

"So, did the cap actually come from her? Do you have any footage of her giving him the cap? There must be new footage to check in the club of the victim wearing the cap?"

Friso spoke up once more in a calm voice. "Just watch the film Arnaud and I will talk you through it, as we have been trying to answer these questions ourselves."

Arnaud relaxed a little, leant over Friso's shoulders now, breathing heavily but remaining transfixed on the computer screen. He was waiting for Friso to reveal his findings, which he did by beginning to tell a story of events.

With the mouse in his right hand, Friso moved it around and clicked away fanatically, and then he began to speak once again.

"Let's start from the beginning." The left-hand side of the screen remained focused on the victim and the right-hand side showed footage from the inside the club.

"We don't have any proof of where Thomas Deckers got the baseball cap, even if we believe that it came from the Magpie. We have checked out all clips of him together with the Magpie, and in all of these, he does not wear a cap. What we have found now, however, is the victim leaving the toilets at 11:57 p.m. wearing the cap. This was forty-four minutes before he exited the club."

Arnaud prompted Friso to zoom in on the guy's face leaving the toilets so that he could be sure for himself that it was really the victim. The close-up shot of his face, even though not particularly clear, confirmed this.

Friso began speaking again. "Where he got the cap from? We don't know. We don't even have clear footage of him entering the toilets as there is a queue of guys crowding around the entrance way and it's very difficult to pick him out. We can assume that it was from the Magpie."

"Of course, it's from the Magpie!" Butted in Arnaud impatiently.

"I agree." said Friso. "But we don't have proof."

"Mmmm." mumbled Arnaud, trying to calm himself down.

Friso spoke up. "We asked his friends if they knew if it was his own cap or if it belonged to one of them. They confirmed that he hadn't been wearing one that day. In fact, they also said that he wasn't the type to wear hats of any kind. This also confirms our beliefs that he must have got it in the club."

Arnaud interrupted once again, "Well, we do know that she likes to conceal herself and cover her tracks, so that cap must have come from the Magpie!"

"I agree Arnaud, but we still need to prove that, and at the moment, we don't have the footage."

"I know." replied Arnaud, running both his hands through his thick unwashed curly hair. He was clearly frustrated.

"We are in the process of calling back the witnesses we have on file, from the Surprise Bar that night, to see if any of them can recall anything about the victim and if they saw him wearing the baseball cap. It would be great if someone had been in the toilets when he put the cap on but we don't expect anything to come from this." said Friso.

Arnaud was looking more and more despondent, so Friso spoke up once more.

"Now, we do have another piece of good news and this is regarding the Magpie."

All three were staring at Arnaud with smiles on their faces.

"Okay guys, what is it? Jesus, tell me!" Arnaud was on edge, as he didn't like waiting and didn't have time for games.

Friso turned back to the screen and clicked on the mouse again.

"Okay, here she is leaving the club."

Arnaud focused in on the screen and Friso zoomed in on the black and white picture.

"She's not wearing a wig! How do you know it is her, Friso?" said Arnaud with a raised voice.

This girl in the picture, leaving the club, had her hair up in a knot on the top of her head. You would expect that you could get a better picture of her face but she was very wary of where the CCTV must have been as she was turning her face the other way. That in itself made Arnaud think that this was the Magpie but he needed more proof. You could also see from the freeze frame that she was walking closely behind the victim as he exited the Surprise Bar with the cap on. The girl in the picture was careful not to hold his hand but stayed very close to him as they walked out. Arnaud knew that this must be the Magpie.

Arnaud spoke again, "Come on. What proof do you have that it's her?"

Friso didn't reply but played around with his mouse, and pulled up a second freeze frame, which he positioned next to the girl and the victim exiting the club. This new black and white picture was of the Magpie in the club and talking to Thomas on the dance floor. It was easy to make out that in both pictures the girl was wearing the same outfit, tight trousers, a sexy jacket, and a pair of black high heels. This confirmed that the photo of the female leaving the club was in fact the Magpie.

Arnaud noticed that in the left-hand picture, the Magpie didn't seem to be looking at the victim as they stood chatting and dancing in the club. He could see that the walls surrounding the dance floor were mirrored, so he assumed that she was probably just checking herself out. Arnaud admired her slender neck that wasn't covered on one side by the long wig. You could also see her immaculate jaw line from a side view. That was about as much as you could see of her facial features from this picture on the dance floor. It didn't help that the picture was in black and white, but this was definitely their girl, as she was in seduction mode in the club, working on her next victim.

In the right-hand freeze frame, the same sexy female, slim but also curvaceous, had done an excellent job of concealing herself from the cameras. Hiding behind the long frame of Thomas Deckers and keeping her head down, she had followed him out of the club without being noticed. Again, the same beautiful neck and side profile of her facial bone structure was slightly visible, but that was about it. Her hair was bound tightly up in a small knot, making it difficult to know what her actual haircut was like. It was definitely her though as she was wearing the same skinny jeans and high heels as the girl inside the club. She had just got rid of the long thick party wig. This was very smart, thought Arnaud to himself. Despite all of this it was still impossible to get a clear picture of her face. She was too clever and wary to be caught on camera.

Friso zoomed in as much as he could on the two head-shots of the Magpie, without distorting the pictures, and clicked on his mouse in order to print them out. He had the killer on two pieces of A4 paper. Friso pinned them up on the back wall where they had all their other clues dotted over the map of Amsterdam.

"Well done, guys!" Arnaud spoke out, impressed with the findings. They could see that Arnaud was lost in thought. He was trying to work out what to make of all of this. He looked a little confused from the new footage that they had as what it showed them was that the Magpie did leave the club through the front entrance with the victim, and that the victim had covered his appearance with this cap, which they believed but couldn't prove yet, had been given to him by the killer.

Friso was the next one to speak. "Well, we are going to take these pictures of the Magpie to the doormen of the Surprise Bar and also to the witnesses from that night who we have spoken to already. Hopefully, these head-shots will jog someone's memory and help us find a further clue. I also think we should go through the footage once more to see if there is any sign of this baseball cap being worn or carried about by anyone else in the club that night."

"Well, good work guys!" Arnaud said once more, looking slightly distracted. "I want to think about things and try and work out if we are missing anything."

The other detectives could see that Arnaud had something on his mind, but didn't know what. It was times like this that it was best not to bother Arnaud with questions and let him just think. He was most productive after new findings, as he fed off of them and normally came up with new ideas.

Arnaud walked over to his desk and turned on his computer. He shouted over to Friso to send him the two freeze frames with close ups of the Magpie's head. When he received the photos in his email, he opened them up and clicked on the one of the Magpie inside the club. He zoomed out on the picture to check the area around her with the tall guy. Was he missing something? Why was she dancing with the victim but not looking at him? Why was she looking at herself in the mirrored wall? Why was she so obsessed with her own reflection? Was she planning her exit strategy? Was she looking at someone else? Maybe she was checking out the victim's friends or perhaps the barman? Arnaud looked at all the possible options and the other people that were also in the picture. He didn't know the answer to this, but believed that whatever or whoever was captivating the attention of the killer, was a big clue. He needed to go through the footage of the dance floor and study it more, as this he believed could be hiding another clue. He was missing something that was potentially very important. Arnaud now needed to do his own digging.

* * *

1:00 p.m.

Fleur sat at a small table in the Struik Bar on the Rozengracht. She was sipping on a glass of fresh mint tea and staring into space. She liked to daydream when she had some free time, which was almost never. In fact, she was trying to avoid eye contact with two twenty-something guy students who were sitting directly opposite her in the bar, whispering to each other and checking her out. She was used to this type of attention, and didn't mind it most of the time, but not now. She was distracted and needed to be alone, and had no time to flirt with these young men.

Fleur was wearing a high cut t-shirt and a thin hoody over the top of that. You could see naked flesh around her mid drift, and from behind, her tattoo crept out from above the tight blue jogging trousers that she had on. It was impossible not to notice her perfectly rounded back-side resting on the wooden stool. When she had arrived in the bar, five minutes earlier, she was wearing a full-length puffer jacket, but had taken it off as it was very warm inside the small café. Everyone stopped to check her out as she sat back down. It was early afternoon and Fleur had just gotten up, stiff and a little bruised from her ordeal at Yab Yum the night before. Normally, she would soak up the attention, but right now, she detested the male sex. She was also distracted as she was keeping a look out for Jade, who was meeting her for lunch at the bar.

Fleur hadn't seen Jade since she had moved out after the fight with Roos. She had received a text from her two days ago asking to meet up for a coffee or some lunch, so they had arranged to go to Struik today. Fleur wasn't really sure what Jade wanted as they weren't close. She expected it was to find out what Roos had been up to since she had left but she really didn't know what to expect, and this type of behavior wasn't like Jade. She was a 'closed book'; very secretive, not friendly at all, and never really spoke to you unless she wanted something. Jade didn't show her feelings or any kind of emotion.

As she mulled over what this rendezvous would entail, in walked the tall slim Amazonian figure of Jade. Fleur admired her olive skin that looked even darker in the low lighting of the bar. Her thick long hair was tied up in a high pony-tail, revealing a beautiful, quite masculine looking face. She appeared as moody as ever, pouting her full lips. Fleur imagined that she too had just woken up. She was wearing a long coat, knee length leather boots, a scarf, and some gloves. She was definitely dressed for the winter weather, but still managed to look sexy. The onlookers in the bar were having a 'field day' as a second pretty girl had just come in. Unlike Fleur, however, Jade couldn't care less about the attention from the beady eyes of the guys. Her exotic appearance and classy outfit made her not look Dutch at all, which was part of the intrigue surrounding Jade. She just ignored the attention completely.

Fleur raised her hand to signal to Jade where she was sitting but Jade had already spotted her and was gliding gracefully around the tightly crammed in tables and chairs, making her way smoothly and quickly over to Fleur. Before she sat down, Jade leant across the table to give Fleur three kisses. This was also unlike her old flat-mate. Maybe she had changed since she had moved out. If this was the case, it was definitely for the better, thought Fleur to herself. Fleur could smell a beautiful scent of perfume on Jade's neck as they kissed.

As Jade sat down, she even had a small smile on her face. "So how are you, Fleur?"

"Fine, thanks." replied Fleur, promptly.

"You look a little tired." observed Jade.

Fleur grabbed the back of her neck and rubbed the part that was aching from the fighting the night before and replied, "I had a tough night at work, you could say!"

Jade sort of nodded in acknowledgment, as she knew that Fleur worked at Yab Yum and had a fair idea about what sort of entertaining she needed to do for the clients.

"So, how are you?" asked Fleur, trying to break the immediate silence. They spoke over each other, by accident, as Jade also began to talk.

"Look, I am sorry about what happened and that I left you alone with her at the house after our fight."

Fleur thought it was strange that Jade couldn't bring herself to call Roos by her name. She must really hate her, she thought to herself.

Jade continued, "It must have been really tough for you having to live with us when we were arguing and fighting all the time. You were in the middle of it."

Fleur looked down, and replied, "No problem, these things happen."

"Well, I am sorry all the same. Are you going to continue living there?"

Fleur was surprised by Jade's apologies and questioning. For the eighteen months that they had known each other, Jade had never spoken this much to her. Did she want something from her or had she genuinely changed since she had moved out? Fleur was not sure and a bit taken back by this.

Fleur and Jade spent the next hour chatting about nothing in particular. Jade continued to apologize about leaving her in the house, and only referred to Roos as 'her' or 'she' and also as the 'crazy bitch'. Fleur thought this was not very nice, even if Roos was really crazy. As Jade talked and talked, it became apparent to Fleur that she had no emotion or feelings surrounding Roos and really didn't care or have second thoughts about the breakup, even though they were together for quite some time. Fleur didn't ask her if she was seeing anyone else but it was very obvious that she had firmly moved on.

Jade always dressed elegantly and today was no exception. Fleur checked her outfit as she listened to her monotone voice. She wore smart skintight Khaki pants, with a simple white blouse and a thin gold chain around her neck with a small crucifix hanging off it. Jade had some subtle make up on to accentuate her dark brown eyes, and a flesh colored lip-gloss to round and thicken her luscious lips.

After finishing her second cup of tea, Jade spoke up again, "So still no boyfriend for you, Fleur?"

"No, no!" snapped Fleur, with a smirk on her face. "I'm a man hater right now." Fleur chuckled and then continued, "But that's a long story!"

"Well, as long as you aren't the Magpie!" replied Jade, with a sarcastic tone to her voice. There was an awkward silence as Jade and Fleur noticed that some girls on the next table were staring at them with stern expressions on their faces. They had obviously overheard what Jade had said and were shocked that she had made such a tasteless comment. Even the guys on the table next to Fleur looked away. Fleur was even surprised that Jade had made such a remark.

"Shit." whispered Jade looking embarrassed. "That didn't go down very well."

Fleur didn't reply but thought it was very strange that Jade would say such a thing.

"Well, I think it's time for us to leave." said Jade, as she signaled to the waitress for the bill.

As Fleur put on her puffer jacket, Jade spoke again.

"This one's on me, Fleur. I owe you this, and again, I am sorry that you had to put up with all the fighting. We put you through hell."

As the girls made their way to the exit, they noticed that the two young guys were staring at them once again, clearly disappointed that they were leaving. Jade came up close behind Fleur and whispered in her ear.

"I think you have some secret admirers!"

Fleur turned back and stared at the gawping students and then spoke out.

"Fucking losers." said Fleur.

This was not the way that Fleur would normally react, and Jade sensed that, as she was normally a young flirtatious chick. It was very apparent that she really wasn't in the mood for any men right now. The two students looked at each other and then down at their beers. Fleur had spoken softly but loud enough so that they could hear her.

As the girls did their coats outside the café and said goodbye. Jade made the move forward to give Fleur three kisses.

"It was nice to catch up and see you again. Let's stay in touch." said Jade in a deep voice, breathing sensually into Fleur's left ear.

Her warm breath sent a chill down Fleur's spine. It was certainly deliberate from Jade and she knew that it had the desired effect.

Jade continued speaking as she pulled away from Fleur. "Let's go out again. I am leaving for Tokyo tomorrow for three days but maybe after that?"

Fleur was surprised by Jade's forwardness. Why was she trying to befriend her? She had lots of friends. Surely, she wasn't trying to make Roos jealous? Fleur didn't know what her motive was but she had enjoyed the lunch and wanted to go out with her again. At least it would be a different night out compared to what she was used to in Utrecht with her student friends or when she was working in Yab Yum. The one thing that she had to take care of was that Roos didn't find out, as that would cause a big problem.

"Yes!" replied Fleur. "Let's do that."

The two girls said their good byes, turned and walked in opposite directions down the Rozengracht, a small street scattered with unusual clothes shops and crowded eateries. Fleur analyzed their conversations as she hurried along in the cold winter weather. She was amazed that Jade had not once asked about Roos. She felt that this must have been deliberate as she didn't want her to think that she cared at all. Maybe Jade thought that Fleur would mention their meeting to Roos? The thought scared Fleur as she knew how crazy Roos was right now and obsessed about her ex. Fleur wanted to take a shower as soon as she got in as she suddenly became worried that maybe Roos would smell Jade's perfume on her and draw her own conclusions. That would be a nightmare for Fleur, which she just didn't need right now. After the ordeal from yesterday evening, she had dealt with enough stress. She had so much going on in her life with exams, a hectic job, and dealing with the break up between her flat-mates. The last thing she needed was for Roos to accuse her of seeing Jade behind her back. She couldn't wait to get in a steaming hot shower as she began running down the narrow street in the direction of her home.

CHAPTER 19

November 1

9:30 p.m.

Dr. Akkermans raised the large crystal wine glass to his mouth once more and tipped his tired head backwards in order to down the remaining wine. Swirling the full bodied red around in his mouth before swallowing he looked down at the kitchen table to see one empty bottle of a Spanish red wine and a half full bottle of Malbec standing there. He was content as he had two glasses left to drink before turning in for the night. This was sufficient to help him sleep well this evening, and he needed this, even if it would result in a thumping headache in the morning.

The judge was sad tonight, more sad than normal. His relationship with his only daughter was getting even worse, which he thought wasn't possible, and this frustrated him. The only way he knew how to cope with this was to have a bottle of wine. He also missed his wife terribly and it was times like this that brought back melancholy, happy memories of them together and then sadness at the state of his existing relationship. He had felt unloved for a number of years and despite his strong, intellectual, and charismatic persona, inside he felt helpless and lonely.

His daughter was cold and blamed him for the death of her mother, his wonderful wife. She used him for everything and it was extremely obvious. Dr. Akkermans also knew that if he stopped helping her financially he would probably never see her again. He had often toiled with this dilemma but always came back to the same conclusion that financing her strange, luxurious, student lifestyle gave him access to his daughter. They would have dinner a couple of times a month and sometimes she would surprise him by just turning up. In these instances, she would be coming over to do a ton of washing and then just go to her bedroom and sleep for an evening. He saw this as her way of staying close to her dead mother.

The other time that he might get an unplanned visit from his daughter was when she needed something. This was normally concerning money and he would always give into her demands in the end. He had nothing else to spend his money on.

The kitchen was dark, lit only by two flickering white candles that sat in sterling silver holders on the long oak table. Dr. Akkermans was in his usual seat at the head of the table. He liked this type of light as it gave off a romantic mood to the room even if he had nothing to be romantic about. It created an air of sadness in the kitchen more than anything else, a mood that oozed dark lost memories. He would never see it like this of course. He was too proud.

The judge sighed and put his empty glass on the table in front of him and reached for his mobile phone, which lay between the two wine bottles. Staring over the top of his gold-rimmed spectacles, he looked to see if he had any text messages. He was really interested whether Mariana had replied to any of the seven messages that he had sent her throughout the last two days. There was nothing. He knew that she must have seen his messages. She was always on her phone. She was simply just ignoring them because she was angry with him, as usual.

His views and opinions irritated her and even though he was just trying to help and steer her in the right direction. All Dr. Akkermans wanted to do was to show his daughter that he cared. She hated him immensely and only wanted his financial support. Mariana had become a hard soulless individual and the only way he could try and justify her terrible behavior was by the death of her mother.

Dr. Akkermans was drunk but he knew that he could handle finishing the second bottle. He needed to forget about things. Soon afterwards, he would be asleep. Maybe Mariana would reply before then. He doubted it.

* * *

10:40 p.m.

Arnaud sat down at his table in De Twee Zwaantjes and looked around him to see who else was in the bar. There were the usual faces that he would expect to see in there at this time of night, and more importantly, there were no surprises. He was always paranoid about journalists or other members of the press following him in there and taking pictures.

As Arnaud took off his coat and placed it on the stool next to him, Noor walked over unnoticed. She placed a beer and a small bowl of nuts in front of Arnaud, smiled and walked back to the bar. He thought her reaction was a bit weird as normally she would stop what she was doing to say hello. Not tonight and the bar wasn't even that crowded. Arnaud was surprised that he didn't get the usual pampering and attention that he was used to from Fleur. He knew how much she liked him but you would never have guessed that by the way she was acting this evening.

Arnaud watched Noor go about her business in the bar serving tables, smiling politely at people having a beer, and picking up the empty glasses. What was wrong, he thought to himself, as she didn't look in a bad mood. He noticed that she had made an effort with what she was wearing tonight and actually looked attractive, with a long black skirt and a white frilly blouse. Noor's hair which was long, dark, and always a little greasy had been cut shorter and looked full of body. She even wore some earrings and a little make-up, which was definitely a first. Arnaud didn't miss anything and began wondering what the catalyst was for this change in her appearance. With his mind wanting to get back to the recent findings on the footage, he quickly drew the conclusion that the changes in Noor's appearance was down to her playing hard to get and making an extra effort to attract Arnaud. She actually looked quite pretty thought Arnaud as he finally fell back into deep thought over the new pictures that they had of the Magpie and the ninth victim leaving the club.

Arnaud's views on why Noor was making an effort with her looks were actually wrong. She had been on her first date with the eHarmony guy. He had contacted her on a whim as his business trip had been delayed. They had been texting and mailing frequently over the last few days so when he called Noor out of the blue to meet up, she couldn't say no. She did have feelings for him so they went on the date, which had actually gone very well.

Jonathan had suggested meeting at the cinema for an early evening film. After this they walked to the Jordaan talking all the way and had dinner in a simple Indonesian restaurant. Noor felt comfortable eating in her local neighborhood and he also liked the idea of seeing the area where she lived. They had chatted non-stop and he was very interested in Noor and her upbringing. Noor couldn't stop thinking about him. He was much better looking than the pictures. She kept kicking herself to make sure that this was really happening. At last, she had met someone that she was attracted to and who really liked her for who she was. She also didn't want to get too carried away as it had only been one date.

Noor's only hesitation about Jonathan was that he was too good for her and she knew that he could get a prettier, trendier, and a more fun girl. He had said on a number of occasions during the date that she had a warm personality. It was this along with her intellect that attracted him to Noor. They had laughed and joked all evening.

As she carried a tray of empty glasses back behind the bar, she thought that she liked everything about him apart from his outfit. She had expected him to dress in a suit or a smart pair of trousers and a coat. Instead he had turned up extremely casual, wearing jeans, trainers, and a hooded top which he wore up half the time. She hadn't said anything to Jonathan because she knew that she was extremely picky and didn't want to put him off. After all, she knew that she was old-fashioned and frumpy herself and needed some modernizing. Maybe he was going to be good for her. He had short hair so the hooded sweat top kept him warm outside even if she didn't like how it looked.

Jonathan had also worn glasses, which he didn't have on in the pictures. He explained that his eyesight had worsened recently and the glasses were a relatively new thing. Noor smiled to herself as she would pluck up the courage at some point in the future to try and persuade him to lose the glasses and hooded tops. Then he would be perfect and she could show him off to her family.

"Oh, stop it Noor." she said under her breath as she washed up some beer glasses. What a blissful and perfect date it had been. Jonathan had walked her home to her apartment and kissed her on the cheek and said goodbye. She would have loved him to come up but didn't want to give the wrong impression. She liked his chivalrous actions and was pleased to see that he had only wanted a peck on the cheek and wasn't just after sex or anything else. This made her like him even more. Maybe next time she could invite him up for coffee. Noor continued to daydream. She couldn't wait to see him again and hadn't stopped thinking about Jonathan since the date.

Having come to her senses, she looked up from behind the bar to see if any of the tables needed another drink. Noor could see Arnaud was in deep thought with his head in his hands staring into space. She also noticed that he hadn't even finished his first beer, which would have normally been drunk in seconds. As she looked over at him affectionately, she realized that she still had strong feelings for Arnaud but right now it was more of a friendship thing. They weren't feelings of lust, like she was having for Jonathan. This made her feel a little guilty, especially as Arnaud didn't know that she was now dating someone else.

As she pondered over the thought of whether Arnaud would be upset if he knew, Noor decided that she would go home after work and get straight on the blog. She hadn't spent as much time as she would have liked to on the website recently. Her mind had been preoccupied. She needed to commit some hours to this as it was her best way of helping Arnaud.

* * *

11:00 p.m.

Fleur sat on the sofa in her usual skimpy jogging pants and a small tight top. She was lying across it, filing her nails and eating from a pack of liquorish sweets, while watching the news on the television. It was late and Fleur was tired and was about to go to bed. She was startled by the front door bursting open suddenly and a giggly Roos walking in. She must have been drunk, thought Fleur. Fleur turned and smiled at Roos and then continued doing her nails and watching the news.

Roos staggered in in high heels and stood in front of the television trying to get Fleur's attention. Fleur was annoyed as she was deliberately blocking her view. Roos wasn't wearing much considering it was freezing outside. She took off her thin coat and dropped it on the ground. Underneath she had on skin-tight jeans and a figure hugging black woolen jumper. Fleur thought that she looked quite nice in her outfit but wasn't really interested in spending any time checking Roos or even speaking with her. It didn't look like Roos was going to budge so

Fleur thought that this was the right time to go to bed. Just as she was getting up, she realized that Roos was actually looking over at the open door. As Fleur turned around, Roos called out in a high-pitched voice, "Come in!"

Fleur tensed up as she couldn't believe that she had got back with Jade. Fleur was taken by surprise and began to feel nervous with anticipation when a girl walked in, probably twenty-two years old. She had short boyish peroxide blonde hair and a pretty face. As she strolled into the living room Fleur observed her outfit which was very tomboyish. With ripped blue jeans and a red checkered shirt, Fleur could see that she had matching tattoos on both wrists. She must have also been drunk as she wobbled over to Roos with a silly grin on her face.

Roos grabbed the other girl with both hands and spoke. "Fleur, this is Iris. Iris, Fleur is my flat-mate."

The young girl's smile disappeared from her face as she checked out Fleur and then nodded. Fleur smiled at Iris as if to say hello, a little embarrassed by this sudden unexpected introduction. She must have met the girl in a bar, thought Fleur. After a few seconds of awkward silence Roos started kissing the girl in front of Fleur as if to prove a point. The girl responded to the kisses and they ended up snogging for a minute.

Whatever the reasoning for this intrusion, Fleur didn't want to stay in the living room with them any longer. Fleur wanted to escape to her bedroom, without coming across as rude or upsetting Roos.

Fleur faked a yawn. "Okay Roos, I'm off to bed. I'm so tired and have lectures tomorrow morning. Nice to have met you, Iris."

With that, she walked past the hugging girls and made her way to her bedroom.

As she shut the door behind her, Roos called out. "Night, night Fleur. Sweet dreams."

How strange, thought Fleur, as she got into bed. Lying curled up on her side, Fleur could hear the two girls whispering in the living room. They then headed upstairs to Roos' bedroom. Surprisingly, Roos didn't shut her bedroom door. She could hear the girls kissing, giggling, and undressing. It was very loud. Fleur realized that Roos hadn't shut her door deliberately. She may have been tipsy but she wanted Fleur to hear all of this. The two girls started making out and the moaning got louder and louder. After a few minutes, Fleur had heard enough. She put on her earphones. Lying back in bed she turned up the volume loud enough so she couldn't hear anything else apart from the sound of one of Adelle's soft ballads.

Soon after, she fell asleep.

CHAPTER 20

November 4

11:00 a.m.

Arnaud sat at his desk drinking a black sweetened coffee and studying the latest comments on the blog, that was obsessed with him and this case. It was late morning and Arnaud couldn't stop yawning, still tired from a bad night's sleep. He scratched the top of his head in despair. The recent evidence that had come from the CCTV footage at the Surprise Bar had been enlightening but it had led to nothing.

On the site, the bloggers were arguing about whether Arnaud and his team were actually making any progress. Happy Single continued to push the point that the Magpie had to have an accomplice. Arnaud agreed with the blogger. When you looked at the pictures of the girl leaving the club, it wasn't physically impossible that she could take these young males down, move their bodies around to work on them, and then dump the corpses after a few days. This work could not be done alone and he was sure of this. Unfortunately, Arnaud had no proof, at least none that he could find at the moment.

Arnaud was frustrated. He had faith that a new lead would come and he just needed to keep searching. The Magpie was extremely calculated and if she had an assistant, they wouldn't be too far away from her when she was working. This was Arnaud's new theory. The killer was a control freak and she would want her accomplice nearby. Arnaud made himself another coffee, as he thought about this more.

* * *

Noor walked out of the hairdressers on the Spui with her new look. She was revamping her appearance. Her hair had been cut shorter, had been highlighted and blow-dried. She was beginning to feel more confident, which was something she had never felt before. She had lost six pounds and if she managed to lose another two she would treat herself to a new dress, one size smaller. Noor was really missing Jonathan, who was away on business, and she couldn't wait for their second date.

* * *

2:30 p.m.

"Don't fucking pick up my father's calls!" screamed Mariana. "You have no fucking right to speak with him."

"But, he…" interrupted Jan, trying to justify calling Dr. Akkermans.

Mariana was red faced and furious. She even had tears in her eyes, which Jan had never seen before. She had never let her guard down and normally didn't show feelings or emotions. Jan sat on the sofa in Mariana's living room, while she stood next to him pointing her index finger down at his head. She was in a rage. Jan didn't know whether she was going to shout or if she was going to poke his eye out. Both seemed possible. There was to be no respite.

"Just fucking listen to me. He has nothing to do with you and you shouldn't speak with him, and definitely not without my permission."

"But I had five missed calls from your father and even some text messages. I'm not going to be rude Mariana."

"I don't give a shit!" she barked back.

Jan had known that she was going to react like this and he also knew why her father had been trying to get hold of him. He hadn't cared in this instance as he saw it as a rare opportunity to speak to Dr. Akkermans and maybe build a relationship with him. Jan knew that Dr. Akkermans had been trying to get hold of his daughter. Jan's long term goal was to stay with Mariana, his true love, and he thought that at some point it would be beneficial to get Dr. Akkermans on his side. It was Jan's view that even though Mariana refused to listen to her father now, he would become more important to her as she got older. Jan always hoped that Mariana would soften somewhat over time but there had been no hints of this happening so far. Nonetheless, Jan believed that she would calm down the longer they stayed together and then it would be good for him to be in favor with her father. This was his plan and it was a risk that he was willing to take. There was no downside to his long-term objective.

As Mariana kept shouting, Jan thought that at least he had an excuse this time. It was Dr. Akkermans who had desperately tried to contact him, worried about his daughter. He was very pleased that Jan had finally responded to him and hoped that they could build a relationship together. Jan's recent conversation with her father had actually been an eye-opener, as Dr. Akkermans had sounded drunk on the phone. He had complained that Mariana blamed him for everything, including her mother's death. He didn't think that she would ever forgive him. Dr. Akkermans had sounded very sad on the phone.

"I didn't have to tell you that I spoke with him," replied Jan, trying to get her to relax a little.

"But you did and you spoke to him without my permission!"

She ran her hands through her hair and took a deep breath. Mariana paused for a second and Jan thought she was going to cry. He was taken by surprise, when she suddenly kicked Jan with her right leg. Her foot hit him square on the left shin. There was a dull thud as her pointed boot connected with his bone. Jan shrieked as he grabbed his leg and doubled up in pain. He had definitely not been expecting this reaction. Jan looked up to see Mariana heading in the other direction towards her bedroom.

"Fucking asshole!" she shouted, before slamming the bedroom door behind her. Jan knew that there was no point chasing after her. He lifted the trouser leg to look at his leg, it was red and throbbing. He would have a big bruise there tomorrow. As he held onto his aching leg, he questioned whether all of this was worth it. Was this what love was really about? He knew for sure that he had one very messed-up girlfriend.

The best thing Jan could do right now was to leave and go home. He stood up from the sofa, still grimacing in pain, and hobbled towards the door. He grabbed his coat and then slammed the door behind him. He wanted her to know that he had left, not that she would care anyway. Jan thought to himself that he would wait for her to contact him this time. Why was he putting up with all of this? Jan got in his van and headed home to the peace of his parents' house in Badhoeverdorp.

CHAPTER 21

November 9

8:10 p.m.

Arnaud's eyes were watering constantly as the biting cold wind blew hard against his face. The tears sprawled down over his red chapped cheeks and almost froze as they dispersed. He struggled to focus as his eyeballs began to dry out battling against the frosty gale. Arnaud was driving along very fast on his moped, in the direction of Hoofddorpplein in Amsterdam South. His right hand gripped on to the throttle and pulled it all the way back in order to go as quickly as possible. He realized that he had forgotten to take his helmet with him when he left the police station. Using his left hand, he pulled the scarf further up over his chin and chattering teeth. As he drove along the icy-looking bike path, Arnaud could hear police sirens in all directions.

He reached Hoofddorpplein and the first police car sped past him around the roundabout, blue lights flashing and siren blaring out in the empty streets. It was heading in the same direction as Arnaud, along with all the other police cars. They were going to the Slotervaart woods, by the International Golf Club and the Nieuwe Meer. These woods were famous as a place for gay men to congregate, and to meet other men randomly.

Arnaud was excited, not because a corpse had been found, but because there had apparently been a sighting of the Magpie. He didn't have any more information than that, and he was very tense and eager to get to the location of the dead body. Arnaud's depression had become so bad recently that he cared more about catching his nemesis, than about anyone else being killed. Of course, they were both connected but the new body that had been dumped was number eleven of the year. It no longer bothered him as much as hunting down this killer.

Realizing that he was almost at the crime scene, he tried to speed up, gritting his yellow teeth as he pulled back down on the moped throttle again. The cold biting wind continued to smack his face and cut through the layers of clothing he had on. Arnaud was pretty good at handling the cold weather, but this was almost unbearable.

Approaching the woods, Arnaud parked his moped next to five police cars that had beaten him to the site. Arnaud walked towards a huddle of policemen and told them to make a line in order to block the entrance into the wooded parkland. Even though this was a well-known pick up area, Arnaud doubted there would be many out here in this weather. Still, you couldn't be sure and there was also the chance that the press would get here shortly. He didn't want them entering the woods and taking pictures.

Friso and his two juniors were already at the woods. Arnaud could see Jim ordering some policemen around, directing them to scale the perimeter of the site. Three of the policemen were busy rolling out the crime scene tape around the woods. Robin was sitting in one of the back seats of a police car interviewing somebody. As Arnaud walked over, he quickly realized that this was the man that had found the body and called it in. He appeared to be a jogger, as he was dressed in black spandex running gear with a bright yellow fluorescent band around his waist. The witness, who was a man in his late thirties, was in shock as he was speaking extremely fast and struggling to get his words out correctly. Arnaud was pleased to see that his team was busy and quickly left the side of the vehicle in which the interview was being conducted. He didn't want to put any more pressure on the witness, who appeared spooked enough.

As Arnaud got to the entrance to the woods, he caught sight of Friso who was standing behind a large tree, speaking into his mobile phone.

"Don't wait up for me, darling. It's going to be a late night." said Friso apologetically. Arnaud knew exactly who his colleague was speaking to. She had clearly put the phone down as he stared at his mobile blankly. The call had ended abruptly. Friso sighed and put his phone back inside the top pocket of his coat. He looked up to see Arnaud and nodded. With a torch shining brightly in his left hand, Friso led Arnaud into the woods along a narrow dark path.

The track was very muddy and the ground had frozen. One could hear their footsteps making cracking sounds beneath them as if they were treading on crisps. Friso kept the torch shining about six feet ahead of them. They could see their warm breaths leave their mouths and nostrils into the cold air and light up in the torch beam. Friso led Arnaud deeper into the woods as they passed thick bushes and low branches from the trees that hung over the dark track. They went past several openings in the parkland where random benches were placed.

After five minutes of silence, Friso began to give Arnaud a detailed briefing of what they had found out already. In his calm methodical tone, he began to speak.

"As you are probably aware, this parkland area is well known for being a pick-up point. Ivar Smit had been jogging passed the parkland about ninety minutes ago and he heard noises and people talking and some rustling inside the wooded area."

Arnaud interrupted Friso, "What was he jogging in here for? I thought everyone knew what went on in these woods?"

"Actually, that was my initial thought as well, Arnaud. But the jogger said that he ran in this area during the winter months when he knew that there would be nobody around as it was too cold. He also said that he only ran around the edge of the parkland."

"Well, what was he doing in the middle of the woods then?" asked Arnaud.

"He said that he heard a number of voices and thought that it was very strange and went in to see what was going on. When the jogger approached the site of the body, he heard and saw people in dark clothing, running away from the opening through the undergrowth."

Before Arnaud could ask the next questions, Friso spoke. "Ivar didn't get a view of their faces and he is not sure if they were male or female."

"Yes, it seemed to him like there was rustling coming from different spots in the woods."

Arnaud looked at his colleague, with a twinkle of hope in his tired eyes. They continued walking along the dark narrow path lit up by Friso's torch.

"The jogger didn't pursue them." continued Friso.

"Why not?"

"He panicked. He just froze on the spot."

Friso and Arnaud stop walking as they came to an opening in the woods, which was lit up by a number of large elevated lamps being run off a noisy generator. The perimeter had been enclosed by crime tape and a number of policemen stood around the edges, wrapped up in long thick coats and keeping an eye out for any noises coming from the surrounding wooded area. There were four forensic staff-members in white outfits, scanning the ground within the lit-up area for clues. One carried a camera with a flash and was busy snapping away. Another one was making notes in a book and the other two carried small plastic bags and pincers searching for evidence.

The two detectives bent down to creep under the tape and walked into the lit-up area. As Arnaud tried to catch his breath, in shock at what he had just seen in front of him, Friso continued talking.

"And the other reason the jogger didn't chase the fleeing people because he had just seen this."

Tied up against a large tree in front of them was a naked body of a dead man. The motionless corpse was strung against the thick tree trunk. His arms had rope tied around them, which were then pulled upwards over high branches on both sides of the tree. It was like a modern-day crucifixion.

The dead male was probably six feet tall. His body was slim but muscular. The head was shaved and slumped forward over his chest in a strange position, giving the impression that the neck was broken. It was not possible to see the victim's face in that position. The man's torso was pale grey in color exaggerated by the bright neon lights that had been erected, and shone over the surrounding area.

Arnaud walked forward and asked one of the forensics for a pair of rubber surgical gloves. Grabbing the dead man's chin, he lifted the head so that he could get a good look at the face. As he raised the heavy head upwards, he heard dull cracking noises coming from the top part of the spine. He already feared the worse having picked up on the familiar signs. Arnaud could see that there was some bruising around the neck area, confirming that it had indeed been snapped. He also saw that there were no other cuts or marks on the body. There was also no jewelry or a watch on the victim. The body was pale and hairless. Arnaud grabbed one of the victim's arms and felt no sign of rigor and concluded that the body must have been dumped recently. As he stared at the man's face Arnaud thought he looked sad. Both eyes were slightly open but his lips were closed. He must have been around thirty years old, thought Arnaud.

Arnaud said nothing, as he stood there staring at the victim. He was sure that the Magpie had strung the body up against the tree so that it could be found easily. She wanted people to know about her work. After all, she took extreme pride in her kills.

Arnaud let go of the dead man's chin and the head slumped forward again, falling to rest onto the victim's chest. He took a step back from the body and continued observing the corpse. He spoke out to Friso.

"Do we know who he is?"

"Not yet. There is also no report of a missing person in the Amsterdam area."

"Maybe he was not from this part of the country." He was thinking aloud. As they walked around the tree, they could see that the victim had a number of tattoos on his back and on his thighs and calves. Some were cryptic writings and others were pictures that wound around the back of his torso. One was of a large dagger and another was of a python. Arnaud was beginning to think that the dead guy was also gay. Apart from the fact that he looked after his physique and had a shaved head and a number of tattoos, it also appeared that both ears had been pierced. One of his nipples also looked like it had once had a ring through it as it hung forward and one could see a hole in it.

One of the forensics stood in front of the two detectives to take some more polaroid pictures. Arnaud turned to face Friso. He had seen enough. He started walking back in the direction of the path. The two detectives first stepped over the police tape that circled the opening in the wood, where the crime had taken place, and then made their way down the narrow track.

"Okay." said Arnaud.

He was drawing conclusions in his head and it was very clear to him that this was the work of the Magpie. Arnaud started walking down the path with Friso in pursuit. He wanted to get back to the office as soon as possible. He wanted to look over the facts and digest all the information with his team, interview the jogger again, and then brainstorm.

"Friso, we need to get the whole team back to the office, as well as the key witness. We need to pick his brain. He may think that he has told Jim and Robin everything but he might still be in shock and might be missing something that is crucial to the investigation. Perhaps he saw something that he doesn't realize is important to us. Let's get him back to the station immediately."

"Okay, agreed." replied Friso.

"How long will it take to identify the dead guy?" asked Arnaud.

"I would estimate three to four hours at most."

"Okay, good. See you back at the office in thirty minutes." Arnaud turned and walked briskly down the path speeding ahead of his colleague. He didn't need the light from Friso's torch to direct him anymore as he was approaching the edge of the woods, where all the police cars were parked and where Jim and Robin were sitting in a car with the witness.

As he got close to the group of policemen who were guarding the entrance, Arnaud spoke, "Gents, I want you to listen to me very carefully, as you have an extremely important job on your hands. This is a very serious crime scene and you need to guard it tonight with your wits about you. If this is the work of the serial killer, then it's possible that she has left some clues at the scene of the crime. She was caught by surprise and had to flee unexpectedly. I believe that she might try and come back tonight to check the area and fully erase her trail. Be on guard and make sure nobody enters the parkland. Nobody."

Arnaud focused in on the six policemen's faces. He could see out of the corner of his eye that Friso had now reached the entrance to the woods as well.

Arnaud turned to Friso. "Friso, please get more policemen down here tonight. I want this whole place ring-fenced with our guys."

Friso nodded and then Arnaud began talking again to the men in front of him.

"The story will be out soon and I also expect the press to be here shortly. Do not let any of them near the woods and arrest anyone who attempts to enter."

The policemen all nodded in agreement. As he turned on the engine to his moped, he shouted back at Friso and the group of police. "Keep up the good work."

Arnaud then sped off into the frosty night, warmed up by the adrenalin running through his veins.

Arnaud arrived back at the office first, and turned on the heaters immediately as it was very cold. One of the benefits of the moped was that it was by far the quickest way to get around Amsterdam.

As Arnaud sat at his desk, waiting for the rest of the team to arrive, a lot of ideas were keeping him occupied. He realized that this was the first time that the Magpie had slipped up and he wanted to take advantage of it. He had an opportunity to catch her. He was also intrigued to know what the jogger had to say, as well as finding out whether the forensics had uncovered any clues at the scene of the crime.

He decided to put his thoughts on paper and just as he started jotting some bullet points Friso walked in with the two younger detectives and the jogger. The witness was still in shock, perplexed, and freezing cold. He was ushered over by Jim to sit with the rest of the team around Arnaud's desk.

"Jim, get this chap a warm drink." said Arnaud.

"Ivar." interrupted Friso, trying to make the jogger feel relaxed.

"Yes, Ivar. Please get Ivar some tea." replied Arnaud, smiling to thank Friso.
"Coffee please." The witness spoke up.

Jim acknowledged the request and walked over to the drinks machine.

Arnaud spoke again, "And please get him a warm blanket as well, Jim. I think it's good for Ivar to relax for a bit in Dijkstra's office while we all touch base."

"Thanks very much for coming in, Ivar. I realize that you must be tired and cold. We appreciate all your help and co-operation. Some of the questions and things that we want to ask you may be repetitive but please believe me when I say that we don't want to leave any stone unturned. All the information that you give us could help catch this murderer and there may be things that you don't feel are important or relevant but may actually be the best evidence that you can give us. So please be patient with the team during this process."

"So, is it the Magpie?" asked the jogger abruptly, taking the detectives by surprise. He almost appeared excited to find out who the killer might be.

Arnaud responded to him in the same calm quiet tone.

"I must say that it has all the traits of a Magpie murder. However, we need to discuss this and go through all the evidence and story so far. We will come back to you with a lot of questions later tonight to assist us with the investigation. We also need to wait for the results of the autopsy, as well as anything that the forensics found where the body was dumped. They may find some new evidence and clues. All this needs to be done before we can be sure that it's the Magpie."

Friso was surprised how much information Arnaud had just shared. He also knew that this was deliberate, as he wanted the witness to feel relaxed and part of the team. After all, he was important to the investigation and Arnaud needed him for fact-finding. Arnaud's attention to detail and clever methods of handling people sometimes amazed Friso. He could see that Arnaud had already worked out every part of the investigation process that needed to be covered quickly and in detail.

Arnaud stood up and pointed in the direction of Dijkstra's office. Robin led the witness there, followed by Jim who was carrying the cup of coffee and a blanket. Just before he started walking behind Robin, the jogger turned his head to face Arnaud again. With a concerned frown on his face, he started speaking.

"But I thought I had already told you everything."

Arnaud smiled and calmly replied to his crucial witness, "Well, we only have a few more questions to ask you so please bear with us, Ivar."

The jogger was ushered into Dijkstra's office and before the door was shut behind him, Arnaud shouted out to Robin. "There is a small heater under the desk, which you can turn on as well."

He wanted his key witness to be as comfortable as possible. You could see through the glass window of the office that Robin had turned on the television and then bent down under the desk to get the heater going.

Arnaud turned back to Friso and then Jim. His face changed from a relaxed one to a serious intense expression. "Right guys. Time is of the essence and we need to go through all the current findings and work out what else we need to do straight away. This is the first time that the Magpie has slipped up and we need to jump on it!"

Both detectives nodded and then looked up briefly to see Robin come out of the office and walk over to them.

"Okay, what do we know?" said Arnaud.

They all realized that this was the start of an intense brainstorming session, with quick-fire questions from their boss. They had to cover a lot in a short period of time.

"It's got all the signs of the Magpie." said Jim.

"She appears to have an accomplice." said Robin.

"That we don't know for sure." interrupted Arnaud.

"I have been over this three times with the witness and he is certain that there were at least two people fleeing the scene of the crime. That he is sure of, even if he had no clear view of their faces. He was not able to confirm whether they were male or female." replied Robin, with much conviction in his voice.

"Well, I guess we are pretty sure that one is a female!" said Arnaud.

He stood up and grabbed a black marker pen. He began scribbling down some bullet points on the board and continued speaking at the same time to his colleagues that sat behind him.

"Okay, so what else?" He wanted all their comments and views now.

"Well," said Friso, speaking up for the first time. "We are still waiting on the results of the autopsy but we know that the body was not frozen so it had recently been dumped. For the body to be still warm at the crime scene, it must have been kept indoors somewhere."

Arnaud continued writing on the large paper.

Friso continued, "The victim was a fit guy. It looked like he worked out. Like the rest of the Magpie's victims, he didn't have any marks or scratches on him. These would have been expected from a confrontation or a fight in trying to restrain him. I would argue that even if the Magpie has an accomplice, she must be drugging the victims."

"Mmm, yes, I agree." said Arnaud, with his back still to the team.

"In fact," said Friso on a roll, "I would assume that the Magpie must be seducing or luring her victims to a point where they are relaxed around her. She must then be drugging them, and once this is done, she takes their life. In this instance, as has been the case with a lot of the killings this year, she has broken the victim's neck. I think that as she goes through this ordeal of stripping the clothes and jewelry off of the body, the victim must already be dead or heavily drugged, so that they can't move or try to protect themselves. After all, each victim has been taken and kept for up to three days before being dumped."

Arnaud spoke up once more. "A lot of assumptions, but again, I agree with you. Can we look into all the drugs that are on and off the market please, which can be used to heavily sedate people? You should include drugs that can either be swallowed or injected."

"There didn't appear to be any marks where an injection was made." said Jim.

"We will look into this anyway, if the victim was injected three days ago, we wouldn't necessarily see it." replied Friso.

Arnaud turned to face his team and took a deep breath before speaking up again.

"So, what don't we know?" He didn't give the detectives chance to answer this question as he spoke up again.

"Who is this guy? Is he gay?"

"He has all the physical traits of being homosexual but we need to confirm this once we find his identity." said Friso.

"Why is this important?" asked Robin.

"Because it would be the first one and so she has deviated from her normal killing pattern. We need to try and understand why she has done this." said Friso in response.

"And if he is gay, and we know where he is from, then we can go to all the gay bars in the neighborhood to see whether he had been spotted with anyone. We can try to see if he had been sighted with a female. Maybe there is a witness out there who saw him with the Magpie."

As Arnaud continued speaking, the detectives frantically wrote down notes in their little pads. When the three detectives had finished scribbling, they looked back up at Arnaud.

The questioning started again.

"Why has the victim not been reported missing? We are obviously making the assumption that he has been stowed away for three days or so."

Arnaud thought for a moment and then continued, "And why was he dumped there?"

"Because it's completely empty at this time of year." replied Friso. "And it's getting more difficult for her to dump her victims, with all the police on the streets waiting for her next move."

"Mmmm. Yes, you are probably right with that one, Friso." replied Arnaud.

"Next to the woods is a car park that you can't see from the main road." said Friso. "If the victim was taken there by car, then the Magpie could have pulled the body out and dragged it into the wood, without any passersby noticing."

"Good point." replied Arnaud, impressed with Friso's thought process. Arnaud began to see that it was becoming harder for the killer to strike and even harder for her to dump bodies without being spotted because she had almost been caught this time.

"Anything else?" said Arnaud again. "Come on, guys. Thoughts?"

Jim spoke up next, "If the victim was gay and we don't know this yet, perhaps he was selected as he was an easy target. Perhaps he lives alone." There was silence, as Jim collected his thoughts before he began speaking again. "If he did live alone and didn't have a partner then it's very possible that nobody would have reported him missing."

"A lot of maybe's." replied Arnaud. "However, I like the way you are thinking, Jim." continued Arnaud. "If the victim was gay then I believe that the Magpie did pick him partly because of what you just explained. It is definitely becoming harder for her to find suitors. Everyone is on their guard as her killing pattern has always been the same. This would explain why she had chosen a gay guy, as he would have been caught off guard."

Jim smiled, pleased with what Arnaud had just said, and happy that he had contributed to the brainstorming session constructively.

Arnaud spoke up again. "But did the Magpie hand pick him? Maybe she knew the victim? Once we can identify the victim, we should put out a report on the local TV network to see if there are any witnesses who may have seen him in the last week. We also need to interview his neighbors and friends, and visit the bars and places that he went out to socially." Friso was making notes in his little black book as Arnaud spoke.

"There may be some more clues at the crime scene that we don't know about yet, especially if the Magpie was forced to flee unexpectedly." said Robin.

"Agreed." answered Arnaud. He turned again to Friso. "We can't allow her to return to the woods in an attempt to get rid of any evidence or to cover her tracks."

Arnaud knew that he had already stressed this point to the police and to Friso. It was essential though that the police guarding the crime scene overnight were alert.

"It's been taken care of." replied Friso, "And if she does return to the woods, she will be in for a surprise, as there are police bordering the perimeter of the woods as well as around the opening where the body was found. There is no way she can come back and not be caught."

Arnaud grunted in response. He had been reassured by what Friso had said, knowing that his colleague would have covered all the bases. Friso was always very thorough and this took a huge weight off of Arnaud's shoulders.

"Okay, tomorrow, when it's light, we will check for more clues. But for now, what else?" said Arnaud. He hadn't finished and wanted more out of his team.

For the first time the three other detectives were silent and stared back at Arnaud with blank faces. Arnaud could see this so he carried on posing questions.

"Any other witnesses? What was their exit route? Were there any cars in the car park? Did the witnesses hear a car speeding away? Are there any tracks left in the car park? Are there any footprints around the crime scene?"

Jim and Robin shook their heads, as they had asked all these questions of the jogger. Seeing their response, Arnaud decided to keep firing questions at his team.

"Did the jogger have anything else interesting to say?"

"We have told you everything that he has told us, so far." replied Jim.

Arnaud continued, "Any idea about what the killer and her accomplice were wearing? Did the witness hear anything that they said? Any names? Why didn't he chase? We need to run these questions by the jogger again. If he heard voices, were they high pitched or low pitched? Please think about other questions for him. We need to work backwards in trying to think about what information we want to find out and then establish the right questions to ask him."

"Okay." said Arnaud, "Let's go through the action points. Jim, once you have completed a second interview with the jogger, you can take him home. Please make sure he understands that he needs to keep quiet about everything that has happened over the last twenty-four hours. No leaking information to the press. Then, I want you to chase up the autopsy and report back to us."

Jim made some notes and then looked up at Arnaud, waiting for him to speak again.

"Robin, I want you to get an ID on the victim and then interview his family and friends. Your goal tomorrow is to complete all this as well as visit the bars and places he hung out socially. We need to know who were the last people to see him this week and where. Pull the CCTV tapes from all the places that he has been to in the last week."

Robin also was busy scribbling down notes. Arnaud then spoke to Friso.

"Friso, you and I will go back to the woods first thing tomorrow to search for clues with forensics. We can't leave any stone unturned. For now, I am going to sit in on the questioning of the witness with Jim as I am sure he must have more important information for us that he is just not aware is critical to the investigation. Friso, can you contact Dijkstra and let him know what's going on?."

With that, all four detectives stood up and started walking in different directions to get on with their tasks. Arnaud saw Robin pick up his coat and head for the exit door. He called out to him.

"Robin, call me as soon as you know who the victim is. We can then put a picture of him up on the news channels to appeal for witnesses to come forward who may also have seen him over the last few days. There has to be somebody who had seen him this week."

"Yep." replied Robin, as he left the room.

Arnaud turned to Jim and patted him on the back and followed him over to Dijkstra's office where the jogger was sitting wrapped in a blanket. Arnaud put on a solemn face as they entered the small room and sat down with the witness.

Ivar began to cry hysterically as he went over the events of the evening once more. Disappointingly, his story didn't result in any further evidence. He hadn't seen anything more than bushes moving and perhaps a couple of silhouettes fleeing the crime scene. He was pretty sure that there were muffled voices coming from two different sides of the opening, making him sure that there was more than one person present. Unfortunately, he had no recollection of whether they were male or female voices. Arnaud was beginning to despair; however, he didn't want the witness to sense his disappointment.

Arnaud could see the cold sweat sit on the outside of the jogger's black lycra outfit. He was for sure freezing, stressed, and tired. What was meant to be an uninterrupted evening run had ended up being a nightmare that would likely scar him forever. He was now drawn into the murder hunt for the Magpie and his life would never be the same again. The jogger had stumbled upon a dead body and if he had arrived there ten minutes earlier he may have been killed himself.

The witness realized, as he sat there in the small office with the two detectives, that he had almost uncovered the identity of the Magpie, nonetheless, he would go a long way in helping the police with their inquest. After all, he had already confirmed that the killer had an accomplice. This was progress in the investigation.

Arnaud made it clear to him that that it was essential that he didn't speak with the press or anyone about the investigation or anything that he had seen. He shouldn't even discuss the ordeal with his wife. Arnaud and his team had to discuss the flow of information to the public regarding the case. Jim explained to Ivar that he would need to come back tomorrow, once his statement had been typed up, and then sign it as the key witness in the case. They wanted him to go home and rest and think. They hoped that the jogger would come up with some new piece of information during the night that he had forgotten about currently.

Arnaud stood up and held his hand out towards Ivar. He shook hands with him and then asked Jim to drive him home. As the junior detective led the witness out of the office, Arnaud rubbed his eyes, feeling just as tired and exhausted as the jogger looked. He needed to go home and get a good night's rest as tomorrow was going to be an early start. They would also have a lot of new information to digest. In the morning, they should have the results of the autopsy and hopefully a positive ID on the victim. If this was the case, then his team would be busy collecting information from the friends and family of the murdered man.

The thought of more witnesses and a clear profile of the victim excited Arnaud. He was sure that something would turn up. For now, he needed to go home. Picking up his jacket and phone, he headed for the exit door.

As Arnaud walked down the stairs that led to the garage, he couldn't help but think about what the Magpie was doing right now. Was she worried? Was she scared that they were getting closer to catching her? Was she going to head back to the woods tonight to cover her tracks? What would her next move be? Maybe she would stop the killing now, while she was ahead? After all, she had almost been caught. Arnaud doubted that she would be thinking that she had made her last killing but he did feel that the noose had tightened around her neck, if only a little bit.

CHAPTER 22

November 10

6:30 a.m.

Arnaud woke up very early excited about the day ahead. In fact, he hadn't slept well at all, tossing and turning all night in his cold apartment. It had been a windy night, with the gale whistling along the canals and banging against his front door and old bedroom window. All he really thought about at the moment was that the strong winds may blow away some clues from the crime scene. At least it hadn't rained last night which was a blessing, as that would have certainly damaged any evidence that may have been around the opening in the parkland where the body had been dumped.

Arnaud got dressed without taking a shower. As he put his clothes on, he was becoming anxious wondering if forensics would find some critical evidence that would lead to them catching the Magpie. He didn't know whether to feel excited or nervous.

He looked at his watch. It was 6:50 a.m. and still very dark outside. He decided that he would head off to the woods anyway as he couldn't wait any longer. The crime scene was lit up and that would help him look for clues in the early hours before sunrise. Arnaud put on an extra jumper knowing that it was going to be freezing outside.

The Magpie had been extremely unlucky that a random jogger had caught her off guard. Arnaud couldn't help but think that the Magpie must be really annoyed with what had taken place last night. It was a tiny victory for the police and the first slip up from this perfectly calculated serial killer.

There was still ice on the cobbled streets in the center of town so he drove a little slower as he made his way through Amsterdam in a southerly direction towards the woods. As he got closer to the parkland, he could hear the stream of cars speeding along the motorway close by. He thought to himself that the Magpie had indeed selected the drop-off zone very well. There was nobody around this area, yet it was extremely noisy because of the motorway next door.

Arnaud arrived at the parkland and he could see that nothing had changed from the night before. The same police stood by the entrance and there were a few extra men parading the perimeter with bright yellow vests on top of their police coats, and all of them carried torches. Some additional police tape had been tied up around the boundary to the woods highlighting that it was a crime scene.

Arnaud got off his moped and walked towards the huddle of policemen.

"Morning." said Arnaud, "Any news?"

"No Sir." came the reply from a couple of the men in unison. They all had red cold faces and looked extremely tired.

"No unexpected visitors last night?" asked Arnaud.

"No Sir. Very quiet."

"Bloody freezing though." said another policeman.

Arnaud breathed a big sigh of relief. "Good. Good to hear. Good work, men."

Arnaud was happy and relieved. He could see that the narrow path into the wood had now been lit up with ground torches and he was able to head down the track without a policeman leading the way.

Now that the muddy path was completely lit up, Arnaud started to get a good understanding of why the Magpie had chosen this place to dump the body. He walked very slowly along the track looking for any clues. Even though he knew that she had fled in the other direction, he still wanted to scan every piece of ground for evidence. He thought to himself that he would also get the forensics to scan this path as well.

After about fifteen minutes of moving slowly along the narrow path he arrived at the very well-lit opening where the body was found. There were, in fact, a lot more police guarding the perimeter than last night, which was a good thing. The forensics, in their white overalls, were also still there taking photos and collecting samples.

"Morning." said Arnaud, which was meant for all those present.

He realized that they had all endured a long cold night and wanted them to know that he appreciated their hard work. Most of the group looked up and over at Arnaud and mumbled back, preoccupied with whatever they were doing. Arnaud then began walking slowly around the opening looking for anything unusual. It was the first time that he could really have a proper look at the crime scene. Arnaud spent a few moments staring at the tall tree with winding branches, on which the victim had been tied. He couldn't stop thinking why had the Magpie hung the body up against the tree. What was she trying to show? All he could think was that she just wanted the body to be found easily, and in stringing it up there, any passerby would see it.

"Morning, Arnaud!" came a voice from behind him along with a friendly tap on the shoulder, taking him by surprise. He turned around to see Roger Zwaart, a senior police forensic officer, who he had known for a long time and had worked with closely on the killings this year. He also regarded Roger as a friend and would sometimes grab a beer with him, if they had been working late on a case.

"Hi Roger." said Arnaud, please to see him. "You made me jump!"

"Sorry." replied Roger with a small smile on his face. He could have had a laugh with his friend, although now was not the right time.

"So, anything?" said Arnaud, getting straight down to business. He knew that he could trust everything that Roger would say to him as he was an experienced forensic, who was extremely thorough. He also knew all the traits of the Magpie as he had been working full time on the murder hunt this year.

Roger turned to face the open space behind them, brightly lit up, and then began to speak.

"Well, we can see by the broken leaves and twigs that the killer fled the scene of the crime through there." Roger pointed to the area behind the big tree on which she had tied the dead body.

"You can also see, along this other well-hidden track, crumpled grass and fallen leaves which have been smoothed down and pushed into the mud. This would indicate that they had entered the woods this way and dragged the body up this path into the opening."

Roger walked over to the other path and shone his torch along it. The flattened undergrowth made it very clear that there had been recent activity along the track and it definitely looked like a body had just been pulled over it.

As Arnaud stared at the second concealed path, Roger began to speak again.

"Interestingly, we followed the track all the way to the edge of the wood and it too winds around and comes out near the car park, which would make sense why they used this one. I would assume that the killer brought the body in a car, then took it out of the boot, and pulled it into the woods. What is very clear is that she must have first tried to carry the body, as the grass isn't so flat near the edge of the woods. Then, once it became too heavy for her, or them, they must have then dragged it the rest of the way to the opening."

Arnaud listened to Roger's every word and followed him along the narrow path, walking on the edge of it, in order not to damage any potential clues. The second track was also lit up by neon lighting on the ground. It was indeed very apparent that something had been dragged over the grass, after about twenty-five meters into the woods. As the two men reached the edge of the parkland, they looked over to see the police standing about forty meters away by the main entrance into the woods.

"Do you think that they fled from the crime scene the same way that they came in?" asked Arnaud.

"I'm not sure, but if they exited via another route then they would have still had to return to this car park to pick up their car and drive off." replied Roger, looking at Arnaud for his next question.

"Mmmm, that's true." said Arnaud.

"We have police scanning the whole perimeter of the woods and working their way inwards. They are checking for any other fresh paths where they may have run along but I do think that they scrambled from the crime scene out behind the tree where the body was hanging, and circled back to this path and headed down here to the car park." continued Roger.

"Okay." said Arnaud, looking around him, and then back at Roger. "That would make sense."

Roger began to speak again, "We don't have the final results from the autopsy that took place last night although I do expect it back this morning. Anyway, I wanted to point out that the body was extremely clean when it was left last night strapped to the tree. What I mean by that is that there were no marks or stains on the feet or legs of the victim, which would indicate that the body must have been dragged in a bag along the path. Otherwise I would have expected dirt on the feet."

"Agreed. Good point." replied Arnaud, scratching his hair.

"The body was indeed immaculate and very clean." re-iterated Roger.

Arnaud hadn't thought about this assumption, which is why he liked working with Roger.

"Unless the ground was frozen last night." replied Arnaud. "Then there wouldn't have been grass and dirt stains on the victim's legs and feet?"

Arnaud was saying this more as a question that he wanted Roger to answer, as he wasn't sure himself.

"True." said Roger. "But there would have been cuts or scratches on the victim's feet caused by scratching of the frozen ground and this wasn't the case."

Arnaud was silent but nodded in agreement with what his friend had said.

"Anyway, the ground wasn't completely frozen last night."

"How do you know that?" answered Arnaud, not really sure where this was going.

Roger turned and started walking back into the woods along the track.

"Follow me." said Roger with an upbeat tone in his voice. Arnaud didn't know what they were going to look at but he sensed there may be some evidence or a clue, which made his heart start beating faster.

They arrived back at the opening in the woods where the body was dumped and Roger walked over to the tree, where the victim was found.

"Come over here." He said to Arnaud as he kneeled down on the ground and took a pencil out of the pocket on the inside of his jacket. Arnaud walked over to him and leant forward to see what Roger was looking at. With the pencil in his right hand, Roger pointed to what appeared to be some fresh footprints. It was very clear that one set of footprints were much larger than the other ones, which made Arnaud believe that there had been a male and a female at the scene of the crime and close to the body. Arnaud was feeling extremely anxious about what was in front of him.

Roger began speaking again. "But the ground is frozen now and we have our clues." He looked up at Arnaud whose mouth was wide open and his eyes were transfixed on the footprints. They were thinking the same thing. The Magpie did have an accomplice and it was a male.

"These footprints are from last night Arnaud and none of the policemen have been walking near this point where the body was hanging. The only people who would have stepped here under the branches of the tree, would in fact be the same people who tied the body up. There is no other reason to stand here. So, we can safely conclude from this that these are the footprints of the killer and her accomplice.

Arnaud was shaking with adrenalin pumping through his body and a rush of excitement filling his senses. They had made a breakthrough, much larger than he was expecting. This brought a whole new dimension to the murder hunt. They would now have to go back to the previous murders and clues to see if there were any suspicious looking men or evidence that could help them. They would also need to go over the footage that they had collated to try and find a male accomplice. They were finally getting somewhere. They were getting closer.

"Is there anything else at this point, Roger?" asked Arnaud with a slightly shaking voice.

"No, that's the only thing worth mentioning at the moment, Arnaud. However, we should have a lot more natural light in an hour and we will do a full scrub of the area once again. The forensics had found a few hair samples in the opening, which have been taken back to the lab for checking. However, knowing what the wooded area is used for, it could have nothing to do with the Magpie." replied Roger.

"Okay Roger. Good work. Thank you. I'm going to head back to the office now and meet the rest of my team there. You have my mobile number, please call me if you get any more evidence." said Arnaud, looking straight into the eyes of his friend. He was very appreciative of his work and thankful that he had made a new discovery. Arnaud held out his hand and shook Rogers.

"Thank you again." said Arnaud before turning and heading back along the wider pathway into the woods.

He wanted to get back to the office and brief his team. They would all be excited by this breakthrough. The day was going to be even busier than Arnaud had originally expected. He walked passed the policemen standing at the entrance to the woods and reached inside his trouser pocket for his mobile phone. He wanted to send Friso a text before he got onto his moped. There was no point for him to come to the woods now. They needed to meet at the office. Arnaud took off his gloves in order to type the message to Friso.

'Hi Friso. Change of plan. Meet me at the office asap and notify the rest of the team. I have very good news. Arnaud."

* * *

8:05 a.m.

As Arnaud parked his moped in the garage of the police station, he could hear the muffled voices of Jim and Robin arriving as well. Friso had gotten the message out immediately to the other detectives. Arnaud turned around to greet the younger guys who were both wrapped up in thick jackets and woolen hats.
"Morning, guys!" said Arnaud.

"Hi boss." They replied, still half asleep. As they walked up the stairs from the garage to their office, they could hear Friso arriving, parking his blue car beneath them. They knew it was Friso, as he had a hole in his exhaust and it made a lot of noise. He sped into the garage, wheels screeching to a halt as he stopped. Friso was always in a rush and Arnaud was pleased that he had got here straight away as well. They didn't wait for him but went into the office and turned on the lights and the radiators. Jim immediately walked over to their small kitchen area to make a fresh pot of coffee, which they all needed. Arnaud took off his jacket and dumped it on the desk and then sat down and waited for the rest of the team to pull up their chairs and come over to where he was sitting.

All three detectives stood by Arnaud's desk. As they waited for Arnaud to speak, Friso's phone rang and he answered it. From the few words that he said to the person at the other end of the call, it was clear that it was the doctor who had carried out the autopsy. They all looked at Friso until he hung up the call after about five minutes.

"Friso, what did they have to say? You go first." asked Arnaud.

"It was the hospital and they have the results of the autopsy. Interestingly, while it definitely appears to be the work of the Magpie, there are a few observations and findings that are different from the previous killings." said Friso.

"What?" asked Arnaud.

He wasn't expecting this response from Friso. Did they have more clues? How could this be? What was different? Arnaud's head was racing, as the dead body had appeared to be exactly the same as all the previous victims.

"What did the doctor have to say? What was different?" Arnaud was very worked up and the rest of the team could see this and hear it in his voice.

"I've asked Dr. Kuipers to call back on your landline. He will be doing that any second. It's better if you hear it from him." replied Friso, believing that he had taken the right course of action.

The phone on Arnaud's desk rang momentarily and Arnaud clicked on the speaker. Friso and the other detectives sat down on their seats and moved closer to Arnaud's desk in order to listen clearly to the doctor on the other end of the line.

"Hello Arnaud, it's Dr. Kuipers. I was calling to give you the results of the autopsy."

"Okay, good."

There was silence, before Dr. Kuipers rolled off his findings in his usual methodical and detailed manner.

"The dead man is Sam Pikkart, twenty-eight years old, and was living in Tussen Kadijken, by the Artis Zoo in Amsterdam."

Arnaud looked over at Jim and Robin to make sure that they were making notes.

"Well, as I just mentioned to Friso, it definitely has all the traits of a Magpie killing. The body is perfectly clean with no markings apart from the ones on the wrists. Here, the skin was red and slightly cut from the ropes that were used to hold the body up against the tree. There was also no jewelry or clothing on the victim either, which I am sure you are aware of already."

"Yes. We saw the body at the crime scene last night. It's good to hear from you though that you see it also as a Magpie killing." said Arnaud. He was keen to hear what else the doctor had to say but didn't want to sound agitated on the phone.

There was a moment of silence before the doctor continued, "Cause of death was a broken neck once more in the fourth vertebrae, where there is some bruising present. Now, despite all these similarities there are some differences that you will be keen to know about."

All four detectives were staring at the dusty phone on Arnaud's desk in anticipation of what the doctor was going to say next. Adrenalin and anxiety filled the detectives.

"The victim has only been dead for a short period of time. I would calculate this at between twenty-four and thirty-six hours. This is different from the previous killings where the victims were dead for considerably longer. Now, that allows me to carry out more tests on the body as it is still fresh. I also wanted to point out that there appears to be an injection wound on the left side of the victim's neck. Such a marking, I would not have been able to spot if the person had been dead for three days, like some of the previous killings. I have done some preliminary blood tests and there are traces of Propofol in his blood."

"What is Propofol?" asked Arnaud.

"It's an extremely strong anesthetic that is used in surgical operations that knocks you out very quickly. It has been used on the victim."

"How was she able to inject him without any signs of physical restraint?" said Arnaud, thinking aloud. It was making sense that the Magpie had been using the drug to sedate her victims. She still needed to stick the syringe in though.

"Well, I'm not sure." replied the doctor. "Maybe the victims were injected when they were sleeping, but that's for you to work out."

Arnaud thought The Magpie must have been seducing them and then when they were asleep, she was injecting the victims. They clearly weren't being pinned down or restrained, as there was no bruising or scratching on the bodies.

"Anything else, doctor?"

"What's also important to note, Arnaud, is that this drug is not easy to get hold of. She must have access to a doctor or a hospital. That is the only place to get Propofol. I assume that she must have used this drug in the past, with the previous killings, and she would require a significant amount of the drug." said the doctor.

Arnaud wondered if the Magpie worked in a hospital or at a drug manufacturer? Was her accomplice a doctor? They could build a better profile of the Magpie now that they had another important piece of evidence. She must have used this anesthetic to sedate the victims before killing them and cleaning the bodies. Arnaud looked over at his team and he could see that they were feeling excited, just like he was.

"Thank you doctor." said Arnaud, trying to see if he had completed his assessment. If the doctor had nothing else to say then Arnaud wanted to get on with his own team meeting.

"Is there anything else at this point?" continued Arnaud.

"No, that's the general overview." replied the doctor. "I will send you the full autopsy report shortly."

"Okay, thank you." He clicked out of the call and turned to look at his team.

"Okay, what do we know? What next?" he said, walking over to his flip board once again. He felt comfort in writing everything down so that they wouldn't miss anything.

Arnaud continued speaking as he wrote bullet points on the paper in front of the other detectives.

"We now know that she has a male accomplice. They found some footprints at the crime scene. One pair is of a female and one set is much larger, almost definitely a male."

"Maybe it's one female with small feet and one female with big feet." responded Friso, questioning the new evidence. Arnaud looked at him but wasn't annoyed by his comment.

"It's possible and that's actually what I said to Roger, however, the forensics are convinced that the larger footprints are from a man because they are much deeper in the ground, which apparently indicates that they are from a much heavier individual."

"Okay, fair enough." replied Friso.

Arnaud continued, "Anyway, now we know that the Magpie is working with a male accomplice, it would explain how she is able to hold the victims down and maybe restrain them whilst injecting them with this sedative drug."

"And that also makes it easier to carry the victim to the place they store the body, as well as when they dump the victim. Corpses are like a dead weight and too heavy for the Magpie on her own to move around." Jim spoke out and the rest of the team agreed with him.

"Agreed." responded Arnaud. "Finding these footprints at the scene of the crime answered a lot of questions we had around the Magpie and how she operates. I also think that it is probably the guy who is breaking the necks of the victims." Arnaud paused for a second before continuing.

"We need to go back over a lot of our old evidence and witness statements to find out if there was ever a suspicious male at the locations where the victims were picked up from, etc. At this point we don't know if we are looking for someone of the same age group as the Magpie but that would be a good starting point. Friso, this is a very important process we need to carry out over the next few days and I want you to lead it with Jim and Robin. I am going to follow up with the forensics at the current crime scene throughout the day to see if any new clues have come up. We also know that the Magpie and her accomplice have access to these anesthetic drugs and syringes. Friso, we need to go to the local hospitals to find out where this is used. Who has access to it? Look for males and females in their late twenties and early thirties."

"Before we do all this, we need to visit the victim's family. I want a character profile on him by the end of the day."

"Friso, can you get Dijkstra here asap? Once he is here, I will get him up to speed on what has been going on. I will also get his view on how to approach the press with the findings."

"Okay, Arnaud." replied Friso.

"And Friso, please oversee the interviewing process of the victim's family and friends with Jim and Robin. I want to know everything about him, including where he went out and where he was last seen. And once you know his favorite bars and cafés pull the CCTV tapes." continued Arnaud.

"Yep." replied Friso, once more.

"Okay guys, let's not let anything slip by. Let's keep sharp." Arnaud watched his tired team nod.

"Let's meet back here at eight tonight." said Arnaud.

The team stood up and started going about their business. The jigsaw puzzle was beginning to fit together and the picture was getting clearer.

* * *

8:00 p.m.

Arnaud sat in a very warm office. The heaters had been on all day and now it was almost unbearably hot. The blinds covering the windows were all closed but it was already very dark outside. The main lights in their room had been turned off and there were only small lamps switched on, around Arnaud's and Friso's desks.

Friso wasn't back yet from visiting the family and friends of Sam Pikkart. He had texted Arnaud to say that he was on his way back to the office. Arnaud was looking forward to see if they had come up with any interesting leads. He was feeling a little disappointed as nothing more had come of the autopsy and there had been no further clues found at the crime scene. Arnaud had been expecting more but in the scheme of things this had been a day of substantial breakthroughs.

Apart from speaking several times during the day with Roger, Arnaud had been in the office talking with Dijkstra who was happy that Arnaud was making some serious steps forward with the case. Dijkstra was genuinely pleased for the team.

Friso and the two other detectives came into the office around eight thirty-five. "Sam Pikkart was twenty-eight years old and lived alone. He was gay but had no serious boyfriend. Looks like it's becoming harder for her to strike and that explains why she had to target a gay guy, who wouldn't have been expecting it. We interviewed his parents and closest friends and family. They are obviously extremely distraught. From the initial conversations, they weren't aware of him having any female friends that fit the description of the Magpie." replied Friso.

"They have given us names of some other friends that we still need to contact and interview. And we also need to retrieve the tapes from the two gay bars in the city, where he regularly hung out." said Jim.

"Wait until we have done the press conference tomorrow morning, and then you can collect the tapes and interview the bar staff. When did he last visit these bars?"

"Not sure. We asked his friends that and they didn't know. He was a bit of a loner so it's been hard to track down his movements." replied Friso.

"Okay, keep working on it." said Arnaud. "We know that he must have gone missing two days ago, so we are looking for anyone who had seen him on Tuesday or Wednesday."

"Yes, for sure. Jim will speak to them tomorrow." agreed Friso.

"Okay, anything more on the victim?" asked Arnaud.

"Well, he worked in Amsterdam for the council. He spent a lot of time at the gym and tended to keep to himself. He would go out once a week socializing or just hung out at home alone. Sounds like he was an introvert."

"That makes sense. Have you checked his apartment yet for clues?" said Arnaud.

"No, not yet. We have the keys and I will go there with Jim once we are done here."

"Once you have completed these interviews and collected the tapes, we can back track and look at the evidence from previous murders this year. I am sure there will be more clues for us to dig up now that we have all this information on the Magpie and her accomplice. We will be doing a press conference tomorrow morning. We don't expect to give too much information away at this stage, apart from the identity of the victim and a recent photo of him. We will appeal for witnesses to come forward on the back of this." said Arnaud.

He took a deep breath and then continued speaking, "We won't be mentioning that the Magpie has a male accomplice at this point. Not until we have been able to go over the old evidence. We don't want to scare her off."

The whole team nodded, understanding this message clearly.

"Keep up the good work and let's report back here at ten thirty in the morning."

Arnaud got up and walked with Dijkstra into his office. Arnaud wanted to finish writing the speech they were going to make to the press.

Through the glass, Arnaud watched the rest of his team disappear, one by one, leaving the office for the night. Around ten, Arnaud decided that they had covered everything and he made it clear to Dijkstra, which questions they were going to avoid. He was done for the night and wanted to get a drink. He needed to wind down and relax.

* * *

11:00 p.m.

Arnaud sat at his usual table. He was on his fourth beer and in a good mood. He was excited thinking about all the evidence that the team needed to look back over now. He kept thinking to himself that if they could identify this guy, then they would be able to find the Magpie. He was also happy that Noor was working tonight. He spent some time chatting with her and hearing what she had been busy with recently. Arnaud was intrigued that she had been on a couple of dates. She didn't say much to Arnaud except that the guy was a real gentleman and was very interested in her. Arnaud was pleased to see that Noor was happy and he also noticed that she was making a real effort with her appearance. Her work clothes were becoming sexy and revealing, and she had lost a substantial amount of weight.

Arnaud had also shared some information around the case but had asked Noor to keep it to herself. He explained that the Magpie had a male accomplice. He also told Noor about the anesthetic drugs that the killer was using.

Noor was very pleased that Arnaud and his team were making progress. She could see in his persona that he was more upbeat than normal. She was also happy to know that she was right about the Magpie having help from an accomplice and that it was indeed a man. These gave her arguments on the blog more credibility.

"I'm pleased to see that you are looking so happy, Noor." Arnaud said with a slurred tone in his voice.

"Arnaud, I am also pleased to see that you are doing well with the case and making progress. I can see that you too are happier and more upbeat. But you are also looking tired and if you have to do this interview tomorrow morning, you should go home and get some sleep."

Arnaud was surprised how quickly the time had passed. He had forgotten about the public address that he and his boss had to make tomorrow and he suddenly felt anxious thinking about answering pushy questions in the morning. He looked at his mobile phone and pager for probably the tenth time that night. He still hadn't received any messages, which meant that there was nothing new to report. He decided to take Noor's advice and go home and get some rest. Tomorrow was going to be another big day.

CHAPTER 23

November 11

9:30 a.m.

Jan was busy cleaning the apartment and for once there was something for him to do. It was messier than usual, which was surprising because there was one less person living there. Jan noticed that Roos was acting quite strange and he had seen a packet of condoms in her room, which had shocked him. While Roos was in the shower, he asked Fleur about it and she had chuckled and explained that Roos had brought this doctor home a couple of times.

Jan could also see that Fleur was unhappy living with Roos now that Jade was gone. Fleur told him that she didn't know if she was going to stay. Jan offered to help her by asking friends if they knew of spare rooms in the city center. He also wondered if Fleur left, maybe Roos wouldn't want him to clean the apartment anymore.

As Jan dusted the top of the chest in Roos' room, he could hear the two girls talking as they sat in the living room watching television. He stopped cleaning for a moment and walked to the top of the stairs and listened to the television. He could make out that the police were speaking about the murder hunt and their latest findings. A body had been dumped in the Slotervaart woods by the Nieuwe Meer. The apartment was still and silent as all three of them listened to the press conference.

"On the night of November 9, the body of Sam Pikkart was found in the woods by the Nieuwe Meer. He was discovered by a passing jogger. The victim was twenty-eight years old. We encourage anyone who knew Sam or may have seen him recently to come forward. We believe this to be the work of the serial killer. It would appear that Sam went missing on Tuesday or Wednesday night this week. We are still collating evidence from the crime scene. At this point, we have nothing else to say and are happy to take a few questions"

Once the detectives stopped talking, a barrage of questions came from the crowd of reporters. "How do you know it's the work of the Magpie?"

Arnaud decided to answer this question. "The body was found naked in the woods, just like the other victims this year and the cause of death appears to be a broken neck."

"Do you have any new evidence or clues, Arnaud?" shouted a Volkskraant junior reporter.

Arnaud paused for a second and then spoke up. "Yes, we do, but at this point we can't discuss them with you."

This seemed to get the crowd going even more as the noise got louder, and the pushing and shoving started.

It was now Dijkstra's turn to speak, "Now, as Detective Van Loo has just stated, we have some new evidence and good clues to help with the investigation. We can't say anymore at this point but what I can tell you is that the team of detectives running the investigation is making progress."

That ended their announcement. Arnaud turned and headed for the entrance to the police station, followed by Dijkstra.

As Jan had finished cleaning upstairs in Roos's apartment, he made his way down into the living room. Fleur was watching the rest of the news, which had now moved on to the weather. Roos was engrossed in the

NRC newspaper. She had the day off and was trying to relax. Fleur looked up and smiled at Jan and then spoke out.

"There has been another murder Jan. It's so terrible. I can't fucking believe it. I wish they could catch the killer." she said, with sadness on her face.
"I know, I heard." replied Jan with a sympathetic voice.

Roos said nothing but carried on reading the paper. Fleur began talking again, brushing her hair back and raising her arms above her head.

"I wish they would catch that crazy bitch and do us all a favor."

"Well, it sounds like they are getting closer." replied Jan, who focused in on Fleur's large chest beneath her tight t-shirt. Even though he was besotted with Mariana, he couldn't help but admire Fleur's amazing body and this distracted him completely from their conversation.

"Okay, I'm off." said Jan.

"Okay, thanks Jan." mumbled Roos. She didn't even look up from the paper.

Jan smiled at Fleur and she smiled back. He then walked towards the door.

* * *

4:00 p.m.

Noor sat at home behind her computer typing away on the blog. She had been spending a lot more time on this recently, now that she didn't need to go on dating websites anymore. She hoped that she wouldn't have to use those sites ever again. She had found the guy that she wanted, the guy of her dreams. Even though they had only met a couple of times, she felt that she had known him for most of her life. They had been emailing and texting constantly over the last few weeks and she was so in love.

Noor drank lemon tea and ate low-calorie crackers as she typed away. She had just taken a shower and washed her hair. Noor was not only pleased with her life, she was also happy with the way the commentary on the blog had been going. Noor took a few sips of her tea as she thought what to write as a final comment before signing off.

"It seems that the Magpie is finding it harder and harder to strike. Why do I think that? Well, now she has had to turn to innocent gay guys as victims. Her killing pattern has been broken. All praise to Arnaud and his team for this. They are getting closer to catching her as she is not able to plan her kills like she used to. The police are close to her doorstep!"

Happy Single switched off her computer, pleased with her final comments for the day.

* * *

6:00 p.m.

Arnaud sat in the office a little frustrated. He had hoped to see some interesting information from all the interviews they had been doing with the victim's family and friends. Unfortunately, there was nothing new to report.

Jim and Robin had pulled the tapes from the bars and still needed to go through them, which they would do tonight and tomorrow. As the two young detectives finished writing up the reports and interviews, they printed them off and made one nice neat pile of paperwork on the edge of Friso's desk for him to read through and sign off.

The silence in the office was broken by Arnaud's cell phone ringing, which made him and the other detectives jump. Arnaud reached for his mobile to see that Friso was calling.

"Hi Friso. Where are you?" said Arnaud.

"In my car, driving back to the office. Where are you?"

"I'm at the office with Jim and Robin."
"I've got some good news, Arnaud." said Friso.

Arnaud stood up, still holding the phone to his ear. He became anxious as he waited for Friso to respond. His hand starting shaking as adrenalin was taking over again. What good news do you have?"

"I can confirm that the only place that this anesthetic drug can be used or found in Amsterdam is at the Vu Hospital. Therefore, the killer or her accomplice must have access into the restricted areas at the Vu. We can do a check at the hospital tomorrow and go through the employee list with this restricted access."

Arnaud rubbed his hand through his hair and spoke back into the phone.

"Friso, this is great!"

"Okay." said Friso with a tired voice. "See you in five minutes."

CHAPTER 24

November 14

7:00 p.m.

Dr. Akkermans stood at the bottom of his beautiful wooden stairway, on the ground floor of his house waiting for Rina to come down. She had gone up to Mariana's old bedroom to see if she could persuade her to come out for some lunch. Both Dr. Akkermans and the maid were worried about her. She had locked herself in her bedroom for the last forty-eight hours and had only come out to go to the bathroom. In the night, her father had heard her sneak downstairs to the kitchen to get something to eat but clearly, she didn't want to see him so he didn't get up.

Mariana had been very annoyed with him recently and when she had let herself in the house two days ago, he was very surprised. At the best of times, Mariana was grumpy with her father but now she didn't even speak to him. In fact, she wasn't even communicating with the maid, whom she loved dearly. Dr. Akkermans was pleased that she was staying in his house but he was lost in terms of what to do about this situation and how to help his daughter.

Mariana had started screaming in the middle of the night and had woken up with her father and the maid besides her. She was inconsolable. It had sounded like she was on the phone with her boyfriend. Later, she just appeared to be crying very loudly to herself. Dr. Akkermans had considered calling Jan to find out what was going on, but he stopped himself from doing so, as this had made matters worse between him and Mariana the last time.

Dr. Akkermans stood there waiting for twenty minutes, head down staring at the purple velvet carpet that ran over and up the old wooden stairs. His tall frame left a long shadow along the ground floor hallway, as dim lighting shone behind him, showing the way up the stairs and also in the other direction, into the kitchen. He was sad and worried. What was wrong this time with his troubled daughter. He had no idea how to deal with her as they had no relationship apart from a blood and a financial aid one. He had seen all sorts of tantrums, rages, and strange behavior from Mariana over the years, but not like this. He decided to walk back into the kitchen and wait there for his maid. Another glass of red wine would help him relax and also pass the time.

* * *

9:00 p.m.

Arnaud and the team had spent the last few days in the office going through evidence from the previous murders. He had thought that the male accomplice of the Magpie would have appeared somewhere in all the previous witness statements or CCTV but so far, they had found nothing.

Friso and Robin had turned their attention to the employees at the Vu Hospital. They would interview everyone who had access to the wards and parts of the hospital where the anesthetic drug, Propofol, was stored and used. Before they started questioning hospital employees, they wanted to do some investigative work behind the scenes so as not to scare off the person that they were looking for. This process was worthwhile but was taking a long time. They hoped that they could start the interviewing next week.

Jim had spent the last thirty-six hours going through footage from bars and restaurants where previous victims had hung out and where they were last seen. He was now working on the footage from the Surprise Bar and would spend tomorrow going through the film that they had taken from the two gay bars where Sam Pikkart had hung out.

The four detectives had slept very little over the last week and the lack of progress with new clues was beginning to take its toll on them. The team was beginning to become despondent and demotivated. Arnaud could see this and had decided to treat them to some takeaway food and drinks. He knew that they were trying their hardest and the fact that there hadn't been any further clues was not their fault. They were crunching data and turning over every stone. It was just that so far, there had been no new evidence, and more specifically, no sightings of the Magpie's accomplice.

"Okay, guys, who is hungry?" said Arnaud.

It took a few seconds for this question to register with his three colleagues as they were all engrossed in their work. One by one they looked over at Arnaud and nodded.

"Okay." continued Arnaud, "How about Indonesian? It's on me?"

The two young detectives nodded with smiles on their faces and Friso spoke up.

"Perfect, thanks Arnaud. Do you want me to get it?"

"No, you stay here. I will go. It's quickest to get there on my moped anyway."

Arnaud put on his coat, gloves, and scarf and walked towards the exit door.

"I will get some beers as well." He thought that food and drinks was a small gesture which would lift the spirits of the guys.

When Arnaud returned back to the office about forty-five minutes later, he was surprised to see Robin and Friso huddled around Jim's desk, staring with bright eyes at his two computer screens. The three detectives didn't even look up when Arnaud came back into the office with the bags of food and drinks. Arnaud began to feel slightly nervous and on edge as he walked over to his team. He kept his coat on as he was still very cold from the freezing conditions outside. Why weren't they speaking to him? What were they looking at? Arnaud speeded up his steps as he made his way around to the back of Jim's desk so that he too could focus on the monitors.

Arnaud took his leather gloves off and placed them on the desk and then brushed his hair back over his head so that he could get a clear look at the computer screens.

"Okay guys, what is it. What have you found? What are you looking at?" said Arnaud. He could see that they were staring at the footage from the Surprise Bar. At this point the three detectives still hadn't acknowledged their boss and had remained transfixed on the screen.

As Arnaud waited for them to respond, he studied the two screens. On the left one was a normal shot of the club and a still of the Magpie in her wig with the victim. This was the still where she appeared to be looking over her shoulder, as she hugged him, probably staring at her reflection in one of the large glass wall mirrors that surrounded the dance floor. On the right-hand screen, were three still shots of a tall slim male in the club. You couldn't see the face but it appeared to be the same person in each frame.

"Guys, what the fuck is it?" said Arnaud with a raised impatient voice. He was getting annoyed that they weren't responding to him.

"Okay Jim, you found this so you explain." said Friso.

"No, you explain it, Friso. I will work the footage."

"Okay, Arnaud. As you can see this is the film from the Surprise Bar on the night that the Magpie took her ninth victim. We have all seen this footage before but this time we have been looking for a male accomplice. It seems like we may have found the guy."

"What?" said Arnaud, slipping off his jacket and pulling over a chair to sit next to Friso.

"On the left screen, you can see the Magpie on the dance floor with the victim. We have studied this shot a lot in the past and always thought that she was looking at herself in the full-length mirrors that hang on the walls." He then leant forward and pointed to the left screen and highlighted the back of a tall male, probably mid-twenties and fit. You couldn't make out his face as he was not facing the camera and appeared to be looking at the Magpie. The guy was standing about ten feet away from the killer and her victim at the side of the dance floor.

Friso continued, "I think that she is making eye contact with this male. We can't make out his face because we only see his back but you can tell that he has very short dark hair and is probably of a similar age to the killer."

Arnaud moved closer to the monitors and squinted his eyes to take a closer, more focused look at the left screen. He tried to follow the line of vision of the Magpie and it definitely seemed very possible that she was indeed looking at this male as she talked into the victim's ear.

"Interesting." said Arnaud. "Do we have any more shots of this guy in the club?" asked Arnaud.

"Yes." replied Friso, "and this is where it gets interesting." He tapped Jim's shoulder. He clicked on the first of three stills that he had saved. The first black and white picture enlarged to show the same male was ordering a drink from the bar. Again, it was a back and side shot of the guy and it wasn't possible to see his face.

"He must be quite tall." said Arnaud. "As the bar area is crowded and he stands out as one of the biggest guys there."

All three members of his team grunted in acknowledgement to what Arnaud said, knowing that this was a good observation.

"Okay." said Arnaud, waiting for Jim to go to the second still shot that he had on his screen.

As Jim enlarged the next photo, Friso started speaking again.

"In this picture, you can see the same male leaving the club about five minutes before the Magpie and the victim. The timing is too coincidental that they would all leave at approximately the same time. He knows where the cameras are positioned as he turns away from them as he exits."

"Just like the Magpie did." replied Arnaud.

"Yes, and if you study the whole tape from the evening," Robin chimed in, "very few party goers turn away from the camera. This is unusual."

"Mmm, true." said Arnaud, a little annoyed. "I think it strengthens the case that this is the male that we are looking for."

"You are right." said Friso with a small smile on his face. He nudged Jim again to get him to click on the final still shot that he had saved on his computer.

"It's too coincidental that they both are looking away from the camera when they left the club, however, the defining proof that this is our man can be found in the picture of him entering the club. This final shot shows the male coming into the Surprise Bar about twenty-two minutes after the Magpie. Again, we can identify him through his clothes and stature, however, what's most interesting is.."

"It's the hat. It's the same fucking hat!" shouted Arnaud, interrupting his colleague.

"Yes, he is wearing the hat that the victim had on when he left the club. Not only does it conceal his facial features as he comes in but it was used to hide the victim as he was led out of the club. Therefore, he must have passed it to the Magpie when they were in the club. We have checked the footage and can't see this, but at the end of the day, it doesn't really matter. This hat links the two together and this is definitely our man."

"You are right. This is the guy. But who is he?" said Arnaud.

"At the moment, we don't know, as we don't have a good image of his face at all." replied Friso.

"Good work, guys. Good fucking work." replied Arnaud. He patted his team on their shoulders.

"So, what now, Friso?" said Arnaud. He really knew what they would have to do but couldn't think straight at the moment.

There was silence as Friso thought for a couple of minutes. "Well, we now have a basic profile of the accomplice as well as an image. We need to go back over all the old evidence and search for this guy again. Hopefully, somewhere we will be able to find a picture of him."

"Do we tell the press now about the accomplice?" asked Robin.

"I think so." replied Arnaud. "We don't want to scare them off but at the same time we need to move fast. At the end of the day, we want to find him and catch them. We will release the pictures tomorrow and a brief explanation of the Magpie having a male accomplice and provide a description. At the same time, we can keep looking ourselves for a face shot. Okay?"

"Understood." replied Robin.

There was silence again in the office before Arnaud spoke up again.

"What haven't we looked into yet?"

Friso replied, "When we go through all the employees at the Vu, we now know we are looking for a male and a female in their mid-twenties, white, and in good shape. We should be able to narrow down the search and interview process quite quickly. Robin and I will do it. Jim, you need to go through the footage again at the Surprise Bar as well as from the two gay bars where the last victim used to hang out. Maybe, the killer or her accomplice were caught on camera there."

"Right." said Arnaud. "Guys, let's eat, drink, and celebrate. We are drawing closer to the killer. I want you all to relax for the rest of the night, if possible. I certainly need to. We all go home after dinner. Let's meet back here tomorrow morning at nine and filter through all the old evidence once more. This guy has to be in there somewhere. I will call Dijkstra later and brief him. We need to get him involved in the press conference tomorrow and release of the photos of the male that we are looking for. If we can't find him ourselves then maybe someone out there amongst the public knows him. Now let's eat. Who wants a beer?"

CHAPTER 25

November 15

10:30 a.m.

Arnaud came back upstairs after the press conference outside the front of the police station with Dijkstra. It had gone well. They were pleased to see that Arnaud and his team were making progress and the announcement of the Magpie having a male accomplice was well received. Arnaud released the freeze frames of the suspect to all the newspapers and television channels. He thought that there was a chance that somebody would recognize the guy, even though they didn't have a full-frontal face shot of him. Arnaud had made sure that his boss hadn't mentioned the anesthetic drug. They didn't want to scare off any of the staff at the Vu Hospital.

As Arnaud arrived in the office, he could only see Jim, who was busy in his usual spot behind his desk.

"Hi!" said Jim, who looked up for a second before focusing back on his computer screens clicking away on a mouse that was stopping and fast forwarding CCTV footage. Arnaud nodded back to Jim, not envying the task he had before him. Realizing that Robin and Friso must have gone to the hospital to look through staff records, Arnaud thought that now was the right time to fill Dijkstra in on their plans and strategies for the next twenty-four to thirty-six hours. Arnaud walked in to his boss' office and sat down. Dijkstra came in behind him and shut the door.

"Arnaud, this is truly excellent work that you and the team have done." started off Dijkstra.

"Well, we haven't done anything yet." replied Arnaud, a bit down beat.

"What are you talking about? You know that she has an accomplice, you know it's a male of a similar age to her and you know what he looks like. This is great!" said his boss in a very encouraging tone.

"Well, it all means nothing if we don't get an ID on the guy. After all we don't know what his face looks like." Arnaud was playing it down as he didn't want any added pressure. He was right though, that unless someone from the public came forward to identify the male suspect they would be no closer to ending this murder hunt.

"I'm sure someone will come forward and even if they don't, I think that one of the two suspects must work at Vu. That is another way we are going to catch them. Come on, Arnaud. Take some credit. You are doing well and I can tell you that the senior members of the police force are happy with your progress."

"Like I said, it's not over yet and we still haven't been able to ID either of them." Arnaud wasn't playing this game and simply didn't want to take any credit right now. He tried changing the subject and spoke up again.

"Okay, let me fill you in on the game plan, as we have a lot to be getting on with."

* * *

1:00 p.m

Noor had the afternoon off from work as she wanted to spend some time on the blog, responding to the hundreds of comments that had been posted in the last couple of hours and directed at her. The general chatter was simply praising Happy Single for working out a long time ago that the killer must have an accomplice and that it was probably a male. Noor had been right and now everyone knew it.

She read through all the comments:

What would happen next? Who was this tall guy? Would they be able to find him? What would happen if they couldn't get a picture of the accomplice's face? Would the Magpie carry on killing or would she stop as it was becoming harder for her to strike? Were the killer and her accomplice boyfriend and girlfriend? Were the detectives managing the murder hunt close to catching the killer?

Noor didn't care about the comments congratulating her for being right. She just wanted Arnaud to come through this and be respected for his hard work. She also wanted the killer to be caught. Noor still cared for Arnaud deeply, even though she had moved on from thinking of him as potential boyfriend.

As she replied to numerous messages, in her usual efficient 'busy bee' manner, very polite but to the point, she tried calling her boyfriend. After three attempts to reach him, she assumed he must be in a sales meeting and decided not to bother him anymore. She left him a sweet voice message and got back to finishing her replies on the blog. Noor then took a shower. She started singing as she washed herself, happy with her life. She was truly in love and her role as the 'secret detective' supporting Arnaud was paying dividends. If they could catch the killer then it would be a perfect year for Noor.

* * *

9:50 p.m.

Jan sat down slumped against one of the steel counters in the family bakery. All the lights were off and he was the only one in there. It was cold and dark and very still. He had spent the day making dough and baking bread. He was in his work clothes and still covered in flour. He sat on the concrete floor, curled up and scared. Reaching into his trouser pocket, he pulled out his mobile phone and proceeded to scroll through the contact names. Finding the name that he wanted to text proved difficult as his fingers and thumbs were cold. He pressed the 'ok' button when he found the right contact.

"We need to talk asap." wrote Jan. Tears were now streaming down his face.

After a minute, a message came back.

"Okay, but I can't now. What's up?"

Jan couldn't believe the reply. He started getting angry as he wrote a new message.

"You know what's up. I am on the front page of every newspaper and television channel. They are close to catching me."
"No, they aren't. They can't identify you."

"Not yet, but I'm fucking scared." replied Jan, wiping tears from his eyes.

"Calm down." came the response. "They don't know who you are."

"Maybe we should stop and disappear now." wrote Jan, which was his real wish.

"No way. We need to kill again. At least one more. Let's meet tomorrow night. I need more Propofol. We have run out. Can you organize it?"

"I can try, but I want to speak with you. I am fucking scared."

"Jan, we will talk tomorrow but chill out for now. They don't know who you are and are no closer to catching you. Just try to relax and we can go over things tomorrow, okay?."

Jan put his head in his hands and continued sobbing. He was just a hometown boy from a loving family in Badovverdoorp. His phone vibrated again as it received another message.

"Let's meet tomorrow at six p.m. Don't forget, I need the Propofol."

"Okay." he replied.

Putting his cell phone on the floor next to him, Jan closed his eyes and tried to control his breathing. He was almost hyperventilating with panic. He wanted to get into bed and sleep and never wake up again.

CHAPTER 26

November 16

8:00 a.m.

Jan woke up early not really sleeping at all last night. He was scared and tired. He also had constant paranoia that someone would recognize him and that he was about to be caught. He sat in his van with the engine turned off but the heating on, parked in the main public car park at the Vu Hospital. Every time he heard a noise behind him or someone walking past his vehicle he jumped and looked down, trying not to reveal his face to any passersby. Jan was convinced that someone would spot him and then call the police.

Jan had bitten his nails right down to the fleshy tips of his fingers and all of them were bleeding. His hands were shaking as well, quite violently, as he tried to get control of his physical state and emotions. He had been asking himself how he had gotten into this mess. He wasn't crazy and it was she who had convinced him to help. It was driving him slowly insane to think that he had been involved in eleven murders this year. Even though he wasn't the one selecting the victims or seducing them, he was certainly her accomplice to murder. He had helped hold the sleeping victims down, as they were injected with the strong anesthetic. In February, they hadn't managed to find the guy's vein in his neck and he had woken during the injection and punched her in the face. If it hadn't have been for Jan jumping on top of him and restraining him, he would have probably escaped.

Jan had also inserted the syringe a couple of times. Once the guy had been killed, it was Jan who would lift the body and carry it to the long table on which the victim would be undressed, stripped of all of his possessions and then cleaned. She would take a long period of time completing this process and didn't want Jan rushing her. It almost amazed him how she could have a dead body being so close to her for two days as she worked on it, taking away all its possessions and stripping it of its dignity. The cleaning was so methodical that she also always took control of this stage. She was so meticulous about making sure that there were no clues or DNA on the victim's bodies that could lead back to her. This was why she was so good and hadn't been caught. She was a professional.

After the victim had been completely cleaned, Jan would put the corpse into a body bag. He would also carry the body into the back of his baker's van and then they would drive together to her dump location of choice. Of course, when they got there, it was Jan who would lift the body out and dump it.

The more he thought about it, the more he realized he was an integral part of this process. But he hadn't actually done the killing. She took great care and pride in ending all of the victims' lives by snapping their necks. As he stared at himself in the mirror above him he could see that he looked very pasty and pale. He had dark rings around his sunken eyes like a heroin addict, although his drug was fear. Jan tried to convince himself that he could still get out of this mess and walk away, but the more he thought about it, the more he realized that he was as guilty as Mariana.

He sometimes thought to himself that he should stop and just walk away, but was there any point? He would eventually be caught and so why stop now? He was equally guilty.

Jan had helped his mother and sister take a large batch of freshly baked bread out of the ovens this morning and box it up for delivery. They could see that something was wrong with Jan, that he was tired and his mind was elsewhere. They always blamed everything on Mariana but didn't mention her this time. They hadn't even asked Jan what was up. They could see that he didn't want to talk. When he sped off in the van they assumed that he had gone to the University or to Mariana's. He either had girlfriend issues or was late with some essays.

The thought had crossed his mind a hundred times last night, whether he should stop while they were ahead and just disappear on his own - go travelling for a couple of years. But he couldn't. If he left her, she would continue killing, and on her own she would get caught. Then, it would be found out that he was involved. For now, he had to continue. He had to help with the next kill, then maybe, he could persuade her to stop and quit. This gave him some peace of mind. As he managed to get control of himself and calm down a little bit, Jan tried to focus on what he had to do next.

What he needed to do now was get some Propofol. He could get the drug from the secure store in the East wing of the hospital by the operating theatres. In order to get into the secure part of the hospital, Jan had originally bought a male nurse's outfit online. He had been able to sneak into building, back in January, and stole a uniform from the men's changing rooms. This helped him blend in with the rest of the hospital staff. Jan had then taken Roos' hospital pass from her bedside table. Roos had unrestricted access to all parts of the hospital. While she couldn't believe that she had lost it, she never accused Jan as she had no reason to. He had no use for it. It wasn't that big a deal anyway because she could just get a new one from the hospital. With the pass, Jan stuck a passport photo of himself over her picture and then changed the name at the top of the plastic from a female name to a guy's name. Jan never had a problem getting in or out of the hospital as everyone was always in a rush. He fitted in very well, like any other member of the medical staff.

He had become very confident walking around the hospital, nodding at other employees and giving flirty smiles to attractive nurses. This time was going to be different though. He was extremely scared and convinced that someone would put two and two together, and associate him with the tall slim man that was all over the newspapers and television. Even though he hoped that this would be the last time that he would have to do this trip, he was paranoid that he would be spotted.

The windows of his van were completely fogged up from the warm air that he breathed. He needed to get out of the van straight away as he might look suspicious sitting in it. He also needed to get some fresh air and relax before going into the East Wing. Jan just needed to check his phone to see if she had tried to call him or send him a text. There was nothing there from her.

Jan clipped the official identity pass of the hospital to the breast pocket of his medical shirt. He got out of the van and walked briskly into the hospital. 'Come on Jan, get a grip. This is a piece of a piss. You have done this routine loads of times. Just chill out!' he said to himself as he moved closer to the building, rubbing his eyes to try and wake himself up a bit more. He felt so weird because he was tired from lack of sleep but extremely wired and on edge from the fear of being caught.

Getting to the entrance of the East Wing, he realized that everyone was just going about their business. He began to relax a little as he made his way inside. Jan walked straight into one of the elevators and pressed the button for the third floor. Once he reached this level, he stepped outside the elevator and froze on the spot. Three policemen and what looked to be a detective were standing by the reception area of the operating department. There also appeared to be a line of nurses and some doctors queuing up to go into a small office room next to the reception area. What the hell was going on? What was happening in that office? He didn't know what to do as a rush of panic shook his body. He didn't turn around but walked backwards into the elevator. His hand was shaking quite dramatically as he reached out with his index finger to press the ground floor button. What the fuck were the police doing there? Were they looking for him? Had they found a picture of him? He got to the ground floor and jogged out of the elevator and through the exit doors of the building.

Once he got back to his van, he sat down, and slowly head butted the steering wheel over and over again as he tried to get his thoughts together. He needed to know what the police were doing at the hospital, and more specifically, why the hell were they on that particular floor. It couldn't be coincidence, surely. The more he thought about it, the more he realized that even if they had found a picture of him, they had no reason to go to the hospital. He didn't really work there and they had no reason to believe that he did, so they couldn't be there looking for him.

Jan began to compose himself as he sat in his van. He still couldn't work out why they were on the third floor where the operating theatres were located. Maybe they were investigating a patient that was having surgery? Jan needed to find out. He decided to drive over to Roos' to ask her innocently what was going on. He would pretend that he thought he was supposed to clean her apartment today. At least, when he saw her he could ask her how was work going and see if she mentioned anything about the police. This was not a bad plan, thought Jan, and it was the only way he would be able to get peace of mind. He was shaking with paranoia.

Before he drove off, he clambered over the front seat and into the back of the van where he had his casual clothes. Jan changed out of the hospital uniform and started driving into the center of town in the direction of Roos' apartment. He needed to calm down and remain collected as he didn't want to give the girls any cause for concern. Jan didn't want them asking him if everything was okay or wondering why he was looking so ill and exhausted.

Arriving at the Singel, Jan parked his van in the first available free spot and walked quickly over to Roos' apartment. It was a freezing day and there was a strange mist coming from the canals, almost like a fog. This comforted Jan as he felt that it kept him a bit concealed from anyone who might recognize him. 'Okay, get control of yourself, for fuck's sake.' He said to himself as he arrived outside the apartment. He checked his phone for any messages or missed calls, but there were none. He took a deep breath before ringing the doorbell.

He heard a noise inside the apartment and within a few seconds Fleur opened the door.

"Hey Jan!" she said sounding a bit surprised that he had come over today.

"Hi Fleur! Can I come in, it's freezing out here?"

"Yes, sure. Is everything okay?" She asked, seeing pretty quickly that he looked very tired and pale.

"Yes, fine thanks. I have just been very busy with my studies, the bakery, and the cleaning jobs." He replied, having already planned this response in anticipation.

Jan walked passed Fleur into the small living room. She closed the front door and turned to face Jan. He sat down on the sofa and was blowing into his cupped hands to warm them up. Jan was shivering quite badly but Fleur didn't know that this was from fear and panic rather than being cold.

"Are you sure you are okay? You are shaking. Let me make you a cup of tea." she said, seeing that he was shivering.

"Okay, thanks. Yes, it's freezing outside and I had to walk quite a way to get here as I couldn't find parking space nearby." replied Jan, quite happy with the lie he had just told.

"Oh, okay." said Fleur, turning and walking into the open kitchen to boil some water.

"So, what are you doing here?" asked Fleur, with her back turned to Jan.

"Cleaning, of course!" he replied.

"Cleaning? You were here two days ago. I know Roos loves a clean house but that's over the top even by her standards! Did she ask you to come today?"

"You know what, you are right. I've made a mistake then." said Jan, lying again. "Where is Roos? Maybe I should ask her if she wants me to clean the apartment now since I am here."

"She has gone out. She wasn't supposed to be working today but she had to go to the hospital to do an interview with the police."

"An interview? What for? Why?" asked Jan, very fast with his response; almost too quick.

"Not sure actually, but she said something about medicine being stolen or missing." said Fleur in a disinterested tone. "Must have been important though, as she had to go in on her day off."

As Jan listened to what Fleur was saying, he started panicking again and a wave of fear and anxiety crashed over him. He looked at his hands and they were shaking profusely. He put them into his coat pockets so that Fleur wouldn't notice them when she turned around. He knew that he must look a real mess and he needed to get out of there as quickly as possible. He didn't need Fleur worrying about him and then talking about him with Roos. He just needed to leave now. 'Why are the police at the fucking hospital speaking with staff about missing drugs? It must be the Propofol they have noticed has gone missing.' Jan thought. It didn't make sense as he had only stolen small doses of the anesthetic and compared to the amount the hospital used in a day, it was insignificant. Did they have another reason to ask questions to the Vu staff and start poking around in the hospital? He stood up from the sofa, wanting to get out of the apartment. He needed to get away and think. He also desperately needed to go and talk with Mariana and share what was going on. He was a paranoid mess.

Fleur turned around and started walking back into the living room with two cups of tea in her hands.

"Oh. What's up, Jan?" she asked, seeing that he was getting ready to go.

"I need to go, Fleur, sorry." he replied, walking up to her and touching her shoulder affectionately in passing.

"But I have made you a cup of tea. Stay, drink it, and warm up. Come on, please stay." she replied, worried about his physical appearance and the state he was in.

"No, I really have to go. I should probably get some rest. I think I am coming down with something." replied Jan, opening the front door.

"Okay, well should I give Roos a message?" asked Fleur.

"No. In fact, please don't tell her that I came round. I don't want her thinking that I am disorganized and don't know what day I should be coming over to clean." replied Jan, with a clever answer that actually worried Fleur even more. He knew that Fleur would stick up for him and he really didn't want Roos to think that he had been snooping around.

"Oh, okay. Sure." replied Fleur, as the door slammed shut. Jan was gone and she was left quite confused as to what was going on with him. Whatever it was, he was looking ill and in a bad way.

Before Jan sped off down the Singel in his van, he pulled out his cell phone again and sent a text.

'Hi – we need to meet now. We need to discuss what the fuck we are doing. There were police at the hospital and I haven't been able to get any of the drugs. See you in ten minutes.'

He waited for about thirty seconds and then his phone vibrated.

'Calm down. Get something to eat and then come over to my apartment in an hour. I will meet you there.'

He looked at his watch and saw that it was a little past ten. He had some time to kill before he could go over to her place. He wasn't hungry so he decided to just wait in the van till it was time and he could head over to meet Mariana.

* * *

11:15 a.m.

Jan rang the brass doorbell of her apartment. He was even colder now and he could hardly feel his fingers. As he waited for her to answer the door, he was thinking through what he wanted to talk about first. As the door opened, he slipped inside quickly to see his beautiful girlfriend standing there, wrapped in a long thick cashmere cardigan. The lights were off in the hallway and it was hard to see her face too well. He could immediately make out that she also looked extremely tired and probably hadn't been sleeping well either. While she still looked stunning, her skin was pale and blotchy, and her beautiful eyes were surrounded by dark grey rings. Mariana's eyes were also red and he knew straight away that she must have been crying. Jan moved forward to give her a hug but she shunned him by turning around and walking into her living room. This was a typical reaction and had nothing to do with this current situation. Jan followed her.

She sat down on the dark red sofa, curling her legs underneath her and pulling a blanket up and over her body. She didn't look up at Jan who was now standing over her, but she could sense his presence.

"Sit down. We need to talk." she said to Jan, giving him a clear order. Whilst he had so much that he wanted to say, he knew that she was also unhappy. It was best to just listen to her and do what she said.

Jan sat on the rug in the middle of the living room. He looked down at the ground and waited to see what Mariana had to say. There was an eerie silence for a few moments and then she spoke up.

"So, you couldn't get any more of that drug?"

"No, I couldn't. The hospital was swarming with police. I'm worried Mariana. I'm scared. I'm sure they know who I am. What are we going to do? Let's just stop now and leave." Jan blurted out all of these phrases, one after another, in a hysterical voice.

"Calm down." she replied in a calm soft voice.

"You are fine. They have no idea who you are but now they have pictures of my back and my side. I'm all over the news. How long before my parents recognize me or someone else we know spots me? What were the police doing at the hospital? They obviously know who I am or they have found the drug that we use on the victims. It's over, Mariana."

"Calm the fuck down!" she shouted back at him in a high-pitched scream, taking Jan by surprise and making him jolt. It also had the desired effect as he shut up immediately and looked up at his girlfriend, sitting above him on the sofa.

As he waited for her to speak, his eyes filled up with tears and he began sobbing.

"Listen, it's not over yet so get that out of your fucking mind now. It's not over. I'm not finished. We are not finished. Our legacy still needs to continue so be clear about that, Jan." said Mariana, in a controlled manner. She could see that he was really scared and decided to be more comforting as she began speaking again.

"Jan, please get yourself together. Take control of yourself and try to calm down. They don't know who you are. In fact they have no more of a clue about your identity than they have of mine. You are just being paranoid and worrying too much."

"Yes, but maybe they will find a head shot of me or someone will recognize me?" replied Jan in a blubbering voice.

"Jan, there are a lot of tall slim men in The Netherlands. That is not much of hunch to go on in filtering down the search for you." responded Mariana in a sarcastic but friendly way. She was trying to relax Jan and at the same time, cheer him up a bit. In this current state, he was no use to her at all.

She continued speaking. "We have both been extremely careful avoiding contact with cameras where we have been over the last year. They won't be able to recognize us without frontal facial pictures. You really need to calm down."

As he cried, looking down at the ground and playing with his hands, he nodded back to Mariana.

"And I have been thinking about the police being at the hospital. It can't be anything to do with you, Jan. You don't even work there. It has to either be a completely separate investigation or they may have found some traces of the drug in one of the victims, probably the latter."

Jan thought for a moment about what she said and agreed with her conclusions.

"Even if they have found Propofol in that dead asshole, then it still doesn't track back to us, so stop worrying. Okay?"

Jan nodded again. Mariana looked at her perfectly painted and manicured finger nails as she thought for a moment.

"Although it does mean that we will need to sedate the next guy differently if we can't get hold of anymore of that drug." continued Mariana, thinking out loud.

"Maybe we will have to wait until the next victim is sleeping before we kill him? That would mean that I will have to seduce them and get them back to my bed. I don't really fancy sleeping with any of these guys."

She was interrupted by Jan. "Baby, let's just stop now. Let's just end this and get away. We could leave tomorrow and both get off the hook, free from these murders. We don't need to do this anymore, darling."

"I decide when we stop. I decide if we kill again. I am not going to have my killing dictated to me by anyone. I am the one who is going to decide whether I end another guy's life or not."

There was silence again as Mariana stopped ranting. Her expression was stern and strong as she looked down at Jan who was blubbering away on the floor next to her. She showed no emotion at all and didn't even try to comfort her boyfriend.

"Understood?" She blurted out at Jan.

He wiped his eyes and nose and looked up at his girlfriend with a pained and sad face. He was infatuated with her even though she was sick in the head. Not only did she show no love towards him or anyone else, Jan still couldn't believe that she had become so messed up that she wanted to kill people. She had become a hater of men and detested the male sex so much that she wanted to take their lives. This fulfilled her and made her happy to the point where she wanted to kill more and more. She insisted on dumping the bodies naked without any jewelry or other items on them, her own sick way of stripping them of anything of value. She wanted the victims to leave the world the same way that they entered it - with nothing. Mariana wanted the dead bodies to be found naked, leaving the victim ashamed and vulnerable for everyone to see.

Mariana had perfected her work as the months had passed, becoming more professional in the way she selected her victims and seduced them before the actual killing took place. She planned this whole process down to the smallest detail, leaving nothing to chance. Jan could see that she not only took pride in the murders but also felt that she had a right to kill these men. He dared not ask her why she did this but was certain that it stemmed from her father and the sadness that she had felt when her mother passed away. She blamed her father for her mother's cancer and had never forgiven him for having an affair and cheating on her.

Jan was afraid that she would try and kill her father, but she was too cunning, and he knew that she needed his support. She needed his financial support, and hence, needed him alive. If he passed away,

Mariana would inherit a lot of money but not until she was forty when the trust fund would be handed over to her. Dr. Akkermans was well aware that she was a spendthrift and didn't want her to have access to cash until she was mature enough to handle it properly. Mariana detested him for this and for everything else that he did and stood for.

As Jan looked up at his girlfriend, he thought about the severity of the mess that they had got themselves into. For her, she was fine with the situation. But she had persuaded him to get involved in this killing spree. She had convinced him to help her, to support her, and to actually become an accomplice to murder. He loved her so deeply. Mariana was everything to him, he would do anything for her, even if it meant risking his own life. She had become an obsession to him.

Jan was taken by surprise by Mariana shrieking out loud again and she made him jump.

"I said, is that fucking understood?"

He couldn't hold back the tears and started bawling again but managed to answer her this time.

"Yes." he replied as he sniffed and sobbed away.

Mariana continued staring at him showing no feelings or compassion. She saw Jan as her assistant and she needed one. She also knew that he adored her and would do anything for her. She needed someone that she could trust and he was this person. She had used this to the fullest - getting Jan to help her in all aspects of the killings. Right now, he was useless to her as he was scared, paranoid, and not able to do or help with anything. Mariana needed to calm him and get Jan to focus. She couldn't operate without him being in control of himself.

Mariana leant forward and put her arms around his neck trying to look like she cared, and spoke to him as she stared into his eyes.

"Okay, come on. Please try to calm down Jan. I am here for you. We will never be caught, my darling. Never. We have covered all our tracks so well and have been so careful. They have nothing on us. Nothing." she said, with a relaxing tone in her voice.

Jan looked at her adoringly with his weeping eyes and nodded. She wiped the tears from his cheeks and continued speaking softly to him.

"I need you to stay focused and support me. I can't do anything without your help, Jan."

"I know." he replied, "But I am so worried that we are getting closer to being caught. It's getting harder for you to find new victims and there are so many undercover policemen on the streets. One of them will get us soon. We almost got caught dumping the last body. They are honing in on us. It's obvious. They will catch us soon. Can't you see that? I don't know how much longer I can do this." Jan was speaking in an uncontrollable way, crying as he rambled with fear in his voice.

Mariana could see that he was a mess and was very frightened. She decided to lie to him in order to get his attention and support.

"Listen baby, I will make a promise to you. Help me with the next killing and then we will stop. I promise."

Jan's mouth opened up wide as he looked at Mariana with disbelief. He wasn't sure he had heard what she had just said correctly. Was she really going to stop? What would this mean for them? Could they escape from this mess and leave Amsterdam together? Would she stay with him after this was all over? Was she telling him the truth? Ideas, thoughts, and questions were flying around Jan's head. He couldn't think straight and just continued staring at Mariana.

"What did you say?" he whispered to her.

There was a pause before she spoke again in her controlled tone. "We will stop after the next one."

"Do you mean that, baby? Do you really mean that?" asked Jan again, still in shock.

"Yes, I do." replied Mariana with a serious expression on her face. She wanted Jan to believe her. She needed Jan to believe her.

He smiled and got onto his knees and fell on her lap and hugged her.

"Oh baby! Thank you!" he said in a high-pitched voice.

She put her hands on his head. She comforted him for a few minutes and then started speaking again.

"Jan, I need you to promise me something now. I need you to get control of yourself. I need you to help me. We have to plan the next kill and you need to have your wits about you. Okay?" she asked him, looking down at him.

"Okay." he replied, still with his head buried into her lap. She lifted his head and made him look at her.

"I really need you to focus now. The next killing will be tougher, with all the policemen everywhere, and the fact that we don't have any of this anesthetic. I need you on the ball and there for me all the time, okay?"

"Yes." replied Jan as he stared into her beautiful eyes. He was infatuated with her facial features. He found her so stunning that she could hypnotize him with everything that she said.

"Okay, good. Well, without you I can't do this- so stay composed. Now, is there anything else that you are concerned about or is there anything else you haven't forgotten to tell me, involving the police or other important information? What else is on your mind that you want to discuss with me?"

He thought for a moment as he sat there. Jan started to feel a little relaxed. He knew that he shouldn't mention his paranoia about the images of him in the newspapers as this would probably annoy Mariana and they had been over this already. Then it came to him.
"Yes, there is something."

"What?" snapped Mariana, "What is it? Tell me."

"It's that blogger. She is worrying me. I'm worried that she will recognize me. We have been on three dates now and I'm sure that she will put two and two together sometime soon. She is obsessed with this murder hunt and spends more time focused on this and blogging about it, than anything else. You know that she is best friends with the lead detective on the case. While he doesn't know it, she is getting a lot of inside information on what's been going on and she uses that to post her ideas and opinions on that blog. She is a pain in the arse and is hurting us. I'm really worried about her. I'm worried that she will recognize me. And I hate kissing her. She's disgusting."

Mariana thought for a moment and then spoke up, "We've been over this. It's good for you to stay close to her. I agree that she is a real threat to us and she is helping those idiots in the police. But you have to stay close to her and if that means kissing her, and sleeping with her, then you need to that. You need to do it for me and for us. She is really our worst enemy in all of this. She is helping the police make progress so you have to stay close to her. We need to know what the police are thinking and doing, especially now."

"I know." replied Jan, with a saddened face.

"But if she becomes too much of a threat, we can get rid of her." said Mariana.

"Get rid of her?" asked Jan.

"Yes, kill her." said Mariana. "If she gets too dangerous, we will kill her as well. I really don't care."

Jan was looking down holding on to Mariana's waist. He was exhausted and needed to sleep. Now that Mariana had managed to calm him down, Jan's eyes were closing with tiredness.

"Okay." he replied.

"But not yet, baby." Mariana spoke again giving clear instructions to Jan. "We will stay close to her and I want you to keep getting information on what the police are planning, okay?"

Jan didn't respond. He was asleep.

CHAPTER 27

November 26

5:10 p.m.

Jan had been busy all day helping out in the kitchen at the bakery. His father was off work with flu, so Jan and his sister had twice as much to do. He had been managing to get some sleep over the last few days, because he had convinced himself that the police didn't know who he was. Jan was also excited that Mariana had agreed to stop after one more victim. It was going to take a big weight off of his shoulders and he hoped they could both go traveling and disappear together. Knowing that there was going to be an end to all this gave Jan peace of mind, and he felt relieved that this was only one month away. For now, he was keeping his head down and trying his best to lead a normal life at home and with his family.

He hadn't had too much contact with Mariana during the last week. He wanted to spend some time away from her. Apart from being concerned that they would be seen together, he knew that she wasn't in a good place, either. She had been staying at her father's house and sleeping all day in her bedroom. Why she wanted to do this, Jan didn't know and he wasn't about to ask her either. She had been extremely unhappy and his conclusion was that she was probably worried and annoyed that the police were getting closer. They were also making it harder for them to strike and Jan was certain that this was also frustrating Mariana. While Jan was pleased that there would be an end to the killings, he was sure that Mariana felt the opposite. Her legacy was coming to an end.

Jan stood in the cold air outside, cooling off from a day next to the hot baking ovens. He took out his cell phone to check if he had received any messages. Interestingly, he had three missed calls from Mariana's father and one text message from Mariana. He opened the text message which just said, 'Call me.' He decided that he would call her back once he got home and was up in his bedroom. He wanted to be in a place where he could relax. The missed calls from Dr. Akkermans were a bit of a surprise. He hadn't left a message so Jan had no idea what he wanted. Jan wasn't going to call him back anyway, because the last time he had done this, Mariana had gotten very angry and upset. With everything that had been going on recently, Jan thought that the best option was to speak with Mariana first and let her know that her father had been trying to get hold of him. Maybe she knew what he wanted. And if she didn't, well she could at least decide whether she wanted Jan to call him back or not.

Jan went back inside to get his coat and then left the bakery. Once he got into his bedroom, he turned on the television and lay back on his single bed. He turned up the volume as they were talking about the murder hunt on the news. The police who were leading the investigation had announced that the killer had been using an anesthetic to knockout the victims before murdering them. The drug that had been injected was Propofol and the police had been carrying out interviews with the staff at the Vu Hospital, which was the only medical facility where the drug was used regularly for operations. While nobody had been charged at the hospital, it was possible that the Magpie had been getting the drug from somewhere else, like Utrecht, where it was also used a lot by surgeons.

Jan turned the television off and lay flat on his bed, looking up at the ceiling. He was relieved that the police had not recognized him at the hospital. He also knew, however, that it was going to be almost impossible for them to use that drug again. Now that the police knew that the victims were put to sleep through anesthetic injections, they would definitely be on the lookout at all hospitals for suspicious people walking near storage rooms and operating theatres. They would have to kill this last victim in a different way and that would probably be harder. Jan hoped that Mariana wouldn't be annoyed too much by this. She always wanted to be in control and the fact that she would have to change her pattern would definitely anger her.

Jan picked up his cell phone and dialed Mariana's number. The phone only rang once and her sexy voice answered.

"Hi, it's me."

"Why are you calling me so late? I have been waiting for you to call?" Mariana said, annoyed.

"Sorry, but I have been working all day. My father is sick so we have been really busy."

There was silence for a few seconds before Jan spoke again.

"Have you seen the news? About the police talking about the anesthetic?"

"Yes." replied Mariana. "Took them long enough to work that out. Pathetic. Anyway, it shows you that you have nothing to worry about. They were at that hospital interviewing staff. They have nothing on you."

"Yes, I know."

"Anyway, that was why I was calling you, Jan. I have an idea and we can use the fact that the police are onto the Propofol lead and the Vu Hospital to our advantage." said Mariana.

Jan had no idea what she was going on about but was intrigued to hear more.

"What do you mean?" He said in an inquisitive voice.

"Well, I have spent the last five days out and about looking for the next sad bastard whose life I am going to take. There are undercover police everywhere. Even if I walk into a bar alone, I look like a suspect now. Every male is wary of being approached by any single white female in their mid-twenties. These fuckers are making it tough for me. Very tough. But they haven't won. They won't beat me. I will get another guy. I have a few more weeks to find my last target for the year." Mariana was mumbling a little and Jan really had no clue what she was talking about or what this had to do with the Vu Hospital.

"Baby, I don't know what you mean?" said Jan timidly, hoping that she wasn't going to get annoyed with him.

"Well, it's becoming almost impossible for me to strike. It's becoming very difficult to find a guy whose life I want to take." said Mariana.

There was silence again as Jan thought about what she had just said. She had actually admitted that she couldn't find a target. This was very unusual of her, to accept defeat, which was what she was sort of doing. Jan didn't know how to answer her without offending her.

"So, what do you want to do Mariana?" he asked, hoping that she would say that this was the right time to stop before they got caught. He knew in the back of his mind that she would never make that decision. He just waited for her to speak again.

"I have a plan. How we can make one more killing and go out on our terms. On my terms. This will make those detectives look so stupid, and at the same time, make me look like a genius."

"Okay, go on." replied Jan in a quiet voice. He couldn't even imagine where she was going with this.

"Well, the only way I can feel comfortable about making a hit and not get caught is if there were a lot less undercover policemen in bars and on the streets. Now, that will only happen if they manage to catch the Magpie." said Mariana.

"Okay?" said Jan, still confused and none the wiser.

"So we help them think that they have caught the Magpie, by framing someone else."

"Okay. Go on." replied Jan still confused.

"It would be very easy for us to frame that bitch whose house you clean. The girl who works at the hospital. At the Vu, you know. What is her name?" said Mariana.

"Roos?"

"Yes, Roos. She works at the Vu and the police already think that the killer must work or be associated with someone at the hospital. Well, we can frame her and she fits the basic description of the Magpie. Nice figure, white, mid-twenties."

"Okay, but how are we going to frame her?" asked Jan. He could see what Mariana was thinking but had no idea how Roos could be accused of the murders. She had been interviewed by the police already and was not a suspect.

"All we need to do is plant some of the jewelry and belongings of the murdered victims in her apartment, along with some syringes. That should be enough to get her charged."

Jan couldn't believe that Mariana had concocted such a plan. It was genius. She was so cunning and smart and Jan felt that the police would definitely fall for this.

"That's amazing Mariana. Amazing." he replied, excited. "But how do we tell them about her? Clearly, we can't do it."

"We can do it anonymously to the police. But first you need to go there and plant some stuff in her drawer. Jewelry, watches, some syringes, maybe a belt of one of the victims. We can really fucking stick her on this one. The police will be so sure that it's her especially since she fits the description of the Magpie and also works at the Vu Hospital. It's perfect." said Mariana.

There was silence as Jan thought for a few moments.

"It is perfect, but eventually, she will be able to prove her innocence. She will have alibis that will prove for her that she was somewhere else when the murders were committed. What then?" asked Jan.

"Well, by then it won't matter, as we will be gone and they will know it's not her anyway as another murder will have been committed in December. I just need a week of peace on the streets to kill. What happens after that I really don't care. If the police think that they have caught the Magpie then they will take the undercover cops off the streets and public will let their guards down because they will think that the bars and streets are safe once more. This will be the perfect time for me to strike. It's perfect. Once we have taken this final victim, we can get out of here, but I need to do this. This is the only way it will happen. I'm sure Roos will get off in the end but that doesn't matter to us. We just need to get the heat off of our backs and the police off of the streets for a few days. Then I can finish what I have started. I can get my job done."

It was a good plan and it would work for sure. Jan was worried that in framing Roos, it would eventually come back to him because he had access to their apartment.

"It's a great plan." said Jan. "I'm just worried that it will come back to me and I will be caught in the end."

"Trust me, you won't Jan. You are just being paranoid. Just trust me okay?" replied Mariana in a firm voice.

"Okay." said Jan, giving in to Mariana. He did trust her, and at the end of the day, even if he thought he was going to get caught, he would still risk it for her. He would do anything for her.

"Right," continued Mariana, "come over to my apartment later and we can plan the next steps. You need to pick up some of the jewelry and personal items from some of these guys. It's all stored away in my cellar. It's probably worth taking a few of the syringes as well and planting them in Roos' room. Just come over to my apartment in an hour and we can decide how and what you need to do tomorrow."

"Tomorrow?" asked Jan, surprised by what she had said.

"Yes, tomorrow. I want to frame that bitch tomorrow." said Mariana, with an evil tone to her voice.

"But it's still November. You have another week before you must take another guy." replied Jan.

"I decide when I strike!" she shouted down the phone. Jan could hear anger in her voice as she panted heavily with rage. "Anyway, I want to take them all by surprise. They won't be expecting this, plus once they have caught and arrested Roos, we need to make the hit immediately afterwards."

"Okay." said Jan, a little confused on why she wanted to frame Roos so quickly. He started worrying that even Mariana was concerned that the police were getting close to catching them. He was also feeling nervous as it was beginning to dawn on him that he was going to have to plant this evidence tomorrow, which was not going to be an easy task, especially if the girls were going to be home. They wouldn't be expecting him to come over to clean.

"See you in an hour, okay?" said Mariana again, wanting his agreement to the plan and confirmation that she would see him shortly.

"Okay, see you then." replied Jan, reluctantly.

* * *

7:02 p.m.

Mariana let Jan in after keeping him waiting at her door step for about five minutes. She leant forward and gave him a kiss, which took him by surprise.

"What were you doing?" asked Jan, wondering why she had taken so long to come to the door.

"Follow me." she replied, walking through the living room towards the cellar door. She opened it and bent over in order to crouch through the small doorway, and down the steep wooden stairs that led to the cellar. Jan followed her down. It was a struggle for him to get through the tiny entrance, stay bent over, and walk down the steps at the same time. The light was on in the cellar, which made him think that Mariana must have been busy down there when he had rung the doorbell.

Jan always found this cellar scary, as it was the place where they would drag the victims once they had been drugged. Sometimes, Mariana would kill them in her bedroom or living room before Jan would have to lug the dead weight down the stairs. Other times she would snap their necks once they were in the cellar and end their lives down there. Either way the body would end up on the large wooden table that was positioned right in the middle of the cellar. Above it were three large lights that were currently not turned on. Mariana would use the strong lights when she wanted to undress the corpses and strip them of all their belongings. The bright light given off by the lamps helped Mariana make sure that she had completely cleaned the bodies.

On the two shelves next to the large table, were a box of rubber surgical gloves and some sharp knives and scissors. These were used for cutting off the victims' clothes. There were also two large bottles of pure alcohol for cleaning the corpses. She took so much pride in what she was doing and it always shocked Jan to see how professional she was, in carrying out these procedures.

On the other brick wall behind them were pictures of every victim, some taken by Mariana with her camera. Earlier in the year, she had been able to stalk her victims and take photos of the targets, before she made contact with them and introduced herself. There were also a number of pictures that were cut out from the newspapers and stuck on the wall as well. This was the equivalent of a trophy cabinet and she was very proud of it. She spent a lot of time sitting in the cellar staring at this collage of pictures on the wall. It gave her a sense of fulfillment and success. She loved her planning, as well as, looking at the victims' photos, and appreciating the results that she had achieved. There were also some polaroids on the wall that she had taken of the corpses once they had been stripped and cleaned, and ready to be dumped. Each victim had his own section on the wall, and all together, they made up Mariana's shrine.

There were even some pictures on the wall of targets that she never ended up killing. How lucky these guys were that they didn't get seduced by the Magpie, thought Jan. Mariana spent a lot of time in the cellar working at the old antique desk that stood against the wall with all the photos stuck on it. The desk had a small lamp on it as well as a map and a notepad. She also had a picture of her beautiful mother on the desk, fitted in a silver picture frame. Jan knew how much Mariana loved and missed her mother but couldn't understand how she could look at her when she was planning a murder or when a dead corpse lay naked behind her on the long wooden table.

From the lower shelf, Mariana had taken a box that was full of the belongings of her victims. She placed it on top of the large table. Jan walked forward to stand next to Mariana and look into the box. In it was an array of jewelry from watches, bracelets, earrings, gold and silver necklaces, and a number of rings. The light of the room glittered on the contents of the box, shining bright rays into Jan's eyes. It made him step backwards and squint. Mariana looked at him and smiled. This was her treasure chest, thought Jan, and this dark, dingy cellar was her nest. This was where the Magpie did her work. This was where she killed her victims and stored them until she was ready to throw them away. He loved her so much, but seeing her happiest in this cellar of hell, confirmed that she was absolutely crazy and her mind was so distorted.

"So, pick some items out." chuckled Mariana with a smile on her face. Why was she always so happy in this cellar? He wondered as he looked back into the box.

"We have to make sure that we select jewelry from a variety of men." continued Mariana in a more serious voice. "If we are going to frame that bitch then we need to make sure that the police find evidence from a few of the victims and not just one."

"Okay, agreed." said Jan. He walked over to the box of surgical gloves and put a pair on. He then started nervously and carefully taking items out of the box, one by one, and placed them into a bag. His hands were shaking and Mariana could see this.

"Isn't it funny that Roos is going to be framed as the Magpie?" she said, trying to cheer up Jan in a sick sort of way.

Jan didn't reply but continued picking items slowly out of the box. He had picked a diamond earring, two watches, a gold necklace, and an expensive-looking cotton bracelet. He looked at Mariana as if to say that he had taken what he wanted to. She got the message, took the box of belongings and placed it back on the lower shelf.

"Right. Let's go upstairs and plan the next steps." said Mariana, leading Jan back up the stairs to the living room. Once they were upstairs she turned the light off in the cellar and shut the small door. Her nest downstairs was her best kept secret. It was her treasure room, her place of study, and her torture chamber, all in one. Only Jan knew about it, her accomplice.

Mariana sat on the sofa and ushered Jan to come and sit next to her. He was surprised that she was dressed so perfectly in a time of distress and panic. She took a lot of care in her appearance and she was both stunningly beautiful and immaculately clothed in tight navy blue cotton trousers, a white blouse, and a grey cashmere jumper. Around her neck and wrists was an array of subtle but clearly, very expensive jewelry, as well as her late mother's gold watch.

She looked at him with a soft smile and then started to speak.

"Okay. This is the plan. Tomorrow you will go to Roos' apartment and say that you have lost your watch and wanted to check if you had left it there."

"What if no one is in?" asked Jan.

"Then you go back later. But it has to be tomorrow. Oh, and don't call them up to say that you are coming as Roos may say that she will look for it. This we obviously don't want." replied Mariana.

"Okay."

"Then, once you are there, plant the jewelry and other items in a chest of drawers in the bedroom, somewhere she won't find it easily. I want you to take some syringes as well and hide those. If we are going to frame her, let's do it properly." continued Mariana, with conviction in her voice.

"Understood." replied Jan, content to take orders from Mariana.

"Okay, once you have done this, you text me and then I can make an anonymous call to the police. I will pretend that I work at the hospital and claim that I have seen Roos go into the secure storage area, numerous times, where the anesthetic drugs are kept. That will make the police interview her again and search her house. That should be enough. That should get her screwed!" said Mariana with malice in her voice. As usual, she had it all worked out.

"Once it's announced that the police have arrested a suspect in association with the serial killings, the cafés and streets of Amsterdam will relax a bit and I can get on with my next steps." she continued.

Mariana was looking up towards the ceiling as she was talking out loud. Once she stopped her orders, Jan butted in.

"Errm, Mariana. There was another thing." said Jan sheepishly.
She focused in on him and spoke abruptly.

"What? What is it?"

"Well, I have had some missed calls from your father. Now, I haven't spoken with him and don't know what he wants. Do you want me to call him back?" Jan wasn't going to take any chances in upsetting his beloved crazy girlfriend.

"Yes." she replied, without thinking about it.

Jan paused for a second to digest what she meant by that.

"So, you are okay with me calling him back?" repeated Jan.

"Yes. Fucking call him back. Just call him back, okay?" barked Mariana, frustrated.

"Okay." whispered Jan. "What do you think he wants?"

"Don't know. Don't care." she responded.

"Okay." replied Jan. She clearly didn't want to talk about it.

"But, try and find out what he wants." came the surprising response from Mariana. "I'm sure he's just worried about me, as I have stayed at his house quite a lot recently and have been planning things from my bedroom. He's just being nosy, I expect."

"Okay, I will call him." said Jan, making it clear what he was going to do. He didn't want any arguments whilst all this other stuff was going on.

"Okay Jan, I want to go to bed. I need to think about what is ahead of us next week. You need to go home and get some sleep. You look like you need it!" said Mariana, who didn't mind being rude and insulting. She had also sent out a clear message that he wasn't invited to stay this evening.

"Okay." he replied and went to kiss her before he left. Mariana surprised Jan by holding his head and kissing him passionately on the lips. She never did this, and it made him feel wanted for once. It gave him a lift and strengthened him. Mariana smiled at him and said good night, waving from the front door step as he walked in the direction of his van.

Her kiss and a small hint of affection towards Jan had had the desired effect. She needed him on his A game tomorrow. She needed him to remember all the instructions that she had just given him. Jan had to calm down and have a good night's sleep. He had to be focused tomorrow and execute the orders that she had given him exactly as she had requested. Jan was critical to her plans. She needed him. If Mariana was going to be able to kill again, he had to frame Roos tomorrow.

Mariana smiled to herself and walked upstairs to her bedroom.

Jan began driving and placed his cell phone on the passenger seat next to him in the van. He decided that he would call Dr. Akkermans once he had arrived back in Baedoverdorp. He had a lot of respect for Mariana's father and felt that he should speak with him once he could give him his full attention. Dr. Akkermans had had a lot to deal with in his life, losing his wife to cancer, and then having to manage his only daughter who hated him, and played with his love and emotions because of money. No one deserved that type of a relationship from their child, and even though Jan loved and worshipped the ground that Mariana walked on, he detested the way that she behaved around her father.

Jan had always hoped that he could build a relationship with Dr. Akkermans. This had not been the case, and she would not allow him to have contact with her father; until now. Mariana wanted Jan to call him. She wanted to know why her father wanted to speak with Jan. Was he upset? Was he worried about his daughter? Was it something else? She needed to know and so did Jan. It was very rare for Dr. Akkermans to call him and Jan felt honored, but also very concerned. Jan was paranoid enough that somebody was going to recognize him and accuse him of being the guy in all the newspapers: the accomplice to the Magpie. Surely, that wasn't what Dr. Akkermans wanted to speak to him about. Jan was getting stressed and anxious again, worrying about being caught. He speeded up as he reached his village and then shrieked to a halt once he arrived outside his family home. Keeping the lights turned off in the van, so as not to draw attention to himself, Jan picked up his cell phone and called Mariana's father.

He listened to the ring tone of the house phone for a few moments, before a deep voice spoke into it. "Dr. Akkermans." came the response.

"Hello Dr. Akkermans, it's Jan." replied Jan politely and a little nervous.

There was short silence and a deep sigh before Dr. Akkermans spoke again.

"Good evening, Jan. Thanks for calling me back. How are you?"

"Errm, good thanks." said Jan. "How can I help you, Sir? I had a number of missed calls." Jan was keen to find out what Mariana's father wanted.

"Oh, yes Jan. Well, I am very worried about my daughter. She has been staying at my house but has locked herself away in her old bedroom for days. It's very strange behavior, even for her." replied Dr. Akkermans, getting straight to the point in his extremely posh voice. Jan thought that he did sound very sad.

"Well, Dr. Akkermans, I am not sure. I think that she is stressed with her studies." It was the only excuse that Jan could think of.

"Come on, Jan." replied Dr. Akkermans. "I know Mariana. I don't have a good relationship with her but she is acting extremely weird. What I didn't mention, is that she is screaming a lot in the night. Maybe she is having bad dreams or perhaps she is shouting at you into the phone. I just don't know but I am concerned."

"Understood, Sir. I will have a chat with her about it and see if I can get to the bottom of it."

"Jan, you are supposed to be her boyfriend. Can you tell me that you haven't noticed that she is acting strange? And please don't tell her that I am asking you to find out what's troubling her, as it will just make matters worse between us!" said Dr. Akkermans with a raised voice. Jan could sense frustration in his tone.

Jan did not know what to say in response and just stayed quiet.

"Listen, Jan, just see if you can subtly find out what's going on with her. This is not normal, even by Mariana's standards. I mean, she hasn't stayed at my house this long since her mother passed away."

"Okay, I get it Dr. Akkermans."

"And one last thing Jan, I would like to invite you next weekend for lunch. Just you and me. I want to get to know you a little better."

Again, Jan was speechless. Did he really mean this? Did Dr. Akkermans really want to build a relationship with him or was he just trying to find out what was wrong with Mariana? Normally, Jan would have done anything for a one-on-one with Dr. Akkermans, but not now. Now, he really didn't want to be scrutinized by Mariana's father. Jan was sure that he would sense that something was wrong with him too and he would use his intimidation skills and experience as a judge to extract information from Jan. He was so paranoid at the moment that Dr. Akkermans would be sure to realize that something was up. That something strange was indeed going on.

"Well, thanks very much Dr. Akkermans. It's very nice of you to invite me. My father is ill at the moment so I am working more hours at the bakery. It might not be possible next weekend."

This was actually true and Jan felt relieved that he was telling the truth and not lying, which he was certain that Dr. Akkermans would smell.

"Okay, Jan, the following week then. But I want to see you soon." came the quick response. Jan knew exactly where Mariana got her ability to give orders from. Her father was very authoritative in nature and had no problem telling Jan exactly what he wanted and expected of him.

"Okay, Sir." replied Jan. "Well, I guess we will speak again soon."

"Yes Jan. We will. I would like you to call me in the next couple of days once you have had a chance to speak with my daughter, and find out what is troubling her. I am worried."
"Understood, Sir. I will call you once I know what the problem is. I really need to go now, Dr. Akkermans. Speak soon. Good night."

"Good night, Jan, and thank you." replied a very sad voice.

Before Jan got out of the van, he thought it a good idea to text Mariana.

'Hi. Spoke with your father. He's just worried about you.'

'Whatever. Did he say anything else?' came the response.

'No.' Jan wrote back, not wanting to mention that her father wanted to have lunch with him. Jan was flattered by the invite and didn't want to annoy Mariana by telling her. He also genuinely wanted to go for lunch at some point, even if they couldn't do it right now.

Jan waited for a few minutes but Mariana didn't reply. He got out of the van and walked into the house. He went straight to bed. Tomorrow was going to be a very tense day and he would need his wits about him.

CHAPTER 28

November 27

11:00 a.m.

Mariana's mobile phone vibrated. She picked it up to read the message. 'It's done.'

'Everything? You planted everything?' she wrote back.

'Yes, just as you had said.'

'Okay, who was there?' replied Mariana.

'Just Fleur. Roos is working all day.'

'Okay, I will make the call this afternoon. Come to my place tomorrow night at nine.'

'Okay. Love you.'

Mariana didn't reply.

CHAPTER 29

November 28

4:55 p.m.

Arnaud and Dijkstra sat on chairs at the front of the large reception area in the police station. As it was freezing and raining heavily outside, the detectives had decided to cram as many journalists and reporters into the reception room as possible.

There were approximately forty people from the press and the room was packed. It was getting very hot and the windows were all steamed up. Everyone was waiting in anticipation for the two detectives to start speaking, although there had been a lot of rumors flying around all afternoon that they had arrested someone in relation to the murder hunt that they were spearheading for the Magpie. No one knew more than that, but this was enough to cause the Dutch and Belgium press to descend on the small police station in Amsterdam Zuid.

Both detectives appeared upbeat as they looked at the clock waiting for it to get to five at which point the press conference would begin. Detective Dijkstra took a swig of water from the glass on the simple wooden table at the front of the room and then stood up to address the audience. As soon as the detective rose, the room became quiet and everyone could hear him swallow to clear his throat before he began speaking. Reading off of some brilliantly white paper, Dijkstra started talking.

"At 1:30 p.m. today, a female was arrested in conjunction with the serial killings that have taken place in and around Amsterdam this year. The police received an anonymous phone call from an employee of the Vu

Hospital who had seen the suspect entering a secure part of the facility without authorization. This is where the drug, Propofol, that had been used in the killings to sedate the victims is stored. We arrested the accused female, a nurse at the hospital, brought her in for questioning and then proceeded to search her apartment. On conducting the search, we found numerous pieces of evidence that link her to the murders of several victims relating to the Magpie. Since then, we have charged the female in conjunction with these killings. We will keep you updated on our progress. We will now take questions for ten minutes."

Before Dijkstra could look up from reading the paper, torrents of questions were shouted out rapidly. He had become good at picking the right questions and was much better at this than Arnaud. Dijkstra pointed to a Telegraaf reporter in the second row, who he had a friendly relationship with, because he asked questions the detective was likely to answer.

"Detective, are you saying that you have caught the Magpie?" came the question from the journalist, who was heard loudly and clearly by the whole room, as an eerie silence filled the space. This was exactly what everyone wanted to ask. Dijkstra looked down at Arnaud who nodded at him and then spoke back to the reporter.

"Yes, we do believe we have caught the Magpie." replied Dijkstra.

There was a roar from the audience and another string of questions and statements were screamed at the detectives.

"But how can you be sure?"

"We have conclusive evidence that leads us to believe that we have in fact caught the Magpie. We will continue questioning her and will keep the press and public updated on our progress."

"Who was the witness who called you to say that they had seen her stealing drugs from the hospital? How can you be sure that the witness was telling the truth?"

"We don't know who the witness was. She made an anonymous call to the police. We do feel that it is a reliable source as the evidence we found lead us to believe that we have caught the killer. Once we are able to release the evidence, which is now with forensics, we will do so."

"So, the Magpie worked at the hospital?"

"We believe so." replied Dijkstra.

"Does the suspect fit the description and pictures of the Magpie?"

"Yes."

"What about the accomplice? Are you close to catching him?"

"We are still questioning the suspect and hope to catch the accomplice as a result of this procedure."

The crowd of reporters continued firing questions at the two detectives, who were both standing up and ready to leave the room. Just before they made their exit, surrounded by policemen, who were clearing the way out, Dijkstra spoke up once more.

"I want to take this opportunity to thank Arnaud and his elite team of detectives who have led this murder hunt investigation all year, and have finally succeeded. I would also like to thank all the other policemen who have been involved in this investigation, without whom we would not have been able to get to where we are today. Finally, I would like to say that we will continue doing press conferences as more information unfolds around the capture of the Magpie. Thank you for your patience."

With that the two detectives left the room, Dijkstra leading the way and Arnaud following, tired with his head down. As this huge weight had fallen off of his shoulders, exhaustion had taken over his body and mind. He had achieved his goal, or at least the first part of it. They still had to conduct more searches of Roos Marijn's apartment. Question her friends and family. Finding the items in the chest of drawers in her bedroom from a number of the murdered victims was compelling evidence. These personal items and jewelry were convincing and the four syringes with traces of the anesthetic drug in them were the icing on the cake.

Arnaud couldn't believe that they had caught the killer so easily in the end, and that it was an anonymous phone call from a colleague that had managed to frame her. The one thing he couldn't understand was why the other nurse wanted to remain anonymous? This question he would try and answer over the next few days. He hoped that they would be able to convince this individual to come forward and act as a key witness.

Arnaud knew that they also needed to interview the Magpie's flat mate, Fleur, as well as her ex-lover, Jade. He didn't want to leave any stone unturned. He wanted to cover all bases and make sure that they had done all their background work and ticked all the boxes. The other thing troubling Arnaud was about the accomplice. They needed to get a confession from the nurse as well. She was currently in shock and denying any involvement with the killings and claiming that she knew nothing about the items found in her bedroom. What made it worse was that they didn't even know who the caller was. This person would be a key witness.

As they left the press conference and walked up the staircase, Arnaud had to try and convince himself that he should be satisfied and that all the other information that he needed would come as a result of more questioning. Today had been the best day of the year so far. They had caught the Magpie.

* * *

8:15 p.m.

Noor sat at home in her familiar spot, at the small desk typing away on the keyboard of her computer. She had taken the night off work, calling in sick. She was too busy and had far more important things to do than serve drinks and snacks at the café. She had to express her views on the blog. There had been a huge amount of chatter on the site, since the announcement from the police that they had found the Magpie. The public and the press were celebrating, and praising Arnaud and his team. They had achieved their goals and ended the murder hunt. At least, that was the unanimous opinion. As Noor read the mails, she ran her hand through her hair, trying to understand how this murder hunt had ended so quickly. How the Magpie had been caught just by chance. It just didn't add up. She just couldn't believe that this calculative killer had suddenly made a mistake after being so precise in the way she went about her business all year.

It made sense to Noor that the Magpie could be a nurse, as she would have access to all the anesthetic drugs and was comfortable around corpses. It surprised Noor, however, that she would be caught sneaking into the secure drug storage rooms at the hospital. Noor also couldn't believe that the killer would leave belongings from the victims, as well as syringes, in her bedroom closet. How could such a professional killer leave evidence so readily available? She had normally covered her tracks so well.

Noor had also spent time this afternoon checking the profile of the suspect, Roos Marijn. Her basic characteristics fitted that of the killer:

white, educated female in her mid-twenties. She also had a nice figure and was pretty. Roos was a local girl from a happy family that didn't seem to have any unusual situation to it, like a death in the family or her parents having an ugly divorce. There was no real explanation for this nurse to be a cold-blooded serial killer. Noor, of course, didn't know her and appreciated the fact that she could just be completely crazy but she still believed that there must be a reason for her hating men and wanting to kill them. She could see from the information that she had on the suspect that she was a lesbian, which was the only possible reasoning for her disliking men but it still didn't fully add up.

As Noor started replying to the chatter on the blog, she got her message across that she didn't believe completely that the suspect fitted the profile of the killer. She didn't want to state unequivocally that the female they had caught was not the Magpie, because she just didn't know for certain. However, she wanted to put her opinion across. She knew that in doing this, it would be questioning the work of the police and in particular Arnaud, but she had to say what she really felt on the blog. She bit her bottom lip as she wrote, not really enjoying throwing out questions to all the readers on the site.

'We don't know for sure that this is the Magpie. Do you really think that such a precise and professional killer would suddenly be caught by a fellow employee at the hospital? Would the Magpie not be discreet when stealing drugs? Why would the killer leave evidence in her own bedroom, readily available for the police to find?'

She knew that throwing out these questions was going to upset the readers but she had to do it. Ultimately, it was the right thing to do. The more she blogged and the more she thought about everything, she came up with a number of points that strengthened her view. How could an anonymous caller frame the killer and not come forward to act as a witness? Why hadn't the police been able to track down the accomplice? That should be pretty obvious. If this Roos-Marijn was really the killer, why was she was denying everything? Noor knew that whether she was right or not, it would be resolved in the next couple of days anyway. The police would be able to track down the nurse's movements over the last year and tie her to the killings or not. The detectives would also still need to find the accomplice as well as the location that Roos-Marijn had used to take the bodies and work on them after they were killed.

Noor thought that she would be happy to be wrong in her opinions, but for now, she needed to let the world know what she really felt. And indeed, if she was right, then the Magpie was still out there and probably planning her next kill. She had a chill run up her spine as she thought to herself about the anonymous caller. Why didn't they want to come forward, but at the same time, were happy to contact the police to frame the killer? If Roos-Marijn was not the Magpie then who was the anonymous caller? There was no way that this was a prank caller who had called the police, as the nurse did in fact have evidence in her apartment that framed her for the killings. It had to be the Magpie that had called the police. And the Magpie must know Roos-Marijn, in order to get in her house and plant the clues.

Noor was impressed with her own trail of thought but she didn't want to put this on the blog, just yet though. This she would keep until the police had announced that Roos-Marijn was not the Magpie. Noor became worried as she thought about this scenario. Maybe it would be too late then, as the Magpie would have had chance to strike again? If she posted her views now, what could she lose? If she was wrong and Arnaud had already caught the Magpie, then everyone would be happy. If she was right, then the murder hunt would still continue and the detectives would be back to square one. Maybe she needed to express her opinions now. She thought for a few moments and then started to type.

'I believe that while it appears that there are enough clues and evidence to charge this nurse, I think that she is in fact not the Magpie. I don't think that this extremely professional killer would let down her guard and be caught in this way. I also don't think that she would leave clues in her bedroom that would associate her with the murdered victims. While the police are interviewing this suspect to try and tie her whereabouts to each killing, I think that the true Magpie is still on the streets trying to strike again. All men should be on their guard.'

Noor sent her message to the blog and went to make herself a cup of mint tea. When she sat back down at her desk five minutes later, there were thirty-two new messages for her. There were two prevailing themes coming out of the chatter. Bloggers were annoyed with Happy Single for supposedly turning on the police and questioning the fact that they had caught the killer.

'I hope that I am wrong and that the detectives have indeed caught the Magpie. That would be the best outcome and in the next few days, we will know for sure, either way. It's my opinion, however, that the killer is still out there, and I think that the Magpie is the female that called the police anonymously to frame the nurse. And this anonymous caller must know Roos-Marijn...'

Noor leant back on the seat and breathed in deeply. She knew that she had done the right thing by posting her views on the blog. She looked up at the computer screen to see lots of messages coming in for her. She didn't want to reply to these now. She had expressed her views and she knew that the public and the press, as well as Arnaud, and the police would read this. Noor hoped that it would at least make Arnaud think twice. Little did she know that Arnaud already had the same view as Noor. None of this added up at all, and he had also thought that this was too easy and obvious.

Noor turned off her computer and picked up her mobile. She wanted to talk to her boyfriend. She wanted to get her mind off this murder hunt and this blog for a while. She would look at it again in the morning. For now, she wanted to speak with Jonathan, and arrange their next date.

* * *

9:00 p.m.

As Jan got out of his van, which he parked on the Herengracht behind the Spui, he checked his phone to see if he had any messages. He was pleased to see that he was exactly on time to meet Mariana. Jan noticed that he had two missed calls from Dr. Akkermans and a text message. This stressed him out. He needed to call Mariana's father and make an excuse for her acting very strange, without Dr. Akkermans suspecting him. That wasn't going to be easy as the judge had seen it all before and would surely be able to see through Jan. He opened the text message and read it as he walked down the canal in the direction of Mariana's apartment.

'Hi Jan! Let me know when you can come for lunch or dinner next week. As you know, I am very worried about Mariana, so please call me back asap. Kind regards, Dr. Akkermans.'

"Shit." said Jan to himself, putting the phone into the pocket of his zipped up jacket. He knew that he had to see him soon. It was really something that he didn't want to do right now. He was very nervous and Mariana's father would sense this for sure. Jan decided not to reply for now. He would see Mariana first, and seek out more pressing issues that were eating away at him and freaking him out.

Like last time, Mariana took about five minutes to open the front door. She must have been down in the cellar again, thought Jan as he stood freezing on the steps outside. The door opened, but this time, Mariana didn't poke her head to make sure it was Jan. Jan was never late, especially when his beloved Mariana was involved. He did everything to please her.

As Jan stepped inside and shut the front door behind him he could sense that something was not right with Mariana. She hadn't even looked at him or acknowledged him. She just walked towards the cellar door. He followed observing her beautiful figure as he walked behind her. Mariana was wearing a long woolen jumper that fell down over her thighs and nothing else. Even though it was ice cold outside, she had the heating turned up in her apartment and it was very warm. Jan took off his jacket and scarf as he got to the bottom of the stairs. Placing them on the table in the middle of the room, he waited for Mariana to say something.

At first she was silent, and didn't even look at Jan. She appeared to be busy clearing out the cellar and had two large black bin bags, which she was filling with garbage. Mariana was wearing a pair of surgical rubber gloves to make sure that she didn't leave any of her own prints on this evidence. Jan looked around the room and noticed that she had taken all the pictures off the walls.

Mariana had put them in the bin bags. She was also emptying her treasure box. Why was she getting rid of everything? thought Jan. Was she panicking and worried that she was going to be caught? Or was she preparing to end all this, as she had promised him. Was she cleaning her apartment before they disappeared together? Jan hoped it was the latter but now wasn't the time to get Mariana to confirm her actions. There were more pressing issues to discuss and he could see from the stern expression on her face that she was in a foul mood.

Seeing that she was solely intent on cleaning the cellar, Jan plucked up the courage to start a conversation.

"So, how are you? How was your day?" he said sheepishly.

Mariana stopped what she was doing and started to speak in a controlled but angry voice.

"That fucking bitch is messing everything up!"

"What?" replied Jan, not sure what she was talking about. He started feeling anxious immediately as Mariana was scaring him. "Who is messing things up?"

"That fucking bitch. That blogger, Noor, is a smart arse!" shouted Mariana. Jan could see that she was shaking with anger.

"What has she done?" asked Jan, completely in shock.

"She's messing everything up. That's what she has done. We had given ourselves a small window to strike again and now she is writing on the blog that the nurse who has been arrested is not the killer."

"That's not possible. You framed Roos perfectly. Brilliantly."

"I know but she has been writing that the arrest doesn't make sense as the Magpie is too smart to be caught like that. She's also saying that the anonymous caller is really the Magpie and that the police should continue looking for the killer." Mariana was in a rage and both her fists were clenched. "I was going to go out tonight to a few bars to have a look around to select another guy for us. A man for December. I'm sure everything will still be on lockdown because of that bitch. She's too fucking smart for her own good."

Jan couldn't believe that Noor had worked out their plan and had already drawn the conclusion that Roos was not the killer. This really was going to make things difficult for them, thought Jan.

"Okay, but you don't know that yet. Go out tonight, walk around, and visit a few bars." said Jan, trying to relax Mariana. He couldn't believe that thirty-six hours earlier she was trying to calm him down and now it was the other way around. Mariana thought for a moment before responding to Jan's comments.

"Maybe you are right and I'm overreacting. But I will go out tonight. I have to. We only have a small window before those detectives realize that they have arrested the wrong girl," replied Mariana.

"Okay, good." responded Jan, pleased to see that she was thinking calmly again.

"But, I'm going to tell you what you are going to do." continued Mariana, looking straight at Jan with tears in her eyes. "You are going to kill that bitch, this week, for me."

"What?" replied Jan, not believing what Mariana had just said to him.

"You are going to kill that blogger. I want her dead this week. She is too much of a risk to us now and is affecting my success. I want you to kill her this week so you better arrange to go over to her place for a date." screamed Mariana. Jan realized straight away that this wasn't a suggestion, but rather an order.

"But do we really have to go that far?" asked Jan, who was really begging her to change her mind.

"Yes." shouted Mariana. "She is a real danger to us and she is damaging my chances of killing again. I want her dead, Jan. This week." She screamed again.

Jan was in complete shock. He had never killed before but had just helped Mariana when she needed and wanted his support. For sure, he was a cold-blooded accomplice to murder but he had never killed on his own. This was different. And with Noor, he would have to do it on his own. He really didn't want to kill anyone, and the only way he could get his mind round being involved in the events of this year was by justifying it as helping and supporting the love of his life. Jan didn't see why it was necessary to kill Noor. After all, they would hopefully disappear in a week. Forever.

Looking over at Mariana, he realized that she wasn't in the right frame of mind to discuss this. She was completely messed up and what she had just asked Jan to do was not a request but an order. He didn't really have a choice. Jan thought quickly to himself and decided that the best thing to do was agree and then hopefully while Mariana was busy planning and making the next kill, she would be sidetracked away from this. Once everything else was done, it would be time for them to flee. After all, Mariana had just instructed him to kill the blogger this week, which meant it didn't have to be done today. He had some time, which was a good thing. For now, he just had to appease Mariana.

"Okay. I will do it this week." replied Jan.

"Okay, good." said Mariana, taking a deep breath and trying to calm herself.

After a moment's silence, Jan began speaking again.

"So, how was your day?"

"It was going well until that Noor started writing her comments on the blog. Roos has been arrested and I was hoping that it would be easy for me to strike tomorrow once I have picked a spot to select a target. That was what I was going to do tonight."

"Well, you can still do that. You should continue with your plan and pick a quieter location to seduce another guy." replied Jan, trying to cheer her up.

"Well, I will see tonight." Mariana replied softly, a lot more relaxed and focused on her next move. "I am going to go out at ten. But first I want to finish cleaning."

Jan looked at his watch and saw that he had been with her for just thirty minutes.

"Okay." he replied. "Why are you getting rid of all this stuff?"

"Why do you think? It's almost over. I told you, didn't I? It's almost done. One more kill and I am done. I have won. I have beaten them all." said Mariana. Jan wasn't quite sure what she was going on about but was pleased that she was going to stop after this murder. He had a sense of joy inside as he thought about drawing a line in the sand and moving on. Both of them moving on. Moving somewhere else. Far away from here.

"Okay. Okay." he replied.

"Jan, I want you to take these two bin bags and burn them somewhere." ordered Mariana. "Tonight."

"Errm, okay." replied Jan, pleased to be able to help, especially since he would be getting rid of evidence that could potentially frame them for the killings. He would take the bags in the back of his van and burn them in woods near his home tonight or tomorrow.

"Good." replied Mariana, pleased that he was following her instructions and doing what she wanted him to do.

"Oh, and your father keeps calling me. He wants to set a date for me to meet him for lunch or dinner." said Jan.

"What does he want now?" replied Mariana, annoyed by what Jan had just said.
"I think he's just worried about you. That's all."

"Well, try and stall this. Avoid meeting him." said Mariana, giving him another clear order.

"Errm. Okay." replied Jan, who was very happy not to visit Dr. Akkermans. Jan would just have to avoid answering her father's calls for now.

"Right. I'm done here. Take these bags. I'm going to take a shower and get changed. Let's speak tomorrow." said Mariana. She didn't wait for Jan to reply.

Mariana hoped that the mood in the cafés was going to be the same as it had been at the start of the year, where she could have seduced ten guys in one night if she wanted to. She would find out soon enough. She only needed one male this time. Just one more guy to end the year and complete her legacy. With that, her goal of beating the police and the rest of the country would have been achieved. She had taken the lives of eleven innocent men in Amsterdam, who she saw as weak, pathetic losers who deserved to die. She had won.

As Mariana headed up the stairs, she didn't even acknowledge Jan or say goodbye to him. She was on a mission. She knew what she had to do now and so did Jan. He walked over to the small box where the rubber surgical gloves were stored and put on a pair. He picked up the two bin bags and took them upstairs, along with his coat and scarf. He could hear the shower running and didn't expect to say goodbye to Mariana tonight. He knew that she would text him tomorrow to meet up or speak. For now, he needed to leave her to get on with what she had to do.

Jan put on his coat and left Mariana's apartment with the two bin bags. He would go and burn them in the woods now and then dig a hole and bury the remains. Even if they were found, there would be no way that the remains could be traced back. After this, Jan was going to go home and sleep. Tomorrow was going to be a busy day and he needed to be ready to act as soon as Mariana contacted him. Tomorrow might be the day that she would take her next victim, her final victim.

CHAPTER 30

November 29

5:15 p.m.

Arnaud sat in Dijkstra's office with his head in his hands. He was tired and completely deflated. He had spent the last two days interviewing Roos-Marijn. Questioning her about where she had been throughout the year when the murders had taken place, in an attempt to pin her to the killings. She not only had proof that she wasn't in Amsterdam when some of the murders took place but she had alibis as well.

Arnaud had doubted from the start that Roos was in fact the Magpie. Not only because he didn't think that this calculated killer could be caught just by chance by an anonymous colleague who had seen her taking drugs from the operating theatre but also because Roos had acted so innocent and unassuming throughout the whole interview process. Arnaud had been doing this job long enough to know when a suspect was lying or not. His hunch was that she was innocent. Roos was not the Magpie.

Friso had spent the whole day yesterday questioning Roos' flat-mates, Fleur and the ex-girlfriend, Jade. Both were convinced that she was not the killer. They not only acted as an alibi in some instances when there had been a killing earlier in the year, but also said that they had not noticed anything strange in her behavior. Admittedly, both females had said that she was neurotic and she did work at the hospital but that was actually her only association with the murder, apart from the jewelry that was found in her room.

The jewelry and watches were the last unsolved part of the puzzle that tied Roos to the killings. How did they get there, if she hadn't hidden them in her room? No one could answer this question. The items also didn't have Roos' fingerprints on them. Whoever had planted it in her bedroom was surely the killer. Everyone knew this. Jade and Fleur were questioned, Arnaud and his team even assumed that they were potential suspects. How could they find out who else had entered the house? If they knew this or even who the anonymous caller was, then they would have their killer. This must be the same person. This had to be the Magpie. So far Arnaud and his team didn't have an answer to any of these crucial questions.

At the moment, the public and the press still believed that the Magpie had been caught. Even though she hadn't been charged, it was assumed by all that she was being kept in solitary confinement and quizzed about all the murders and interrogated about her accomplice. This was another reason why Arnaud was convinced that Roos couldn't have been the killer. She didn't have any long-term relationship or friends that were male. This was confirmed by Fleur and Jade.

Soon, Arnaud would have to let the outside world know that they had the wrong person in custody. They hadn't arrested the killer, but actually the Magpie had framed an innocent girl, and in doing so, had made the police look silly. The killer was playing games with them. As soon as the press and the rest of Holland got wind of this, there would be an uproar.

Arnaud was feeling stressed out and as he sat in the small office opposite Dijkstra. He explained the complete situation to him. After thirty minutes of going through all the points, he drew his conclusion.

"So that's it. She is not the Magpie." said Arnaud with a deflated voice. "We have been through everything. She has a string of perfect independent alibis. It's not her."

Dijkstra stood up for a second out of frustration and started speaking again with a raised voice. "Okay. You know that blogger is right again. She was stating just last night that we had the wrong person. The blogger said the same thing as you. We have arrested the wrong person. The nurse is not the Magpie. We are going to be the laughing stock of Amsterdam!"

Arnaud had heard from Jim, who was monitoring that blog on a daily basis that Happy Single had come to the same conclusions as them but without the intel that they had. The blogger didn't know that Roos had alibis that cleared her. Dijkstra was worked up and disappointed to hear the truth that they didn't have the killer. As he sat down Arnaud could see that his boss was also feeling completely gutted.

"Okay." continued Dijkstra, rubbing his hand through his thinning grey hair, "What now?"

"Well, someone has clearly framed her, and we need to find out who that is. Whoever planted those items in her bedroom was probably the same person who made the anonymous call to the police. My belief is that has to be either the Magpie or the accomplice. We need to pick Roos' brain to see who could have been into her house. I think that it has to be someone she knows that is trying to frame her."

"You think that the nurse knows the killer?" asked Dijkstra, reading Arnaud's trail of thought.

"Yes." replied Arnaud, with a deadpan expression on his face. "I don't think Roos realizes it but she must know the Magpie."

"Okay, so what are the next steps?" said Dijkstra.

"Well, she is in a bit of a mess at the moment but we will explain that she is no longer under suspicion. We will then brainstorm on who she thinks may be a possible suspect and fits the description of the Magpie or the accomplice. This is the starting point and probably our best chance of catching them."

"Okay, when do we let the public and the press know that Roos is not going to be charged?"

"I think soon. It should be today. The public needs to know that the killer is still out there and will probably strike again, and soon."

"Okay, shall I set up a press conference?" asked Dijkstra.

"No, not yet. Give us another hour or two with Roos." Arnaud stood up and looked out of his boss' office in the direction of Friso and the two younger detectives. They were speaking to Roos and making notes.

"Okay, Arnaud." replied Dijkstra softly. He was looking as stressed as Arnaud, knowing that they would shortly announce that they had messed up. In admitting their failures, they would have to explain that the killer was still out there. He was not looking forward to that.

Arnaud walked out of Dijkstra's office slowly and back over to his team and to a distraught innocent nurse.

* * *

7:10 p.m.

Jan sat on his bed at home, staring at his phone. He had a number of missed calls from Dr. Akkermans but nothing from Mariana. What was she doing? Why hadn't she called or sent a text? He could only assume that she was busy trying to target and grab her next victim. He didn't want to disturb her, however, as she could be busy.

Jan couldn't stop thinking about what Mariana had instructed him to do yesterday. The thought of having to kill Noor was eating away at him and making him scared. She hadn't really done anything wrong. She didn't deserve that. Jan realized that he would have no choice in the end. If it was a case of Mariana and him getting away free, or Noor surviving, he would take her life. After all, Mariana was right. The blogger was causing them a lot of problems right now. He would wait for Mariana's instructions again but hoped that the moment wouldn't come.

As Jan sat there, he scratched the small amount of stubble on his chin and could feel that his jaw muscles were sore. He had been grinding his teeth at night. Seeing the seven missed calls from Dr. Akkermans didn't help. Mariana's father must be thinking that Jan was extremely rude as he had not called or messaged him back. Any chance he had of befriending him in the future was becoming slimmer and slimmer by the hour. Jan realized that once this was all over, they probably wouldn't see him too much, anyway. Hopefully, Mariana and he would be long gone, far away. They would disappear and cut themselves off from this life and the events that had taken place this year.

Jan reached across to his bedside coffee table and picked up his laptop. He wanted to check what Noor had been writing on the blog. As he clicked on the website of Amsterdam Living, he couldn't believe the amount of chatter based around the arrest of the Magpie. Jan couldn't understand how Noor had worked it all out. How could she go against everyone else's opinions and state that the police had arrested the wrong female? How could she defend her arguments when the police had found evidence framing this nurse for the serial killings? Jan was so surprised by the blogger's trail of thought. He also knew that Noor had no other information to go by. She was making judgement calls on pure instinct. Annoyingly, she was right. The more he read, the more he understood why Mariana was so angry with what Noor had written.

As Jan continued to read the chatter, his phone began to ring, which made him jump. It was Mariana so he pressed the answer button immediately.

"Hi. How are you?" asked Jan

"Not good. Not fucking good!" replied Mariana, sounding very upset. "It is as I expected. I can't do anything at the moment. Fucking nothing. I went out last night and the bars are full but I am sure that there are policemen everywhere. Maybe I am being paranoid but I can sense it."

"You are probably being paranoid. Bide your time."

"We don't have time. I don't have any fucking time. I'm sure tomorrow that nurse will be released and then it will be impossible to strike. I'm sure of it!" Mariana was fuming and ranting into the phone.

"Then go out tonight. I will come and wait at your house for when you need me." said Jan, trying to encourage her and offering his help.

"No. It's not happening tonight. I haven't been able to plan it yet. I haven't selected a café yet and I need to check out the targets. It's just not going to happen tonight. These fucking police are everywhere. I can feel it." she shouted back.

There was a silent pause as Jan tried to think what he should say and how he could possibly help. It didn't look like Mariana wanted to be comforted.

"Well, don't stress." continued Jan. I can come over if you want and stay with you. We can make a plan for tomorrow." He waited in anticipation for a response from her.

"No. I'm going to stay at my father's house. I want to be alone. I want to think."

Jan thought it was strange that she was going to her father's house, especially since she knew that Dr. Akkermans wanted to talk to her and try and understand why she was acting so strange. He was definitely going to do this and Jan was worried how Mariana would react when confronted by her father.

"Okay, do you want me to come to your father's place with you?"

"No!" came the immediate response. "No. Just wait for me to call you tomorrow." Jan could hear that she was crying, which didn't happen often.

"Okay, but what…" said Jan before realizing that she had clicked out and disconnected the call. Even he thought that she was acting extremely strange now. Was it because she couldn't achieve her final goal? Was it because she couldn't kill and it was all coming to an end? Whatever the reason was, he thought that Mariana was bound to go into a rage if her father started asking too many questions.

Jan didn't know what to do so he lay back on his bed and tried to think. Normally, when they were about to do a kill, everything was planned precisely and he knew exactly what he needed to do to assist Mariana. This time, however, he had no idea. He didn't know what was going to happen tomorrow and what was more concerning was that apparently neither did Mariana.

* * *

10:00 p.m.

It was getting late and all five of them were still in the office. Friso and Jim were busy typing up all the interviews and questioning that had taken place over the last two days with Roos, Fleur, and Jade. Robin was hunched over his desk staring at old video footage and clicking away on his mouse.

Arnaud and Dijkstra sat opposite each other in Dijkstra's office. They had spent the last hour or so writing out their speech for the press conference tomorrow morning. They were both fully aware that tomorrow's statement would cause a massive stir in the news.

Arnaud was feeling extremely fatigued and depressed. It had been a long three days and he thought from the start that the person they had arrested was not the killer. Not only had they wasted a lot of time, they had been tricked by the Magpie. She had made a mockery of their work and they had given her some free time to look for her next victim. Arnaud was wondering if she had already struck again.

Arnaud was taken by surprise when Friso beckoned them. Friso's eyes were wide open and he looked shocked. What had he found? Thought Arnaud, as he jumped up out of the seat and opened the door to the small office.

Friso walked over to Robin's desk where he was sitting with Jim, huddled in front of the computer screens. Friso appeared excited and clearly wanted to share their findings with his boss. As Arnaud followed his younger colleague, he could feel anxiety building up inside him. He hoped it was good news, as he definitely needed a 'pick me up'.

Arnaud and Dijkstra moved in close behind the other detectives trying to get close to the computer screens. On the left hand screen appeared to be the still shots of the male accomplice that they were trying to hunt down. The screen was split in two with both a picture of the back of the guy, standing on the dance floor in the Surprise Bar, staring at the Magpie, as well as a picture of him leaving the club, with his head turned away from the CCTV camera. On the right hand screen was a front still picture of a tall slim male standing in another bar. Arnaud hadn't seen this shot before, and couldn't make out the café either. What he could see immediately was that there were a lot of similarities between the guy on both screens, so he knew where this was going.

"Well, you have seen these pictures on the left Arnaud. They are taken from the Surprise Bar." said Friso with an excited tone. He was speaking very fast which was unlike him. "The picture on the right screen is taken from the camera in one of the gay bars where the most recent victim used to hang out. Robin has been going through the footage over the last week and he just came across this guy." continued Friso, pointing to the male in the middle of the screen. All of them focused in on the male and his face, which they hadn't seen before. It wasn't a perfectly clear picture of his face, but you could make out that he was good looking and had a prominent bone structure and jaw line. He had a crew cut and didn't appear to have any wrinkles on his skin, putting him in the age bracket of early twenties. The male was wearing a pair of large thick rimmed glasses, which hid his nose and eyes somewhat.

As the detectives flicked between the two screens, observing the similarities between the two men, Friso started talking again.

"We believe that this is the same guy. You can see that they have the same haircut and body shape."

Robin clicked on the mouse and enlarged the two pictures from the shoulders upwards and Friso was indeed correct with what he had just said.

"You can also see that the jacket that the guy was wearing is exactly the same one that he is wearing in this other café." said Friso, and as the detectives checked what he had just said, they realized that he was correct again. "The glasses are probably a disguise."

"Agreed." replied Arnaud. "What is the date of when this film was taken?"

"It was three days before the last victim was abducted. I can only assume that the accomplice was in the gay bar to check out the potential targets. It's definitely the accomplice."

"Yes, I agree." said Arnaud. "So, what now?" He had been so busy all night working on tomorrow's press conference that he wanted some input from his team.

"When you hold the press conference tomorrow, you should also release these pictures and explain that it's the suspected accomplice. Hopefully, someone will come forward and recognize him. It's not a clear photo of his facial features but somebody has to know who this is. I really think some people will recognize the person in this picture." said Friso.

Arnaud looked across at his colleague once he had stopped talking. He was right. This picture would definitely generate some identification. It was in fact a very good lead for them. It might also take some of the pressure from them when they do the press conference in the morning.

"Okay." Arnaud said. "I agree that this is a great lead for us and we will release this new picture tomorrow. Try and clean up the image as much as possible."

"Okay Arnaud. I'm just going to run this guy's profile and image through the police database to see if we get any similar matches. Unlikely, but I don't think it hurts to do it." said Friso.

"Fine." replied Arnaud. "I'm heading home. Good work today and I will see you all here at seven in the morning."

One by one, the detectives put on their coats and left for the evening. It had been a long tiring day.

CHAPTER 31

November 30

1:30 p.m.

Jan sat in his work van in the middle of Amsterdamse Bos by the rowing lake. He had parked in a small lane but kept the engine running to keep the heating on. It was a frosty day with the temperature in the minuses and he was freezing cold. This was partly because of the outside temperature and the fact that he was dressed inappropriately. It was also because he was shaking with fear. Jan had been working all morning in the bakery and listening to Sky Radio. The news had come on and it had been announced that the police had released the suspect who was being held in custody.

The detectives running the murder hunt confessed that the nurse was not the Magpie. This was not a surprise to Jan as he had been expecting this. What had taken him by complete surprise was the announcement that the detectives had found images of the Magpie's accomplice and they were to be released to the press. Jan had run immediately out of the bakery and back home, up to his bedroom. He had turned on the television, and just as he had feared, they had found pictures of him.

"Shit, shit!" He whispered to himself as he watched the television in his room. "I'm fucked. I'm really fucked now. Shit!"

On the news, they had blown up Jan's facial shot and even though he had put on a thick-rimmed pair of glasses, his bone structure and mouth were very clear. He was panicking as he was certain that someone would now recognize him from these photos. He didn't know what to do as he sat on his bed, cursing himself, and biting his finger nails. Was it all over? Jan thought to himself. He tried countless times to call Mariana but she had turned her phone off. He was on his own for now. He made the abrupt decision to get out of his house and go away from home and the bakery as quickly as possible. He was extremely paranoid that either his mother or sister would recognize him on the news. He didn't know what he would do if they questioned him about this. He just needed to flee the house and be alone. Jan had to think and devise a plan as quickly as possible. This time, he didn't have Mariana to tell him what to do. He had to think on his own two feet.

As he sat curled up in the driver seat of the van, he held his mobile phone in his hands. He flicked between speed dialing Mariana and checking his phone for any other messages. So far he had attempted to call Mariana twenty-seven times and he had received a text message from his sister asking where he had disappeared to. They had finished the dough preparation for the following day's bread deliveries. Jan took some comfort from the fact that his sister hadn't mentioned anything about the pictures that had just been released. He was sure that his family might have made the connection between Jan and the images all over the news.

Apart from his family, his biggest fear was that Noor would be able to identify him. She was always following the murder hunt. She would have definitely seen these images already. She was also obsessed with Jan and he could imagine that she had his face tattooed on her brain right now. He could picture her watching the news and then spotting her boyfriend. She would quickly put two and two together and then realize that he had wormed his way into her life so that he could get closer to the enemy.

Jan realized that Noor was now his biggest threat. He had to eliminate her today. With a clear plan in his mind, Jan decided to text Noor. 'Hi Noor. It's me. I have a meeting this afternoon in Amsterdam and I was hoping to see you. Can I come over around six-thirty, seven?'

Jan waited about five minutes and then his phone began to vibrate. 'What a nice surprise! I'm supposed to be working in the café tonight but I can see if it's possible to cancel.' replied Noor, who was obviously keen to see him. Jan was relieved as she obviously hadn't recognized him on the news yet.

Jan immediately responded. 'Okay great. Please try and cancel work. I really want to see you and I have a surprise for you as well!'

'Oh really. I'm excited! Will confirm in a bit. See you later. xx.' came the reply

Jan was pleased that he had sorted out the first part of this plan. He leant back in his seat and thought about how he was going to do this. He couldn't imagine killing someone, and now he had to take the life of someone he knew, and it was someone who loved him. He was dreading it even though he knew that it had to be done to ensure his and Mariana's survival. Would he use a weapon or just his hands and strangle her. He just didn't know but he would have to put together a plan before he went to her apartment. He knew that he would be taking Noor by surprise and she wouldn't be expecting this at all.

Jan looked at his phone again to see if he had any other messages. There was nothing. He was becoming paranoid that Mariana was ignoring him on purpose. What could she possibly be doing? thought Jan to himself. He desperately wanted to share his plans with her. She would be pleased that he was eliminating the blogger from the equation. That would make their lives a lot easier. But there was nothing. Mariana was radio silent. As Jan sat there, cold, tired, and stressed, he decided that he would stay there for the rest of the day until it was time to visit Noor.

* * *

3:00 p.m.

Mariana sat in her old bedroom at her father's house in a terrible state. She was extremely angry and frustrated. The last two nights were spent trying to find her next victim. In her usual style, Mariana had dressed up in a beautiful but understated outfit to attract an innocent bystander. She looked sexy but conservative. Any guy would definitely notice her and she was able to move under the radar as she wasn't wearing anything too striking. Mariana had worn her hair down so that she could use it to cover her face if she needed to conceal herself from a camera. She had put on some simple diamond earrings and a small pearl necklace, which made her look elegant and innocent. It was very difficult for anyone to look at this stunning young lady and believe she could possibly be the sick serial killer that was haunting Amsterdam.

Nothing had changed in the way that Mariana approached her next victim, apart from the fact that she was stressed that she was getting closer to being caught. She needed to get this last kill before she stopped. She wanted to be the one who decided when this was all going to end. Neither the police nor anyone else was going to decide this for her.

She also had a lot more on her mind than usual, which was acting as a distraction. After the kill and dumping the body, she needed to make a decision around what she was going to do next. Was she going to really leave Amsterdam with Jan, or go on her own? She didn't love Jan but he had his uses and would do anything for her. Maybe he could help her in whatever she decided to do next. First though, Mariana needed to decide what she wanted to do and where she wanted to go. She had cleaned up her entire apartment and got rid of all the evidence but she was still paranoid that there was DNA in there that could come back and hurt her in the future. This was a concern that was eating away at her, and she needed to address this soon, but after the next kill.

Mariana had visited seven bars and cafés in the Jordaan, and five bars in the Spui area. She had also gone to several hotel bars around Amsterdam as well as some student cafés. She had been extremely unsuccessful in finding a target. Whilst the bars and cafés were busy, she still thought that there were many undercover policemen on the streets. A lot of the men in the bars were in groups and it was difficult to single one out. It was also apparent that there seemed to be more cameras installed in the bars, which made her paranoid. Mariana was wondering if she was losing her touch. She also kept thinking that maybe men weren't attracted to her anymore. While this was not the case, it was clear that everyone had their wits about them and this was making it virtually impossible for her to find an unassuming male. The longer Mariana spent in the cafés, the angrier she became.

Mariana had managed to chat with a businessman in the bar at the Okura hotel but she had been asked to leave by the barman as he accused her of being a prostitute. This had made her annoyed but she left very quickly and didn't make a scene. Apart from talking to a very drunk student in another bar she had had no success. Mariana had thought that the student would have been a perfect target but he was so drunk that she would not have been able to get him back to her apartment.

As she sat on the floor in her old bedroom, she started crying hysterically. She looked at a small picture she had of her mother in a silver picture frame. She always had this next to her bed in her apartment and also took it with her to her father's house. She liked to be next to her mom and it was the first thing she saw when she woke up each day and the last thing that she would look at before she fell asleep.

Mariana felt like she had nowhere to run and nowhere to hide. She felt helpless and that she was a failure. She couldn't strike and take another life. She desperately wanted to do this, not only to show her position of control over the police and the public, but also for her mother. Her dear mother, who had died of cancer, was killed by the male race. She didn't just blame her father for his affair that her mother never recovered from. Mariana blamed all men for this. She saw all men the same way. They were all cheaters and disrespectful to women, and most importantly, they had betrayed the most important person in her life, which was her mother.

She thought about her mother all the time, every day. She cherished the memories she had. She was sexy, smart, and kind. She had also been supportive and loyal to her father who had betrayed her. He broke her heart and ruined her happiness, which caused her untimely death. Her father had ruined her mother's life and her own life, too, by his actions.

Her fond memories of her mother were tainted by what her father had done. Now she thought more often about sad things from the past and how he had poisoned and divided their family. This sadness had been cultivated into hate over time and then revenge. Through her hatred she wanted to put things right for herself and for her dearest angel, her mother. As Mariana sat there on the cold wooden floor, she cried uncontrollably. She felt beaten by the police. She couldn't see how she could strike again. It was all coming to an end. She had failed her mother. She had been beaten once again by men.

Exhaustion and emotion filled her body and she continued to cry loudly, as she wiped tears from her cheeks and eyes, smudging her faint makeup.

Dr. Akkermans sat at the bottom of the stairs in the hallway with the NRC Handelsblaad in his hands. He was looking at the front page of the newspaper that had a picture of Magpie's accomplice on it. As he looked in the picture, he was sure he knew who it was. Dr. Akkermans could see past the thick-rimmed glasses and could clearly make out Jan's face. This wise old judge had looked at and studied a lot of criminal evidence in the past and it was very apparent to him. Jan was the accomplice. As he thought about this, he put his head into his huge hands and pondered over the dreadful thought of who could possibly be the Magpie. While he knew that Mariana was a very angry, unhappy, and unstable girl, he could not believe that she was the killer. She couldn't possibly be the Magpie, surely.

Lots of thoughts started going through the wise man's head, as if he was weighing the prosecution's and the defense's arguments in a serious murder trial. First of all, he didn't know Jan very well but his first impressions had been of a young chap who was nice, and probably too kind for Mariana. He was from, what appeared to be a simple happy family, quite the opposite of his daughter's messy and broken upbringing. He really couldn't believe that he was involved in these killings but then he didn't know him very well and with many murder trials that he had been involved in the past, a lot of the vicious criminals were not what or who you would have expected.

Dr. Akkermans had looked at these pictures in the paper numerous times and he was convinced that it was him as he even recognized the coat that he was wearing. What he was more concerned about was that if Jan really was the accomplice, then who was the Magpie, and more importantly, was it his daughter? Even though he didn't want to believe that she could do something so evil, Dr. Akkermans knew that his daughter was psychologically a mess, and she hated men. It sort of made sense why she would get involved in this crazy killing spree, as she had a cause. Could his beautiful daughter really be that sick and twisted? Certainly her recent behavior would lead you to believe that she was very upset about something. Perhaps Jan was involved and she knew it but couldn't say anything about this to anyone as she was scared. Maybe Jan was the accomplice to another female and was using Mariana as an alibi. Dr. Akkermans thought this highly unlikely as he knew his daughter was extremely strong-willed and controlled Jan like a puppet. If he was the accomplice and she wasn't involved, then she would have reported him to the police, if she knew about it.

Maybe she wasn't involved but if that was the case then something else was seriously wrong. She did at least have a real hatred for her father, which was sufficient to turn this into a general disgust towards men. But was this bad enough for her to want to kill a man? Dr. Akkermans didn't know the answer and didn't really want to find out. He was more concerned about his daughter's unhappiness and was just trying to help her. He decided that he would approach the subject by questioning Mariana directly about Jan's pictures in the newspaper.

He sighed deeply, weighing up the information that he already knew as he listened to his daughter sobbing on the top floor of his house. He had never really understood his daughter, even in her brighter days. Over the last few years their relationship had broken down completely. He knew her reasons for hating him but her behavior over the last year had gotten dramatically worse. Her general demeanor had become one of a young lady filled with hatred. He did not understand this deterioration and while he had wanted to confront her on this many times, he knew that she would never open up to him.

Dr. Akkermans thought that he had seen it all in terms of how Mariana had become such a selfish, cold individual, but he had never heard or seen her show emotion like this. She was crying uncontrollably. He felt like he couldn't listen to her sadness anymore. He had to do something and he felt drawn to help his daughter. Even if she hated him, he had to try and do something. He couldn't just listen to her pain and sadness. He was her father after all. Dr. Akkermans stood up and quickly walked upstairs. He not only wanted to console her but also needed to confront her. He needed to know if she was involved in these killings with Jan. He needed to know desperately, and as he thought over things to himself, he scuttled up the long stairway to the top floor.

He walked over to her bedroom, making loud steps on the wooden floor boards as he wanted Mariana to hear that he was approaching. As he got to her door he could hear her sobbing inside so he knocked three times with his knuckles. For a second, the sniffing stopped and there was silence from inside but no answer. Dr. Akkermans took the initiative and spoke up.

"Mariana, darling, are you okay?" He said in a stern voice.

There was no response so he knocked again, "Mariana, I'm going to come in now." He took a deep breath and walked in slowly. Dr. Akkermans could see his daughter curled up in a ball on the wooden floor, sobbing away. He couldn't see her face as she hid it from him. Clearly, Mariana didn't want her father to see her crying. He thought that she looked so unhappy and helpless. He kneeled down next to her and tried to comfort her with words, knowing that she wouldn't appreciate a cuddle from him.

"Mariana, what's up my darling? Are you okay? I'm really worried about you."

Mariana didn't want to look up at her father. She was desperate for him not to see her sadness. She started questioning what he wanted and why had he come upstairs. Was it because she had been crying and wailing loudly? She could see through her hair that was draped down over her face that he placed the newspaper that he had been carrying on the floor next to him. Glancing over at it, she also noticed that it was open on the page with a large picture of Jan on it. She immediately knew that the game was up. Her father must know. He had made the association between Jan and the picture. What next? thought Mariana to herself. Did her father assume that she was the Magpie? Could she lie and say that it wasn't her and pretend that she knew nothing about it and say that she too had just found out after seeing the news? Should she tell her father that she knew and that she was too scared to inform the police? Should she try and kill her father as he would report them both to the police? She needed to make a decision immediately. She needed to react now.

Dr. Akkermans was getting ready to question his daughter again, when he was suddenly taken by surprise. Mariana looked up at her father and then she put her arms around him, something she hadn't done for a very long time.

"Oh Papa. I am in so much trouble. Oh papa, please help me!" said Mariana, squeezing her father tightly and hysterically sobbing once more. Dr. Akkermans began hugging his shaking daughter in an attempt to try and console her. He had never seen her so upset and she never went to him for comfort. She grasped him tightly with both arms for about ten minutes and didn't stop crying the whole time. When he realized that the sobbing had stopped he spoke softly into his daughter's ear.

"My darling Mariana, please tell me what has happened? If you don't, I can't help you."

Between sniffling, Mariana replied, "Papa, I am in so much trouble." she sobbed. Mariana wanted to test her father and see what he would read into this.

"Why, what is it? Is it to do with the picture in the news? It looks very much like Jan, you know." Dr. Akkermans didn't want to accuse his daughter of anything but wanted to get to the point.

Mariana was right. Her father knew. The only thing that she wasn't sure of was whether he thought that she was also involved. She needed to respond quickly.

"Yes Papa. That's it. I'm in so much trouble." She started crying uncontrollably again, hugging him tightly, wrapping her arms and body around him like a child. Dr. Akkermans loved his daughter immensely and even though he knew that she really was in trouble, he felt drawn to her and wanted to comfort her and protect her. He hadn't had this moment of closeness with Mariana for as long as he could remember. Even though she was extremely upset, he felt like a father again.

"My darling, please tell me what's the matter. I can try and help you. Tell me everything." replied Dr. Akkermans, holding his daughter close to him and rubbing one of his hands over her back. She needed to decide what she was going to say. Mariana had to reply and pick a route which she was going to take and what the story was going to be. She needed to decide now.

"Papa, it's Jan. He's the one who has been involved in these killings. I'm so scared." said Mariana, as she started crying and shaking again.

"I know. I recognized him from the picture. I need to know though, my darling, are you involved?" asked Dr. Akkermans. There was silence as he waited for Mariana to respond. "No Papa, I wasn't. I knew about what he had been doing but he threatened me and I was too scared to do anything or say something." replied Mariana, still holding her father tightly as if she was really frightened and needed his protection. Dr. Akkermans was taken back by his daughter's fragility, and he liked finally being the father figure and a comfort to Mariana. He was also very relieved that she wasn't involved in the killings, even though she should have reported Jan to the police or at least said something. He wasn't going to criticize her for what she should have done. He was just pleased that she wasn't the Magpie and he felt a strong urge to support her and help her get out of this mess.

"Okay, you are safe now, my darling. He's not going to hurt you." said Dr. Akkermans, as he hugged his daughter. "Do you know who this Magpie is?"

There were a few moments silence as he waited for her to reply and Mariana thought about what she was going to say next.

"No Papa, he was very secretive about this. He would just disappear days upon end and I wouldn't see him. I questioned him about what he was up to and he was extremely secretive about everything. I thought he was having an affair so one night when he went out and I decided to follow him. I followed him and watched him go to some warehouses in Amsterdam East. When I questioned him later he told me everything but threatened to kill me if I ever said anything. He is a real beast, Papa. I have been so scared all year and didn't know what to do. I know I should have told you, but I was just terrified." Mariana started crying again and waited to see how her father reacted to what she had just said, and more importantly, whether he believed her or not.

Dr. Akkermans digested everything that his traumatized daughter had just told him. He then held her face with both hands and looked straight at her.

"Are you sure you weren't involved in any of this, Mariana? I need to know either way. I will stand by you and support you whatever it is. But I need to know the truth."

He looked into her big brown eyes and watched as they started to well up with tears. "Of course not, Papa! I know I am not a very nice person a lot of the time but I am not a murderer!" replied Mariana, as she started crying again. Dr. Akkermans pulled his daughter towards him and hugged her again.

"Oh, my little girl. It's okay. You don't need to cry anymore. You are safe and it's all over now. You are safe with me." said Dr. Akkermans in his deep authoritative voice. Mariana had managed to convince him of her story. "I guess this is why you have been behaving strangely recently and have been very unhappy?"

"Yes Papa. That's why I have been coming to stay here. I feel safer here, away from Jan. I'm just sorry I didn't have the courage to tell you about it." replied Mariana. She lied so easily and was able to make up an excellent story to convince her father. Little did he know that she came around to get away and think about her next killing. She also washed all her sheets at her fathers that contained DNA from the victims. She didn't want to do this at her own house, just in case she was ever caught.

"Thank you, Papa." continued Mariana, sounding very sad but relieved. Mariana cuddled her father back with affection, something he hadn't felt from her in a very long time. Dr. Akkermans pondered over the fact that in sadness they had been drawn closer together. He was happy but he knew he needed to sort out this situation in the correct manner to get Mariana off the hook for being aware of a string of murders and not notifying the police. There was a moment of silence.

"Right, Mariana," started Dr. Akkermans, "this is what we are going to do. We will go and see the police immediately and tell them everything. Once we explain what Jan has done, they will understand your position in not saying anything. They will also be able to catch the killer quicker as well once they have him charged and have been able to interrogate him. But we need to get your name cleared. We need to act now and do the right thing. Once Jan is arrested, you will be safe."

As Mariana listened to her father explaining what he saw as the appropriate course of action, she realized very quickly that she couldn't let him tell the police, at least not yet. She needed to dissuade him from contacting the police. It wouldn't ruin her plan.

"But Papa, we can't tell the police yet. Jan made me hide belongings and jewelry from the murder victims in my apartment. If the police find these, I am sure that I could be accused of being an accomplice to murder. I need to get rid of these items or give them back to Jan, first."

"Mmmm." said Dr. Akkermans, as he pondered over what Mariana had said. She was indeed right. This made it a lot more complicated. He knew the right thing was to tell the police. In his high profile role as a judge this was definitely the route to take but he wanted to help his daughter and he didn't want her to go to prison. The most important thing for him was that Mariana got out of this with no charges. That she was safe, and that they would become closer once more. He didn't know what to do and was quiet for a number of minutes while he weighed up what his heart wanted him to do versus what was legally and morally the correct way to proceed with this dilemma. He was a highly regarded judge in the Netherlands but was at the end of his career. His daughter's wellbeing and happiness were so much more important to him than whether he was doing the right thing. After all, he had spent his whole life upholding the law and trying to make correct and morale decisions. Realizing that her father didn't know what to do, Mariana decided to speak up and put thoughts into his head.

"Papa, I don't want to go to prison. I want this to be over. Let me get rid of the jewelry and these items then we can go to the police. Then it will all be over." Mariana hesitated, not knowing how her father would react.

"Mmm," he said again, "You know that is illegal." Dr. Akkermans didn't like the idea of doing this and he wanted Mariana to know that. It was, however, probably the best way to get his daughter off any suspicion of being an accomplice. He really didn't want her going to prison either, especially as he had the chance to get close to her again. "But what about Jan? I don't want you near him, my darling. I want the police to get him as soon as possible." replied Dr. Akkermans, with a fair comment. Mariana didn't know how to respond to this.

"I will stay here with you Papa, until this is all over. I am safe here with you. I will just go to my apartment to collect this bag of jewelry and belongings from the victims. Then I can dump it and come back here."

Her father thought about what Mariana had just said and then decided to go along with her plan. "Okay darling, but I want you to stay with me at all times from now on. Okay?" replied Dr. Akkermans.

"Okay, Papa." She hugged him again, pleased with the plan. She had a chance to get things done but she needed to move fast. There was still a lot to do.

"I'm so glad that I could talk to you about this Papa. I feel so much closer to you now." she said with a sad tone in her voice. She was so fake and cunning.

"Me too, my darling." replied Dr. Akkermans, who was crying with tears of happiness that they had made up and become closer as a result of this mess. He would protect Mariana even if he needed to lie to the police. His knowledge of her planning to destroy criminal evidence was also a serious offence but he didn't care.

"Papa, can I have a few moments on my own please? I want to take a shower and get changed and then I'm going to come down and have some tea with you." said Mariana. Dr. Akkermans couldn't believe what he was hearing. Mariana never wanted to spend time with him. He thought to himself that he really needed to protect his daughter from what Jan had done and make sure that she didn't get dragged into it. She was innocent and he would do whatever he could as a father to keep it that way.

"Of course, darling! Take your time and I will see you downstairs in a bit." replied Dr. Akkermans. He kissed her on the forehead and left the bedroom, shutting the door behind him quietly. Mariana listened to him making his way down the stairway to the ground floor. She saw this as her chance to call Jan. Picking up her phone, she pressed the speed dial and waited for him to pick up, which he did almost immediately.

"Where have you been, Mariana? I have been worried. Where the fuck have you been?" said Jan in a panic.

"Don't speak to me like that, and calm down." Mariana snapped back in a low voice.

"It's over, Mariana. My picture is out. Have you seen the front page of every newspaper? It's over I tell you. Someone is going to recognize me now. I'm fucked." said Jan, in a real mess. Mariana needed to get him to relax a little bit. He was no use to her in this state of mind and she really needed him now.

"Jan, listen to me. Stop talking and listen to me!" replied Mariana with a raised voice. She wanted to get Jan's attention but couldn't shout too loud as she didn't want her father to hear downstairs.

Apart from heavy breathing on the phone, there was silence. "Okay, you really need to calm down Jan. Has anyone recognized you yet? No. I didn't even think it looked like you in the newspaper, so relax."

"My sister has been calling me all day. I'm scared to go home." responded Jan, still stressed out.

"She is probably worried about you and wondering where the hell you are!" said Mariana. Jan thought for a second and realized that she might be right. He was supposed to be working at the bakery and his sister would have been both concerned and annoyed that she had to do all the dough preparation on her own. Jan relaxed a little as he listened to Mariana.

"Okay but I'm sure that Noor knows it me, and if she doesn't yet, she will do soon. I have to go and deal with her tonight. I'm going to get rid of her this evening." Mariana listened and was pleased that Jan was taking initiative. He was actually going to take care of the biggest threat to their success. If Jan killed Noor, Mariana would probably be free. She had her father's backing now and he would support her and act as an alibi. She couldn't possibly be caught but she did want to kill one last time and she needed Jan for this.

"Okay good. When?" replied Mariana.

"Tonight, at seven."

"Okay, once that is done I need you to do some other stuff for me."

"What?"

"Tomorrow I want you to burn my apartment down. We need to destroy any evidence there. I am going to stay at my father's tonight and tomorrow so I will be safe."

"Why?" asked Jan. This new plan was a surprise to him. They hadn't discussed this and so he was taken back by this new instruction from Mariana.

"If we are going to run away together, we need to make sure that we have covered our tracks and left no evidence behind."

* * *

7:00 p.m.

Noor was busy skipping around her apartment happy and excited that Jonathan was coming to see her. Jonathan had even put three kisses at the end of the text message which was a new thing from him, which she interpreted that he must really like her and their relationship was blossoming. Noor was in a mad rush to get ready. She had cancelled work by calling in sick, and had gone to get her hair cut. She hadn't even looked at the blog today. She just didn't have time and since she knew that she would be seeing Jonathan tonight that took priority over everything else.

Noor was standing in her underwear by her wardrobe trying to decide which dress to wear with what shoes. She picked a long red dress, which made her look quite slim, and put on a flat pair of shoes. She couldn't wear heels as her chubby ankles were quite swollen from walking around all afternoon. She also didn't want it to appear that she was trying too hard to impress him. As she stood in front of her bathroom mirror, she thought that she liked how she looked. She added a small amount of blusher to her cheekbones and a faint lipstick. She was ready.

Noor walked to her small kitchen and opened the fridge. She had bought some beer for Jonathan and wanted to check if they were cold enough. She was expecting him any minute and was getting more excited by the second. Would he kiss her as soon as he came in or would she have to wait for that moment? Noor had missed him a lot as she hadn't seen him for quite a long time. Even though they messaged frequently and spoke regularly, she was frustrated that they didn't see each other too often. There was nothing she could do about this as it was a consequence of his sales job.

Noor had decided that they were going to get Indonesian takeaway from her favorite restaurant. Noor left the kitchen and walked into her tiny living room. She turned off the lights and lit some candles on her coffee table and her desk. She looked at the clock on the wall above her computer and could see it was 7:05 p.m. and her boyfriend would be arriving any second.

Noor started looking over the food menu when the doorbell rang. She froze for a minute, ran her hands through her hair and looked down at her dress to check that it fell nicely over her curvaceous body. She turned and started walking towards the front door.

She opened it excitedly to see a very different man. Jonathan was wearing flour-covered blue trousers and a sweaty T-shirt. Normally, Jonathan was always clean shaven and looked very handsome with a big smile on his face. Now he looked tired with big dark rings around his eyes and his complexion was pale and pasty. He had a lot of stubble, which was also out of character. Jonathan was also wearing surgical rubber gloves, which was also extremely strange.

Jan could see that Noor was taken back by his appearance. He needed to get in the apartment so he smiled at her and leant forward to kiss Noor on the cheek. She blushed and let him in.

"Hi Noor! How are you?" said Jan nervously following Noor into the living room and looking for something to hit her with. His hands were shaking violently with adrenaline.

"I am fine, thanks. I wasn't expecting you to come dressed like that. What have you been doing today? Painting?" replied Noor, mistaking the flour for white paint.

"Errgh. Something like that." Jan was just happy that he had an excuse for his appearance, even if it was a poor one. "I have been helping a friend paint his apartment so I am pretty tired. Is it possible you could get me a glass of water?" asked Jan. He wanted a few moments alone to scan the apartment to work out how he was going to attack her.

"Yes sure, are you okay?" said Noor as she walked into the kitchen to get him a glass of water.

"Yes, thanks, just a little tired." replied Jan, who noticed a large glass paperweight on her desk, which sat on top of some folders. It looked heavy enough to strike Noor over the head with and do some serious damage.

"Okay. I'm going to make a cup of tea. Maybe you would like that as well?"

"Yes, please. That will warm me up. Thank you." This gave him a few more minutes to plan his next move. He reached into the inside pocket of his jacket to feel for the knife he was carrying. Jan had gone to the red light district before coming to Noor's and bought a 12-inch long hunting knife, which was extremely sharp and had a serrated edge on one side of the blade. Jan was not experienced in using such weapons but it looked like the perfect weapon and the shop assistant had told him that it was designed for gutting and skinning a rabbit or a deer.

Sitting on the small sofa in Noor's living room, Jan was getting worked up as he planned his next move. He decided that he would wait for Noor to sit down at her desk where the computer was and then he would walk up behind her and hit her over the back of her head with the heavy paperweight. This would at least knock her unconscious. Then he would take her life with the knife that he had just bought. His hands started to shake uncontrollably as he realized that within ten minutes he would be a cold-blooded murderer.

Jan walked over to Noor's desk, picked up the paperweight, and walked back to the sofa with it. He took off his jacket and covered the paperweight. He was ready. Noor came back into the living room carrying a small tray which had two cups of tea, a glass of water, and some cookies on it. She put the tray down on the small coffee table.

"There you go." said Noor, hoping her boyfriend would be happy with this. She sat at her computer desk and turned her chair to face him. This wasn't good, thought Jan. He needed her to look the other way in the direction of her computer. He needed to surprise her.

"So, are you sure you are okay?" asked Noor once again. She was genuinely concerned about him and could see that he was shaking.

"Yes, thanks. I'm fine. Just extremely tired and overworked." replied Jan. "What's the latest with this murder hunt? Have they caught her yet? I've been so busy these last few days that I haven't been able to follow the case."

"Well, they did arrest a female suspect but it turns out that she wasn't the right one." replied Noor, who was still staring at her man and thinking that although he looked exhausted, she still fancied him and wanted to take care of him. "Maybe you would like a bath?" she asked.

"Errm, no thanks." snapped back Jan, who was getting frustrated that she wasn't turning on her computer. "Can you see what the latest is on the internet please? I would really like to catch up on the murder hunt."

"Sure." replied Noor, a little surprised by his sudden interest in the Magpie killings. "Let me go online." With that, Noor turned her chair around to face the computer screen and she switched it on. This was Jan's chance. He needed to move quickly. As Noor stared at the screen, he stood up from the sofa and grabbed the paperweight in his right hand. He walked quickly towards her and before she could turn around, he raised his right arm above him and then thrust it downwards into the back of her skull with the paperweight crunching her head. There was a crack and then a dull thud as he struck her with all of his force. Noor's head immediately dropped forward and then she fell to the left and slumped to the ground motionless.

Jan was breathing extremely fast with adrenalin pumping around his body. He dropped the paperweight to the ground and leant down to see if she was still alive. He could see that her thick black hair was matted with the blood that oozed out of the back of her head and onto the wooden floor. The room was still as he listened for her breathing. She was still alive even if her breath was only faint and there was a gurgle in her throat every time she took air in. This meant that she had blood filling up her throat. Jan thought to himself that although she was still alive, it wouldn't be for long. The blow to the back of her head must have smashed her skull.

Jan needed to make a decision whether he was going to finish her off or let her die slowly. He started to think about Mariana and how Noor was a threat to their future and their happiness. He realized that he had to kill Noor now. Jan stood up, walked back to the sofa, and picked up his coat to get the knife. Feeling inside his pockets, he couldn't find the weapon so he bent over the sofa to see if it was on or under one of the cushions. Where was the knife? He couldn't think straight. He started to panic a little as he couldn't find it. He reached down the sides of the sofa to see if it had slipped in there and to his relief he could feel it under the cushion. Pulling it out, he walked back towards Noor who was still unconscious. As he stood over her overweight lifeless body, Jan took the knife out of its leather sheath and gripped it hard by the handle.

He could see that the pool of dark red blood around Noor's head was getting bigger by the second. Jan didn't think that he actually needed to use the knife on Noor as it appeared that she would be dead shortly anyway. She was losing a lot of blood and was struggling to breathe. He thought for a few moments as he looked down at her. Jan had to be sure that she was dead. Noor had brought this on herself. She was the one who couldn't stop blogging about the Magpie, and the fact that she had an accomplice. She was the one who had put the heat on Jan and Mariana. As he mulled over these points, Jan was getting angrier with Noor and he decided that he needed to kill her properly.

Jan knelt down besides Noor and grabbed a handful of her thick black hair. He picked up her limp head with his left hand and stared at her white face and lifeless eyes. Jan could hear her barely breathing. He could also hear something else and it startled him as it sounded like a distant voice shouting, 'Noor, Noor, Noor.' Jan turned around and scanned the room to see where the voice was coming from. He heard the faint voice one more time and looked down to see that it was coming from the body itself. Jan was shocked to see her mobile phone next to Noor's left hand. The phone was lit up. Jan saw that she had called Arnaud. Jan needed to get out of the apartment as soon as possible, just in case this Arnaud called the police.

"Fucking bitch!" shouted Jan in anger as he slid the knife against Noor's chubby throat. It ran sideways across the skin and pressed inwards as he sliced through her jugular. The knife was sharp and it cut through her skin so easily. Jan knew that she was now dead as the flow of blood from her neck to the floor was so fast that he had to jump up and step away in order to avoid being caught in it. Jan let go of her hair and the skull dropped on the wooden floor with a thud. He picked up her mobile phone and ended the call. Placing her phone in his jacket, he left the apartment, trying not to walk too quickly. He didn't want to draw any attention to himself but at the same time he needed to get away from the building.

Jan put the bloodied knife back into the pocket of his jacket along with Noor's mobile. As he walked in the direction of his van, he could hear Noor's phone ringing over and over again. He looked at it to see who was calling and it was no surprise that Arnaud was trying to get hold of Noor. After the fourth call, Jan decided to throw the phone into the canal.

Despite it being freezing cold, Jan was so pumped up from killing Noor that he was feeling very warm. He was surprised that he didn't feel any remorse from taking this innocent lady's life. He didn't even have any feeling of guilt or sorrow for Noor, which was quite shocking as he knew her and had a somewhat intimate relationship with her.

Jan got to his van that was parked in an unlit spot on the Herengracht. He went inside the back of the vehicle where he had some blankets to wrap around himself. He decided to stay the night in the van as he didn't want to go home and face his family. He didn't know what they knew at this point but Jan certainly wasn't in the mood to answer a string of questions.

Jan lay down on the broken cardboard boxes that he had flattened in the back of the van and used them as a mattress. He wrapped himself in the blankets and tried to think about what tomorrow would bring. He knew that he needed to torch Mariana's apartment but he wanted to speak to her before he did that. He wanted to tell his dearest friend and lover that he had done exactly what she had wanted. He had killed Noor. Once he had her apartment down, he didn't know what her next steps would be. Jan needed to know that because he was becoming anxious. Would Mariana try and kill tonight or would she plan on doing it tomorrow? Would she want Jan to help her? Jan just didn't know. He took his phone out of his jacket pocket and tried calling her but it went straight to voicemail. She was either asleep or looking for her final victim. Jan didn't like the fact that he had no idea what she was doing. At a time like this he needed security and her instructions. Mariana was distant from him right now and he didn't like it. His whole body was shaking now from the crime he had just committed and also from the cold.

As he pulled the blankets around his neck, Jan could smell the dried blood on his hands. Outside he could hear sirens passing by on the other side of the canal. There were a number of them and they appeared to be heading in the same direction. Maybe they were going to Noor's house. Within minutes, Jan was asleep.

* * *

8:12 p.m.

Arnaud screeched to a halt on his moped outside Noor's apartment. He took the keys out and ran in the direction of her front door. He didn't know exactly why she had called him but she definitely had someone in her apartment. Arnaud could hear that she was in trouble and that she couldn't speak but only mumble and breathe very faintly. Something had happened and Arnaud was extremely worried. He was sure that she was in a lot of trouble and he needed to get to her as soon as possible.

Arnaud had heard someone walking in her apartment and it sounded like heavy steps on the wooden floor. Then he had heard a deep voice say "Fucking bitch". Was this guy a burglar? Why was she at home? Why wasn't she at work? Had the intruder attacked her? Arnaud didn't know the answer to any of these questions and that frightened him. He feared the worse. He feared for Noor's life. What made him even more concerned was the fact that she had not picked up her phone when he had tried calling back a number of times. And now it was switched off.

The front door to Noor's apartment was closed and after ringing the bell twice Arnaud couldn't wait any longer. He took a step back and then kicked the door in. It opened easily as the lock broke. As he started walking up the steep stairs, he could hear two police cars pull up outside the building and then men rushing in behind him with torches. Before leaving the station Arnaud had told Friso to bring back up to Noor's apartment. The policemen lit the dark stairwell and followed Arnaud closely up to Noor's apartment door. Both Arnaud and the other police had their pistols out and cocked, ready to meet an aggressive intruder. Arnaud was ready to shoot, not knowing what was inside the apartment.

Arnaud shouted Noor's name before entering the apartment. There was no reply from Noor so he pushed open the apartment door with his foot. He had managed to smash the lock with his forceful kick. He took a deep breath and walked in slowly and quietly, holding his pistol out in front of him with both hands. The policemen who were following Arnaud turned off their torches as they weren't necessary.

Arnaud had never been to Noor's apartment before. As he turned left through the hallway and by a coat stand, he came directly into the living room where Noor was lying in a large pool of blood. Arnaud started shaking with sadness and it was clear that she was dead. Noor lay on the ground in her smart red dress. Her body wasn't moving and she didn't appear to be breathing either. There was a big dark pool of claret-colored blood surrounding her head and from the matted hair at the back of her skull, it seemed like this was where she had been struck. There was also a large amount of blood near her neck and in front of her body. Arnaud could see that she had a large gash in her throat. What a terrible murder. His friend had been killed. Arnaud began to cry as he looked down at her. He couldn't touch her as the forensics would need to scan Noor and the surrounding area for clues and DNA from the killer. He could only stand and stare at her lifeless body. Her eyes were still open but motionless.

The other policemen ran around the apartment and checked the other rooms to see if the intruder was still there. No surprise, he had already left. They started calling in the forensics to come to the crime scene, as well as more police back up.

Arnaud could see, next to Noor's outstretched right hand, that she had drawn what appeared to be a line with her blood. Her index finger had dried blood on it so she must have used this to make the line. Arnaud kneeled down to look at it more closely and he could make out an arrow sign at the end of the line. Why did Noor do this? Was she trying to send a message? Arnaud followed the arrow in the direction that it was pointing. He noticed that it was aimed at the computer that sat on the desk. Arnaud could see that the computer was turned on.

Arnaud put on a pair of rubber surgical gloves. As he moved the mouse, the Amsterdam Living website flickered on the screen, specifically on the blog about the Magpie. This wasn't too much of a surprise for Arnaud, as the whole city was obsessed with this right now. As he looked closely and read the messages on the site, it became apparent to him that Noor was logged in as 'Happy Single.'

Arnaud paused and thought for a while. A cold chill ran up his spine as it dawned on him that Noor was the blogger who had defended him throughout the year. Arnaud was in shock. Noor had been a true friend both in person and also behind the scenes and now she was gone. He put his head in his hands and cried loudly. What bastard had done this to her? Arnaud was so sad right now, he couldn't even be angry. After a few minutes, one of the policemen who was in the apartment touched his shoulder and spoke softly to Arnaud.

"Are you okay, Sir?"

Arnaud didn't have the strength to speak but just nodded in acknowledgment. Arnaud looked up once again at the computer screen and saw that Noor had been posting recently. He found it hard to focus with so many tears in his eyes. He started to wonder why Noor wanted him to see this? Did she want Arnaud to find out that she was the blogger, 'Happy Single?' That would sort of make sense, as it showed how much she really cared for him.

Arnaud noticed some pictures of a guy above the computer screen. There were five photos, some of which were head shots and others were full body shots of a young man. He was tall, short haired, quite good looking, and slim. As Arnaud looked at them, he realized that they were of the same person. He realized that it must be the man that Noor had recently started dating. It couldn't be anyone else. Arnaud thought for a few moments in silence and then turned around to face Noor. He looked down at the dark red arrow on the ground again and it dawned on him that maybe Noor was pointing to the pictures and not at the computer. Maybe she wanted Arnaud and the police to see this young man in the pictures. Arnaud needed to find out who he was immediately. Even if he wasn't the intruder, he may be able to help them. At the back of his mind, Arnaud had a bad feeling about the man in the photos. They needed to find him soon. There would be no other reason why Noor was trying to send them a message.

The more Arnaud thought about it, the more he thought that the guy was their suspect. There had been no forced entry into the apartment, there were two cups of tea on the coffee table and Noor was all dressed up. She had been expecting a visitor, thought Arnaud.

He shouted to the policemen behind him and asked them to get Detective Friso Bos on the phone. He pulled one of the pictures off the wall. As he stared at the young slim man, he began to draw a lot of similarities between him and the pictures of the accomplice. Arnaud could feel his heart beating extremely fast as the more he looked at the picture, the more the man's face and body shape resembled that of the male that they were hunting down in association with the Magpie murders.

How could Noor's boyfriend be the accomplice, thought Arnaud? It didn't make sense and couldn't possibly be a coincidence. Arnaud was absolutely certain that Noor wasn't the Magpie, after all he knew that she was the blogger who had been helping them on the case. Arnaud could not understand how this was possible. How did the Magpie's accomplice get close to Noor? Arnaud would need Jim and Robin to go through Noor's emails to see if they could find a trail of how the two had originally met. None of this made sense, thought Arnaud to himself.

Arnaud typed on Noor's computer and brought up the online newspaper of the Volkskraant. On the front page was the photo of the accomplice in the gay bar. Arnaud held the picture of Noor's boyfriend next to it and examined the pictures side by side. It was definitely the same guy. Noor's boyfriend was the man that they had been trying to hunt down. Noor's boyfriend was the accomplice to the Magpie. All they needed to do now was find out who he was. Hopefully, they would find his name from Noor's emails tonight.

Arnaud sat at the desk feeling sad. He couldn't bear to turn around and look at Noor anymore. Why had she had been brutally murdered? She was too nice to hurt or harm anyone. The only thing that he could think of was that Magpie's accomplice had somehow befriended her and taken her life as she was a threat to them.

Arnaud jumped as his mobile started to ring and vibrate at the same time. It was Friso, thank goodness, thought Arnaud.

"Arnaud, it's me. What's up? What has happened? One of the police men told me to call asap." said Friso in a panic.

Arnaud couldn't hold his emotions back and just cried loudly into the phone. He was so sad that he couldn't stop himself.

"Arnaud. What's up? Please tell me. What has happened?" asked Friso again, now in a panic.

There was a pause as Arnaud tried to compose himself. Friso could hear sniffling down the phone as Arnaud cleared his throat and nose from all the tears.

"A friend of mine has been murdered. I'm not going to explain what has happened as I don't know myself really, but it's very strange." said Arnaud in a stuttering voice. He began sobbing again.

"Arnaud. What's going on? Can I help?" responded Friso, very worried.

"I don't know but I think the guy we are looking for killed my friend." replied Arnaud.

"What do you mean? The accomplice?" said Friso.

"Yes." replied Arnaud. He sounded exhausted and helpless.

"What? How?" said Friso, frustrated that he didn't have more information.

"Let's meet at the office in half an hour, Friso. We need to get to the bottom of this and I don't have much energy left right now."
"Okay." replied Friso.

"And I will get two of the policemen here to bring back this computer from my friend's apartment. I am sure there will be some clues on how we can track this guy." said Arnaud.

Friso was completely confused.

"Okay, Arnaud." he replied.

"You know, Friso, I think I have clear pictures of the accomplice. We just need to find out who he is now. See you at the station." said Arnaud. "And get Jim and Robin to meet us there as well. We have a lot to do tonight."

"Okay, Arnaud. See you soon." said Friso.

Arnaud clicked out of the call and started crying again. He would really miss Noor. Arnaud took the rest of the pictures off of the wall and put them in his pocket. He gave clear instructions to the sergeant to get the computer brought to his office immediately. Arnaud put on his coat and left apartment. He managed to hold back the tears as he was going past all the policemen. He got on his moped and drove off along the canal. He started to cry again. One of his only friends had been taken away from him. She had been killed and he needed to clear his head and think straight as it all seemed to intertwine. He couldn't believe how close they were to the accomplice and the Magpie. With the pictures he had now, they should be able to catch him soon. The next few hours would be critical for the case. He needed to focus in order to unravel the story.

Arnaud pulled back on the throttle of the moped and sped in the direction of the police station.

CHAPTER 32

November 30

11:05 p.m.

The four detectives sat in the cold dark office working very hard, against the clock. They wanted to ID this guy as soon as possible. Arnaud had explained the story to the rest of his team and they had all come to the same conclusion. The guy in the pictures at Noor's house was not only her boyfriend but also the accomplice to the Magpie. After scanning all her emails, Jim and Robin confirmed that Noor was the blogger 'Happy Single.' They established that she had met the boyfriend recently on a dating website. He had reached out to make contact and they had started a relationship.

There was no question that Noor's boyfriend was the accomplice. The detectives assumed that he had tried to contact her because she was a threat. Noor had come up with very good explanations of who the Magpie was and what her profile was like. The detectives had spent the last hour discussing these points and had all come to the same conclusions.

From Noor's email history and running a background check on the guy's name, they found out that he was using a false identity. Jim and Robin were also running the pictures through the police national database for any matches. They would have some answers shortly. Friso was sure that if they put the pictures on the news, they would definitely get people to identify this guy. Arnaud didn't want to wait for this. They were too close now and if they waited till morning the guy might try to flee the country. If this happened they would miss out on getting the Magpie as well because the accomplice would certainly lead them to their prized target.

As the team waited for the results of the data search, Friso tried to console his boss, who looked distraught and completely exhausted. Arnaud was extremely pale and his eyes were bloodshot from all the crying. He had never showed emotion before, thought Friso, but he needed his support now. Friso would be there for him always, especially now. He could see how upset Arnaud was and how much he was hurting from this tragic turn of events. The best thing that they could do to help the situation would be to catch this bastard, and also track down the Magpie.

CHAPTER 33

December 1

7:02 a.m.

Jan woke up in the back of his work van, tired and cold. He had a crick in his neck from sleeping on broken cardboard boxes. It had been freezing last night and he only had a thin jumper and his coat to keep him warm. His teeth were chattering as he swallowed to try and clear his dry throat. Jan was extremely hungry and thirsty. His last meal was around lunchtime the day before and he had been too scared and preoccupied to leave the van during the night to get something to eat or drink. The pain he was feeling in his tight stomach was a combination of fear and hunger.

As he sat up against the inside of the van, Jan picked up his phone and turned it on. He needed to know what the time was as well as to see whether Mariana had tried to contact him. He was desperate to speak to her for comfort and security. Jan also needed guidance about what the plan would be today. Right now, he felt alone and scared. They were in it together and he desperately needed to hear Mariana's voice.

Jan wiped his eyes so that he could focus on the lit up screen of his phone. To his surprise, he had one text message and one voice message. Jan decided to look at the text first and he was shocked to see that it was from his older sister, Doreen.

"Jan. Where are you? Call me asap. Urgent. Doreen."

As he read the message, Jan could feel the rush of panic sweeping across his body once more. What did she want? Was she just checking on him to see why he had left the bakery early yesterday or why he hadn't come home? Jan didn't know the answer to these questions and hoped that the voice message would clarify this. If not, he would have to take a decision on whether he should reply to Doreen.

As Jan listened to the message, he started crying. What Doreen had to say was far worse than he had expected. His sister was weeping and was in a complete state of panic. "Hi Jan. Please come home. You need to speak to the police. They are looking for you. They came to our house this morning at 5:30 and wanted to arrest you. They said that they need to speak with you urgently regarding the serial killings that have taken place. Please call us Jan. Please come home and talk to the police. They are saying that you are the accomplice to the Magpie. I hope you are okay. Please come home."

Jan couldn't believe it. They had found him, just as he had feared. It was all over. How did the police come to the conclusion that he was the Magpie's accomplice? They must have found some new evidence. It was all over for them; Mariana and he were finished. Their dream to disappear together would never happen now. He had no idea what he should do. He needed Mariana. She was the one he had done all this for, after all. He had supported her throughout the year and done whatever wanted. She had needed him then and now Jan needed her. As he tried calling Mariana's phone again, he started biting the skin around the end of his fingernails. It wasn't possible to actually bite a nail as he had taken these all the way down to the tips of the fingers and had even chewed away at the skin as well. Two of his fingers started bleeding as he reopened old wounds. Jan didn't feel this anyway as his mind was elsewhere.

As Jan had feared, Mariana's phone went straight to voicemail. Why was she doing this? He needed to tell her about last night and more importantly, he had to explain to her that it was over and that the police were searching for him. He threw his phone onto the floor and hit the back of his head against the steel side of the van in despair. He felt helpless and very alone. He looked out through his watery eyes and tried to think about what would happen next. The police had pictures of him and had tried to catch him at home. He couldn't run from this, not for very long anyway. What should he do? He had to speak to Mariana, his true love, the one he had sacrificed everything for. The sides of the van looked like they were closing in on him. He had nowhere to go and nowhere to hide apart from his van. Jan had no choice but to sit and wait where he was. He needed to speak with Mariana before he could do anything else. He was supposed to meet her today. The safest place for him to be right now was probably in the van.

Jan lay back down on the hard cardboard boxes that had been flattened out on the floor of the van. He was cold and tired, but most of all, frightened. He curled up under his coat and closed his eyes. He wished that this was all just a nightmare but he was shivering so much that he knew he was going through a living hell. He had done all this for Mariana and now she had left him alone to deal with his worst fears. He could feel his heart racing inside. His life was going to change forever. It was going to change for the worse.

Bicycles rode past his van, waking him up from his light sleep. Jan was paranoid that it was the police but as the noise of the cyclists and a car disappeared into the distance, he was able to drowse off once more. He had decided to stay where he was and just wait until he was able to speak with Mariana. He had no choice.

* * *

8:30 a.m.

Arnaud sat in his office, next to Dijkstra, and opposite Friso and the two younger detectives. Arnaud was chewing on some gum to calm his nerves and also his excitement. The team was strategizing, as they knew that they were close to making a big step forward in the case, and perhaps very close to ending the whole murder hunt. It was very clear that if they could catch the accomplice, then they would be able to get the Magpie.

Arnaud looked both exhausted and wide awake at the same time. He hadn't slept much last night as he was still so upset about Noor's death. He had also been extremely wired from the fact that he knew they were so close to finding the murderer. Arnaud was also still in shock that his dear friend Noor was actually Happy Single. He had never expected that.

They had followed up last night with the pictures that they had found in Noor's apartment. Luckily, they had been able to find out his real identity. The male was Jan Meijer, a local twenty-four year old male from Badhoeverdorp, who lived at home with his parents and studied at the University. Arnaud and the team, along with armed police, had gone to the family house early in the morning in order to catch the man off guard. On arriving there, the detectives were surprised to see that the whole family was already up but this was because they were busy preparing bread, as they ran a bakery. It was also very clear that the family had no clue that their son was part of a sick killing spree.

Arnaud and Dijkstra spoke to the family and explained what they needed to speak with Jan about. They appeared to be a simple, warm family, and it shocked Arnaud that the son could be a twisted murderer. Arnaud knew that he would have to interview both the sisters in detail as potential suspects for being the Magpie, even though the one who lived at home did not match the description of the killer. Every female that they came across, who had some association with Jan, would have to be interviewed at length.

The parents and the sister began crying and looked shocked when Dijkstra broke the news to them. They were not faking their feeling of disbelief or anguish; they clearly had no idea. Arnaud and Friso showed them pictures of the accomplice in the newspapers as well as the photos that Arnaud had taken from Noor's apartment last night. This confirmed what the detectives were saying and the family said that they would do their best to help the police find Jan. They wanted their son to come forward and explain himself and hopefully prove his innocence.

The parents had allowed the detectives upstairs to search Jan's bedroom for clues. The forensics and the police would do a complete DNA sweep of the house in due course but Arnaud was keen to see if there was any initial evidence or things that he could spot straight away that would either lead them to Jan or confirm that he was involved in the serial killings. As he expected, there was nothing in there that would tie him to the murders. There was, however, one very interesting observation that Arnaud picked up on immediately.

The bedroom was a typical student's room. It was quite small and plain in appearance, with stacks of books on Art History. There was a laptop by the bed, which they took away as potential evidence. Arnaud was most interested in the pictures of the beautiful girl that he had stuck on his wall and in various picture frames around the room. She was young and probably Jan's age. She was also extremely pretty and very well dressed. Arnaud couldn't take his eyes off the girl and he needed to know who she was. He assumed that it must be Jan's girlfriend, this needed to be confirmed by the family, but perhaps she would lead them to Jan. It was also possible that she was the killer, although she looked far too young and innocent to be involved in the murders. One thing was for sure, thought Arnaud, that Jan obviously adored her as he had so many pictures of this girl up in his bedroom. He had created a shrine.

The parents confirmed that the pretty girl in the pictures was his girlfriend. Her name was Mariana Akkermans. Arnaud noticed that when he asked the family about the girl, their faces twisted up and began to snarl. It was clear that none of them liked her. Arnaud had asked them why this was, and the sister was the only one who had wanted to say anything. She explained that her brother had completely changed over the last year since he had started going out with her. This sent shivers down Arnaud's spine as the killings had begun approximately one year ago. Was this girl, Mariana Akkermans, the killer? Was she the Magpie? He tried keeping his cool as a lot had to be done before they could draw any conclusions but he had a hunch that they were close. First, they needed to find Jan and then they could focus on finding the Magpie.

The detectives got Mariana's address from Jan's parents. Arnaud sent Friso and the two young detectives to her apartment to see if she or Jan was there. The four policemen, who were assisting them, surrounded the possible exits from this nice-looking building on the canal. There were no lights on in the apartment and nobody answered the doorbell. Friso took a look through the letterbox and the ground floor windows. It definitely looked like there was no one at home. The detectives could see that it was an expensive property. This was quite unusual for a University student, thought Friso. Nonetheless, they didn't hang around the apartment for too long, not wanting to draw any attention to themselves. They needed to report back to Arnaud and plan for the rest of the day.

Arriving back at the police station Friso and the other detectives went up to their office where Arnaud and Dijkstra were waiting. As they entered the office, Arnaud looked up with a tired but excited expression on his face.

"Anything?" he said.

"No." replied Friso. "The apartment was empty. There was no one there."

"Are you sure?" said Arnaud, with disappointment in his voice.

"Certain, Arnaud."

The three detectives sat next to Dijkstra on the opposite side of Arnaud's desk. Dijkstra could see that they were all cold, so he went to make some coffee for them.

"So, what now?" asked Friso.

This was directed at Arnaud. They knew that he had to be the one to make all the decisions today. They were so close and the next twenty-four hours were crucial. Right now, they were in a waiting game but that wasn't good enough for Arnaud. The worst thing that could possibly happen would be for the accomplice and the Magpie to escape. This was possible, as this morning's newspapers and television channels were showing new pictures of Jan Meijer from both the gay bar with those glasses on and also the photos taken from Noor's house.

They had to catch him today and then hopefully he would give up the identity of the Magpie through interrogation. But first they had to catch Jan, which was proving difficult so far.

Arnaud thought for a few moments and then began speaking. "Okay, I want to put a team in Badhoeverdorp, near Jan Meijer's house. I also want a team waiting close to his girlfriend's house. It's important that the team wait in an unmarked vehicle. When you were at Mariana's apartment, I did a background check on her, and interestingly, she is the daughter of Dr. Akkermans, a well-known judge in Holland."

"Yes, I have heard of him." replied Friso.

"Well, we should give him a call, as maybe he knows where his daughter is." said Arnaud.

"Okay." replied Friso. "Good idea."

"I will do that." continued Arnaud. "He is high profile and an important person in Amsterdam. I don't want to alarm him or start making any accusations regarding his daughter. After all, we can't make the assumption that she had anything to do with these killings yet."

"Agreed." replied Friso. "But if he has read today's papers then he has also seen the photos of his daughter's boyfriend on the front pages, so he may know already."

"Yes, that's true. We need to call him right away." said Arnaud.

"Where does he live?" asked Robin.

"On the Keizersgracht, in the center of the canals, very close to his daughter's house. Maybe she is there? Well, even if she isn't, he may know where she is. Anyway, let's call him now." said Arnaud.

He looked at the piece of paper that lay on his desk in front of him. On it was the address and telephone number of Dr. Akkermans. As he dialed the number, the rest of the team listened in silence.

* * *

9:40 a.m.

Mariana opened her eyes and looked across at the small bedside table. On it was a beautiful silk scarf, her watch and the silver-framed picture of her mother. All three things reminded Mariana of that beautiful lady.

She had slept well considering everything that was going on right now. She immediately started to think about the fact that she hadn't been able to find any victims over the last few days. She felt useless and helpless. Mariana knew that her reign of terror was coming to an end. She needed to make an exit plan. The good news was that she felt that she had her father wrapped around her little finger now, and he believed her. He wanted to protect her and would probably defend and support her. Mariana was fully aware of how important her father was now as her alibi and this would definitely help her if she came under the spotlight.

After checking the time on her watch, Mariana turned on her phone. It was no surprise to see numerous text messages and missed calls from Jan. She flicked through a few of them and they all said the same thing. Jan wanted to know where she was and why she hadn't returned any of his calls. He was worried that they were going to be caught and that the police were looking for him. This was the reason she had turned off her phone. She couldn't handle speaking to him when he was like this and she needed to rest and plan what she was going to do next. She didn't need Jan stressing her out.

Mariana sat up in her bed and propped another pillow behind her slender back. She pulled up the blankets to her shoulders to keep her warm. It was freezing outside and the heating had only just come on in her bedroom.

She picked up the remote control that lay on the bed and pressed it whilst pointing at the old fashioned television on the other side of the room. After a few seconds the television turned on and a picture appeared, which took Mariana's breath away. The channel was RTL5 and the news was currently showing at 9:45 a.m. She was extremely concerned by the photos of Jan that were being shown on the national news.

Mariana turned up the volume to listen to the reporter. She couldn't believe the headlines and she knew that it wouldn't be too long before her pictures would also be on the news, as well. The reporter was saying that the police were searching for the male suspect, Jan Meijer, who was not only accused of being the accomplice to the Magpie but also for killing a female in Amsterdam yesterday evening, named Noor Lumas. They were showing the CCTV footage of Jan in the gay bar as well as some very clear pictures of him on holiday and in a suit. Mariana froze and couldn't think straight. She had no idea where they got these new pictures from but there was no mistaking who Jan was. They also knew his full name and so it was definitely over for him.

Mariana didn't care about Jan or the fact that he was going to be caught. All she was concerned about was that he might give her up to the police. Maybe he would deny that she was actually involved in any of the killings, thought Mariana. She couldn't take this risk but at the same time she couldn't do much about it. Mariana wiped some tears from her eyes and cheeks and shook her head violently from side to side. She needed to clear her head and think straight. She didn't have much time and needed to take action immediately. She had to be on the right foot if she was going to have any chance of getting out of this.

As she jumped up, out of bed, she continued watching the news as she got dressed. Slipping on her skin-tight jeans and a putting on a jumper over the t-shirt she had slept in, Mariana thought about what would happen next. The police knew who Jan was and they would surely go to his parent's house to find him. If he wasn't there, his family would definitely tell the police about her. It wouldn't be long before they came to her father's house. She needed to go and speak with her father immediately.

Mariana put on some socks and flat shoes and ran down the stairwell to the ground floor. As she skipped quickly down the stairs she tried to think sad thoughts and squeeze out more tears to show her father that she was upset and scared.

Mariana arrived in the kitchen where Rina was clearing the breakfast dishes. She scanned the room but her father was nowhere to be seen. Mariana looked across at Rina and gave a small smile.

"Morning Rina." said Mariana, sniffling as she spoke. "Where is Papa?"

Rina said nothing but responded to Mariana's question by looking over at the door to her father's study. Mariana stared at Rina wondering why she didn't say hello or smile back. Did she suspect that she was involved in all of this? She knew Mariana better than anyone else and probably wasn't fooled by Mariana's acting and games. However, Mariana didn't have time to ponder over this now. She had to move fast and think about what she needed to do next. For this, she had to get her father's help and support.

Mariana walked quickly over to the large oak door to her father's study. She took a deep breath and then turned the door handle. As she pushed the door open, it gave a loud whining creak, announcing her entry into the room. Mariana walked in slowly and shut the door behind her. She had her head down as she walked in and her hair fell forward over her face. She looked up slightly through her long silky hair and could see her father sitting in his usual spot behind his desk with the newspapers laid out in front of him and a cup of coffee in his right hand. She could just make out that he had looked up and was staring through the round gold-rimmed spectacles that sat on the bridge of his long Roman nose.

"Good morning, Darling." he said, realizing that she had been crying and was shaking slightly as she sniffled away. "How are you? Did you get any sleep?"

Mariana started crying very loudly and ran over to her father and sat on his lap, throwing her arms around him.

"Oh Papa, I'm really scared. I just saw the news and they know that Jan is involved in all of this. I'm worried that he is going to come and get me."

Dr. Akkermans hugged his daughter. "You are safe here, my darling. He won't come here."

"I think we need to go to the police now, Papa. I think I need to tell them everything." continued Mariana.

"Yes, you do Mariana. That will help getting Jan arrested. It also gets you completely off the hook. You need to tell them everything and have your story fully worked out." replied Dr. Akkermans, stroking his daughter's back as he spoke.

"But maybe they will think I am involved, Papa. I was Jan's girlfriend so they might accuse me of being in on it. Oh Papa, I'm so frightened." Mariana stared crying uncontrollably once more.

"Listen, my darling. I will be on your side and act as your alibi. You don't need to worry about anything. I have thought it through and I will stand by you. You do need to prepare your story though, so calm down and get your facts together. I will support you through the whole ordeal." replied Dr. Akkermans in his deep calming voice. Clearly, Dr. Akkermans had been strategizing all night about how best he could protect his daughter. He had a game plan.

"Okay, Papa. Shall we call the police now?" she asked.

"We don't need to do that my darling. They called me this morning. They know that you are Jan's girlfriend and they want to see you today." said Dr. Akkermans.

Mariana's heart started beating very fast. They were on to her, just as she had expected. She needed to get control of herself and devise her next steps. She didn't have much time.

"Oh, okay. Are they going to take me away for questioning? Are they accusing me of being involved?" said Mariana.

"You don't need to worry about anything, Mariana. They are just trying to find Jan. The police went to his parent's house this morning and they told them who you were and where you lived. We just need to tell the police that you are staying here because you are scared to go home in case Jan comes round. I will tell the police everything that you have told me. I have already told them that you knew that Jan was involved in these murders and that you have been in hiding here for a few days. So don't worry, the police don't suspect you at all. You just explain everything to them just the same way that you have told me."

Mariana was pleased as her father had not only fallen for her story but was also backing her up all the way. He would be able to support her and act as an alibi if necessary. She just needed to think through the rest of the details and plan a complete story for the police. She was going to frame Jan and hopefully get out of this. The only risk now was if Jan would tell the police that she was also involved in the killings.
She sniffled and then started speaking again.

"Okay Papa, thank you. I am going to take a shower and get changed. What time will the police come over?"

"Ten-thirty." replied her father.

"Okay, Papa. Please come and get me when they arrive. I will be upstairs." said Mariana.

She stood up and wiped her eyes. Looking down at her father with a sad face and with a quivering bottom lip, she spoke once more. "Thank you for helping me, Papa. I will never forget this, as I wouldn't know what to do without you."

Dr. Akkermans smiled at his daughter, with a concerned look on his face. She leant forward and kissed him on the cheek and then turned and left the study. Walking into the kitchen Mariana could see Rina wiping the long wooden table in the center of the room. Mariana tried to get Rina's attention as she walked through the kitchen towards the hallway. Annoyingly, Rina didn't look up, which made Mariana think that she didn't believe her tears. She began to feel extremely paranoid.

She didn't think that Rina knew what was going on, but she was sure that she knew Mariana was acting and playing with her father. This was not good but she had too much to worry about and she couldn't let this bother her. Once Mariana got to the hallway she started running towards the stairs and then quickly skipped up towards her bedroom.

When Mariana got into her bedroom, she shut the door and picked up her phone. She dialed Jan. The phone only rang once before he answered it.

"Where are you? Why haven't you answered any of my calls? What the fuck is going on?" shouted Jan through the phone. He was in a mad panic.

"Calm down, Jan." replied Mariana.

"No, I won't calm down. I've been trying to call you all night and all morning. I have left you loads of messages and you haven't called me back. What the fuck is going on, Mariana?" said Jan in an absolute rage.

"I have been busy at my father's house, Jan. I have been planning our exit. Our exit together."

"What do you mean our exit together? What have you been planning? Why didn't you tell me about this?" Jan wanted answers.

"It's time for us to leave soon, Jan. We have spoken about this already. I have been planning where we are going to go. Where we are going to escape, away from all of this." said Mariana in a calm voice.

In reality, the only thing she had really been planning was her made up story to frame Jan but he was hysterical right now and had no idea what to think.

There was silence as he thought about what Mariana had just said. She could hear him breathing heavily on the phone. It sounded like he was having an anxiety attack.

"Where are we going, Mariana? When are we leaving?" asked Jan, in a quieter voice.

"It doesn't matter where, Jan. But soon." she replied.

"I need to know when. It does matter as the police are breathing down my neck. They are fucking on to me, Mariana. It's over, I tell you. If I don't get out of here today, I am fucked." He was getting worked up again.

"It will be tomorrow Jan, so try and calm down." replied Mariana.

There was silence again, as Jan thought about what she said. Mariana decided to keep speaking.

"Where are you?" she asked.

"I've been hiding in the back of my van. I'm parked up in a small side street off of one of the canals." replied Jan.

"Oh, okay." said Mariana.

"I killed Noor last night and now the police are onto me. I don't know how exactly but my sister has been trying to get hold of me. She said that the police have been to my house and are looking for me. It's over. I'm truly fucked unless I can get out of here soon." Jan continued with a raised voice.

"Well, we will leave tomorrow. I have it all planned out. I'm at my father's house now and will be picking up our train tickets later, so don't worry about anything." Mariana knew that Jan hadn't seen the news or the papers and she didn't tell him either. She didn't want him more scared than he already was. She needed Jan to do one last thing for her. "Baby, I need you to relax and calm down. You need to do one more important thing for me and for us. I need you to go to my apartment and burn it down. We need to wipe out all the evidence that may still be in there. We need to get rid of any DNA. Then we are clean. Then we will be free."

"How am I supposed to do that? The police are looking for me." shouted Jan.

"Don't overreact. You will be fine. It's almost ten in the morning. I want you to stay in the van until eleven-thirty and then go to my apartment. There are three industrial size bottles of lighter fluid in the cellar. Pour them all over the three floors of the apartment and torch everything. Then, I want you to come over to my father's and text me when you arrive. I will let you in and we can hide out in my bedroom until tomorrow. Then, we can get up early, head to Central Station and get on the train. We will be free." Mariana gave clear instructions to Jan.

"But I'm scared." replied Jan, in a desperate tone.

"So am I, Jan, but we need to clear the trails behind us. Then we can disappear together and be safe." said Mariana. Mariana knew that she was framing Jan to save herself. There was no way that Jan could sense this. He was just listening to what she had to say and the instructions that she was giving him.

"Is that clear, Jan.? Go to my apartment at eleven-thirty." continued Mariana.

There was silence again as Jan digested what she had just said. "Yes. Eleven-thirty." he replied.
"Good. It's almost over, Jan."

"I miss you, baby. I can't wait to be with you. I love you." said Jan as he started to cry.

"Me, too, Jan but now you need to get hold of yourself and do this last job. Burn my apartment down to the ground. Set it on fire. Please don't mess up." she replied.

"Yes, I know what I have to do. I will text you afterwards, once I am outside your father's house." said Jan.

"Okay. Let's speak later. Bye." replied Mariana and she clicked out of the call.

* * *

10:20 a.m.

Mariana took a shower and changed into clean clothes. As she looked into the misted mirror, she saw a beautiful young lady who had failed to achieve her only goal. She had wanted to get men back for how they treated women. She needed to feel that she had taken revenge for her mother's death. Mariana had spent a lot of time in mourning. As she had got older, this feeling of melancholy and grief had turned to hatred. She detested all men, including her father, and what she had done over the last eleven months had given her peace of mind. She had carried out all the killings for her mother and it made Mariana feel content. It had made her feel good.

What the future would hold for Mariana now, she just didn't know. She couldn't bear the uncertainty of not being able to see what lay ahead for her. She liked to be in control, and up until one month ago, she really was in the driving seat and deciding her own destiny. Now, however, everything had changed. The walls were closing in on her. Mariana knew that it was not going to be possible for her to fulfill her dream of ending the year with another kill. That wasn't going to happen anymore. The police were onto her, and while they didn't know that she was actually the Magpie, they weren't far away from drawing those conclusions. Mariana had spent some time devising a plan to get her 'off the hook' and now she just needed to execute it.

She had her father on her side, which she knew would help a lot. She just needed to convince these detectives that she wasn't part of the serial killings and then get Jan framed. Unfortunately for Jan, just being caught by the police wasn't enough. Mariana needed Jan dead. That was the only way she could be sure that she could get away from all of this as an innocent individual. She had only a few hours to implement her strategy but first she would need to act out her character to the police. She had to pretend to be the fragile girlfriend, caught in the crossfire of a crazed boyfriend who was working with a mass murderer to commit numerous calculated killings.

Mariana decided not to put on any makeup. She wanted to look as simple and as weak as possible for the detectives. She put her hair up in a tight ponytail, which revealed the full beauty of her face. Even though she was looking tired and pale by her standards, she was still stunning. Mariana put on her petite diamond stud earrings and tied one of her mother's silk scarfs around her thin neck in a knot. She turned on the cold tap, and with cupped hands, collected some water and then poured it onto her eyes. She wanted to give the appearance that she had been crying a lot.

Mariana looked at her watch and saw that it was almost ten-thirty. She took one last look at herself in the mirror and pulled a solitary pout. She headed out of the bathroom and down the long stairway to the ground floor. Arriving in the hall at the bottom of the stairs, Mariana walked towards the kitchen. The kitchen was looking spotless, thanks to Rina, who was still cleaning up. She could tell from Rina's face that she knew something was up. Mariana was sure that Rina didn't believe her.

Mariana needed to focus on the job on hand now, which was tricking the police. Mariana turned and headed towards the study. As usual, she knocked before entering and then walked into the study with a sad and frightened expression on her face. She could see her father sitting at his desk with his head resting in his hands. He looked up as she walked towards him.

"Hello, Darling. How are you feeling now?" he asked, seeing straight away that his daughter had been crying again.

"Fine, Papa. Just nervous and scared. I'm worried that the police will be angry with me for not informing them about Jan." replied Mariana in a sad voice.

"Listen, you had your reasons for not doing that. You have been extremely frightened and Jan threatened you. The police will understand. You don't need to worry. Just tell them everything you know." said Dr. Akkermans.

"Okay but I am still worried that they will think I am involved in all these killings. I have been thinking and I can't remember where I was on certain times and days when the murders happened. I have no idea, Papa." replied Mariana in a panic.

Dr. Akkermans paused for a moment before replying to his daughter.

"Listen to me, my darling. Don't worry. I will vouch for you. You have nothing to worry about. Nothing is going to happen to you. I will tell the police that you have been staying with me a lot during the year and certainly during the periods when murders took place. They are not going to accuse you of anything. I can assure you." Her father raised his voice as he spoke.

It was clear to Mariana that her father was going to defend her under any circumstances. Dr. Akkermans was going to protect his daughter and act as a witness and an alibi. This was good news. All these years of making him feel guilty for what he had done to her mother had really paid off. Dr. Akkermans would do anything to defend her innocence even if it meant lying to the police. This was something he had never done before. Dr. Akkermans had spent his whole career upholding the law. Now, he was going to throw all of that away to ensure that his daughter remained free. Mariana felt a warm glow fill her body and she walked up to her father and hugged him again and kissed him on the cheek. She knew he loved this.

"Thank you, Papa. Thank you for being there for me." she squeezed out some tears as she held him close to her.

"It's okay, Mariana." He replied in a more serious voice. "I want you to sit on the couch now and compose yourself as the detectives will be here shortly."

Dr. Akkermans ushered her over to the old sofa that was positioned on the side of his study. Mariana sat on it and pulled the blanket that was lying on the sofa over her legs. She wanted to look as innocent and helpless as possible for the detectives. She took a few deep breaths and rested her head back on the wall behind the sofa. She was ready.

The doorbell rang through the house at ten thirty-five. Dr. Akkermans stood up from his desk and checked himself. He tucked his perfectly-ironed shirt back into his navy blue suit trousers and adjusted his gold cufflinks on his shirt so that they looked symmetrical and smart. As always, he was dressed immaculately and his expensive business attire along with his very tall frame made him intimidating. Dr. Akkermans ran his hands through his grey, slicked back hair and then headed for the door of the study. Just before he left the room, he looked back at Mariana and gave her a reassuring smile.

"Everything will be fine. That I promise you."

With that, he left the study and walked through the kitchen in the direction of the hallway and over to the front door of the house. Mariana could hear his hard footsteps on the wooden floorboards as he made his way through the house.

Dr. Akkermans stood up tall and straight and took a deep breath before opening the front door to his house. Standing on the steps outside was Detective Arnaud Van Loo and another detective whom he ushered politely indoors. He recognized Arnaud from the television and welcomed the two detectives in a formal manner.

"Good morning detectives. Please come in." said Dr. Akkermans. He led them through his house in the direction of the study. As they followed the judge, Dr. Akkermans began speaking in his articulate methodical manner.

"My daughter is in the study and waiting to speak with you. As I mentioned on the phone, she is extremely frightened and worked up. She is very worried about Jan coming to find her, as he is fully aware that she knows about everything he has been doing this year. I would like you to get some police protection here at my house if at all possible."

Dr. Akkermans glanced round at Arnaud as they walked through the kitchen to see if he was going to agree to this request. Arnaud nodded at Dr. Akkermans and then looked at Jim as if to say please arrange this.

"I'm sure we can get that sorted out straight away, Dr. Akkermans." replied Arnaud.

"Good." said Dr. Akkermans. "Thank you."

He stopped by the closed door to his study and turned round to face the two detectives. He began speaking again, but lowered his voice, as he knew that Mariana was sitting on the sofa on the other side of the door. "My daughter is very upset and worried because she hadn't notified you earlier about Jan. You have to understand that she is terrified of her boyfriend. Please go easy on her detectives. I have spoken in-depth with her today and yesterday and she is willing to cooperate fully with you. So please go easy on her."

Arnaud looked up at the daunting torso of Dr. Akkermans that towered over him. He was going in there with an open mind and wasn't going to be influenced or told what to do by this judge, but for now, he just smiled and nodded at Dr. Akkermans.

"Understood." replied Arnaud, wanting to get into the study as quickly as possible to speak with the judge's daughter.

Dr. Akkermans had heard what he wanted to from the detectives. He opened the door to his study and led them in. Shutting the door behind them, he pointed to the two seats that were positioned on the other side of his desk.

"Please take those seats." said Dr. Akkermans.

Arnaud and Jim looked around the study, observing all the shelves of books and pictures on the walls. Dr. Akkermans sat down next Mariana on the leather sofa. She was curled up in a ball under a blanket, with her head down and her body shaking as she cried softly.

Dr. Akkermans put his hand on his daughter and spoke, "Mariana, I have told them that you are going to help as much as you possibly can with their investigation."

Mariana looked up at her father and tried to pull a small smile. She then turned her head in the direction of Arnaud and Jim. She had tears streaming down her face but her natural beauty was still there for everyone to see. Both Arnaud and Jim spent a few moments just staring at this emotional girl. She was stunning.

After a minute or so, Arnaud began to speak. He was in a rush and wanted to get as much information as possible. His immediate concern was to find Jan Meijer. Arnaud needed to take it easy on her and try and extract as much information as possible without working her up more than she already was.

"Good morning, Mariana. I am Detective Van Loo. You can call me Arnaud. I am responsible for the murder hunt and investigation into the serial killings that have taken place this year in Amsterdam."

"I know who you are." replied Mariana in a soft innocent tone, as she looked straight into Arnaud's eyes.

She had to try and come across as innocent and as fragile as possible, even though her blood was boiling inside. She was sitting one meter away from two of the arse holes that were trying to track her down. This detective was the one who was ruining her legacy. As much as it killed her to sit there in the same room as these men, who had almost won, she had to think about her future. That meant that she had to play the role of the traumatized victim and the angelic-threatened girlfriend of a murderous beast.

Arnaud gave Mariana a soothing smile and began speaking. "Mariana, thank you for speaking with us now. Thank you also Dr. Akkermans for letting us come round to your house so quickly to talk with your daughter."

Dr. Akkermans smiled back at Arnaud in acknowledgement of what he had just said.

Arnaud carried on speaking. Whilst he didn't want to make her more upset than she already was, he needed to get straight to the point. "I understand that you are feeling distraught and worried. You are safe here, so you don't have to feel threatened anymore. We really do need your help now and I know that discussing some of these issues about Jan might be difficult for you, so please bear with us."

Mariana said nothing but continued staring at Arnaud with a sad face.

"Now, do you know where Jan is at the moment?" asked Arnaud.

"At the moment, I don't know. I assume that he is at home." replied Mariana. Her naivety came across convincing.

"He isn't at home and hasn't been there since yesterday morning. When was the last time you saw him?" continued Arnaud.

"I haven't seen him for quite a while." replied Mariana.

"How long is a while?" asked Arnaud.

"Errm. I am not sure but at least a week to ten days." said Mariana, caught off guard by the question. "I have been staying at my father's house. I have been trying to avoid him. I have been sleeping here for a couple of weeks now."

This was clearly a lie, but even though Arnaud didn't know this, he could sense that Dr. Akkermans was looking at his daughter in a strange way. Something wasn't right and Arnaud felt that she wasn't being completely honest. He looked back over at the judge who then nodded at him in agreement to what his daughter had just said. Arnaud couldn't spend any more time thinking about the strange mannerisms of Dr. Akkermans. He would come back to this later.

"Do you know where he might be, if he isn't at home?" continued Arnaud. Jim was making notes in his little black book, which was annoying Mariana. She felt like the detectives were busy taking evidence, which they may use against her in the future.

"If he is not at home then I am not sure. He used to disappear for days at a time. I was sure that he was having an affair with another girl, but he denied it. Then I found out that he was involved in these murders and I assumed that he was going to see the girl that he was helping. This Magpie."

This was very clever of Mariana, as she knew that Jan had been supposedly seeing Noor, and was using her ignorance as an excuse for not knowing where Jan was hiding out.

"Okay." said Arnaud. He had a lot of thoughts going through his head right now but needed to focus on listening to Mariana. Mariana clearly didn't know that Jan had been seeing Noor, even if she sensed it. He would have to break this to her but wasn't sure if now was the right time. The judge's daughter was clearly distressed enough. Before Arnaud could speak again, Mariana started talking again.

"I expect he is with the killer though. Where that is, I don't know. He would never tell me. He always warned me not to ask questions and keep my mouth shut. He used to threaten me and sometimes he would hit me. I was so scared of him Detective."

Mariana started crying again and her father gave her a hug to try and console her.

"Okay. I understand, Mariana. Please try and relax, as it won't happen again. Like I said earlier, you are safe now. We just need to find him asap." said Arnaud.

"So you have no idea where he is now or where this other girl lives?"

Mariana paused for a moment and then spoke up.

"No, Detective. I tried to stay away from his involvement with this killer. I followed him once to the Marnixstraat in the Jordaan but I don't know if that was where the Magpie lived. Anyway, Jan did call me yesterday evening and he said that he needed to speak with me today."

Arnaud's eyes lit up as she said this. He was very surprised that she had kept this information back until now. The two detectives looked over at the beautiful girl, waiting for her speak again.

"Go on." said Arnaud.

"I told him that I didn't want to see him but he did say that he needed to go to my house today and pick up some clothes. Anyway, I told him that I couldn't meet and that I was staying at my father's. That's why I wanted to speak with you as I am worried that he will come here. He wants to talk to me and he said that he would be going to my house around eleven forty-five this morning. I am so scared of him. He is violent and frightens me."

Mariana began crying again, quite uncontrollably. Her father hugged her tightly and stroked her hair. Arnaud could see how much the father adored his daughter and how upset he was as well.

"Okay, Mariana. We will send some police over to your house again and hide out and wait for him to come." replied Arnaud.

He knew that there were undercover police already waiting across on the other side of the canal but he didn't want to tell Mariana that as she might think that they were spying on her. Arnaud just needed to notify the police now to be ready. He nodded at Jim, who stood up and went out of the room to make a call to Friso and the rest of the team.

"Okay, detective." said Mariana in a calmer voice. She thought for a moment and then continued speaking. "There is one other thing, Jan has a pistol with him most of the time so tell your colleagues to be careful."

Arnaud thought this was strange as a gun was never used before in any of the murders and it hadn't been used to kill Noor, either. Nonetheless, this was good information to have and they would need to send some police from the firearms squad over to Mariana's house as well.

As Arnaud looked across at Mariana, wrapped up under the blanket and in her father's arms, she seemed to be more relaxed now as she spoke up again. "Where did you get these other pictures of Jan from? I saw them on the news this morning, and I have never seen them before?"

"Well, Mariana, we took the pictures from a flat in the Jordaan. It was the apartment of the female who was killed last night, Noor Lumas. They were on the wall in her living room."

"Why were they there?" asked Mariana immediately in response.

Arnaud paused as he knew what he was just about to say would upset Mariana. "We believe that Jan was having an affair with her."

Mariana froze for a moment before falling onto her father's lap. She began crying very loudly. "I knew it. I knew he was seeing someone else." sobbed Mariana.

"And the female in question was killed by Jan last night." continued Arnaud.

Mariana sat up suddenly, as if in deep shock. "How do you know he killed her?" asked Mariana.

Arnaud didn't want to tell her about Noor calling him on her cell phone and that he could hear Jan attacking her. "We just know that it was him. That's all I can say about it right now."

Arnaud started choking up as he talked about Noor's death. It was fresh in his mind and he couldn't stop himself. Mariana just stared at the detective, enjoying his pain.

As there were a few seconds silence, Dr. Akkermans saw this as his chance to talk. "Okay, detectives. I think you have enough information to be getting on with the search. Mariana is happy to help more but you should first catch Jan in my opinion. Mariana has been through enough for now and has cooperated fully with you and will continue to do so."

Arnaud looked over at the giant sized judge and nodded. "Okay, Dr. Akkermans. Thank you for your assistance and thank you, Mariana, for your cooperation. We will keep you updated on our progress with the case and let you know when we have arrested Jan."

"Thank you." said Dr. Akkermans.

"One last thing, please stay here Mariana. We will need to speak with you in more depth about what you know." stated Arnaud clearly. "Understood." said Mariana.

With that, Arnaud and Jim stood up and walked towards the front door. The judge showed them out of the house and shook both their hands as they left.

As the two detectives walked in the direction of the police car, waiting for them outside, Arnaud pondered over their meeting with Mariana and her father. Something didn't add up. He felt that Mariana was too innocent and feminine to be true. He also found it strange that Jan had a pistol and hadn't used it to kill Noor. Maybe he didn't want to make any noise in her apartment. That was the only explanation he could think of. As they got into the police car, Arnaud knew that once they had caught Jan, he could have plenty of time to ask these sorts of questions.

They drove in the direction of the Singel, looking for a place to park the car. They would hide with Friso and the rest of the police and wait for Jan to turn up. They were close to the end.

* * *

11:29 a.m.

Arnaud sat in the back of an unmarked silver VW Golf on the opposite side of the canal from Mariana's apartment. He was in crammed next to Jim. Friso and Robin sat in the front. Parked behind them on the Singel was a large black van with six undercover cops in it. In another car, about fifty meters from the apartment were three armed policemen. They were all waiting for Jan. Everyone knew what he looked like and all had been briefed about him carrying a gun. The plan was very clear. Arnaud had explained that he wanted Jan to go into the apartment and then they would seal off all the exits of the building. Once they had him inside, it was Arnaud's view that it would be very difficult for him to escape.

Arnaud and his team were both excited and nervous at the same time. They had been working towards this moment for eleven months and now they were going to come face to face with one of the two people responsible for all the killings that had taken place this year. Arnaud looked at his watch and the time was eleven-thirty exactly. Jan should be arriving any minute he thought to himself, unless he had spotted them. This was probably unlikely as they were parked like any other vehicle and there wasn't a sign of a police uniform in site.

One could literally feel the tension in the air and Arnaud tried to install a calming influence on his team. "Everyone okay?"

The three other detectives just nodded as they continued focusing on the pedestrians walking by outside, trying to spot Jan.

"There he is!" said Robin, in an excited tone.

"Where?" said Arnaud quietly.

"Walking towards us. He is about fifty meters behind our car, coming in our direction." continued Robin.

"He's going to walk right past us." said Jim.

All the detectives looked in the front wing mirrors and could see the tall slim frame of Jan approaching the vehicle from behind. He had a coat on as well as a baseball cap. Whilst his head was down, you could see that it was him. He looked tired and jaded, and his face was very pale. Jan had stubble and large dark rings around his eyes. It looked like he hadn't slept for a while. You could see that he was checking out Mariana's building on the other side of the canal. He was probably looking for policemen, thought Arnaud.

"Okay guys, let's look as inconspicuous as possible." said Arnaud, paranoid that they were going to be seen.

Friso pretended to be asleep in the front of the car, while Robin picked up the newspaper from the floor of the vehicle and pretended to read it. Both, Arnaud and Jim slumped down in the back of the car and pretended to be sleeping, too. Arnaud turned his face in the other direction from where Jan would walk past them, as he was concerned that Jan may recognize him.

After a few moments, they heard Jan's footsteps approach and then walk quickly past their car. He hadn't stopped and didn't appear to spot them. The four detectives stayed slumped down in their seats but tracked Jan as he moved further up the cobbled street of the Singel. It was clear that he was going to cross the bridge, which was a few hundred yards ahead of them, and then walk back down the other side of the canal to the apartment.

"Shit. That was close." whispered Jim.

"He didn't see us." said Robin.

"Do you think he has his gun?" asked Jim.

The four detectives checked out Jan's back as he walked away from them. His hands were in the pockets of his long coat, which could be where he was hiding the pistol.

"He could be holding it in his pocket." said Friso.
"Yes, we have to assume that he has it on him." said Arnaud. "Tell the guys on the other side of the canal that he is approaching, and appears armed."

Arnaud was feeling extremely anxious, as he knew that if this siege went according to plan, then they would catch the accomplice in about ten minutes. Once this was done, he knew that he would be close to finding out the identity of the Magpie and then catching her, too.

Arnaud and his team watched Jan cross the bridge and walk down the other side of the Singel towards his girlfriend's apartment. He went past the undercover police van and reached his destination where he stopped and looked up at the building once more. Jan looked very normal thought Arnaud, despite his weary face. He definitely didn't stand out as guilty accomplice to multiple murders.

After a few moments of checking his surroundings, Jan took his hand out of his pocket and looked at his wristwatch to see the time. It was eleven thirty-seven and he was a little early. Without hesitating, he walked briskly up the steps to the front door of Mariana's apartment and let himself in.

As Jan shut the door behind him, Arnaud thought that it was safe to speak through the radio system to the other police. "Okay guys, hold on please. Wait for my order to move."

"Roger that." came the reply on the radio.

You could see through the apartment curtains that Jan had turned on the lights inside. After about three minutes Arnaud gave the instructions to move. "Okay guys. Let's get into position. Be quiet and go to the agreed spots and wait for further instructions. I want all the possible exits to that building closed off immediately. Assume that he is armed, so have your guns ready. Ideally, we want him alive so shoot only as a last resort."

The four detectives watched the armed police creep slowly out of the back of the van and scurry off around the building into their places. After about a minute, Friso spoke up. "They are ready, Arnaud."

It was completely quiet and still inside the detectives' car as they all looked across the canal at the lit up apartment.

"What now?" asked Friso.

Arnaud continued staring over at Mariana's apartment, surprised that there didn't appear to be any movement inside. Suddenly Arnaud sat upright in his seat, making the rest of his team jump. "What the fuck is that?!" said Arnaud with a raised voice.

"What?" responded Friso.

"It looks like there is smoke coming out of the cellar door." shouted Arnaud, in a panic.

All four of them were focusing on the small exterior door, which was below the steps going up to the front entrance to the building. There were large streams of black smoke billowing out from under this door and rising up out over the canal. You could also see licks of bright yellow and orange flames through the cellar window.

"My god, the apartment is on fire!" shouted Arnaud, as he watched the flames and smoke climb up from the ground level of the apartment. Arnaud opened the door to the car and jumped out. Both Jim and Robin did the same. Friso picked up the walkie talkie and spoke into the radio.

"Everyone, the building is on fire. I repeat. The building is on fire. Wait for the suspect to exit. It should be any second. Do not enter the building. I repeat, do not enter the building."

"Affirmative." came the crackled responses through the radio.

With that, Friso also stepped quickly out of the vehicle. The four detectives started walking briskly towards the bridge. They were on autopilot, and as they moved swiftly along in silence, they all continued staring at the building. It was now difficult to see the front of Mariana's apartment as it was shielded by a large black smoke screen. The flames were now rising up to the second floor and you could hear the glass breaking as windows smashed open.

"Speed up guys." said Friso in a raised voice.

They needed to get to the apartment before Jan came out, which had to be any second. The detectives were now about a hundred yards away and they could hear fire engine sirens in the distance. Neighbors were coming out of their buildings to see what all the commotion was about. Arnaud didn't want or need this attention. They had to focus on the job at hand. Suddenly, the front door to Mariana's apartment burst open and out jumped Jan, coughing and spluttering. Clouds of smoke gushed out behind him, as the cold air sucked the fire from the building.

Jan's face was hard to recognize as it was tar-colored from the smoke. Once he finished coughing, Jan wiped the smoke out of his watering eyes and looked up. Jan could see all the locals who had come out of their buildings staring at him. He also spotted the three undercover policemen standing there, armed with pistols. There was no mistaking them as they all had earpieces and bulletproof vests. Jan knew the game was up. There were loads of witnesses to what he just had done. It was over. He was trapped.

He stopped in his tracks and froze, looking from side to side, wondering who would move first. Apart from the noise coming from the roaring fire, there was silence on the canal. As the four detectives approached the building, Arnaud saw this as his chance to speak. At the top of his voice, Arnaud shouted over at Jan.

"Jan Meijer, you are under arrest for murder. Please raise your hands above your head and come peacefully. If you have a gun, then drop it now."

Jan opened his mouth in shock. He had nowhere to run. He was trapped. How did the police know he was in there? He would be interrogated and then they would force him to talk about Mariana's involvement. He didn't want that. He couldn't handle the thought of his girlfriend being caught. He could put up with the aftermath that came with his arrest and his family being heartbroken but not Mariana. He didn't want her involved. Even after all of this, he wanted her to be free.

Tears started streaming down Jan's face as he began sobbing and crying out loud. Everyone stood still waiting to see what he would do next. He looked genuinely shocked as he broke down on the doorstep with black smoke engulfing him from behind. The armed police stayed focused on Jan's movements just in case he was going to pull out his gun. Suddenly, he wiped his face and ran back into the apartment, slamming the door behind him.

"Shit!" shouted Friso. "What's he doing?"

They could hear Jan screaming inside the apartment as the flames and smoke grew larger. The detectives started running towards the steps leading up to the door but the smoke and the heat was too much. They couldn't get close. If they tried to go up the steps they would be in danger themselves.

"It's over!" said Friso.

The front door suddenly blew open and giant flames roared out. They all jumped backwards away from the building. The crying had stopped. Jan was surely dead. They all knew it, none more so than Arnaud. They had lost the accomplice, their lifeline to the Magpie.

The fire engines arrived and pushed the onlookers away from the building. The police and the detectives huddled around their unmarked van, which was parked fifty yards away. Everyone was in shock and didn't know what to say. Friso looked round, expecting Arnaud to speak up but he wasn't there. He ran back to the burning building and could see Arnaud walking over the bridge back to their vehicle. His shoulders were slouched forward giving the impression that he was exhausted and about to fall over. Friso began running in the direction of his boss. Friso knew that Arnaud would be completely deflated now that they had lost the accomplice. He had to help him.

As Friso speeded up and drew closer to his friend he shouted out. "Arnaud. Arnaud. Wait!"

Arnaud carried on walking and so Friso shouted again, "Arnaud. Wait! Please wait!"

Arnaud stopped in his tracks and Friso could see him run his hands through his thick mop of hair. He also noticed that his whole body had started shaking. It was clear that he was crying. Arnaud broke down. He had lost one of his closest friends yesterday and now he had lost the accomplice. Maybe the hunt for the Magpie was over. Maybe they would never find her now.

Arnaud fell to his knees as his crying turned into a complete emotional breakdown. He was exhausted, extremely upset and now he felt helpless. It looked like they had lost their only possible lead. He was pleased that Jan was dead as he had killed his dear friend but at the same time, it was now going to be very difficult for them to uncover the serial killer. Who was she? They would probably never find out. The Magpie had escaped thought Arnaud to himself.

He continued crying as Friso tried to console him. "It's okay Arnaud. It's okay." said Friso as he leant down and patted Arnaud on the back. He didn't know what to say. No words could comfort Arnaud at this moment. He also didn't have a solution. Friso had no idea what they were going to do now. The only lead they had that could perhaps share some light on Jan and his past movements was his girlfriend, Mariana. Friso knew that he and Arnaud would have to speak with her tomorrow to let her know about Jan's death and to see if she could help them with their ongoing search for the Magpie. He hoped that she wouldn't be too upset or shocked by what had happened to her boyfriend.

"Okay, come on Arnaud. Let me help you up. Let me take you home. You need to rest, mate. Have the afternoon off. We can meet up tomorrow and talk next steps. I can deal with this mess with Jim and Robin. Let me take you home. Come on."

Arnaud said nothing but stood up and shuffled slowly over to the car. Friso opened the passenger door and let Arnaud in. He began driving down the Singel slowly swerving around the crowds of people that had now congregated on the canal to watch the building that was burning down. Fortunately, nobody knew that someone had just died inside it and that it had been a suicide. The fire brigade was busy shooting powerful jets of water at the flames and this seemed to controlling the blaze. Friso had to honk a couple of times in order to move some people out of the way. He looked across at Arnaud, who was curled up in the passenger seat, still shaking and staring motionless out of the window. He was in bad shape thought Friso to himself.

As he drove along, he called Jim and told him what he was doing. He also asked the two young detectives to stay at the crime scene. There could potentially be a lot of clues in the building, once they could actually get inside it.

He then drove Arnaud home to the Jordaan. Parking on the Tuinstraat, Friso helped Arnaud out of the car and walked him to his small house. He wanted to go in with him to make sure he was okay. He also didn't want Arnaud going to a café and getting drunk. He wanted him to rest, as he definitely needed it. As they walked to the front door, they could hear sirens from police cars heading to the Singel from all directions. Friso wanted to get him inside as quickly as possible. He wanted Arnaud to switch off.

"Have you got your keys?" asked Friso, in a sympathetic voice.

Arnaud just stood there silently. He had switched off. Realizing this, Friso reached into Arnaud's coat pocket and felt around for his keys. He found them pretty quickly and opened his front door.

"Okay, Arnaud, let's go inside. Come on, it's freezing. Let's get inside."

He ushered Arnaud in and turned on the lights in his living room. Arnaud sat down in his familiar leather seat and put his head into his hands. Friso walked over to the two radiators in the living room and turned them on. The house was very cold. He then went into the kitchen and boiled some water. He wanted to make a cup of tea for both of them. Having done this, he went back into the living room and sat on the sofa facing Arnaud. Friso put the cup of tea into Arnaud's hands. He hoped this would warm him up and bring some life back into him. Arnaud looked briefly at Friso and then nodded in acknowledgment. He sipped on the tea, which Friso saw as a good sign.

For the next twenty minutes the two detectives sat in absolute silence. Apart from the sound of slurping tea, the room was completely still. Friso was happy to be with Arnaud. They had been through so much in the last year, most of which were not success stories. They were constantly chasing shadows and their friendship was the only thing that had kept them going and motivated. Today had been a showstopper. They had hit a serious roadblock and they both knew it.

Friso was taken by surprise as Arnaud began to speak, "What now? What do we do now Friso?"

Friso looked across with a blank face. He wasn't expecting him to speak or ask a question. "I'm not sure, Arnaud. But for now, you need to rest."

"Okay, I will rest but what then? What do we do next?" came the helpless reply.

Friso didn't know how to respond. There was silence again as both men collected their thoughts.

"We have lost the accomplice. There is no way we can find the Magpie now." said Arnaud in a depressed tone.

"You don't know that, Arnaud." replied Friso.

Arnaud looked over at Friso. His eyes were completely blood shot from all the crying. "Our best source of information has gone. I can't see how we can ever find the Magpie. The only inroad we have is the judge's daughter. If she had known anything, she would have already told us. The information we are going to get out of her now is going to be very limited."

Again, Friso just looked at his boss and remained silent. Arnaud was probably right. "The only thing that doesn't make sense is why that young guy killed himself? Why did Jan Meijer go back into the burning house, knowing that this was going to be the end? It takes a lot to do that. What was he hiding? And why did he set the building on fire in the first place? He knew Mariana wasn't there otherwise he wouldn't have done that. What reason did he have to burn the building down? He must have known that he would draw attention to himself. This I don't understand. Knowing that she wasn't in there, why didn't he just wait for her to return?"

Everything that Arnaud had just said made sense. These were all the unanswered questions, thought Friso. It was good to see that Arnaud was still able to think methodically, even though he was so distressed. Again, Friso didn't know the answers to these important questions. He hoped that maybe Mariana would be able to shed some light on this when they got round to questioning her again.

"I don't know Arnaud. I really don't know. I just hope that the judge's daughter might be able to help us. We should go and see her tomorrow when you have rested. Then we can ask her a load of questions."

There was silence for a moment and then Arnaud spoke up again.

"We will go and see her this afternoon." He replied, in a dead serious tone and with a real focus in his eyes.

Friso could see that Arnaud meant business. He wanted to get on with things straight away. This was a good sign. "Okay Arnaud, we will go there this afternoon."

CHAPTER 34

December 1

6:05 p.m.

Arnaud and Friso sat in Dr. Akkermans' study looking across at father and daughter who were next to each other on the sofa. The room was very warm and still. The silence was broken only by the ticking of the large grandfather clock in the corner of the study. They had been there for over an hour and were wrapping up the meeting.

Arnaud and Friso had explained the events of the day to the judge and Mariana. Surprisingly, she didn't show any emotion at all. Admittedly, she was over Jan and had been scared for her safety. She must have been relieved as he was now gone but it did seem strange that she wasn't upset at all.

The detectives were lost for words and frustrated as Mariana had shut down and wasn't helpful at all. She had answered every question with 'I really don't know.' For such an intelligent girl, it was peculiar that she had no idea who Jan really was and what his whereabouts had been throughout the year. Friso had ended the meeting by saying that he would contact them with a list of dates that he would need explanations of where Mariana was. They made it clear that they weren't accusing her of anything but just needed to cover all the bases. Dr. Akkermans promised to help with this. Arnaud was surprised to see that the judge was already being an alibi for his daughter even though he didn't know the dates yet.

Arnaud looked across at the immaculately dressed judge and his daughter and began to speak. "Well, I think that's it for now. Thank you for your co-operation and we will be in touch."

"What more do you need from us, detective?" asked Dr. Akkermans.

Arnaud paused before continuing to speak. "Well, I don't know but something may come up. Mariana is now our best lead with the investigation so I am sure we will be in touch."

The judge didn't reply. Arnaud could see that Mariana stared straight at him with no expression on her face. She was both beautiful and cold and he couldn't work her out.

The two detectives looked at each other and then said their goodbyes.

Friso dropped Arnaud off home. Arnaud got undressed and climbed into his cold bed. He was so tired and needed to sleep. He had no idea what tomorrow would bring. They had no leads and it seemed like the case was still open. Maybe the killer would stop now that her accomplice was dead. Part of Arnaud hoped that this was the case as it would all be over then. The other half of him wanted the Magpie to continue as that would give him the opportunity to catch her. If she did nothing, then she was as good as gone.

As he lay there, he thought about Noor. What a surprise that had been. She was 'Happy Single', the internet angel that had been helping him throughout the year. She must have really loved him. Now, she was gone forever. Arnaud wiped a tear from his eye. He then started thinking about Jan again and picturing his face as he looked at all the people and police standing outside the burning apartment. Arnaud still couldn't get his head round the fact that Jan had run back into the burning building. Why did he do that? What was he hiding? Was burning to death better than going to prison? Arnaud didn't know the answer to this, and would never know.

Tomorrow they would have to do another press conference explaining the events from the last twenty-four hours. This included the murder of

Noor Lumas and the death of Jan Meijer. He didn't want it known that Noor was his friend and the infamous blogger 'Happy Single.' He wanted to keep their close friendship private if at all possible. It was stressful to think that it may have to come out anyway. There was still so much to be done. Within minutes, he was fast asleep.

CHAPTER 35

December 25

7:12 p.m.

Arnaud sat in Cafe Prins on his sixth beer and fourth Geneva. He hadn't gone back to De Twee Zwaantjes since Noor's death. He couldn't face it. He was well on his way to being drunk. He had spent the day with his ex-wife and daughter celebrating Christmas at their house. Normally, his ex wouldn't allow him over but after all the stress he had been through this year she made an exception.

It had been a nice day and it had lifted his spirits somewhat. After the death of Jan Meijer, he had to do a press conference with Dijkstra and explain that the young man killed in the apartment fire was in fact the accomplice. They had managed to find his identity but were not able to arrest him as he chose suicide over being captured. The public and the press reaction to this was favorable. They had made progress and had managed to get rid of one of the two killers, even though they were not able to identify the Magpie and catch her. The fact that there hadn't been another murder since Jan Meijer's death made the public believe that the killer had fled. This was also seen as a success for Arnaud and the police, and had taken a lot of pressure off of him. For Arnaud, however, he had sunk into a serious depression as he felt that that he had failed because he had not caught the killer and he had lost a dear friend in Noor.

Arnaud couldn't get comfortable with everything that had happened since early December. There were too many unanswered questions that didn't sit right with him. He was sure he was missing something but couldn't get to the bottom of it. Too much had happened that was eating away at him. Arnaud wasn't sleeping well and had spent most of the month pondering over these points. As he sat in the bar he couldn't help going through all the events again in his head. He could feel himself getting tense.

Jan had been burnt to the bone in the fire and any possible DNA on him was gone. Nothing substantial was found in the remains of the house. It was clear and they couldn't find any links to associate either of them to the killings.

Arnaud still had no idea why Jan had burnt Mariana's apartment apart from maybe to try and kill her. This seemed strange though as Jan was in the building for a few minutes before setting it alight so he knew that Mariana wasn't there. This made Arnaud think that he had done this for another reason, especially since the forensics confirmed that the blaze started in the cellar. Was Jan trying to get rid of something? Some evidence perhaps?

Why had Jan chosen to kill himself as opposed to being arrested? Did he do this because he wanted to protect the identity of the killer? Was he worried that the Magpie would end up being captured as well? If this was the case, then he must have really cared for her, as he was willing to die for her freedom.

There was also no gun found in Jan's possession. This seemed strange since Mariana had said that he would be carrying a pistol. If there was one time when you would have expected him to have his weapon with him, it would have been then especially since he knew that the police were looking for him. Did Mariana just want the police to shoot Jan? There was no pistol found at Jan's home or in his van. Did he actually have one or was Mariana making it up?

DNA evidence found in Jan's bedroom and in his van linked him to the victims, who were murdered throughout the year. He was definitely the accomplice to the Magpie and his van was used to transport the dead bodies around. But who was he working with? Who was the serial killer? Who was the Magpie? Surprisingly, there was none of Mariana's DNA in the van.

Jan's distraught family was convinced that Mariana was involved. They were sure that she was the killer. When Jan wasn't studying in his room or working in the bakery, he was with Mariana. He had spent all his spare time with her. His parents believed that she manipulated their son and had changed him. Jan had been obsessed with Mariana and his bedroom proved it. His walls were covered in pictures of her. It was like a shrine. How could it be possible that he had another woman in his life, thought Arnaud. Why would he burn her apartment or try to kill her? None of this made sense. What the parents didn't know was that Jan was supposed to be dating Noor. This also didn't add up especially since he was in love with Mariana.

Arnaud started thinking about Mariana again. He had met her and Dr. Akkermans four times this month. She had not been helpful in providing any new information on Jan. She always came across as cold and fragile and too distraught to be of any use. The one thing that Arnaud couldn't get to grips with was that she always dressed and looked beautiful whenever they met, even though she was supposed to be traumatized. How was this possible? How could she get dressed in the morning in such expensive outfits and cover herself in diamonds if she was so stressed and sad?

Her father, Dr. Akkermans had acted as an alibi for all the times there was a killing throughout the year. This cut any association between her and the Magpie. Nobody could question his integrity as a top judge and if he said that she was at his house on specific times and dates then he was a legitimate alibi. There was also no DNA or items found in the remains of the burnt down apartment that could link her to the killings.

The other thing that was strange was that they had asked to see her mobile phone to check text messages. Arnaud had found out from her phone bills that they communicated via text. Surprisingly, Mariana had lost her phone and didn't know where or when. It was never recovered.

Dr. Akkermans had since encouraged his daughter to take a long well deserved holiday. She was unhappy and extremely distraught and he had agreed with Mariana that she could go travelling on her own around South America for a few months. She was going to take a year's sabbatical from her University. Her father wasn't sure where she had gone but had received a postcard from Brazil. She was no longer available for future questioning but Arnaud and his team didn't really have anything else to ask her.

Mariana hadn't been particularly helpful and they had no reason or proof to associate her to the killings or Jan, she was free to do her own thing. Dr. Akkermans had also been extremely defensive of his daughter and had made it clear that they had to be very careful how they trod around Mariana especially since she was innocent and distraught. Arnaud felt helpless. There was nothing he could do. He also had no idea how he could get to the bottom of these unanswered questions.

As the months passed, no more killings occurred. Arnaud didn't expect there to be another one. He was sure that The Magpie was gone. As he swigged down the last drops of his beer he thought about how the press were portraying him as a hero. The killings had stopped. He, however, felt like a failure. He hadn't caught his nemesis. He may have stopped her killings but she had escaped. The Magpie was free.

In a sick sort of way, Arnaud wished that she would kill again. This would at least give him the possibility of catching her. But he knew that this wasn't going to happen. They had gotten too close to capturing the Magpie. Too close and she knew it. She was gone and Arnaud had to accept this. He needed to try and get over this case and move on. There had to be closure otherwise this would haunt Arnaud forever. He had to accept that the Magpie was gone.

* * *

9:45 p.m.

Dr. Akkermans sat at the long oak table in his kitchen. He was alone in his large canal house on Christmas Day. Rina had made him a wonderful dinner of roasted turkey with a variety of vegetables and all the trimmings. She had cleaned the kitchen and then left for the night to visit some friends. The judge had spent the last three hours drinking numerous glasses of red wine and thinking. The more he drank the sadder he became. Since Mariana had left for South America, he had received just one postcard from her. He was extremely upset because they had seemed to bond strongly earlier in the month. Once she travelled abroad, their communication had stopped and he didn't feel close to her anymore. Dr. Akkermans was beginning to feel used again, just like the old days.

In front of him sat three empty bottles of wine and a phone. The expensive bottles of red wine belonged to him and he had polished them off during the evening. The phone wasn't his. It belonged to Mariana. Rina had found it lodged between some loose floorboards in the corner of her bedroom. It wasn't lost, as Mariana had explained to the police. Rina had not turned the phone on. She didn't want to see the messages on the phone. It was as if Rina knew that the phone would reveal some secrets. Instead, she had just put it on the desk in Dr. Akkermans study. It was the judge who pressed the power button on and read through his daughter's messages and call log.

The kitchen was dark and the flicker from a few candles gave some light to the room. Dr. Akkermans was tired and drunk. He was also very sad.

The sadness was not just because he hadn't heard from her for a while, but also because she had lied to him. He had suspected that she might have known more about what Jan had been doing than she was letting on. He just didn't think it possible that she was the killer. His daughter was the Magpie. She had committed multiple murders and had gotten away with it. She was a coldblooded, calculative killer. She was his daughter, his own flesh and blood. How could she have become so evil? How could she be so crazy? What made matters worse was that she had played him as well as the police. She had also played Jan. Dr. Akkermans felt sorry for her boyfriend. He had loved Mariana and would have done anything for her. In fact, Jan had done exactly this. He had helped her with all the killings, and in the end, he had committed suicide just to protect her.

In fact, this was no different than Dr. Akkermans. He had lied to the police to protect his daughter. He hadn't known that she was the killer but he certainly wasn't sure about where she had been at specific times during the year. Acting as her alibi, he had got Mariana off the suspect list. Now he felt very guilty as well as tricked. He also felt very lonely. He had nobody. Was all this his own fault? Of course, he was to blame in part for his wife's death from cancer. But did his actions from such a long time ago help to create such an evil crazy monster?

Dr. Akkermans began to cry. His daughter was gone, probably for good. She must really hate him, he thought. She probably blamed him for everything. He wiped some tears off of his cheeks and picked up the phone that lay in front of him. Flicking through some of the text messages, he broke down again. He was now facing a dilemma. He could put a lot of things right if he called Detective Van Loo and told him the truth. This was the right thing to do and by giving Mariana's mobile phone to the police, they would have sufficient evidence to arrest her. They would be able to track her down and bring her back to The Netherlands for sentencing. They would have caught the Magpie.

If he did this, then he may also be arrested for lying to the police. His reputation would be tarnished in the high legal circles of Amsterdam and his daughter would go to prison for life. Dr. Akkermans leant back in his chair and thought, closing his eyes and running his hands through his grey slicked back hair. The wine was making him emotional and it was difficult to think straight at the moment.

The judge stood up from the kitchen table and took a deep breath. He picked up his daughter's phone and tossed it into fireplace. Strong plastic fumes rose out of the flames as the evidence melted away. Dr. Akkermans began crying once more as he walked out of the kitchen in the direction of the stairs. He was going to sleep. He wanted to forget about all of this. He needed to move on from these grave mistakes he had made. His daughter had gone and would probably never come back. He hoped that this whole nightmare would now be over forever. As he climbed the stairwell, he was not only feeling sad but also guilty and extremely lonely. He knew that this was all his own fault.

As Christmas Day was drawing to an end, Amsterdam was a safer place once again. The serial killings had ended and things were back to normal in the liberal city. Some people's lives had changed forever, some for better but most for worse. Many had lost innocent loved ones and others had lost guilty loved ones. The scars caused by these serial killings would last for a lifetime. At least the killings had ended. The Magpie was gone.

www.ingramcontent.com/pod-product-compliance
Lightning Source LLC
Chambersburg PA
CBHW051204120726
47905CB00004B/982